P9-CRT-021

A Prince of a Guy

SHEILA RABE

BERKLEY BOOKS, NEW YORK

A PRINCE OF A GUY

A Berkley Book / published by arrangement with
the author

PRINTING HISTORY
Berkley edition / August 2001

Visit our website at
www.penguinputnam.com

ISBN: 0-425-18098-0

BERKLEY®
Berkley Books are published by The Berkley Publishing Group,
a division of Penguin Putnam Inc., 375 Hudson Street,
New York, New York 10014.
BERKLEY and the "B" design
are trademarks belonging to Penguin Putnam Inc.

PRINTED IN THE UNITED STATES OF AMERICA

10 9 8 7 6 5 4 3 2 1

For Big, Bad John

ACKNOWLEDGMENTS

Okay, all you great experts out there. Here is the page you show to your friends and say, "See? I do know something after all." Thanks to Luke Burbank, producer at KVI radio, who gave me lots of good information. You're not the dashing hero, Luke, but, like Waldo, you're in the book. Where's Luke? Thanks to John Wachsmith for explaining this stock market stuff in such a way that I could almost understand it. Thanks to brother Sam for helping me with that nasty football stuff. Thanks to Lisa at Ski Master Water Sports, the only person who would take five minutes during the boating industry's busy season to explain to me the difference between a speedboat and a ski boat, and to Melissa Christopher, who shared her foolproof method for teaching someone how to water-ski. (The falling-down part I did all on my own: I already knew how from personal experience.) A big thanks to Sherri and Steve from the Seattle Seahawks, who both made me feel like a V.I.P. when I visited the team's headquarters. Thanks to Officer Hansen of the Bainbridge Island Police Force for taking time to answer a lot of dumb questions, and to Mike Swenson, ace mechanic, who had to put up with even dumber questions. A special thanks to Lee at San Carlos. No one in their right mind would waste that award-winning food the way the characters in my book do! Thanks to Shirley Shneckloth for the free title consultation. You are a princess. Thanks to Penny Jones for sharing her investment expertise and to Corrine at Washington Mutual, who gave me interest rates even when she knew I

didn't want a car loan. And special thanks to my friend
and critique partner, Lisa Hendrix, for letting me tap into
that amazing hard drive inside her head on a regular basis.
For everyone who helped me with this book, may your
love life always be great and may you never have to call
Dr. Kate.

Hello, Doctor Kate

If you don't use common sense when choosing Mr. Right, I guarantee that when you get home with what you thought was a prince, you'll find you only fell for a frog with a glass slipper.

Dr. Kate Stonewall,
author of *The Frog with the Glass Slipper*

"SUSAN, IT'S NOT EXACTLY A SLAM DUNK TO PRE-dict that a man who wants to try and arrange his wedding date around next year's NFL playoff schedule is going to end up as an ESPN couch potato," said Dr. Kate Stonewall. "In fact, I don't predict it, I guarantee it. Been there. Done that."

"But I love him," said the caller in a small voice.

Kate looked at her producer, Wallis Frank, seated next to George the board operator on the other side of the glass, and rolled her eyes. Wallis just shook her head.

"Actually," said Kate, "the question you have to answer is not if you love him now, but will you love him in ten years? I'd be willing to bet a honeymoon in the Bahamas that you won't." Silence filled the air waves as Susan tried to digest the unpleasant truth. "Susan, if your man is already pulling this kind of stuff when your relationship is at that stage where you can't keep your hands off each other," continued Kate, "what do you think he's going to be like in a few years? He's already showing you clearly where his priorities lie."

"Well, I'm sure once we're married it will be different," said Susan hopefully.

"Yes, it will," agreed Kate. "Instead of watching those playoffs in his living room, he'll be watching them in yours, which I've been getting the distinct impression doesn't appeal to you. Susan, this man is doing you a real favor: he's already showing you his true colors. And it sounds like he's not your prince. He's a frog in Nikes. If I were you I'd wait to order the wedding cake."

"It's already ordered," said Susan, and from her tone of voice, Kate could tell canceling the wedding to Mr. Wrong was not on this caller's list of options.

"Then I hope you told the bakery to be sure and add plenty of flies to those frosting roses for the groom, because you are about to marry a frog. Ribbit and good luck."

Kate terminated Susan, quickly checked the screen in front of her for the name of the next caller on hold, then punched the appropriate control button. "Kristin. Welcome to the program."

"Hello, Doctor Kate? Oh, I can't believe I'm really talking to you," gushed the woman.

"How may I help you?" asked Kate, cutting to the chase.

"I want to know what I can do to get my husband's attention."

"What's the competition?"

"The Mariners," said Kristin.

"Well," said Kate, "this seems to be our afternoon for sports-related troubles." No surprise there. As long as American men were the way they were, every afternoon would be an afternoon for sports-related troubles. "Tell me more."

"Every time there's a game, he's either at it or listening to it on the radio, or if it's on TV, he's watching it," said

Kristin. "And it's not just the Mariners. He loves football, too. He's really awful during football season because we've got the Huskies and the Seahawks."

"I know," said Kate, her voice empathetic. Boy, did she know. She'd been married to just such an animal. "Well, first things first. Let's take the pulse on this marriage. Do you love him?"

"Oh, yes."

"Other than the sports barrier, would you say you have a good relationship? You communicate well, get along, have other interests in common?"

"Yes," said Kristin.

"And you're committed to your marriage?"

"Yes."

"Then you have two choices," said Kate. "You can start going to the games with your husband or you can pursue other interests when he's doing his sports thing. On game day, go see a movie or go shopping with a friend. Just don't leave him in charge of the kids, whatever you do."

"But I'll never see him," protested Kristin.

"Well, then, plan A is your best bet," said Kate.

"But I hate sports." Kristin's voice was turning whiny, a sure sign that she was not open to any advice other than dynamite the television and chain your husband to the bed.

Kate took a firm hold on her impatience. "But, Kristin, the man you married loves them. And I've got news for you: he's not going to change. So, you've reached the stage where you realize that life at the castle isn't one never-ending ball. That's the reality of living with the prince you've chosen. Now you have to cope with reality. Do what you can to make your kingdom a place you can be happy in, too. Do some things for you."

She cut off Kristin before she could protest any further and spoke to the audience in general. "Women, remember, what you don't see is what you get. So take off those blinders and check Mr. Right very carefully before you commit to living with him. Just about anyone can stir up your hormones, so use your brain and find someone who can make the rest of you happy as well. Look behind that great face to make sure it's not a mask and you're not getting a frog.

"Speaking of frogs, we're going to have to quit now because the Mariners are playing this afternoon, and *Jock Talk* will be starting an hour early. Oops! That was rude. Nothing personal, Jeff, really. See, people? Even psychologists aren't perfect. But we'll have to save my imperfections for another day because I'm out of time. We'll meet tomorrow for more life strategies. And remember, in real life we don't get to go back to start, so let's make the right moves along the way."

George started the bumper music that signaled the end of the show and Kate picked up her empty coffee mug and well-scribbled tablet and headed out of the air studio, rubbing the tight muscles in her neck.

She loved her job; it was perfectly suited for a woman on a personal crusade to save American women from themselves. If she could prevent even one woman from making the same mistake she had made, her life would not be in vain. But today, with baseball season in full swing, and the abundance of sports-related questions, she had felt like she was fighting a losing battle.

"Good show, Kate," said Wallis. She reached over and plucked a long-forgotten pencil from Kate's brown mane.

As usual, Kate's thick hair was sneaking out of its scrunchy, and what little makeup she'd worn at the beginning of the program had long since evaporated, revealing the freckles she hated. She knew she'd chewed off her lipstick, too.

"If your fans could only see you now," teased Wallis. "What a difference from that perfect, together woman whose picture is riding around on the Metro buses."

Kate eyed her producer, who was looking svelte and polished in her linen suit, then took in her own loose-flowing dress with the stain on the skirt—a memento of the jelly donut that had landed there earlier.

"That is the Seattle me," said Kate. "This is the real me. Anyway, nobody cares how you look on Bainbridge Island. Speaking of which." She checked her watch. "If I hurry I can make the three-fifty ferry and get home in time to actually see something of my kids before Robbie's Little League game."

"Little League," hooted George. "I thought you hated sports."

"I do," replied Kate, rushing for the door. "But I love my son."

In her haste, she collided with Jeff Hardin, who was just coming in to start his show.

"Sorry," she said, feeling flustered and stupid.

"No problem," he replied. He held the door open for her, adding, "I can always grow a new toe."

Kate slipped past him, refusing to dignify the crack with a response. Anyway, she didn't have time. It took exactly eight and a half minutes to get from KZOO's downtown radio station to the waterfront. If she flew like the wind and if there wasn't a huge line for the boat, she might just be able to squeeze on.

In her dreams. As she watched the Volkswagen two cars ahead of her putt into the last available space, her thoughts turned to the other irritation in her life: Jeff Hardin, host of the marathon sports talk show, *Jock Talk*. She really had nothing against him personally. After all, she barely knew the man. It was what he stood for she detested so strongly. And it aggravated her no end when an afternoon ball game cut short her midday program so that Jeff could squeeze in a pregame show and devote even more air hours to the sick male obsession of sports. Drive times, those morning or late afternoon hours when commuters were surging to work or wending their way home and listening to the radio in their cars, were the plum times, and Jeff had the afternoon one. Three to seven, every Monday through Friday. But he wasn't happy with that, the pig. Oh, no. He had to gobble part of her show to float yet more insignificant babble onto the airwaves when there were people out there in genuine need of her help.

The last Arbitron rating had showed that her program had gone up a whole share. She was a five now, which was good, and she thought it was exceptionally good, considering the fact that she'd only been at this a year and a half. But Jeff's rating was a seven, which put him right up there with the big boys—a sad commentary on Seattle's taste in radio talk show hosts. A woman with a best-selling book who had just signed a big syndication deal shouldn't have to play second fiddle to a drool king whose only claim to fame was knowing the batting averages of a bunch of tobacco-chewing, crotch-scratching baseball players. Now that she had signed with the Premiere Radio Networks, the program director at KZOO had better smarten up.

First Jeff, now the missed ferry. Next, a Little League baseball game, the perfect ending to a perfect day. Kate watched the boat sail off without her and swore.

One

OKAY. DEAL WITH IT. SHE FISHED HER CELL PHONE out of her purse and called her next-door neighbor, Grace Morrison, who graciously allowed Kate's children to demolish her house every weekday afternoon.

"I almost made the three-fifty," said Kate. "Which means I'll be on the four-forty and I'll be coming through the front door at a dead run."

"Won't that be fun," said Grace.

"Robbie's supposed to be at the field at five-thirty. So can you turn the little dears into latchkey kids at five and tell them to be ready to go the minute they hear me pull up? Amanda can put together some turkey sub sandwiches for us to eat there."

"Do you want me to just feed them?" asked Grace.

"Nah. At ten and a half Amanda is perfectly capable of putting together three sandwiches."

"Okay," said Grace. "It's your blood pressure."

Kate turned off her phone and did some quick calculating. The ferry would unload her at five-fifteen. She could be home in ten minutes, well, more like fifteen at the rate the commuter traffic moved. That would put her at the front door right when Robbie was supposed to be at the field. But if the kids were ready to go, they could just hop in the car and tear off and they'd only be five minutes late. She could do this.

It was five–twenty-eight when Kate ran through the front door, wishing fervently they didn't have to be anywhere and could just stay home and play a board game. All this stress and hurry, and for what?

"I'm home!" she called.

She heard a bedroom door slam, followed by thundering feet. Robbie bounded down the stairs, ready to roll. "We gotta go, Mom."

Her son had not been having a good season—no hits, no runs, and a hundred errors—but hope sprang eternal, and here he was, eager as always to get to the field. Just the opposite of the way his mother felt.

"Okay," said Kate. "Amanda!" she called.

"Just a minute, Mom."

Kate followed the voice to its source: the kitchen. There stood her daughter, carefully laying turkey slices on hoagie buns. Amanda's blonde hair had been freshly done, clipped up with her favorite butterfly-shaped hair clips, and her fingernails sported a fresh coat of neon blue. It wasn't hard for Kate to guess how her daughter had spent her time since she got home. Confused priorities. That particular flaw had been her father's contribution in making her.

"Oh, Amanda," moaned Kate. "Those sandwiches were supposed to be ready. We've got to go."

"I'm hurrying," replied Amanda, continuing to move at the same plodding, meticulous pace.

Kate rushed to join her at the white-tiled work island and grabbed the jar of mustard.

"Mom," urged Robbie.

"I know, I know," said Kate. "We'll make it."

All this fuss for a waste of time, she thought irritably. Adorable as her seven-year-old was, she believed in facing facts. And the fact was, that with his father's husky frame, Robbie was just not baseball material.

"Football," Rob had prophesied, "a fullback." Even though she tried to blot out the image, Kate could still see Rob tossing a small, sponge football at Robbie when he was barely walking.

Thank God Robbie hadn't shown any interest in that Neanderthal sport! Baseball was bad enough. He could have been doing Boy Scouts or singing in the island kids' choir, but instead here he was, going for the world's record for the boy who struck out the most, and ruining his self-esteem, and Rob was probably turning in his grave.

Well, let him turn. If he hadn't drunk too much and choked to death on a peanut on Super Bowl Sunday six years ago, he'd be around now to help his son.

On second thought, maybe it was just as well he wasn't. Kate was already unhappy over that moment of weakness when she had caved in to her pleading son and allowed him to enter the portal to the world of male idiocy. Rob would have kept him in there, turning her bright, talented child into a sports nut like himself.

Just thinking about Rob made Kate's blood pressure rise. Subject closed, she told herself, and began digging in a drawer for plastic wrap.

"Amanda," she barked, "get the Thermos and pour some lemonade into it."

"Geez, Mom, you don't have to yell," said Amanda.

"You're right," said Kate. "Sorry." Bad moods brought on by encounters with sports-crazed imbeciles and over-crowded commuter ferries did not need to be shared with one's offspring.

"Do you think coach will want me to keep track of how many runs we get tonight?" asked Amanda as she carried the pitcher of lemonade to the kitchen table.

"Most definitely," said Kate. "You did a great job last time."

"We're gonna be late," fretted Robbie.

They already were late. "We'll be fine," Kate assured him, and put the wrestling match between her and the plastic wrap into high gear.

"But I have to be there to warm up," Robbie reminded her, his voice edged with hysteria.

"Okay. Go get in the car." Kate stuffed the sandwiches into a plastic grocery bag. Now in the throes of out-the-door-itis, she strode to the table. "Thanks, Amanda. I'll finish."

"I can do it, Mom," insisted Amanda, jerking away from her mother's outstretched hand and slopping lemonade on the floor.

"Oh, Amanda!" exclaimed Kate in exasperation, grabbing for a paper towel.

"I was doing it," said Amanda in her own defense.

Kate sighed as she watched the quicker picker upper suck up the liquid. She wished it would also pick up the sticky residue off the floor. That would just have to be dealt with when they returned. *This is not a big deal,* she reminded herself.

"I know," she said, and patted her daughter on the shoulder. "Put the lid on the Thermos and let's get out of here."

They made it to the field in five minutes flat. Bill, the coach, was already at home plate, hitting balls to kids positioned around the baseball diamond.

"Rob, my man," he hollered. "Come on out here."

Robbie ran around the chain-link fence to the inner sanctum. Amanda followed him, strolling casually toward the dugout, where Kate knew she'd wait for the coach to notice her and find her some task to make her feel important. The men play and the women keep score, thought Kate irritably as she took her place on the bleachers next to Bill's wife, Janet.

"You were great today," said Janet. "The advice you gave Kristin was right on."

"I thought so," said Kate.

"To listen to you, nobody would have thought you were prejudiced. Well, not until that crack about Jeff Hardin."

"I'm not prejudiced," said Kate. "If I were, my son wouldn't be here. And as for that one little slip, it proves I'm human. Anyway, it ticks me off when they end my show early so Mr. *Jock Talk* can come on and chatter about something that really doesn't matter."

"Not everyone feels that way," said Janet. "Show me a man who doesn't worship the golden glove and I'll show you a misfit." She pointed to a father seated at the end of the bleachers, wearing a set of headphones. "I'll give you one guess what he's listening to."

"Oh, brother," said Kate in disgust. "Don't these guys realize there are other things in life besides baseball games and pregame shows?"

Janet nodded in the direction of the dugout. "Tell that to Bill."

Kate had tried telling it to her own husband. "But this is an important game, babe," he'd say. Every game—baseball, football, basketball, volleyball, and any other ball—had been an important game. And while Rob had been watching important games, his children had been growing and his wife had been getting an education—in more ways than one!—and drifting away from him. And then he was gone. Damn him!

"Most men are into some kind of sport," continued Janet. "It's a testosterone thing."

"Another reason to stay single," muttered Kate.

"You fell in love once, and if somebody fabulous came along, you'd fall again, just like the rest of us, Doctor Kate."

"Not like the rest of you. I have no intention of being one of those women who doesn't think when it comes to choosing a man."

"Hey, we don't all blow it."

"Enough of us do," said Kate. "If I could, I'd make *The*

Frog with the Glass Slipper required reading for every woman in America."

"Well, we'll see if you can continue to practice what you preach when someone comes along and hot-wires your hormones," goaded Janet.

"There's not much chance of that happening here. Every heterosexual male on this island who's our age is married."

"Yeah, but not in Seattle. One of these days you might just meet someone in the big city."

"It would have to be someone who's not a Mariners or Seahawks fan, so I'd say that reduces the odds to nil."

"A man would have to be from the moon not to be into some sport," said Janet. "Besides," she added with a sly smile, "don't you at least want someone who plays tennis?"

"I don't want anyone. Anyway, tennis is different. That's a gentleman's sport."

"Right. Ever hear of John McEnroe?"

Kate rolled her eyes. What did Janet know?

Another set of parents came and joined the growing flock perched on the bleachers, and all around her Kate saw people visiting with each other about their day-to-day lives. Two rows in back of her, the Williamses were telling the Franklins about the house they were building. Further to her right, she heard three moms discussing plans for the end-of-school picnic. This was the one thing she did like about Little League games, she thought. It was so friendly, so like living inside a slice of American apple pie.

Warm-up time ended, and the game began, and most of the dads dropped out of the conversation, either to plug earphones into portable radios and tune in for particulars on the baseball game about to begin in the city, or to leave the bleachers and pace alongside the chain-link fence that edged the field. The chit-chat kept on, but an underground stream of tension suddenly seemed to bubble beneath it. Here came the part Kate didn't like, where the apple pie got left behind, and everyone became obsessed with the handling of one little ball. It might be a game to the kids out there on the field, but to the parents it was life-and-death.

Kate tried to keep up her conversation with Janet, but when Robbie stepped up to the plate she caught life-and-death fever, too. She held her breath, gritting her teeth along with her son, as the father standing by the pitching machine held up the ball for him to see. *Nothing up my sleeve.* Then the ball went into the machine and Robbie stood, bat poised, concentrating on the hunk of whirring metal as if it were a fire-breathing dragon he needed to slay. The ball shot through the air at him, and he swung his bat a good six inches above it.

The umpire held up the first dreaded finger. "Strike one!" Two fingers to go.

"That's okay, Robbie," yelled Janet.

"Swing level," called Bill.

"I can't watch this," groaned Kate, holding up her hand and shielding her eyes from the whole ugly scene.

"You have to watch," said Janet, yanking it away. "What if he looks up here and sees you hiding? What will that do to his psyche?"

Good point. Kate clasped her hands tightly together and dutifully watched her son's public humiliation. *This is sick,* she thought. *What am I doing?*

Another ball went into the pitching machine. Kate switched from tooth gritting to fingernail gnawing. Again, the machine spat out the ball. Again, Robbie swung and caught nothing but air. Up went another finger.

Here came his last chance. *Oh, please, God,* prayed Kate, *let him at least touch the damn thing.*

Robbie's third swing wasn't any more blessed than the first two.

"Strike three," announced the ump.

Not for the first time, Kate felt suddenly thankful for her widowed condition. If Rob had been here, he'd have camped out at the fence, alternately shouting instructions to Robbie and yelling at the umpire. And things were bad enough as it was. She watched her son's shoulders slump and felt a dull ache in her chest.

"It's okay, Robbie," she hollered fiercely as he went to the dugout to get a consoling slap on the back from Coach Bill.

"It's his first year," said Janet. "He'll get the hang of it by next season."

There won't be a next season, Kate vowed. They weren't going to go through this nonsense again. Robbie had only wanted to play baseball because all his friends were doing it. If he insisted on participating in a sport next year, she'd let him take tennis lessons at the racquet club. He'd find it easier to hit a ball using a racquet instead of a skinny little bat, and he'd feel better about himself.

What was she thinking? Forget tennis. Sports were archaic and unhealthy. She'd get him involved in cultural activities where he'd make new friends, ones that might just grow up to become something other than living couch cushions.

By the time Robbie had basked in the glory of shared victory and inhaled more than his share of postgame cookies and pop, he seemed to be feeling just fine about himself. Running on a sugar high, he bounced into the backseat of the car already talking about next week's game. That was his father's sanguine nature coming through.

Acting, Kate thought suddenly. Robbie was so outgoing he'd be a natural. She'd put him in the kids' summer theater program with Amanda, and that should effectively wean him off sports.

"Hey," she said brightly as they drove past the island's performing arts building, "how'd you like to take acting classes with Amanda this summer?"

"Mom!" protested Amanda, and Kate gave her a "Be quiet" frown.

"Is James gonna do it?" asked Robbie, referring to Bill and Janet's son.

"I don't know," said Kate.

"If James does it, I will."

"Honey, Amanda will be there," said Kate.

"I want to go with James," said Robbie firmly.

"Well, I'm sure James will want to go," Kate assured him. She'd offer to pay James's fee, of course, and if she promised to drive the kids . . .

"Okay," said Robbie. "Did you see the home run James hit? Coach said that when I connect with the ball I'll be able to hit like that."

Thank you, Bill, thought Kate sourly. As if that was ever going to happen.

They were almost to their driveway on Pleasant Cove Road when Amanda pointed to the For Sale sign next to their neighbor's drive. "Look, Mom. It says sold."

Sure enough, the sign had been covered with a blue banner with the word *sold* emblazoned on it.

"What do you know," said Kate. "New neighbors."

"I hope they have kids," said Amanda.

"That would be nice," Kate agreed, and entertained a vision of her children finding best friends right next door to grow up with. By the time they'd gotten out of the car and headed into the house, she had the kids and their new friends grown to the teenager stage and happily sailing boats together around the cove.

She sent Robbie off to the tub and Amanda to her room to start her math, and went to water her roses.

Although the lots along the cove were long, sloping in unfenced grandeur down to the water, most of them weren't wide. Towering fir and cedar trees hid the houses from the road above and each other, however, which gave most of their owners a feeling of privacy. Kate's house and the vacant one next door were the exception. In spite of a big cedar that stood between the two houses, the occupants could pretty much know each other's business. Kate cast a glance in its direction as she walked to the corner where her hose sat curled, hoping that whoever moved in would be easy to get along with.

"Home from the war?"

She looked up to see Grace Morrison approaching. Grace was divorced, in her midfifties. Although she now sported two chins and her dark hair was generously salted with gray, it was still easy to see traces of a once beautiful woman in her high cheekbones, big brown eyes, and full lips. She enjoyed life at a slow pace, occasionally doing some substitute teaching at the local grade school and helping Kate out with her kids. Mostly, Grace loved to garden and bake. From what Kate could tell, her mission in life was to make sure her neighbors never lacked for goodies. Like many of the residents of this casual place, Grace had long ago moved past the desire to be *Vogue* beautiful, opting, instead, for comfortable. Today she wore baggy sweats, and a T-shirt topped with a shapeless, gray sweater.

Kate acknowledged Grace's approach with a friendly wave.

"How was the game?" asked Grace.

"Awful as usual," Kate replied. She nodded toward the house next door. "It looks like we're going to have new neighbors."

"Neighbor," Grace corrected. "I heard all about it this afternoon."

"So, tell."

"Do you want to pour yourself a stiff drink before I break the news to you?"

"I'm tough. I can take it. Anyway, it can't be that bad."

"It's not," said Grace. "Just remember that."

Grace's words set off warning bells in Kate's head. Someone much worse than Dennis the Menace was about to move in next door.

Kate braced herself. "Who's my new neighbor, Grace?"

"Jeff Hardin."

Two

KATE BLINKED. SHE HAD HEARD INCORRECTLY, that was it. "Jeff Hardin?" she repeated.

Grace nodded.

Denial wasn't a good thing, but right now it looked much better than reality. "This isn't happening," Kate insisted. "I'm having a nightmare."

"You're awake," said Grace, "and it's not really that bad."

"No. It's worse," said Kate. She strangled the water supply to her hose and threw it down in disgust. "Of all the neighborhoods in all the world!"

"He had to walk into mine," finished Grace in her best Humphrey Bogart voice.

"Funny."

"Actually, it is. Just a little."

An angry throb began inching its way across Kate's forehead. "I need to go take an aspirin."

"Take two," said Grace, "and call me in the morning."

Kate's headache was gone by morning, but not her sour mood. She managed to hide it from the kids while she got them off to school, but by the time she arrived at the radio station it was back in plain sight.

"You look like you should call yourself for advice," observed Wallis.

"I couldn't give me any that was impartial," said Kate. "Why, oh, why couldn't it have been you who bought the house next door to me?"

"Because I like living in the city, near civilization. So, who's moving in next door, the Antichrist?"

"Worse. Jeff Hardin."

For a moment, Wallis's expression stalled on stunned. Then her mouth cracked into a smile, which quickly deteriorated into a laugh.

Kate endured Wallis's merriment, reminding herself that the situation really was ludicrous. If she wasn't the one in it, she, too, would probably see the humor.

"I'm sorry," said Wallis at last. "That is just so bizarre."

"Yes, isn't it?" Kate shook her head. "The man follows me around like a bad smell. First work, now where I live."

"That's not quite accurate," corrected Wallis. "He beat you here by a half dozen years."

Kate indulged herself in a long-suffering sigh. "Yes, you're right."

"So, Doctor Kate, how are you going to handle this?"

"The same way I would advise anyone in my situation to handle it: with good manners. I'll smile politely at him when he crosses my line of sight, just as I do here. And if I happen to see a burglar entering his house, I'll call the police. As a neighbor, that's all I owe him, and that's all I intend to pay."

"That sounds very wise," said Wallis. "I'm impressed."

"So am I," said Kate. "I hope I can follow my own advice."

"And meanwhile, here's something to do your heart good," said Wallis, picking up a copy of the *Seattle Post-Intelligencer.* "You're news."

Kate read the headline. " 'Popular Local Radio Shrink Expands Her Practice.' Shrink. Ugh, I hate that slang."

"Okay, so shrink is not so good, but popular, that's definitely good," said Wallis. Looking over Kate's shoulder, she read aloud, " 'Dr. Kate Stonewall, psychologist at Seattle's KZOO talk radio, has just signed a syndication contract with the Premiere Radio Networks. Starting in September, the good doctor will be heard on radio stations across the country, joining such big radio names as Rush Limbaugh and Dr. Laura Schlessinger at a company that syndicates more than sixty radio programs to more than seventy-eight hundred radio affiliates.' "

"And who says everything you read in the news is bad?" murmured Kate.

"You've hit the big time, and that should console you for your personal troubles."

"What will console me for my personal troubles is when our nitwit of a program manager stops allowing my program to get bumped for pregame drivel."

"We can work on that," said Wallis. "But just remember, a prophet is without honor in her own land."

"Thanks, I feel wonderfully consoled now," said Kate.

"Don't mention it," said Wallis.

B Y THE TIME KATE CAME TO PICK UP HER CHILDREN from Grace's house, they had heard the big news. "Guess what, Mom? Jeff Hardin is moving in next door!" announced Robbie, hopping around her like a demented Slinky.

"Really?" said Kate, doing a fair imitation of a person who was willing to give a stranger a chance. *Bad news travels fast.* She shot a suspicious look at Grace, who was suddenly very busy straightening a stack of papers on her kitchen counter.

"Do you think he has any kids?" asked Amanda.

"It would be better for the world if he didn't," muttered Kate.

"I bet he can get us tickets to the Mariners." Robbie's voice was rising. So was the level of his bouncing.

"Thanks," Kate said to Grace.

"What could I do? They asked."

"You could have told them he's a child molester."

"He is?" cried Amanda, eyes wide.

"No, of course not," said Kate.

"He's just a perfectly normal, healthy male," added Grace. The smile she turned on Kate was positively wicked. "That's why your mom has such a hard time relating to him. She's only at her best with maladjusted people."

"That's why we're such good friends," Kate retorted.

"What's maladjusted?" asked Amanda, wrinkling her nose.

"Never mind," said Kate, steering her daughter toward the door. "Let's get you hoodlums out of here so Grace can have some peace and quiet. First one home gets to pick what we have for dinner."

The kids stampeded out Grace's back door, and Kate turned to her. "I can cope with this," she said. "After all, I'm a trained psychologist. I know how to handle problems."

"I know," said Grace, walking with her to the door. "And when it all gets to be too much, you can come over and I'll break out the vanilla tea."

Kate nodded. "Stock up."

THE NEW NEIGHBOR MOVED IN ON THE SATURDAY of Memorial Day weekend. Robbie and Amanda both had wanted to be around to witness the momentous event, but, as it turned out, they each got a better offer. Amanda was sailing with her best friend, Sommer, and her family, and Bill and Janet had taken Robbie camping with them to keep James company.

It was just as well, thought Kate. The kids would have been over there, getting underfoot or, worse yet, getting acquainted.

She heard the crunch of gravel as the U-Haul backed down the driveway at ten A.M., but she told herself she had no interest whatsoever in her new neighbor's doings. And to prove it, she poured herself a second cup of coffee and headed for the spare bedroom that doubled as her office. *The Frog with the Glass Slipper* had gotten her hooked on writing, and her second book, *How to Separate the Men from the Boys,* was due to hit the bookstores in July. Now she was well into her latest labor of love, *How to Pick the Gems from the Junk Pile,* and could hardly wait to get at it.

But once seated in front of her computer, she found she couldn't concentrate. Well, who could string together a coherent sentence with the sounds of thumps, whumps, grunts, and male laughter drifting in through the open window?

She looked out and, for the first time, it bothered her that she could see past the massive but misplaced trunk of the cedar tree and right into the living room next door. And her office wasn't the only place that provided an unwanted view of the new neighbor. She could see his front lawn and dock from her dining room and her deck, as well as the balcony off her bedroom, all of which faced the water. Then there was that bedroom window that stared right across into his. Great. Just great. She'd have to get window shades, shutters, locks, bars.

Stop it, Kate, she scolded herself. *You're being irrational.*

She let her gaze drift and caught sight of two men in T-shirts and shorts moving a couch into the living room. One of them she recognized as Jeff. Almost against her will, she found herself studying him—something she never did at the station. She watched his biceps bunch with the effort of holding the massive, well-worn thing. He had nice muscles, she would give him that. He wasn't very grace-

ful, though. Of course, it was hard to be graceful when lug-
ging around a heavy piece of furniture. Watching Jeff and
his friend maneuver the couch across the room, Kate noted
that in spite of the sweating and straining, the goof was
smiling.

Only the dim-witted smiled constantly. Kate shook her
head in disgust. What had she done to deserve inheriting
someone with the I.Q. of a mule for a neighbor?

When the Petersons, a sweet retired couple, had lived in
that house, they had placed the couch opposite the fireplace. Why was Jeff putting it along that particular wall? It
would look so much better facing the fireplace.

What was she doing? What did she care? Disgusted
with her nosy self, she reined her wandering thoughts back
to chapter two: "Dead Giveaways That He's No Gem."

By one o'clock, she realized she was hungry. She didn't
hear any scuffles, crashes, or grunts from next door and
wondered if the movers had all collapsed from their hard
work. Maybe there was a game on and they'd all stopped
life to watch it.

She fixed herself a sandwich and stepped out onto her
deck to grab a breath of fresh air.

And saw the blonde. The woman wore denim shorts and
a bikini top, and was heading down to Jeff Hardin's dock.
She had a great body: slim waist, nice, long legs, little
buns. Kate watched her walk, slinging her hips with the
confidence of a woman who knows she's perfect, and
Kate, conscious of the unwanted aftereffects of too little
exercise and too many of Grace's home-baked brownies,
felt a sudden, petty desire to run over there and force-feed
the woman an entire box of chocolates. The woman turned
to look back up the sloping lawn and, seeing her face, Kate
realized that she was young: twenty, twenty-two at the
most. Her laughter floated across the lawn and invaded
Kate's space.

A man came running to join her, and Kate immediately
recognized him as her nemesis. He was probably a good

ten years older than his consort, Kate guessed. He had shed his shirt, giving Kate a view of nicely formed pecs. Aside from that there was nothing all that remarkable in Jeff Hardin's looks. He was average height, average weight, even his hair was an average brown. But he did have great muscles. Kate had always been a sucker for muscles.

Which was what had trapped her the first time. Kate wondered if this poor girl was thinking clearly. She should give her a copy of *The Frog with the Glass Slipper*.

Jeff scooped up the girl and hustled her to the dock, where he pretended he was going to throw her in. She kicked her feet and squealed, clinging to him in fake alarm, and he finally set her down. Kate watched as the girl hung on him, smiling up into his face. He circled his arms around her waist and kissed her.

Watching the kissing couple, Kate felt suddenly old at thirty-five. She turned and went back inside the house before they could come up for air and catch her spying on them. *I'm too young to feel this old,* she thought sadly.

A new thought followed that one in short order. What kind of neighbor was this guy going to make? Like her, he was a radio personality. But, taking in the cute young girlfriend, Kate decided that was probably where the likeness ended. *Wild* and *party* were the two words that instantly came to mind. Kate hoped fervently that she was wrong.

By quarter to one in the morning she knew she wasn't. The party next door was now in full swing, with raucous laughter and loud, obnoxious country music taking over the once quiet atmosphere of Pleasant Cove. Kate flopped onto her side and pulled her pillow over her head. Someone let out a shriek and she gave a start.

This was ridiculous. There were laws, after all. Should she call the police? That would be a rotten thing to do to someone their first night in a new neighborhood, at least without warning.

Of course, her new neighbor wasn't exactly being considerate of the rest of them, and somebody needed to set him straight about how things worked around here. Grace wouldn't do it. She was too mellow to let anything bother her. Besides, she'd once said she could sleep through the end of the world, so while the civilized world of Pleasant Cove was coming to an end she was probably snoring happily, oblivious to the racket. Since the neighbors on Jeff Hardin's other side were away for the weekend, that left only Kate to do the job. She got up and yanked on her bathrobe.

Like Kate's and most of the houses along the cove, the one Jeff Hardin had bought boasted a reversed floor plan, which put the front door at the back of the house to take advantage of the view and make a good impression on passing boaters. A few people perched on the railing and steps of the porch that ran along its front, but most of the party was spread out over the lawn and on the dock. Kate pushed past the laughing, dancing people and made her way to the dock, where Jeff Hardin stood, holding court. The same blonde Kate had seen earlier stood next to him, a beer can in one hand, her free hand twisting a lock of her hair around a finger.

Kate stepped into the circle and faced him. "Excuse me," she said, using the voice that always made impertinent callers to her program stammer their apologies for offending her.

Jeff's eyes widened. Perhaps it was coming as just as much a shock to him to learn who his neighbor was as it had to her. "Kate Stonewall? Oh, my God."

"No, just your neighbor. Do you have any idea what time it is?"

He looked her up and down, taking in her ratty bathrobe, making her instantly aware of how well worn it was.

"No, but it was real neighborly of you to come over here to tell me," he replied, and the blonde and another woman stifled giggles.

Jerk, thought Kate angrily. "Did it ever occur to you that some people might be trying to sleep?"

"On Saturday night on Memorial Day weekend I figured most people would either be camping or partying."

"Not everyone," Kate informed him.

He looked at her pityingly. "Didn't anybody invite you to their party? You can join us if you want."

As a matter of fact, Janet had invited her to come camping with them. She was not some pitiful, friendless soul, for crying out loud. She was Dr. Kate Stonewall!

"I don't want to come to your drunken brawl. I want you to shut up or I'm calling the cops."

"Whoa," he said in mock horror, and Kate felt an uncivilized urge to push him off the dock. "Well, I guess we'll take the party inside. Sorry we bothered you," he added in a tone of voice that told her he was anything but. "By the way, I caught the last half of your show Friday. I really liked the advice you gave that woman about getting along with her coworker."

Did he honestly think he could twist that situation to apply to this one?

Kate smiled sweetly at him. "Thank you. It's always a good idea to try and get along, which is why I'm going to give you a chance to quiet down before reporting you."

He arched an eyebrow at her, and the simple gesture made her feel small. Which made her even angrier. He was the one being rude here. Why should she feel guilty? She shouldn't.

But she did.

Disgusted with both herself and the whole ridiculous situation, Kate turned and walked away, wrapping herself in self-righteous dignity as she went.

She could hear a woman saying, "What's her problem?"

Hardin amplified his voice for her benefit. "She's just mad because we're having fun and she's not."

Kate picked up her pace, trying to escape the eerie sensation of being stalked by the same nasty voice that always followed her program, saying, "Hey there. Pop a beer, kick off your shoes, and kick back. It's time for some *Jock Talk.*" The man was a prole, and his presence next door had probably dropped the value of her house by at least ten thousand dollars.

Back in her bedroom, she looked at herself in the full-length mirror. Her hair was a tangled mess, and the comfortable bathrobe she had kept until it was too worn even for the Goodwill now offended her greatly. She supposed the unnamed blonde had something short, satiny, and floral. No, probably black. Fredericks of Hollywood.

Kate tore off the bathrobe and hurled it on the floor, then climbed between the sheets and gave her pillow a punch. Why was it that in every other aspect of life and with every other human being—except, of course, deliberately obtuse callers—she was a perfectly rational, warm human being?

She knew the answer to that. It was because she resented Jeff Hardin. But she really didn't resent him out of petty jealousy over the fact that he had a bigger market share than her. And she certainly didn't covet his time slot. She wanted to be home with her children during the dinner hour and early evening. No, what she resented was what he represented: a society filled with immature men who elevated sports to a high level of respect even while they took their women for granted.

Moving the party inside hadn't done much to muffle the whoops and laughter coming from next door and she still had too much adrenaline pumping through her blood to sleep. She should get up and work. No, she didn't want to turn her night and day upside down like *some people*. She closed her eyes.

A male partier had sneaked back onto Hardin's porch and was now howling some horrible song about liking his women just a little on the trashy side. Kate flopped over onto her stomach. Just relax. She heard a splash from the cove, followed by a chorus of laughter. Someone had probably just fallen off the dock. Hopefully, it was Hardin.

The minutes dragged on, and she lay in bed watching her clock and dreaming up ways to avenge herself on Pleasant Cove's barbarian invader. Her ideas ranged from poking her garden hose through his open window, then turning it on full bore and dousing the revelers, to waking him at six A.M. with a boom box blaring the cries of Wagner's Valkyries.

She should just call the cops. If they weren't quiet in another five minutes, she would. She didn't care what Jeff Hardin and his idiot friends thought of her. And her advice to that caller could not be applied to this situation. No, sir. She had given Mr. Hardin plenty of opportunity to behave like a rational, mature person. If he insisted on acting like an adolescent boy whose parents were out of town, then he should be treated like one.

As if on cue, the noise began to lessen. Or was it just that she was getting used to it? No, the revelers were definitely subduing themselves. Which meant she could finally sleep. She shifted onto her back and stared at the ceiling.

Go to sleep, she told herself. She began to hum. The humming took on words. *Now I lay me down to sleep. I live next door to a creep.*

That sort of silliness was getting her nowhere. She needed to think about something pleasant. *A meadow filled with wildflowers. Amanda and Robbie making daisy chains. And there comes a handsome man in a three-piece suit at the far end of the field, walking your way. He's holding out a hand to you. . . .*

Kate finally drifted into sleep, and by early morning her mind had manufactured a lovely dream as an incentive for her to stay prone a little longer. It began just as the vision in which she had indulged herself earlier (knowing, of course, that dreams and fantasy have their place; a woman simply can't mix them up with reality). She was back in a meadow, but unlike the one she had imagined before falling asleep, this one was carpeted with voluptuous red poppies like the ones the witch in *The Wizard of Oz* spread out to trap Dorothy and her friends. Now here came her hero, who swept her off her feet, literally. This hero looked suspiciously like Jeff Hardin, so, obviously, in this dream she had no taste in men. As he carried her through the meadow she threw back her head and laughed, her long, brown hair trailing over his arm in a glorious cascade. The glorious cascade thing was always nice, since in real life her hair was much too ornery to cascade properly.

Suddenly, the dream took a turn for the worse. The poppies gave way to freshly mowed grass, and beyond that, Kate saw a diamond-shaped plateau of dirt, dotted with men in baseball uniforms, who stood scratching themselves and spitting.

"No!" she screamed, and started to kick and squirm, but her dream man merely chuckled maniacally and kept walking, past the scratching players in the outfield and onto the infield.

He stopped in front of the pitcher, saying, "I couldn't get to first base with her. She won't play hardball."

The pitcher, a brute with a foot-long chin, narrowed his beady eyes at Kate, who was still squirming helplessly, and said, "She will now."

Her captor tossed her to the pitcher, then walked to home plate and picked up a bat. With a mighty heave, the pitcher shifted Kate so she sat in the palm of one hand. He raised his arm, bringing her back as though she were a javelin he meant to toss, or . . .

"Oh, my God," she cried. "I'm a human baseball."

The huge man threw Kate, and she began hurtling through the air. In front of her she saw Jeff Hardin standing, bat poised, ready to swing. She was almost to him, his bat was moving—

With a strangled shriek, Kate sat up. Untangling her legs from the sheets, she pushed back her hair from her damp forehead and forced herself to take deep breaths.

This was ridiculous. What was the matter with her, anyway?

She turned to her bedside clock. Almost ten A.M. Good grief, it was past time to get up. Maybe in giving her a nasty dream like that, her subconscious was doing her a favor and making sure she didn't sleep her whole morning away. After such a dream she certainly had no desire to stay in bed any longer.

She got up, not bothering with her bathrobe since the morning was so warm, and padded across the worn rag carpet that had been her grandmother's to take her usual morning dose of fresh, salty air.

The spring breeze embraced her as she stepped out onto her balcony. Pleasant Cove lay before her in all its lazy beauty, its blue water sprinkled with dazzling sunshine diamonds. Here and there a small boat bobbed. An eagle swooped past her, and she smiled and let her gaze follow its progress down the cove. That was when she caught sight of him.

There stood Jeff Hardin on his front porch, binoculars pressed against his eyes and sighted right on her. She put her hands on her hips and glared at him, and he jumped as if he had just seen a terrifying sight. Then he quickly turned, fastening his attention on something across the cove.

My new neighbor, thought Kate bitterly as she ducked back into her bedroom. He's not only rude, he's a pervert!

And since he was a rude pervert, it didn't matter that he had caught her looking her absolute worst, wearing a faded pink, oversized cotton nightshirt that proclaimed, "I don't do mornings."

He wasn't going to catch her again, she'd make sure of that. She went downstairs to the kitchen and pulled the island phone book out of the junk drawer and laid it on the kitchen counter. It didn't take her long to find what she was looking for. She made her call and placed her order, then hung up wearing a smile. That took care of that.

Half an hour later, Kate answered a knock at her back door and found the pervert standing there. He hardly looked preppy in his faded jeans and black T-shirt sporting the Nike logo, but he did look . . . not sexy. Sexy was a man in a three-piece suit. Well, whatever his look, it was turning her brain schizophrenic. Here was one side, taking in his slim torso and the cute way his hair insisted on flopping over his right eye, and demanding to know why she hadn't ever noticed that. The sane half reported that there was no need to take any interest in the physical attributes of a man so completely disgusting. Jeff Hardin, it insisted, was a prime example of what any woman with a brain did not want. That, it reported, was why she had not noticed, and that was why she didn't need to pay any further notice now.

He craned his head forward a little and gave her a tentative grin. "Hi."

"Hello," she said, keeping her voice neutral.

He shifted his weight from one foot to the other and cleared his throat.

"Did you want something?" she asked.

"Yes, actually. We've never really gotten a chance to get to know each other at the station."

"I suspect we move in different circles."

He took no offense at her words, which was good. None was intended. She wasn't trying to be a snob, really. She was just stating a fact, letting him know that the words *good neighbors* and *good friends* were not synonymous.

"But since we are neighbors now, I thought I should come and apologize. I think we might have gotten off on the wrong foot."

What a gross understatement! Was this his idea of an apology? "When?" she inquired sweetly. "Last night at your drunken brawl, which kept me up all night, or this morning, when you were spying on me?"

His lips moved sideways and his eyebrows shot up, indicating he had now gone into think mode. Kate waited to see the results, not expecting much.

He didn't disappoint her. "Look, I'm sorry about last night. And as for this morning, I wasn't spying on you. I was watching that eagle."

"The eagle flew south," said Kate. "You were looking north."

"All right, I admit it. I got distracted from the eagle when you came out on your balcony. I'm sorry. I'm not a Peeping Tom if that's what you're worried about."

"So you say."

"I have someone in my life," said Jeff. "I don't need to get my kicks watching strangers parading around in their . . . whatever that thing was."

The nerve of this guy! "Since when is standing on your own balcony parading around?"

The only reply Jeff gave her was an arm waving her argument away in disgust as he walked back to his house.

Kate slammed her door shut. "It was a nightshirt!"

Three

BOTH THE CHILDREN GOT HOME FROM THEIR TRIPS too late on Memorial Day to meet their new neighbor and, thankfully, they were so full of their own adventures that the subject never came up. But Robbie introduced the topic the next morning at breakfast.

"I don't want either of you over there," said Kate, eating the last bite of pancake off his plate before putting it into the dishwasher.

"Why not?" asked Robbie.

"Because he's not a nice man, and it wouldn't benefit you to be around him."

"We can't even say hello if he says hi to us?" asked Amanda.

"Of course you can say hello. There's no need to be rude. But this man isn't anyone with whom we're going to want to become friends."

"Why?" persisted Robbie.

"Because he lives a different lifestyle than we do. There is nothing we are going to have in common with him."

Kate glanced at the clock. "You guys better get going or you're going to miss the school bus."

There, she thought after she had kissed the kids good-bye and hustled them out the door. Never give children more information than they need, and at this point they didn't need to know about Jeff Hardin's wild lifestyle or the kind of scenery he liked to watch with his binoculars.

The idea of herself as any man's sex object almost made Kate laugh. After Rob's death, she'd let herself go, and these days her hairstyle was simple, her makeup sparse, and her weight, well, less than spare.

The phone rang, saving her from having to think about the diet she knew lurked just around the corner.

It was Grace. "I just took my cinnamon rolls out of the oven. Want one?"

"Sure," said Kate. She had to eat, after all. "Come on over and I'll provide the coffee. But don't bring enough for seconds."

"Sure," said Grace.

They were on their second cinnamon roll when Grace brought up the subject of Jeff. "I met our new neighbor."

"Someone new for you to fatten besides me," said Kate.

"I like him."

"You may have him. Want to trade houses?"

"Have you actually talked to him?"

Kate nodded. "Yes, I have. We met Saturday night."

"And?"

"And he is the reincarnation of Rob. Just what I need living next door."

"Maybe he is," said Grace thoughtfully. "Maybe having him in your life will prove to be therapeutic."

"I don't need therapy," said Kate. "I give it, remember? And I sure don't need another Rob in my life. One was quite enough. More than enough."

Grace looked sad at the mention of Kate's deceased husband and shook her head. "Poor man."

"Poor man!" shot back Kate. "Poor me. I don't know

which was worse, his ignoring me while he was alive, or his dying and leaving me to raise these kids on my own."

"He didn't commit suicide, Kate," said Grace gently.

Kate sighed. "I know. It's not fair to blame him for the fact that I'm on my own. And the truth is, with the way we were drifting, I'd probably have wound up single anyway. But surely you can see why I don't care to be around men like him. That doesn't show I need therapy; it shows I know how to protect myself. And if more women would learn what kind of man is harmful to them and just stay away, we wouldn't have the high divorce rate we have in this country, or the huge amount of domestic violence."

"You're absolutely right," said Grace.

"If there's one thing I've learned," said Kate, "it's how to size up men. And I can tell you right now, Jeff Hardin and Rob Stonewall were both cut out of the same piece of cloth."

"You're absolutely right again," said Grace. "And what a nice piece of cloth it is."

IT WAS SATURDAY, AND SATURDAY WAS MOW THE lawn day. At least, that was how it had always been with Jeff's dad, and Jeff saw no reason not to carry on the tradition. This was his first lawn, and since the property had cost him a bundle, he wanted it to look good. With no fences to divide the lots, only a tree here or there, it looked like one gigantic park, and since his neighbors all maintained well-manicured lawns, Jeff figured he'd best do his part to keep things looking good.

He whistled as he pulled out his brand-new lawn mower from the garage. Condos and apartments were okay for guys just starting out, but real men had houses and mowed lawns.

And had kids playing on those lawns, came the afterthought.

Kids. Thank God he hadn't had any with Leslie. What

an ugly mess that would have been, having to fight with an alcoholic mother for custody of his own children. He'd have kids someday, he told himself, but right now he was happy enough with just the house.

Dad would like this place, thought Jeff. He'd have to get the old man over soon to check it out.

The old man would probably tease him over picking a house next door to a single woman. But sharp-tongued, aggressive women who slept in pink T-shirts didn't fit Jeff's definition of perfect neighbors. Neither did know-it-all shrinks. He didn't know anything more about Doctor Kate than the hype he'd seen in her press kit, but she was obviously divorced, which meant that although she sure liked to run other people's lives, she wasn't much good at managing her own. It wasn't hard to imagine her husband leaving her. She must have been something to try and live with.

Halfway through his mowing, Jeff caught sight of a boy standing on the edge of his property, watching him. The kid looked fairly young in spite of his height and husky build. He wore a baseball cap and had a glove in one hand, and brought back good memories of Jeff's own childhood. Jeff turned off the mower and strolled across the lawn to him.

"Hi."

"Hi," said the boy, and smiled.

Cute kid, thought Jeff.

"Are you Jeff Hardin?" asked the boy.

Jeff nodded. "That's me. Who are you?"

"I'm Robbie Stonewall."

The good doctor's son. Odd. He looked normal.

Jeff pointed to the glove. "You like to play ball?"

The boy nodded.

"What position do you play?"

"Outfield," said Robbie.

At this age, there were only two reasons why a boy played outfield. Either the kid could actually catch and had an arm on him or the coach had stuck him as far away from the action as possible. Jeff wondered which it was in Robbie's case.

"Outfield's an important position," he said.

"Yeah?" asked the boy eagerly.

"Sure."

Now the kid looked a little embarrassed. "I'm not very good at catching fly balls. I mean, I try, but . . ." He bit his lip, as if holding in a deep, dark secret.

"Some of 'em get by ya, huh?" guessed Jeff.

Robbie nodded and stared out at the water, unable to look at Jeff.

"Don't worry about it, kid," he said. "Everybody misses some." He started back to his lawn mower.

"They scare me," Robbie blurted.

Jeff stopped and turned around. He knew the reason for that, remembered his own fear as a kid. "See somebody get beaned?" he asked.

"Donny French got a concussion."

"Well, Rob, I'll tell you, there's only one way you can keep from getting konked on the head."

"What?" asked Robbie eagerly.

"You've got to keep your eye on the ball all the time and have your hands up, ready to catch it." He took Robbie's glove and demonstrated. "See, you make a well for the ball to fall into."

"Wow," breathed Robbie.

Jeff smiled down at the kid, and handed back the glove. He could tell by the scuffing foot and hesitant expression that another confession was forthcoming.

"What else?" he prompted.

"I can't hit, either."

"You can't?"

Robbie shook his head. "Coach says when I connect with the ball I'll hit homers."

Jeff put his hands in his back pockets and studied the boy. He belonged to the terror of the airwaves, who probably wouldn't appreciate Jeff taking her son under his wing. Maybe the kid's dad, wherever he was, wouldn't, either. The boy was looking at him as if he were convinced Jeff kept the keys to baseball success on his key ring.

Jeff came to a sudden decision. "Come with me, kid," he said.

Robbie hesitated.

"Well, come on," said Jeff, and headed for his garage. The boy trotted after him.

Jeff had a collection of bats propped in one corner. He picked up his smallest wood one and grabbed a ball and an ancient life jacket his dad had given him for the day he got a boat to go with his dock. He handed the bat to Robbie, then led him back to the middle of the half-mowed lawn, where he dropped the life jacket.

"There's home plate. Show me your stance."

Robbie sidled up to the improvised plate and held the bat over his right shoulder.

"Don't crowd the base," advised Jeff. "You've gotta give yourself some moving room."

The boy complied.

"That looks good." Jeff walked to an imaginary pitcher's mound and tossed the kid an easy ball.

Robbie swung with all his might and completely missed it. No wonder, thought Jeff, the kid's not watching the ball. His coach should have caught that.

"Hey," he said, as he ran to fetch the ball, "this can be fixed."

Robbie's discouraged expression turned hopeful. "It can?"

"Yeah. There's one thing you've got to remember in baseball or any other sport that involves balls. You know what it is?"

Robbie shook his head.

"It's like I told you about catching the thing. You've gotta keep your eye on the ball. You've got to always know where that baby is. Now, I'm gonna throw you another, and this time I want you to watch the ball all the way to your bat. Watch the ball hit the bat, okay?"

"Okay," agreed Robbie.

Jeff returned to his pitcher's mound and held up the ball. "All right now. You're gonna watch the ball hit your bat."

The boy nodded.

Jeff threw the ball and the kid swung again, but took his eyes off it at the last minute. It bounced behind him and rolled away, and he looked at Jeff as if they had both just seen a dog get hit by a car.

"That was a good try, man," said Jeff, loping to retrieve the elusive target once more. "But what happened was, you took your eyes off the ball at the last minute. This time I want you to watch it hit the bat."

Robbie caught his lip between his teeth and nodded.

Jeff pitched the baseball again. The boy watched it as if his very life depended on it. Again, he swung hard. This time he connected, and the ball rocketed through the air, past an astonished Jeff and right through the window of Robbie's house.

Uh-oh, thought Jeff as his new neighbor's face appeared on the other side of the shattered glass. To the boy he said, "Great hit, man!" And it had been. This kid had huge potential.

Robbie had been looking worried, but with Jeff's words he beamed. "I've never done that."

"Well, now you're a real guy," said Jeff. "Nobody's a real guy until he's managed to put a baseball through a window."

"Mom's gonna be mad," said Robbie in a small voice.

"Don't worry. I'll talk to your mom," Jeff promised, then realized that would probably make things worse for the kid, who was at the moment regarding him as if he were Saint George, Superman, and the Lone Ranger all rolled into one.

Now Kate was marching across her lawn toward them,

looking like a small general leading her army to battle. But this woman didn't need an army. She was scary enough all by herself.

"Sorry about your window," said Jeff as soon as she got within earshot.

She ignored him, turning, instead, to her son. "Robbie," she said sternly, "what were you told?"

The boy's head dropped. "I'm sorry, Mom. I didn't mean to."

"We'll talk about it when we get home," she said, and put a hand on his shoulder.

"I really didn't mean to," the kid insisted as she gave him a nudge.

"Sweetheart, you know it's not the window," said Kate. "Go on back to the house. I'll be there in just a minute."

Jeff watched the kid's slumping shoulders and felt like an informer who had just sent someone to their death. "I'll be glad to pay for the window," he offered.

"It's okay," she said. "My homeowner's insurance will cover it." She turned and started to follow her son back across her lawn.

Jeff felt there was more to be discussed here. "Your son says he hasn't got a hit all season."

"There's more to life than baseball," she replied, and kept going.

This woman was not going to get the last word. "He could be good," Jeff called.

That pronouncement made Robbie stop. He turned and looked at Jeff, a world of hope in his eyes.

Kate had frozen in her tracks at Jeff's words. Now, she closed the distance between herself and her son. She bent over and said something to the boy, then patted him on the back and sent him shuffling toward the house. Slowly, she turned and walked back to Jeff, wearing the expression of a severely tested kindergarten teacher.

"He just needs somebody to train him to keep his eye on the ball," he said, sure that if he could only explain things this woman would see the whole episode in the proper light.

"Well, I appreciate your doing that," she said, and from her tone of voice Jeff could tell she was trying to be fair. Good. Now they were making progress.

With a little kindness on her face she was attractive, he thought. There was something about freckles that made a woman look so damned adorable. Add some more lipstick, put her in something other than that oversized tee and those baggy sweats . . .

"Now if we can just train him not to hit balls through windows we'll be in business, won't we?" she continued, making Jeff's good feelings toward her vanish.

"That would have been a home run on a baseball field. The kid's got a lot of power."

"I guess you proved that," she said in a snippy tone that made Jeff scowl.

"Hey, I was just trying to help."

"Well, thanks to your help I've got glass all over my living room floor."

"And a kid who feels good about himself. I would think, being a shrink—"

"Psychologist," she corrected.

"Whatever. I would think that you'd figure a little broken glass is a small price to pay for your kid's self-esteem getting a boost."

Kate's cheeks flushed and she stiffened. "You don't know me well enough to make that kind of slam."

"And I don't want to," snarled Jeff, and returned to his lawn mower. He gave the starter cord a ferocious pull and the thing came to life with an obnoxious roar. He'd take the company of a sharp-bladed lawn mower over Kate Stonewall any day.

LATER THAT AFTERNOON, JEFF WAS SITTING ON AN Adirondack chair on his front porch, enjoying the view, when he saw Grace Morrison crossing his freshly mowed lawn, bearing a pie.

"Is that for me, I hope?" he called.

"It is. I promised you one, and I always deliver on my promises."

Jeff stood up and saluted her with his can of beer. "Grace, you're my kind of neighbor. Heck, you're my kind of woman. Marry me."

Grace chuckled as she came up the porch steps. "I hope you like apple."

"That just happens to be one of my favorites," he said. "Want a beer?"

"No, thanks," said Grace, "but I wouldn't mind sampling a piece of my handiwork." She followed him into the kitchen, filling the house with the aroma of apples and cinnamon, and set the pie on the counter. She eyed the cardboard box overflowing with canned chili, stew, and Kraft Macaroni and Cheese on the floor.

"I was going to get around to that later today," said Jeff.

"I assume you've unpacked the cutlery?"

"Oh, yeah." He pulled open a drawer. It looked as though the utensils had been dumped in. Come to think of it, that was about what had happened. He gave a helpless shrug. "It's in there somewhere," he said, and began rummaging around. He brought up a knife and displayed it like a trophy.

"Very good," said Grace, taking it from him. "How about forks and plates?"

"I can do that," he said.

She cut him a generous piece of pie, put it on the plate he'd produced, and handed it over.

"This looks great," he said. "At least someone around here knows how to be neighborly." He cut off a chunk and stuffed it in his mouth. "Good."

"Thanks. So, how are you settling in?"

"Okay," said Jeff. "Most of my neighbors are nice."

"You and Kate haven't exactly hit it off, have you?"

"Have you talked to her?" he hedged.

Grace took a step back, crossed her arms, and examined him from head to toe. "I've got to say, you don't look like a drunken pervert. But then, looks can be deceiving."

Jeff whistled. "I did make an impression, didn't I?"

"You are definitely a presence in the neighborhood," said Grace diplomatically.

"Well, she hasn't made much of an impression on me, either," said Jeff. "It's no wonder she's divorced."

"Divorced. Who told you that?"

"Nobody. I assumed—"

"You assumed wrong. Kate's a widow."

Jeff sobered. "No."

"Yes. In fact, I should tell you something of her background. You'd probably find her a little easier to understand."

"I'm listening," he said, and loaded more pie in his mouth.

"Kate married her high school sweetheart, who was the star of the football team. His glory years ended with a bad injury his second year in college."

Jeff let out a low whistle. "Tough break."

"It was for both of them," said Grace. "Rob's hard knock took its toll on their marriage. I think the two of them got unbalanced. Kate kept plugging away at her education, while he just . . . settled."

"Doing what?"

"Working for his father as a real estate appraiser."

"Nothing wrong with that," said Jeff.

"It's a long way from a pro football career," said Grace. "Anyway, when he wasn't working, he was glued to the tube, watching every sports event he could find. He died when the kids were really little. I don't think Robbie was much older than one at the time. It hasn't been easy for Kate."

Jeff picked up his beer. "How'd her husband die?"

"He choked to death on a peanut."

Jeff coughed out the beer and grabbed for a paper towel. "Are you making this up?"

Grace shook her head. "Swear to God. It was Super Bowl Sunday, and Kate had left the kids with her mom and gone shopping with a friend. Rob's buddies were plastered just enough to not figure out what was happening until it was too late."

"Geez," said Jeff, stunned. "Poor lady."

"Kate's so worried Robbie will grow up to be like his dad it's a wonder he got to even try baseball."

Jeff shook his head. "And I just helped the kid put a ball through her window."

"Yes, and you and your show represent everything she is on a crusade against."

"Yeah, men."

"Not all men, just ones who take women for granted and are sports addicts. And who preempt her show, which she thinks is useful and important, for pregame shows, which she thinks are silly and useless."

"But what I do isn't useless," protested Jeff. "Sports serve a very important purpose in our culture. They help guys let off steam, make them feel good about themselves. And I'm not addicted," he added.

Grace smiled. "I believe you. And I'm sorry you two got off to such a bad start. I think you'd like Kate if you got to know her. She's got a great sense of humor."

That she keeps hidden in her underwear drawer, thought Jeff cynically.

"She's generous."

With her complaints, he mentally added.

"She's really a nice woman," finished Grace.

Compared to Cruella DeVil. "I'll take your word for it, Grace," said Jeff. "Anyway, it's too late. She's had her chance and she blew it. I'm already in love with another woman."

Grace looked disappointed. "Oh?"

"Yeah. She lives two houses down and makes great pies."

Grace took the hint and cut Jeff another slice. "Kate could use a nice man in her life," she said casually.

"Well, that lets me out," said Jeff. "I'm a drunken pervert." *Thank God.*

K ATE KEPT MENTALLY REPLAYING HER LATEST CLASH with Jeff Hardin. Really, for someone who was supposed to know so much about human behavior, she was making some incredibly stupid mistakes. The more she thought about it, the more she realized that she might have been unfair to her new neighbor. The fact that she disliked him to begin with had probably made her less tolerant of his rowdy party than she would have been if it had been hosted by someone else. And looking back on the great binocular incident, she realized she was blowing out of proportion something she might normally have found silly and amusing. Then there was the way she'd jumped all over him when he'd tried to help her son. That had been cute. She had come across like a combination of the Ice Queen and the Wicked Witch of the West. Still, the man had no right to tell her how to raise her children.

When her mother made her weekly check-in call from San Diego on Sunday, Kate told her about the new man in her life.

"I can't imagine fate coming up with a crueler trick than to stick this man next to me," she finished. "And he's already proving to be an attractive nuisance. I'm having a hard time keeping the kids away from him."

"Is he attractive?" asked Carol Hewitt hopefully.

"That's not what I meant," said Kate. "He's like an unfenced swimming pool."

"But is he nice looking?" persisted her mother.

"Oh, I suppose. In an average sort of way. But I don't want anything to do with him. He's another Rob."

"Kate, you hardly know the man," protested her mother.

"Believe me, I know all I need to know. When a man hosts a talk show dedicated to sports it says something about him."

"Yes," put in her mother. "It says he has a steady job. There's nothing wrong with that."

"It also says he's emotionally stuck at seventeen," argued Kate. "I mean, what kind of a career is sitting around talking about baseball scores all day?"

"Maybe as enjoyable a one as sitting around poking your nose into other people's business," suggested Carol.

"Oh, Mother. You can't even compare the two. What degrees did he need for what he does? And what kind of smarts does it take to do it? I use my brain."

"I'm not sure you're using it now," said her mom. "Think about it, darling. If you make him completely off limits to the kids, you'll turn him into forbidden fruit, and that will make him all the more attractive to them. And it's not exactly in your best interests to snub him, either. Good neighbors are hard to find. It pays to be one, because you never know when you might need one."

Her mother was right, of course. She didn't need to become pals with Jeff Hardin, but she didn't need to start a feud, either. "Oh, you're right, and I know it. Where is my common sense these days, anyway?"

"I don't know, but until you find it you're welcome to borrow mine. And mine says that you ought to make an effort to mend your fences while you still can. You may be stuck next door to this man for many years. There might even come a time when you need help, and he's the only one around to give it. Better to eat a little crow now than the whole bird later."

"Good point," Kate admitted. "I guess I'll make some cookies and take them over."

By late afternoon, Kate was standing at Jeff's back door with her peace offering. She told herself she was simply wearing a nice pair of slacks and a blouse because she was tired of constantly getting caught looking dumpy. It put her at a psychological disadvantage.

He opened the door and blinked in surprise. Then he smiled. It looked like a gloating smile to Kate, but remembering her mother's words, she tried to ignore it.

She held out the plate and said, "Chocolate chip olive branch."

His smile widened into an appreciative grin, and he took it. "I like your taste in olive branches."

"I think you're right. We definitely got started on the wrong foot," she said, "and I figured since we're going to be neighbors, maybe we ought to try again and see if we can find the right one."

"Thanks. You know, I meant what I said. I'll be happy to pay for that window."

Kate shook her head. "You don't need to. Really."

"You've got a nice kid."

Kind words about one of her children. Kate already liked Jeff Hardin better.

He stepped away from the door. "Want to come in?"

Something inside Kate gave a shiver of anticipation, and she slapped it down. Being neighborly did not include entering Jeff Hardin's den of stupidity.

"No thanks," she said. "I've got to get home."

"Working on a new book?" he asked.

She was not about to discuss something with Jeff Hardin that would be completely over his head. She merely nodded politely. Time to go.

He spoke before she could turn her back on him. "Another self-help book for women?"

"Yes, as a matter of fact, it is."

"You should write a self-help book for guys," suggested Jeff.

"Men seem to do pretty well at looking out for themselves."

There went the eyebrow again. He nodded slowly. "Oh, that's right. We're all selfish droolers."

You're the one who said it, thought Kate, but she refrained from voicing her thought. They were going to be good neighbors whether he liked it or not, and she was not going to allow him to pull them into another stupid squabble.

"Enjoy the cookies." She gave him her polite but aloof smile, turned her back on him, and walked away. There. She had done her part for diplomatic relations, and that was that. Now she didn't need to have anything more to do with Mr. *Jock Talk.*

ON MONDAY, SHE FINISHED HER PROGRAM AND gave Jeff a brief nod and a polite hello as they passed each other in the hall. The gesture showed what a civilized, rational human being she was. The brevity of it reminded him that while no fence separated their houses, there was such a thing as a property line, and she expected them each to stay on their respective side.

He wasn't quite as proper. "Nice suit," he added as she hurried past him. "Got a hot date?"

She kept on walking. "No." And if she did, Jeff Hardin would be the last person on the planet whom she would feel the need to inform.

She did have an engagement, though. Tonight she would be speaking at a banquet, addressing a gathering of the city's professional women, and proceeds would go to the new battered women's shelter under construction downtown.

She knew that Jeff made his share of personal appearances, too. He could be found at grand openings of pubs and supermarkets all over the greater Seattle area. What a guy.

KATE SAT DEMURELY WHILE THE MISTRESS OF CERE-monies listed her degrees and accomplishments, including a Matrix Award for Achievement in Education and the International Women's Forum Award in Career Achievement in Washington state.

The introduction ended and the women burst into enthusiastic applause as Kate made her way to the podium.

"It is a pleasure to be here tonight," she said, "especially since I know that you all have put in a long day. Each one of you, I am sure, works hard at your job. You give great thought to how you manage your time. You pay careful attention to how you deal with your coworkers, how you present proposals, and how you ask for a raise. But let me ask you this. Can you honestly say that you give the same amount of attention to how you run your love life?"

A reverent hush fell over the room as the last of the banqueters set down her dessert fork and leaned forward, her attention effectively captured. Good, thought Kate. This was important. Once women mastered the art of thinking practically when choosing a man, the happier both sexes would be.

She went on to explain the importance of not being fooled by a mask of charm or good looks, of making sure that you shared common interests with a man, and common goals for life. Even as she gave her audience a checklist, going over the differences between a frog and a prince, she mentally shook her head over the sad fact that so many women had such a difficult time differentiating. They were ignorant, of course.

Just like the young and foolish Kate who had once picked Rob Stonewall for her Mr. Right. The Kate Stonewall of today would never be so stupid.

She concluded her speech, and the women gave her a standing ovation. As she looked out at the sea of faces, she hoped that her words had, somehow, sunk in.

A swarm of women wanted to speak with her after the banquet, and by the time she left, it was close to ten. So much for making the nine-fifty boat. She'd be stuck waiting for the ten–forty-five. Ugh.

This was the only thing she didn't like about her job: the extra appearances, the late nights, all of which kept her away from the kids. They were growing so fast, and her time with them was precious. But there was only her to provide for them. And there was only her to wise up American women on how to pick a mate.

When she first got her degree she hadn't planned on becoming a guru to thousands of American women. Studying psychology had begun as a way to try to understand herself better and make sense of her less-than-perfect life with Rob. The more she had learned about human behavior, the more fascinating she had found it, and the more she had wanted to know. And the more she came to know, the more she realized she couldn't, with a clear conscience, keep that knowledge to herself. Now, years later, here she was, a woman with a mission.

On the ferry, Kate stayed in her car and dozed until the boat bumped into the pilings of the dock on Bainbridge Island. Good. Home, sweet home was only a few minutes away now. She could hardly wait to get out of her panty hose and into bed.

She followed the parade of cars off the boat and got about two miles past civilization when her car started cathwunking its way down the highway, doing the automotive equivalent of a limp. There could be only one explanation for this kind of uneven ride. She pulled onto the shoulder and the last two cars from the boat zipped uncaringly past her. She got out, hoping her diagnosis of the problem was wrong.

As usual, she was right. There it sat, under her left rear bumper. A very flat tire.

"No," she moaned. It was always something with this car, and always at the most inconvenient time.

She watched the taillights of her fellow ferry passengers disappearing into the darkness. Here she was, alone, at eleven-thirty at night on a dark road, in heels and a suit. Not the most ideal situation for changing a tire.

Ah, but she had her trusty cell phone. She got back inside the car, pulled it out of her purse, and dialed Andy's Garage. Andy wasn't the only mechanic on the island, but he was the best, and his services included twenty-four–hour towing. Cars were his life.

"This is Andy," said a prerecorded voice. "I'm probably out on a tow, so leave a message where you are and I'll get there sooner or later."

Knowing Andy and his propensity to want to try and diagnose on the spot, then lecture the owner on the importance of vehicle maintenance, it would be later rather than sooner. Kate left her number anyway, hoping she might get lucky.

Meanwhile, she couldn't just sit here. It wasn't that she was worried about the kids. Grace was with them, and was probably at this moment sacked out on the couch, lullabyed to sleep by Jay Leno. But Kate longed to be sacked out, too. She was so tired her head felt wuzzy and her eyes stung. She wanted her bed. She needed her bed.

There was only one way to get to it. She climbed back out of the car and went to the trunk and opened it, hoping she remembered after all these years how to put the jack together. She was pretty sure she had a flare in the trunk as well. She could set that off so no late-night drunk would plow into her and turn her into morning news. The trunk was capacious, and, naturally, the flare was hiding in its farthest recess.

She bent over, stretching out her hand to reach it and coming up a good foot and a half short. She leaned over further, but still had no luck. Determined, she laid herself out inside the trunk. The pressure this put on her abdomen was not pleasant. She could feel her skirt creeping up her thighs, and could imagine what a spectacle she made. Well, at this hour of night there was no one to see. No one to help, either. She was on her own. She reached for the flare and almost touched it. She wriggled farther into the trunk, whanged her thigh, and felt the zing of a run racing up her panty hose. A shoe slipped loose and dangled from the ends of her toes. Fun. This was just too, too fun.

She had finally succeeded in wrapping her fingers around the flare when she heard a car pulling onto the shoulder in back of her. Company. Great. Here she was, wedged inside the trunk of her car with her skirt hitched up and her rear in the air. She could only imagine what sort of pervert that had attracted.

She began to scramble back out of the trunk, losing her shoe and banging her shin in the process.

"Got a problem?" asked a familiar male voice.

Four

KATE TRIED FRANTICALLY TO EXTRICATE HERSELF before Jeff Hardin could take it into his head to get chivalrous and help her.

Too late. He probably couldn't spell the word, but he seemed to understand the concept. Two big paws hooked onto her waist and hauled her out. The contact sent a nervous shock jolting through her and made her squeal in protest.

He set her down immediately, saying, "Sorry. I didn't mean to scare you. You looked like you were having trouble getting out of your trunk."

"Nothing I couldn't handle," she said. Why, God, of all the people to catch her in such a ridiculous position, did it have to be Jeff Hardin? She covered her embarrassment by straightening her suit. Jeff had left his car headlights on, and she felt like she had been trapped in a spotlight.

He picked up her shoe and handed it to her. "Flat tire?"

Keeping her dignity, she took it as if she were a queen and he a courtier offering her a valuable present. "I'm afraid so. I was just about to set off a flare."

"And change the thing yourself. In those clothes?"

No. In my bra and panty hose. Twit. "Unfortunately, I forgot to pack my mechanic's overalls."

Jeff fished the jack out of her trunk. "Well, I guess jocks are good for something."

"I guess so," agreed Kate. That had sounded snotty and ungrateful. "Thanks for stopping," she added. "This really is kind of you."

"Hey, no problem. I'd have done as much for anyone."

She supposed she deserved that. But this ingrate in the rumpled suit wasn't the real her. Being around Jeff Hardin was like drinking Doctor Jekyll's famous potion. It turned her from sane, lovable Doctor Kate into irrational, unsociable Ms. Hyde.

Jeff had the jack under her car now. She stood off to the side and watched him work. It took less than a minute for her to find the silence uncomfortable.

"What are you doing out so late?" she asked.

"I stayed in town to visit a friend."

The blonde bimbo, of course. "She's cute, your friend."

"Yeah, she is," agreed Jeff, unscrewing a lug nut.

"Thinking of marrying her?"

"Thinking of giving me advice?" he countered.

"I'm off duty," she said.

"Oh, so you were just being . . ."

"Polite," she supplied.

The last lug nut came off. "Polite. So that's the word for it."

Kate capitulated. "All right. Nosy."

He stopped operations to grin up at her. "You really are human. I was beginning to wonder."

"I think you've already found out how human I am," said Kate.

He shrugged. "Some of my best friends are humans."

Kate smiled. Jeff Hardin was pretty funny. For someone with the I.Q. of a guppy.

She watched as he hauled off her tire and replaced it with her spare. "I really do appreciate this," she said.

"What are neighbors for?"

Kate listened for sarcasm in his voice, but couldn't detect any.

"It looks like I'm going to owe you more cookies," she said.

"Cookies work." He put the dead tire in her trunk, and tossed the jack in after it. "Your spare tire looks a little flat. I'll follow you home."

She caught the glint of humor in his eyes, and the hint of a smile. "I wouldn't want you to go out of your way."

"No trouble, ma'am."

"Thanks again," said Kate, and climbed back into her car. She realized she was smiling. Well, of course she was smiling. She had just been saved from ruining her suit. This small, momentary euphoria had nothing to do with bantering with Jeff Hardin. Nothing.

The next morning she made good on her promise. It didn't look like he was up, so she left the plate on his back porch. There. She had paid her debt and now they were even.

AND THAT, SHE TOLD HERSELF, WAS WHY SHE WAS smiling when she entered the studio. She was simply happy that she hadn't been stuck out on the highway half the night, glad that she was doing what she could to foster good relations with the new neighbor, glad that she was coping so very well with the five-foot-ten thorn in her side.

"You look happy today," observed Wallis. She eyed Kate suspiciously. "Am I imagining it or are you wearing more makeup than usual?"

"You're imagining it. What kind of interesting faxes did we get?"

"Okay," said Wallis. "I can take a hint."

They turned their attention to business and sorted

through the faxes and e-mail messages, deciding which ones Kate would honor by reading on the air. Then Kate got her customary cup of coffee and headed into the air studio to settle in for another day of solving other people's problems.

Her first caller was a woman named Debbie, whose husband resented the fact that she read romance novels.

"Well, Debbie, I suspect that it's not what you're reading he objects to, but how much of your time those books get. Think about it. Don't you feel ignored when he sits on the couch, glued to the TV?"

"That's why I'm reading," protested Debbie. "Because he does sit on the couch and watch TV."

"Well, one thing that will get him off the couch is probably you, feeling romantic. After you've read an especially sexy scene in your book, you might try hunting him down and telling him you are hot. If he sees some positive effects from all that reading, he might just change his tune."

Kate moved on to the next caller. "Adrianne, welcome to the program."

"Oh, Doctor Kate, I'm your biggest fan," said Adrianne.

"That's always nice to hear," said Kate. "How can I help you?"

"Well, my husband's daughter is getting married next month and . . ."

Adrianne launched into a complicated three-family soap opera that left Kate blinking. Good God, how did people manage to mess up their lives so much?

"So, should I go to the wedding?" Adrianne finished.

"Yes, you should," said Kate.

"Even if . . ." Adrianne brought out her laundry list of excuses for hating her husband's first wife.

Kate cut her off. "Adrianne. You are not the Hatfields and the McCoys. Don't ruin this bride's day by being petty. Go to the wedding, act like a grown-up, and be polite. That's what being civilized is all about."

"Okay," said Adrianne, all of her initial friendliness drained from her voice. "Thank you for your time."

"My time and not my advice," observed Kate after the woman had hung up to go throw darts at her picture. "I think I just lost my biggest fan." She brought up another caller. "Megan, welcome to the program."

On and on the questions went, and Kate was amazed at how many of the situations simply required that the caller be polite. Just like she had been with Jeff last night. It was really quite simple, and it made life so much easier.

An image of him crouched next to her car, his jeans hugging a very nice set of buns, sprang to mind. Good God, what was the matter with her? What was this preoccupation with Jeff Hardin's physique all about, really?

Sex, pure and simple. But not with Jeff Hardin, just what he represented: the half of the population with different body parts. Her body appeared to be telling her it wanted contact with the male of the species again. It looked like she was ready to let down the walls she'd built around herself, start dating, give love a second chance, enjoy the company of someone with a voice lower than hers.

Maybe. First and foremost, however, she had her children to consider. That made even the thought of picking a new mate seem daunting. After all, she wouldn't subject her children to just any man. Mr. Right had to be someone intelligent, kind-hearted, well-off materially—she certainly wasn't going to marry a sponger—and good father material. That would be a big order to fill.

Her show was winding to an end when she caught sight of Jeff. He was wearing jeans again, with a Mariners T-shirt tucked into them, and Kate wondered if he owned any other kind of clothes. He smiled at her from the other side of the glass, and waved a hand in greeting, and she waved back and wondered if any of her makeup was still left on her face.

Not that it mattered. She wasn't interested in someone

so completely unsuitable. Anyway, he had a girlfriend, a bimbo who was his intellectual and emotional equal. Bimbo and himbo, a perfect match.

Jeff looked Kate up and down as she came out of the air studio. "Lookin' good today, Doctor Kate. Well, from the neck up, anyway. You ought to lose those baggy dresses. They don't do a thing for you."

"Thank you," she said. She looked pointedly at his jeans. "Anyone can see you have a handle on sartorial excellence."

He took a John Wayne stance and slipped his hands in his back pockets. "Well, little lady. I'll bet you think I don't even know what that word means."

Kate cocked her head. "Do you?"

"Nope." He sauntered past her. "And I don't care. By the way, you might want to wear a slip with that one."

Kate's cheeks caught fire. She glared at his back while her mind whirred, trying to come up with some scathing reply before he could put himself out of earshot.

"Hey, man," George called to him. "Caught your interview with Keith Griffin last night. That guy is great."

"Yeah, he's something," agreed Jeff.

Something, thought Kate in disgust, storming down the hall. Animal, mineral, or vegetable? If the man had anything to do with Jeff Hardin's program, it was probably vegetable.

Out in the station's parking lot, she used more pressure on the gas pedal than was necessary to start her car. It coughed to life and she jerked it into gear. Changing a flat tire for a woman didn't qualify a man to be her fashion consultant. What made him think she cared what he thought about how she looked? And that smart remark about the slip had been totally unnecessary. Like Jeff Hardin's presence on the planet.

• • •

JEFF WAS ABOUT TO ENTER THE AIR STUDIO WHEN HE heard the sound of a squealing car. He looked out the half-open window and saw Kate Stonewall laying rubber as she left the parking lot.

He let out a low whistle. "Guess I should have known better than to offer the good doctor advice."

"You could stand to take a Dale Carnegie course," suggested Wallis.

"That dress was butt ugly," said Jeff. He shook his head. "What's she trying to hide, anyway?"

"Twenty pounds," guessed Wallis.

Jeff let out a snort. He supposed Kate thought she was too fat, and that those loose-flowing folds hid the fact. Fat and pregnancy. Women seemed fond of hiding both facts of life.

He smiled appreciatively, remembering the way the light had hit her as she'd walked to the door. He'd been able to see her whole figure silhouetted under that otherwise useless dress. And she hadn't looked all that bad.

Enjoyable as he had found it to play peekaboo with what she was wearing today, he definitely liked Kate better in the suit she'd had on last night. He had appreciated the way it had hugged her butt, and how the skirt had hiked up her thighs as she struggled to climb out of her car trunk. The woman had nice legs. Maybe a little thick in the thighs, but, hey, it showed she wasn't obsessed with the fat and calorie content of everything she ate.

So, Ms. Perfect liked to eat. She was human after all.

It had been great fun catching the stuffy, perfect Doctor Kate in such an interesting position. Remembering it made Jeff grin. What he would have given for a camera. Put her in a few more situations like that and she might become almost normal. She'd given a pretty good imitation of it last night. And she'd actually been likable.

That was because her circumstances had demanded a truce. Well, the odds of them enjoying a truce very often weren't high. And it was just as well. Women like Doctor

Kate were wired crazy. It wasn't worth the effort of trying to figure them out. Better to leave them to men who were equally squirrelly. Women like Bambi Hooterman suited him much better.

Yes, definitely, he thought as he sat on Bambi's couch later that night, with her tucked under his arm, watching Van Damme slaughter the occupants of cable TV. She was cute and sexy, and happy to do whatever he wanted whenever he wanted. She didn't tax him in any way. She was the perfect woman. He took a chug of Hale's Ale, then relaxed into a satisfied smile. Life was good just as it was. One thing a man didn't need was people who would complicate it and turn things upside down.

KATE STOOD ON HER BALCONY, ENJOYING THE warm, early June night and taking one last, loving look at the new addition to her yard. The order she had placed with the island nursery on the day of the great binocular incident had arrived at five-thirty, and been safely installed by six. The lovely, six-foot-tall Leyland cypress was guaranteed to more than double in size in three seasons. Now, when her new neighbor came out on his porch, instead of her, he'd be seeing green. And red, probably.

There was nothing wrong with what she'd done, nothing at all wrong with wanting privacy. And Jeff Hardin's obnoxious behavior today had served to confirm her action as right and sensible. The new tree would not only give her privacy, it would send a strong message. Hopefully, Jeff's weak brain would be capable of receiving it.

JEFF HAD TAKEN A LATE FERRY HOME, PASSING THE commute time by reading the Civil War history book he'd found that morning at a downtown used book store. He'd gotten into it and had taken it to bed with him. The last thing he remembered was laying it on his chest to rest his eyes for just a minute. At nine in the morning, he'd hammered his clock radio into silence, turned off the lamp on his nightstand, and then fallen back into unconsciousness. But now, an hour later, the sunlight had finally succeeded in creeping behind his eyelids and pulling him away from the World Series, where he was pitching a winning game for the Mariners.

He shook the cobwebs loose, shoved himself out of bed, and staggered to the kitchen in his favorite tattered blue silk boxers. He pulled the orange juice carton out of the fridge and took a swig. Still carrying it, he went to his living room to survey his domain.

Glancing out the window, he suddenly discovered that things had changed overnight. His view to the north had been disrupted by the presence of a six-foot tree that portended the growth ability of the man-eating plant in *Little Shop of Horrors*. *Feed me, Seymour!*

"What the hell?" He glowered and slammed the orange juice container down on the coffee table, then marched out of his house and across the lawn.

He found Kate just about to get into her car.

She smiled that fake smile of hers and said, "Good morning." She nodded at his boxers. "Going swimming?"

"What's with the tree?" he demanded.

"Oh," she said airily. "I ordered that some time back."

"You've ruined my view."

"Only your view of my balcony."

"Is that so? Did you stand on my porch to see what it would look like to me? Did you look out my living room window?"

"It is just one tree," she said through gritted teeth. "I could have planted a laurel hedge."

Jeff gave a snort of disgust. "I'm surprised you didn't."

"It might not have been a bad idea, considering the fact that I'm living next door to a Peeping Tom."

Jeff shoved aside the memory of enjoying her silhouette

under that stupid dress she'd worn yesterday. Instead, he rolled his eyes heavenward. "Oh, for God's sake."

"Look," she said, her tone of voice turning patronizing. "Our houses are practically on top of each other. Whoever designed the landscaping around them didn't take into consideration—"

"That one of us is a bitch."

Her eyes flew wide and she fell back a step as if he had just slapped her. "Are you calling me . . . ?"

"You bet. And I do know what *that* word means. I'm living right next door to the definition."

Her face shut down, the only traces of emotion left showing in the red on her cheeks. "I'm sorry you don't like the tree," she said in a tight voice. "I tried to place it where it wouldn't affect your view but would still give me some privacy. I hope, once you get used to it, you'll think it's pretty."

"I think it's pretty right now," snarled Jeff. "Pretty small, pretty immature, and pretty hypocritical, considering the fact that it was planted by a woman who claims to have it so together. You, Doctor Kate, are a joke."

The red drained from her cheeks and tears rose in her eyes. "I'm sorry you feel that way. If you'll excuse me, I have to catch a ferry."

She was barely able to choke out that last sentence before climbing into her car, and Jeff knew she was going to indulge herself in a crying jag as soon as she could get away from him. Good. He hoped she drowned in her tears.

He stalked back across his yard and into his house, slamming the door as he went. The realtor who'd showed him this place should have told him who his neighbor was. He'd rather have lived next door to a prison, a cemetery— anything but her. He'd move. That's what he'd do. Let someone else deal with Kate Stonewall.

Wait a minute. This woman had been winning battles all her life, bludgeoning people with her credentials. Everybody kowtowed to her, gushed over her, did what she said.

He'd be damned if he'd become another Kate Stonewall victory. No, he'd stay right here and make her life miserable, and love every minute of it.

K ATE REMAINED ON THE FERRY'S CAR DECK DURING the crossing to Seattle, watching the waters of Puget Sound through blurry eyes. Damn him! She only wanted privacy. She only wanted to get away from him. How dare he say those things to her!

Of course, he'd thrown his little temper tantrum to manipulate her. As if that kind of immature behavior would have any such effect. He was a childish, hot-tempered jerk, who would just have to grow up. She hoped her new tree grew another six feet over the summer.

Jeff's epithets assaulted her memory. Hypocrite? Joke? Bitch. Jeff Hardin had called her a bitch. She had never in her life been called that word. At least, not to her face. There were probably people who thought she was one, people who confused strength with bitchiness. She *was* strong. She'd be the first to admit it. She'd had to be, left with two small children to raise single-handedly. But that didn't make her a . . . she would not use that word again. It didn't apply to her. She had nothing to be ashamed of. She had climbed out of hell and carved out a niche for herself in the world, and it was a valuable one. She helped people work out their problems.

That was more than Jeff Hardin could say. He didn't help anyone with their problems. He was a problem.

By the time she drove off the boat, she felt better, more in control. She checked her reflection in the mirror on her sun visor, then wished she hadn't. Her eyes were red and puffy from crying. She looked like a hag instead of a woman still in the prime of her life. Jeff Hardin was aging her before her time.

Never mind, she told herself. The tree will grow quickly. Soon you can pretend he's not there.

Wallis looked at her suspiciously when she came in. "Are you okay?"

Kate nodded. "Just a little morning crisis combined with a mild case of PMS, but I'm recovering."

"I've got chocolate," offered Wallis.

"Good. I feel better already."

The chocolate did wonders. So did getting on the air, and being able to help people. Twenty minutes into the show, Kate had already helped a mother take a step toward healing the breach between herself and her estranged daughter and steered a woman away from a man who obviously only wanted her for her body. Feeling in control of her world once more, she checked the computer screen for her next caller.

"Don, welcome to the program. How can I help you?"

"I've got a problem," said Don.

Wait a minute. Kate knew that voice, and just hearing it shot adrenaline into her bloodstream. What was he up to?

She smiled smugly. It didn't matter. She'd tie him in knots.

"Hey, Doc. Are you there?"

Her eyes narrowed. "I'm here. Just waiting for you to tell me what your problem is." Narrowing it down to one thing should be a challenge.

"I've got a real nasty neighbor," said "Don."

The chocolate began to churn in Kate's stomach. "Really?" she said, her tone of voice encouraging him to tell her more.

"She's rude and arrogant. I've never done anything to her, but she's got it in for me."

"And you have no idea why?"

"No," he said, sounding self-righteous and persecuted.

"So, when you first moved into the neighborhood, you did nothing to make her dislike you?" probed Kate.

"Well, I had a party that got a little noisy. But I apologized."

"And that's all?"

"Yeah. Pretty much."

"Mm-hmm," said Kate. Any listener with half a brain would be able to figure out that there was more to this story than good old "Don" was letting on. "And how can I help you?" she asked.

"Just last night, for no reason, she put a tree between our houses that blocks my view."

"For no reason?"

"Yes," he said, anger slipping into his voice. "For no reason."

"Have you talked to her?" asked Kate.

"Yeah."

"Well, she must have given you some reason for her actions. What was her explanation?"

"She wants privacy," said "Don" shortly.

"I see," said Kate. Probably, so did the entire listening audience. The much-maligned neighbor in this story had her reasons, even if a certain caller wasn't sharing them. "Don, what, specifically, is your question to me?"

"I want to know how to make this person think like a rational human being and move that tree."

"Behave like someone she can stand to see," said Kate, and cut him off. "We've got to take a break for some news, people, but we'll be right back."

"News!" Wallis's squeal came through Kate's headphones. "What are you doing? We have three minutes 'til the news."

George punched a button and started a commercial rolling, and Kate leaned back in her chair and let out her breath.

"Sorry," she said to Wallis. "I needed a minute to bring my blood pressure back down."

"You handled that great. What's the big deal?"

"The big deal is that 'Don' was good old Jeff Hardin, being cute."

"You're the crazy neighbor?" Wallis's voice was disbelieving.

"I will be before he's through with me," said Kate.

"Great," said Wallis. "We've got World War III brewing right here in the station. Next thing you know we'll be sweeping for grenades when you come in."

"Nah," said Kate. "The station is neutral ground."

She recovered her aplomb and made it through the rest of the show. And when she passed Jeff on her way out of the studio she managed to look unruffled and nod politely even though she could feel unpleasant emotions rippling through her.

"Great show, but you were a little hard on some of your callers," he sniped.

"I'm only hard on my callers when they have it coming," she replied and kept walking. If this was how the guy thought he was going to get her to move her tree he was even stupider than she'd originally thought.

SHE MANAGED TO KEEP HER CONTACT WITH JEFF Hardin to a minimum for the rest of the week, and by Saturday her equilibrium had been restored. Until she piled the kids into the car to head for Robbie's baseball game and tried to start it. It coughed, then shuddered into silence.

"Come on," she muttered, and tried again. She looked over at her son, who was wearing a worried expression, and smiled encouragingly. "Just a little temperamental this morning," she said.

This car was only eight years old. It was too young to be acting temperamental. She tried again, but with the same results. Robbie began to fidget.

She patted his leg. "We'll get there. I'll just call Grace and see if she wants to go to a ball game."

"Grace isn't home," piped Amanda, who was sitting in the backseat with her friend Sommer.

Kate let out a breath. "Okay."

Robbie brightened. "Jeff's home!"

"No," said Kate firmly. "We are not going to bother

him." *We wouldn't bother him if I were bleeding to death.* "I'll bet Janet hasn't left yet. I'll run and call her."

Fortunately, Janet was just going out the door and had no problem with swinging by to get them.

"Thanks," said Kate. "I owe you."

"I'm going to remember that when I want free marriage counseling," quipped Janet.

After hanging up, Kate called Andy the mechanic. "It's Kate. My car won't start."

"What a surprise," said Andy. "Didn't I tell you when you brought that dead tire in that we should be giving her a checkup? Kate, I tell you, you wouldn't put off getting your kids to the dentist, now, would you?"

"Andy, I really don't have time for this right now," protested Kate. "I have to go to Robbie's game."

"How are you going to get there, fly?"

"Yes. I'll leave the keys under the mat. Can you come get the thing before I dynamite it?"

"Hey, now, talk nice about your car," cautioned Andy.

"Don't worry," said Kate. "I'm in the house and it can't hear me. Just come get the thing."

"Okay. I'll send somebody out. If all goes well, you can have it back Monday morning."

Kate returned to the car hoping all would go well. "Okay, guys. Our limo is on the way. Everybody out."

Janet arrived a few minutes later, and they all piled into her minivan, making it to the field in time for Robbie to stumble around the outfield after some practice fly balls.

"So, how's it going with the new neighbor?" asked Janet as they watched the kids settle themselves in the dugout for their first inning at bat.

"He's not what I would have chosen if I could have gone neighbor shopping," said Kate, watching the lead hitter on Robbie's team step up to bat.

"That's too bad," said Janet. "Bill listens to him all the time and thinks he's great."

"He is. As long as you don't have to have anything to do with him," said Kate. "Hopefully, the tree will help."

As soon as she'd uttered the words she regretted it. She could almost hear the wheels spinning in Janet's brain, feel the moment when the lightbulb went on.

"You're the neighbor!" Janet crowed.

Kate sighed. "It's not quite the way he made it sound on the radio."

"I'm not stupid. I could read *behind* the lines." Janet chuckled. "So Don was really Jeff Hardin."

"You wouldn't mind if we moved on to some other topic, would you? I mean, my day hasn't exactly started out great here."

Janet took pity on her. "Okay. Oh, hey. Here comes Robbie."

Kate sucked in her breath and tensed her muscles as her son stepped up to the plate and took a practice swing.

"Looks good," commented Janet.

The next swing looked good, too, even if it didn't touch the ball. Strike one.

Robbie set his jaw and waited for the next ball. It came. He swung and cracked it good, sending it sailing right past the shortstop's head and into the outfield.

"Go, Robbie!" screamed Kate, jumping up.

Robbie went. To first base, second base. He finally stopped at third.

Kate bounced up and down and screeched like a maniac. Janet, who had been cheering, too, finally decided they'd used up their quota of cheering time and pulled Kate back down onto the bench.

"Did you see that?" cried Kate. "He actually hit the ball."

"I told you he'd improve," said Janet.

"That wasn't just improvement. That was a great hit," Kate insisted.

Janet smiled. "I see you're hooked."

Kate sobered. "I'm just proud of my son. That's all."

"He did fine," said Janet. "I think Bill finally got through to him."

Kate remembered her broken window and knew who had gotten through to her son.

The family came home in high spirits, and Kate's improved even more when she saw that Andy had towed off her lemon. To thank Janet for rescuing them, Kate invited Robbie's friend James to stay for the afternoon. Amanda was quick to pounce on her mother's generosity, and Sommer, too, was adopted for the rest of the day. Kate turned the four kids loose to play frozen tag on the lawn and went inside to do some cleaning.

Half an hour later, she looked out her kitchen window and saw that Amanda and Sommer had strayed onto Jeff's lawn and were doing some kind of dance routine. She caught sight of long, tan legs on the lawn chair propped in front of them and knew who their audience was.

Great. One more link forming with the Neanderthal next door. She was going to have to put her foot down. She left the house and headed for enemy territory.

"Hi, Mom!" called Amanda as Kate walked across the grass toward them.

The blonde in the lawn chair turned and waved. "Hi!"

"Hello," said Kate. "I came to drag my daughter back home."

"Oh, Mom," protested Amanda.

"Please don't," said the blonde. "We're having fun."

"Bambi taught us one of her routines," said Amanda.

Bambi? There is really someone in this world named Bambi?

"We haven't met yet," Bambi informed Kate, then blushed. Kate, remembering the circumstances of their first encounter, felt her cheeks warming, too.

"That is, not officially," the girl corrected herself. "I'm Bambi Hooterman, Jeff's girlfriend."

"Nice to meet you," lied Kate.

"Bambi says you can get cheerleading scholarships to college," said Amanda.

"That's what I did," said Bambi. "I went to Idaho State."

"Oh? What did you major in?" asked Kate.

"Well, actually, I didn't get as far as declaring a major. I went a year, then decided to try out to be a Sea Gal. I didn't really like college that much, anyway."

Kate hid her disgust behind a mask of politeness. A cheerleader for the Seahawks, that sounded like a Jeff Hardin kind of woman. Kate had hated cheerleaders when she was in high school, with their perfect hair, their plastic smiles, and their football player boyfriends. She'd gloated for weeks after stealing Rob away from Pam Wells, the prima cheerleader. Mom had always said that the way to a man's heart was his stomach. Stomach had worked. So had helping Rob pass Language Arts.

"I've been a Sea Gal for two years," said Bambi, "and I'm back in school again now. I want to be a personal trainer."

"What's that?" asked Sommer.

"It's someone who helps other people get into shape," said Bambi.

"Could you help us get into shape?" asked Amanda, the last child on earth in need of any such help.

"Sure," replied Bambi.

The two girls grinned at each other as if they had just landed front row tickets to 'N Sync.

"It's really not that hard," Bambi continued. "And exercising can be fun."

For who? thought Kate.

"It's especially fun when you see how good it makes you look," she added. Her smiling gaze took in Kate now. "If any of you guys want help, let me know. It's my specialty."

Kate hated getting sweaty, and she knew she would especially hate doing so in the presence of a size five. "How about something to eat to give you energy for getting in shape?" she said to the girls.

They nodded in unison.

"Come on back to the house and I'll find you and the boys some Popsicles."

"All right!" whooped Amanda, and she and Sommer scampered off across the lawn, calling their good-byes as they went, the promise of a treat driving all thoughts of fitness from their minds.

"Nice talking to you," Kate said to Bambi. Wouldn't Miss Manners be proud!

"Yeah," agreed Bambi. "Come on over later and have a diet Coke."

"Thanks," said Kate noncommittally and followed the girls back to the house. She would have to point out to Amanda later that Jeff Hardin's girlfriend wasn't any more acceptable company than he was.

She slipped back onto her own property, relieved that Jeff hadn't come out and caught her on his lawn. Bambi had certainly been friendly. Kate could hardly believe he hadn't told his girlfriend that Kate was the enemy and to shoot on sight. Maybe Bambi was more broad-minded.

Kate shook her head. Somehow, she couldn't get the words broad and mind to match up when picturing Bambi Hooterman.

Back at the house, she passed out Popsicles and cautioned the kids not to run with them in their mouths, then started her attack on the refrigerator, where she had been growing mold in a variety of plastic leftover containers.

She was well into the job when a shriek of pain carried up from the lawn and through the open windows. She dropped her sponge and dashed to the door, colliding with Amanda.

"Mom! Robbie fell on his Popsicle stick and it went through his mouth."

Five

KATE RACED OUT TO THE LAWN AND FOUND A shrieking, bloody-faced Robbie doing an Indian war dance around Bambi, who was trying to calm him. She looked up at Kate, her expression a mixture of horrified empathy and relief at seeing the approach of reinforcement.

"I think you're going to have to take him to the emergency room," she said.

This served to freshen Robbie's hysteria, and his dancing grew even wilder and his face bloodier.

Kate told herself not to panic. Her son looked like an extra from a slasher movie, but it probably wasn't as bad as it looked. His vocal chords, obviously, hadn't been damaged.

"Okay," she said, putting an arm around Robbie and shepherding him toward the house. "Everybody go get in the car. Hurry!"

"Mom, the car's not here," Amanda reminded her.

Kate's heart plummeted to her toes and stopped her in her tracks.

"We can call my mom," offered Sommer.

"No, we'll call a taxi," Kate decided.

"We should call 911," said Amanda.

It was tempting, but 911 seemed a bit like overkill. No one was having a heart attack. Yet. But if she didn't resolve this soon . . . *Stay calm!*

"Jeff can take you to the emergency room," said Bambi decisively. "He's a great driver and he'll have you there in no time. I'll watch the kids. Come on." She took off for Jeff's house at a run.

Of course, she was right. That was the quickest, most sensible thing to do. Kate would have rather ingested nails than ask Jeff Hardin for a favor, but this was not the time to be small.

"Come on, sweetie," she said, turning her son a new direction. She called over her shoulder, "Amanda, get me a towel. And hurry!"

JEFF HAD BEEN TRYING TO IGNORE THE COMMOTION outside and finish his phone interview with an up-and-coming golf pro. He knew it was a lost cause when Bambi burst into the living room and announced, "The neighbor's kid just got hurt. You've got to take him to the emergency room."

Her words were punctuated by approaching screams of agony, followed by the entrance of Kate Stonewall and a bloody-faced hysterical Robbie.

Jeff terminated his conversation and crossed the room. "Hey, man. What'd you do?" he asked, squatting in front of Robbie.

Robbie was too busy caterwauling to answer. His mother spoke for him. "He fell on a Popsicle stick."

"Didn't your mom ever tell you not to run with those things in your mouth?" teased Jeff. He could almost feel the heat from said mom's glare, but ignored her. "Here, let's see the damage. Open up." Robbie gulped back his cries and complied, and Jeff inspected the damage.

Kate bent to look, too, and gave a whimper, which set her son off again. *Thank you, Doctor Kate. Way to stay calm.*

Jeff frowned at her, then directed his attention back to the kid. "Hey, now," he said in soothing tones. "It's not that bad."

Robbie quieted and stuck an exploratory finger into his mouth. "What's that thing hanging down?" he asked.

"Just part of the roof of your mouth," said Jeff.

The kid broke into a fresh wail.

"That's enough," said Jeff sternly. "You're not gonna die. Be a man and quit upsetting your mother."

Kate emanated enough outrage at that remark to nuke Jeff right on the spot. Let her bristle, he thought. There were some things women just didn't understand about being a man.

The kid did, though. He got himself under control, hiccuping into small sobs.

"Okay," Jeff said to him. "Whaddya say we get you to the doctor to put you back together?"

Robbie nodded and Jeff picked him up.

Amanda made her entrance with the towel, too late to prevent Robbie from leaking blood all over the floor. It wasn't a big deal to Jeff, but he suspected that would be one more thing to upset Kate.

Sure enough. "I'm sorry about the mess," she said as she held the towel to Robbie's mouth.

"Don't worry. I'll take care of it," said Bambi.

Jeff carried the boy to the garage, saying, "I hope you like to ride real fast. I bet I can get you there quicker than an ambulance."

•

KATE HURRIED IN JEFF'S WAKE, NOT SURE IF SHE should be encouraged by those words or more worried still.

Jeff's sporty red Jeep Cherokee seemed to be waiting

for the opportunity to race down the road. Feeling nervous already, Kate climbed into its front seat. Jeff settled Robbie onto her lap, strapping them in together, then went to the driver's side and slid behind the wheel.

True to his word, he shot them out of the garage and up the drive at a terrifying speed, spewing gravel every which way.

Robbie's crying had already settled to a whimper. This fresh excitement seemed to numb his pain, for it shut him up completely.

Jeff roared them onto the road, then looked at Robbie. He smiled and rumpled Robbie's hair, saying, "Hang on, kid. The doctor'll have you fixed up in no time."

They turned onto the main highway and Jeff really hit the gas. At the rate they were speeding, Kate worried that the doctor would have more than one person to mend. She felt like she was in an airplane, taxiing down the runway. If Jeff went even a fraction faster, they'd be airborne. She braced herself against the seat, clutched her son to her, and prayed that the island's few remaining deer would stay safely hidden in the woods they were racing past.

True to his word, Jeff got them into town and to the island's medical center in only a matter of minutes. Kate let out her breath in relief as they pulled into the emergency entrance parking lot. She watched him stride quickly around the car and yank open the door. He lifted Robbie from her lap and headed for the door, leaving her to follow as best she could.

And it felt good to do just that: to follow and let someone else take the reins of management for just a moment. She hadn't realized until now just how heavily the burden of single parenting had sat on her shoulders.

It was a brief enough moment. There was insurance information to be gathered that only she could give. Then there was the doctor to see, and although Robbie was happy enough to have Jeff carry him into the examination room, it was his mom he wanted next to him to hold his hand when the doctor put in the stitches.

Except for one relapse into hysteria at the mention of the "S" word, which Jeff calmed with the promise of a baseball autographed by the Mariners, Robbie comported himself bravely. Forty-five minutes later they were back on the road, this time moving at a more leisurely pace. Robbie leaned, exhausted, against Kate and she stroked his damp hair.

She stole a glance at Jeff, who was keeping his eyes securely on the road. "You seem to be rescuing me a lot lately," she said.

He didn't say anything, just nodded.

She blundered on. "My car was in the shop, otherwise I wouldn't have bothered you. Actually, I had no intention of bothering you at all. I'm afraid your girlfriend volunteered you."

"She's got a big heart," said Jeff.

Kate would concede that. She nodded.

Now Jeff slanted a look her way. "Nobody may ever ask her to leave her brain to science, but she also doesn't have a mean bone in her body."

"Unlike some of us, who are a veritable skeleton of meanness?"

Jeff said nothing and Kate looked down at her tired son and sighed. She was tired, too, suddenly very tired of coping with the complexities of life. She wanted to be a pretty Bambi, with nothing more difficult to deal with than stretching out on a lawn chair and drinking diet Coke. She looked out the window and watched the trees slide past.

They got home to find Bambi in Kate's kitchen, feeding the kids hamburgers and chips. Kate realized she had been dreading having to cap off her afternoon ordeal with preparing dinner.

"This might be a little earlier than you normally eat, but I thought you wouldn't want to have to cook when you got home," Bambi explained.

"You are psychic," said Kate gratefully.

"Did you have to get stitches?" asked Amanda, slipping out of her chair to come peer into her brother's mouth. Robbie opened up to show off his wound and Amanda wrinkled her nose. "Yuck."

"He probably can't have anything, can he?" guessed Bambi.

"I think he just needs to hit the showers and go to bed," said Kate.

"And we should get going," said Jeff. "We've got a party in town tonight."

"Oh, my gosh! I forgot." Bambi's hands flew to her hair. "I've got to get ready." She waved good-bye to the girls, who gave her an enthusiastic send-off, then hurried out the kitchen door.

Jeff started to follow her.

"You won't forget about the baseball, will you?" asked Robbie.

Jeff smiled at him. "Of course not." He reached for the door.

"Jeff," Robbie called, rushing after him.

Jeff turned.

"I got a hit today. I did just what you told me and I got a hit."

Jeff's face lit up as if Robbie were his own son. "All right," he said, holding out his hand for a high five.

Robbie complied and smiled the first smile Kate had seen since his close encounter with the Popsicle stick.

"How far did you get?" asked Jeff.

"Third base," said Robbie proudly.

Jeff nodded. "I knew you could do it."

"Will you come to one of my games?" asked Robbie hopefully.

Jeff shot a questioning look at Kate.

She owed him a lot for what he'd done this day. But he wasn't Rumplestiltskin, and she wasn't about to give him her son. She'd give him cookies for life, though. Bambi could use some fattening up.

"Mr. Hardin has to work in the evenings when you have your games. Remember?" she said to her son.

Robbie's face fell, then brightened. "Coach says our last game is next Saturday. He could come to that."

Kate couldn't quite read Jeff's expression, but she was sure she caught a hint of taunting in it.

"We'll see," he said, then left.

Great, thought Kate.

By the time she finally got the kids settled she was exhausted. Even sitting in front of the television seemed to be too much effort, so she went to bed and stretched out, ready to sleep.

That was when her brain decided to rise from the dead. The events of the day kept insisting on replaying themselves for her. And with each replay, the crumb from next door emerged looking more heroic. All right, so maybe he wasn't as useless as she'd thought. And he sure deserved more than just thanks. More than cookies. He deserved a good neighbor.

J EFF HAD JUST SETTLED IN TO WATCH A SUNDAY AFTERnoon baseball game when somebody knocked on his door. He opened it, hoping it was Grace with another pie. It was Kate Stonewall, with a shovel. She was wearing a pair of worn jeans covered by—what a surprise—a baggy T-shirt.

"You're not going to hit me with that, are you?" he asked, eyeing it.

She smiled. The woman had a real cute smile. "The thought hadn't crossed my mind," she said. "Yet." She looked at him. "Were you busy?"

"Just watching a game."

"Oh. I could come back later."

"No, that's okay. Do you need a hole dug?"

She nodded. "I'm moving a tree."

Well, what do you know, thought Jeff, the doc has a heart after all.

"I thought maybe you could help me find a spot that will still give me some privacy, but keep your view."

"Good thought."

He let the game play on without him and walked with her across the lawn. "How's Robbie?"

"It looks like he'll live. He ate five pancakes for breakfast."

"That's always a good sign," agreed Jeff.

They reached the tree. "I thought we could dig it up. . . ."

"We meaning me," guessed Jeff.

"Well, yes. Then you can go stand on your porch while I move it to the east by degrees. You can tell me when it's not blocking your view. Deal?"

"Deal," said Jeff, and plunged the shovel into the sod.

It didn't take long for him to uproot the thing. He presented it to her saying, "There you are, my lady."

She nodded regally. "I thank you, Sir Knight. Now, why don't you trot back to your castle and direct me in the repositioning of this thing."

"Your wish is my command," he said with a bow.

"Genies say that, not knights."

Jeff shrugged. "Well, whatever. You get the idea."

She smiled and he caught a hint of a dimple. It distracted him, and for a moment he forgot he was supposed to be heading for his porch.

She raised her eyebrows. "What's the matter? Has your horse gone lame?"

Jeff hauled his thoughts back to the subject of views and trees. "No, just my brain." He turned, jogged back across his lawn, and bounded onto his porch.

Kate was standing on the property line, facing him with the tree propped in front of her and looking like Johnny Appleseed's girlfriend.

"Okay," he called. "Move her."

She took one small step to her left.

"You're going to have to move a little more," he called.

She took another step, this one smaller than the first.

Jeff didn't want to tick her off, but she wasn't exactly giving a lot here, and her grand gesture was shrinking with every baby step. He scratched his head. How to handle this diplomatically?

"You can take one more step," he called. "This time make it a big one."

"Mother, may I?" she replied sarcastically.

"Yes, you may."

She took two big steps.

All right, Doctor Kate. He could live with that.

"It looks good," he hollered, then jumped off the porch and came back across the lawn.

He took over the job of holding the tree upright, saying, "Okay now, why don't you run up onto your balcony and see if you have any privacy left."

K ATE HURRIED INSIDE THE HOUSE AND UPSTAIRS. She stopped and looked out her bedroom window. The new placement of the tree would at least shield her here. In fact, it actually did so more effectively where it now stood than where it had first been.

She proceeded to the balcony and assessed the view. Well, she probably wouldn't be able to stand out here in her nightshirt anymore. But what the heck. To ever think she was private here had probably been a mistake. For all she knew, someone on the far side of the cove could just as easily have had binoculars trained on her for the last three years. She turned and saw Jeff looking up at her.

"What light from yonder balcony breaks," he bellowed. "It is the east and Kate Stonewall is the sun."

Of all the people in the world to be almost quoting Shakespeare! Maybe Jeff Hardin was an idiot savant. Kate hurried back out of the house before he could shout any more declarations and embarrass her further.

She couldn't resist correcting him when she got within earshot. "It wasn't a balcony."

"I know," he said. "It was a window. But balcony worked better in this case. So, what's the verdict?"

"I can live with it," she said.

"Okay. I'll dig the hole and you can play road construction worker and supervise."

"That works for me," said Kate.

His grin was teasing. "Somehow, I thought it would."

"I do know how to pitch in," she informed him.

"Yeah, but if you had to choose between being one of the peons pitching in and being the supervisor, which would you pick?"

"Supervising, of course. Someone has to."

"Right-o," said Jeff, driving the shovel into the ground.

Kate watched him work. "You don't strike me as a Shakespeare kind of guy. How is it you can quote the Bard?"

"Most people know that one," said Jeff.

"So, that's all you know."

"I didn't say that."

"Are you going to answer my question?"

"Well, it's like this," drawled Jeff. "My pappy only let me have a third-grade education down there in the foothills. But my ma, she cleaned house for a real nice rich lady who let her bring me along. And while I was washing the lady's underwear she'd read Shakespeare to me."

Kate made a face. "Funny."

"I knew you'd think so," he said, sounding pleased with himself.

"Now, the real answer, please."

"I took a few Lit courses at the U."

"What U?"

"The University of Washington. That's why I'm so partial to the Huskies. I like to support my alma mater."

Kate found it hard to think of Jeff as an educated man. "What did you major in?" she asked suspiciously.

He stopped work to lean on the shovel. "I have a master's in communications." Something in his face changed as he said the words. It was as if a mask had slipped, revealing a side to Jeff Hardin he obviously preferred to keep hidden. Kate suddenly caught a glimpse of the sharp mind of a man who was nobody's fool.

Like a chess player who sensed he had given too much away, Jeff shuttered his gaze and turned his attention back to the task at hand.

"You're smarter than you let on, aren't you? This dumb jock thing is an act."

"Most of the jocks I know aren't dumb," said Jeff. "They just have their own brand of smarts."

"So do you. Why do you hide it?"

He shrugged. "I don't. People choose not to see it. Some people, that is. They look at how I make my living and they jump to conclusions about me."

Here he stopped to give Kate a pointed look, and she felt her cheeks warming in response.

He continued. "Part of the problem is my temperament. I'm friendly and open—"

"With part of yourself," interposed Kate. "I think there's a lot of you that you keep sealed up tighter than beans in a tin can."

"Is that so?"

"Yes, that's so."

"Well, thanks for the insight, Doc. Am I going to get your bill in the morning?"

"No charge," said Kate. "So, let's pretend I don't know the truth. You're friendly and open."

"I am, actually. And I'm a pretty happy guy. People who are happy and friendly sometimes get mistaken for idiots. The ones who are moody and ruthless or who act superior are the ones who get the intellectual's seal of approval. At least, that's been my experience. A smart guy sees a guy like me smiling for no other reason than the simple fact that the sun is out and he's glad to be alive and says, 'What's he got to smile about? He must be a real dork.' "

"And a guy like you says in response to that?" prompted Kate.

"A guy like me doesn't say anything because he knows that everyone loves a dork. I'm a hero to the common man, every guy's friend. That's why I have no trouble getting interviews, because I'm a nice guy. People like to talk to nice guys because they make them feel good. That's why people love to call my show. And you know that saying about nice guys finishing last?"

"Yes."

"Well, I can tell you why they finish last. It's not because they're stupid or naive. It's because they've been busy stopping along the way for a pickup game of basketball or for a beer at the local tavern while the hotshots just run and sweat, thinking they're going to find a pot of gold at the end of the race." He shook his head. "Most of them only find the medics." He stood aside and gestured to the hold he'd dug. "I think we're ready."

Together, they settled the tree into the cavity, then Kate held it in place while Jeff tipped the dirt in over it.

"Okay," he said when they'd finished. "Why don't you give the thing a drink and I'll fill in that other hole so nobody lands in it and breaks an ankle."

She fetched water for her tree while he filled in the hole.

"Thanks," he said as he handed her back the shovel.

The softness in his voice touched her. Seeing the sheen on his face, Kate decided it would only be right and hospitable to offer him something to drink.

"How about some lemonade?" she asked.

"Sounds good," said Jeff.

"Would you like to come up to the house, or have it on my dock?"

"The sun feels good. I'll meet you at the dock."

As Kate hurried back to the house she realized there

was a spring in her step she hadn't felt in some time. Well, naturally she was happy. She had done the mature thing and reached a compromise with her neighbor.

She mixed frozen lemonade in a glass pitcher, which she set on a serving tray with two glasses filled with ice, then headed to the dock, where Jeff was now stretched out on his back.

"Just in time," he murmured as she bent to set down the tray. "Another minute and you might have found me lying here dead of thirst."

He raised up on one arm to take the glass she offered, balancing easily. Kate settled next to him and poured herself a glass.

"You know, some of this wood is rotten," he said. "You really ought to replace it."

"I guess I should," said Kate.

"If you buy the materials, I'll do the patch job," he offered.

"That's sweet, but not necessary." Not even desirable. One more good deed and she'd be so in debt at the Jeff Hardin kindness bank, she'd never get out.

The way he cocked his head and studied her made her uncomfortable. He may as well have said, "I know what you're thinking, and don't you think that's being a little silly?" She gave him her "Kate's in control" smile, then took a sip of lemonade.

"I tell you what," he said. "Why don't you cook me dinner one night in exchange for my labor? Then you won't have to feel like you're taking advantage of me."

"That's hardly a fair trade-off," pointed out Kate.

"Okay, dinner and free psychiatric care for the rest of my life."

"I couldn't take it."

"Then it will just have to be dinner," said Jeff. "You'd be doing me a favor, you know. I'm itching to do some manly man things, and my dock doesn't need mending. So, while I'm waiting for it to start falling apart, I can practice on yours."

Kate still hesitated.

"Come on, Doc. I wouldn't offer if I didn't want to do it. Deal?"

It would be small to turn down his generosity.

She nodded. "Okay. Deal. I'll call in my charge card number to Lumberman's and you can go get what you need." That was a little too much of a carte blanche. "Under a hundred dollars, that is," she added.

"I should be able to fix it for that," he said, and took another chug of lemonade. He held out his glass for more, saying, "I love this stuff."

"Me, too," said Kate. She refilled the glass, and he took another deep drink, then set the glass down with a contented sigh.

He looked so casual, so much a part of his surroundings, so comfortable in them. No, it wasn't his surroundings he was comfortable in, it was his own skin. Jeff Hardin was a contented man, and easy to be around. Good company, actually.

Good company, a glass of lemonade, and the sun warm on your back. It was a golden moment. Kate relaxed into it and smiled.

"Hey, don't do that," Jeff cautioned. "People won't think you're smart."

"That is the silliest theory I've ever heard," said Kate.

"But true." He looked out at the boats bobbing gently next to their moorings. "Before the summer's over I'm going to be out there in a boat."

"Oh?"

"Yeah, a ski boat. You know how to water-ski?"

Kate shook her head. "I've never tried."

"I could teach you," Jeff offered.

The image of herself in a bathing suit was not a pleasant one. "We'll see," she said noncommittally.

Jeff gave a knowing nod. "Oh, yeah. The bathing suit

thing. You know, you women worry too much about your bodies," he observed, still watching the water.

His remark made Kate feel like a turtle that had been pulled out of its shell. She decided to bluff it out. "What makes you think I'm worried about my body?"

He twitched the sleeve of her T-shirt. "Just a wild guess. I bet you'd rather have your fingernails ripped off than be caught in a bathing suit. And I'll bet you'd look fine in one."

Kate shook her head. "Fine is your girlfriend. I've had two kids. My fine days are over."

"How about your life, Doc? Is that over, too?"

"There's nothing wrong with my life," said Kate. She knew she sounded defensive. "It's great," she added, keeping her tone of voice light.

"Well, that's good," he said.

Kate continued, feeling compelled to explain just how good her life was. "I've got two wonderful children, nice friends, a good job."

"Yeah, you've got it pretty good," he agreed. "Speaking of your kids, where are they?"

"At friends'. They should be home soon."

Jeff took his eyes off the water and looked at her and, even though there was nothing remarkable about those hazel-colored eyes, something in them made her heart flutter. "When your kids are gone, what's your life like?"

"Busy, full."

"Happy," he said. "You forgot happy. In fact, you haven't said that word yet."

Now it was Kate's turn to look out at the water. She'd had her happy moments, especially with the kids. But was *happy* a word she would use to describe her life? Well, so what if it wasn't? She had something more important than happy: she had purpose. And purpose was what gave life meaning.

"There is more to life than being happy," she said.

He nodded and took a slug of his lemonade. "That's

true, but there's nothing wrong with enjoying yourself, either."

"You seem to have taken it in your head that I don't enjoy myself."

"You're right, I have. And you don't. Not really. You're busy being responsible, and practical, busy solving the world's problems. But when was the last time you enjoyed yourself? If I treated one of Grace's pies the way you treat your life she'd throw it in my face."

"What is that supposed to mean?" demanded Kate.

"It means that you're just going through the motions. You're living, but you're not savoring anything."

Oh, brother. Here was the grasshopper telling the ant how to get its life together. And it was easy for Jeff to talk. What had he ever lived through?

"There are more important things in life than knock-knock jokes and sports trivia," said Kate. It was true, so why did she sound so prissy and unreasonable when she said it?

"Yeah, you're right," he conceded. "But sometimes it's kind of fun to tell knock-knock jokes."

"Oh, brother," said Kate in disgust.

"No, it's true," insisted Jeff. "I'm sure you've read those studies that prove laughter is good for you."

"Of course I have," said Kate. "But I haven't been impressed with a knock-knock joke since I was ten."

"So, what do you do when your kid tells you one?"

"That's different," said Kate. "He's the right age for knock-knock jokes. But aren't you a little old for that kind of childish humor?"

"You're never too old for knock-knock jokes," said Jeff. "And I'll prove it to you."

"Go ahead," said Kate. "Try."

"All right. Knock-knock."

"Nobody's home. Go away."

"I'm a salesman, and we never give up," Jeff retorted. "Knock-knock."

"My mother told me never to open the door to strangers," said Kate.

"Come on, knock-knock," he insisted, playing with the ice in his lemonade.

"Okay. Who's there?"

"Ice."

"Ice who?"

"I only have ice for you," said Jeff, pulling out a cube. Before Kate could react, he had slipped it down the front of her T-shirt, making her jump and sending him into up-roarious laughter.

"Oh, that was funny," she snapped, standing and shaking the ice cube free.

"It got a reaction out of you," he observed.

"Yes, it did," she said, fishing in her own glass.

"Hey, now," he said. He jumped up and began moving away, his voice still tinged with laughter. "Let's not get carried away here."

Kate advanced on him, backing him to the edge of the dock.

"Okay," he said, pulling on the neck of his T-shirt, "okay. I give up. Just drop the damn thing and be done with it."

"All right," she said, and dropped the ice cube off the dock. It landed in the water with a tiny plink.

"Well," he said. "It's a wise woman who knows how to accept defeat. I'm glad to see—"

She pushed against his chest, catching him off guard and toppling him off the dock and into the nippy water. "And it's an even wiser woman who knows when not to," she called after him, then burst into impolite guffaws. Now, that was funny.

And it felt good. It felt amazingly, refreshingly good to be silly and laugh a deep belly laugh.

He was spluttering, shaking the water from his face. "You were right," she said, leaning over the edge and smirking down at him. "Laughter is indeed good for the soul."

"Yeah, and he who laughs last laughs best." He rose from the water like a sea lion and his hand caught her ankles in a vise grip.

The next thing she knew, Kate was hitting the water with a splash. It surrounded her, smothering her and brushing her skin with icy fingers. She suddenly realized that other fingers were touching her, too, sliding up her thigh, wrapping around her waist, heaving her toward the sunlight.

She broke the surface, squealing, and Jeff laughed, his voice rich and deep. And then another voice joined them to make a trio.

"Having fun?" asked Bambi.

Six

THE IRRATIONAL FEELING THAT SHE'D JUST BEEN caught in bed with Jeff brushed warmth across Kate's face. She hoped Bambi would mistake the pink she felt growing on her cheeks for sunburn.

She heard the guilt in Jeff's voice as he tossed her away from him and said, "Hi, babe."

Even with his welcoming words, the normally sunny Bambi still looked a little overcast, so Jeff hauled himself onto the dock and gave her a soggy embrace.

She stepped out of it, wrinkling her nose and protesting, "You're all wet."

"Yeah, that's what the doc's been telling me. I was just showing her how to loosen up and live," he added as Kate waded out of the water.

"Actually, we were celebrating the moving of my tree," added Kate. She walked onto the dock and plunked herself down, trying to look as innocent as she was. Nothing had happened here. Really.

"Want some lemonade?" asked Jeff, offering Bambi his glass.

Bambi was ready to forgive and forget. "Sure," she said, and took a slug, and Kate breathed an inward sigh of relief. "There's a game on," said Bambi.

"Oh, yeah," said Jeff.

"How come you're not watching it?"

"Well, we had to move the tree," he replied. He grinned at Kate. "And quote some Shakespeare."

"Misquote," she corrected.

Bambi nodded slowly. It was a suspicious nod, and Kate felt guilty all over again. Which was ridiculous, because there was nothing to feel guilty over. Nothing at all.

"Your TV's still on," said Bambi.

This conversation was not rolling along well with three wheels. Kate decided it was time for her to go back to being the invisible neighbor. Anyway, she was getting cold.

"I think I'll go put on some dry clothes and let you get back to your game," she said.

"You're welcome to come watch it with us," offered Bambi.

Kate knew she was either being polite or wanting to further observe Kate and her boyfriend together. Whatever the motive, it wasn't a good idea.

"Thanks," said Kate. "But I have plans for the afternoon." It wasn't a lie: when the kids returned home they would . . . do something.

"Okay," said Bambi, trying to sound regretful.

"Thanks again for moving the tree," said Jeff.

"Supervising moving the tree," she corrected, and he grinned.

Bambi was smiling, too, but it was a fragile one.

Kate picked up the pitcher and glasses and made her getaway, leaving Jeff to cement both Bambi's happy expression and their relationship.

Back inside her house, she felt restless, unable to concentrate. She went to her bedroom, peeled off her wet clothes, and examined her reflection in the mirror. Just as she'd suspected: she still looked the same. Bambi Hooterman didn't have a thing to worry about. There was no way Kate was going to attract Jeff Hardin's attention.

Or anyone else's, for that matter. She needed to get serious and take this weight off now, before it got any worse.

She put on dry clothes, then marched downstairs to the kitchen. She grabbed the plate of fudge brownies Grace had sent over the day before and stepped up to the sink like a batter ready to hit a home run. These were going right down the drain.

She got as far as holding the plate over the sink and remembered the old saying: waste not, want not. It would be a shame to destroy a whole plate of helpless brownies. They seemed to be begging her not to do this terrible thing. She'd save one. As a sop to her conscience, she rescued the smallest and took a dainty bite, making both her taste buds and her psyche instantly happy. Who needed a man, anyway? Past thirty it was silly to be vain about your looks.

Strike one.

Okay, get a grip, Stonewall. How can you help other people learn to master their bad habits if you can't master yours? She put the rest of the brownie back on the plate.

Well, that was stupid. She'd already eaten half of it. Anyway, she was going to destroy all the others, so what did it matter if she ate just one? She retrieved it and took another bite, savoring the rich chocolate taste.

Strike two.

What was she doing? She returned the last bite of brownie to its condemned brothers. Then she turned on the water full blast, flipped the garbage disposal switch, and tipped the plate, sending the fat larvae to their grisly end.

Yes, home run! Er, rather, success!

JEFF HAD ENOUGH EXPERIENCE WITH WOMEN TO know when one was dying to launch into a potentially unpleasant conversation, and his was sending off "Let's talk" vibes nearly strong enough to render his satellite dish useless. He had avoided the Talk by hurrying to his room for dry clothes as soon as they got in the door. Then he'd distracted Bambi by offering her some potato chips, although he already knew she would refuse his hospitality: when it came to food, she was more rabbit than female, preferring carrots and celery to chips and salsa. Still, discussing food made a good diversionary tactic. After that, he had planted himself on the living room couch and riveted his gaze to the game in the hopes that Bambi would get the hint and not bring up the subject of his neighbor.

Not that he minded talking about Kate—he and Bambi had shared some good laughs after Kate crashed his Memorial Day party. And, in the wake of the Popsicle stick episode, they had found much to discuss in regard to her child-rearing methods. But this had been a good day, and he didn't want his peaceful feeling uprooted by female jealousy, especially since there wasn't anything to be jealous about. He and the doc had just been being neighborly.

Granted, he had felt a little more than neighborly back there in the water. His close encounter with Kate's curves had given him quite a zing. But that didn't mean anything. Bambi ought to know by now that he wasn't the kind of sleezoid who got his kicks juggling two women at once. Just keeping one happy was enough work.

Bambi managed to maintain silence until the beer commercial. Then she nonchalantly tossed out her opening volley.

"It looks like you and Doctor Kate are getting along better."

"Yeah. She's okay," said Jeff, hoping that would end the dialogue.

Bambi nodded. "She's nice. I like her."

This was not, exactly, the tactic he had expected and it threw him. What was that remark supposed to mean, anyway—that he didn't, that he should?

"Well, so do I," he said, and it sounded defensive.

"Now that she moved her tree?"

"It shows she's got a heart after all."

"She's kind of cute, actually," added Bambi.

Now we were finally getting to the main event. "Yeah, she's not bad," said Jeff. "But she's not my type—too sharp-tongued."

That was what she'd wanted to hear. Those great lips of hers turned up at the corners, and she cooed, "What is your type?"

He pulled her against him. "What do you think?"

Her smile faded a little. "I think she's nice and she's really smart, and she lives next door."

Jeff felt himself tensing. Was Bambi just feeling threatened or was she fishing for an invitation to move in? And why did the thought of her coming to stay make him squirm?

Listen to this! Now he was sounding like Doctor Kate. He didn't have any deep psychological reasons for not wanting his girlfriend to move in. He just wanted his space, that was all.

"You know what I think?" he asked.

"What?" Now she was looking at him with those big, blue, trusting eyes as if he could do no wrong.

"I think you think too much." He kissed her, and she sighed happily and settled in for a nice seventh-inning-stretch worth of necking. After the game, they'd get down to serious business.

ON MONDAY MORNING TEMPTATION ARRIVED AT Kate's doorstep in the form of Grace, bearing freshly baked coffee cake.

"Had breakfast yet?"

"Yes," said Kate, "plain egg whites, scrambled, and you can check your weapons at the door before you come in." She lifted the plate from her friend's hands and set it on the porch. "That goes back home with you when you leave."

"What's this all about?" asked Grace, following her out to the kitchen. "Did you join Overeaters Anonymous over the weekend?"

"Something like that," said Kate. "Want a cup of coffee?"

"Yes, and I would've liked to have had a piece of raspberry coffee cake to go with it."

"By all means, have one, but please don't bring that plate in here to tempt me. I'm not strong enough yet to sit here and just look at it."

"I feel somehow rejected," complained Grace.

Kate gave her a hug. "Don't. I'm not rejecting you, personally, just the fat pills you brought. I've got to get a grip on my bad eating habits before they grow too big to grab."

Grace nodded. "I understand. You're still young, and having such good-looking motivation living right next door—"

Kate cut her off. "This has nothing to do with Jeff Hardin, believe me."

Grace raised both eyebrows at her.

"Well, in a way it does," Kate amended. She set a mug of coffee in front of Grace and sat down opposite her at the kitchen table. "I have to admit, he and Bambi make good catalysts. Seeing them together has made me realize it's time I open myself up to the possibility of giving the opposite sex a second chance. And to do that I need to give me a second chance. I need to be the kind of woman I'd want to spend time with."

"You already are," said Grace, reaching across the table and patting her arm.

"Thanks," said Kate, and returned the gesture. "But you know what I mean. I've gotten sloppy. Unless I have a public appearance, I dress like I really don't care about myself. And my eating habits say the same thing. I think it's time I pulled it together and got interactively involved with life again."

"You're harder on yourself than anyone I know," said Grace.

"Maybe. Or maybe I haven't been hard enough. It happens when you spend most of your time fixing other people's lives."

Grace's mouth turned down at the corners.

"What?" said Kate.

"You and your becoming the kind of woman you want to spend time with. Now you've shamed me out of eating my coffee cake."

"That's not right. I'm sorry. Go ahead and have a piece. I'll try not to embarrass myself and salivate over your shoulder while you eat it."

"No, that's okay. We foodaholics don't like to eat alone. And the image of you drooling on me has just done wonders for my appetite. After I drink my coffee I'll take it over to Jeff."

"Tell him to feed it all to Bambi and let's see if it shows up someplace on her body other than her breasts," Kate suggested, making Grace grin. "Oops. Now who said that?"

"I can't imagine," said Grace. "I thought you let the cat out." She snapped her fingers. "Oh, that's right, you don't have one."

"Obviously I don't need one."

AS SHE GOT READY FOR WORK, KATE REMEMBERED how kind Bambi had been when Robbie hurt himself. On her way out to the car, she stopped by her office and dug out a copy of *The Frog with the Glass Slipper*. Inside it she wrote, *For Bambi. Hold out for your prince.* She signed her name beneath with a flourish. There. That made a nice thank-you gift. She'd give it to Jeff at the station today and ask him to pass it on.

He seemed to be in earlier than usual. She saw him pass

by during the last half of her show and, somehow, lost her train of thought.

"So, do you think I should move to Yakima, Doctor Kate?" prompted her caller.

Kate jerked her attention back to Lois. Yakima, Yakima. Oh, yes, the lady with the cowboy.

"Lois, what you have here right now is a pleasant romantic fantasy. You and this man see each other on weekends. You get to play cowgirl at his ranch, and when he comes over to Seattle, you show him the sights. But the reality is, you have two very different lifestyles. In order for this relationship to work, one of you is probably going to have to make some big changes."

"He couldn't leave the ranch, it's the only thing he knows," said Lois.

"Okay, what about you? Do you work?"

"Yes," said Lois.

"What do you do for a living?"

"I'm a teacher."

"Great," said Kate. "Then why don't you try this: instead of burning your bridges and leaving everything, look into renting a place east of the mountains for the summer and get a good idea of what life on the open range is really like. Of the two of you, you're the most flexible. If it turns out you like it over there, you can probably look into getting a teaching position."

"Oh, that's a good idea," said Lois.

"And while you're visiting, work alongside your friend whenever possible, observe him in as many different circumstances as you can. It will give you a clearer picture as to whether this cowboy is a prince or just a dusty, old frog in chaps."

"Great. Thanks, Doctor Kate."

Jeff had slipped in to stand behind Wallis now. He leaned over and used her mike to send a message into Kate's headphones. "Ribbit."

Kate couldn't help feeling smugly pleased. With just

one kind gesture, she had turned them from antagonists to buddies.

She stuck her tongue out at him playfully, and brought up her next caller. "Lisa, welcome to the program. How can I help you?"

"I want to know how I can stop my husband from working such long hours. I'm afraid he's going to kill himself."

Jeff turned and hopped off, and Kate burst into a very inappropriate guffaw, making Wallis scowl.

"Oh, Lisa, I am sorry," she said. "Our afternoon guy, Jeff Hardin, is in here clowning around and distracting me. Let's start again so we can give your problem the serious attention it deserves. First of all, you need to know that no person can make another do anything. Your husband is going to have to decide for himself that he wants a more balanced life. So, you get to say something just once, then after that you have to keep your mouth shut. Agreed?"

"Agreed," said Lisa.

Kate went on to help Lisa brainstorm ways to be supportive of her husband, took two more calls, then ended the show.

"Well," said Wallis after Kate had joined her, "it looks like you've not only negotiated a truce with the enemy, but you've succeeded in establishing friendly relations."

"Things are going much better," admitted Kate. Wallis regarded her with a knowing smirk. "What?"

"Just how much better are things going?"

"I know what you're thinking. But it's not as good as that. Jeff Hardin is hardly my idea of Mr. Perfect. Anyway, he has a girlfriend, a cute, blonde Sea Gal."

"A romantic triangle!" exclaimed Wallis. "This should prove very interesting."

"You've been going to the movies too much lately," said Kate, moving to her desk to gather her things. She picked up her book and headed for the door.

"Who's the book for?" asked Wallis.

"Jeff's girlfriend."

"Going to try and convince her he's a frog?"

"Just giving her a thank-you for helping out with the kids when Robbie stabbed himself with that Popsicle stick."

"Very neighborly of you," said Wallis.

Kate ignored her and went in search of Jeff.

She found him just emerging from the break room.

"Good show today," he said. "I listened to you on the way in."

"I hope this doesn't mean I have to return the favor on the commute home."

He grinned. "You might learn something."

"Yes, but ignorance is bliss." She handed over the book. "I have a present for Bambi. Can you see she gets it?"

"Sure," said Jeff. He studied the cover.

"No wisecracks," warned Kate. "It's been a long day and I might forget I'm an expert in human relations."

"Hey, I was just going to say it looks interesting. I still think you should write one like this for guys. You know, we don't always know what we're doing."

"Yes, but you rarely admit it, so who would buy the book?"

He grinned good-naturedly. "You've got a point there." He headed down the hall toward the studio. "Thanks, Doc. I'll make sure she gets it."

Kate proceeded down the hall and out of the station, a smile on her face. Her mom had been right. It paid to be a good neighbor.

JEFF WENT UP TO THE PASSENGER DECK OF THE *Walla Walla* with Kate Stonewall's book tucked under his arm. He slumped across a seat next to a window and began to flip through the book. It seemed to be a mixture of romance horror stories and how-to's, and even included a checklist, captioned "Does the Slipper Fit?" He could imagine Bambi reading this and checking the spaces provided. He read down the list.

Do you have common interests?

Sure. They both liked to laugh and have fun, and Bambi enjoyed sports. Well, she at least liked football. She had to. She was part of the Sea Gals, and that dance troop performed at all the Seahawks' games. How could you do that if you didn't like football? And she watched baseball games with him. She didn't eat the same food, of course, because she was always dieting, and he wasn't sure she got as into those action movies as he did. The History Channel didn't do anything for her, either, but she did like *Biography* on A&E, and biographies counted as history. And she liked parties. So did he.

Without common interests, you will have little to keep you close once the sexual attraction wanes, and nothing to talk about other than the kids when it's just the two of you out together. It is hard to establish a bond of oneness without the glue of common interests.

Yeah, yeah. Next question.

Do you have similar life goals?

Well, sure. They both wanted . . . to . . . have a good life. That counted as similar goals, didn't it? He was pretty sure Bambi wanted kids someday, same as him. She'd make a good soccer mom or den mother.

It's hard to pull together when you both are pulling in different directions. A man who is driven to have a successful career may not be your prince if you are hoping for someone who will hurry home to play with the kids at night. Conversely, if you are ambitious yourself and are looking for the good life, someone who has no desire to climb the corporate ladder with you will not be able to help you achieve it, and you will find yourself constantly frustrated by that man's lack of ambition.

Jeff was happy where he was. He had career success; in fact he lived the average Joe's dream life: talking sports, hanging with guys who had actually made it as athletes,

and getting paid for it. But he could get into the family
man thing, too. He had a good, balanced life. What you
saw was what you got. And Bambi seemed to like what she
saw. He didn't think she had any particular ambition. She
was happy enough where she was, enjoying her stint with
the Sea Gals, which she could do for the next ten years,
probably. Some of those women had been around for a
long time. Between that and studying to be a personal
trainer, she seemed happy enough. She wasn't an overly
ambitious, Type A woman, like the writer of this book,
which suited him fine. If there was one thing he didn't
want, it was some woman always nagging him to do better, do more, and die early from a heart attack.

Will he share his real self with you?

Oh, please.

*It is also hard to pull together when you don't know
what motivates each of you on the deepest emotional level.
A real prince not only wants to know your hopes and fears,
but also trusts you enough to share his.*

In other words, he should be just like a woman. How
had the doc managed to get this fairy tale published?

Can you discuss ideas, books, movies?

They discussed . . . next question.

*Do your personalities and temperaments complement
each other? Do you work well together and bring out the
best in each other?*

Well, there was an easy one to answer. Absolutely! He
was an easygoing guy, and Bambi was sweet tempered.
They got along perfectly.

*It is important that you be able to not only communi-
cate, but solve problems and compromise. To do this, you
don't need to be Siamese twins. Many women pick their
prince because he is just like them, then find themselves in
a stagnant relationship with a life going nowhere. You can
pick someone similar, but make sure there is enough of a
difference that you each challenge each other to be better.*

Jeff frowned. That was biased Type A drivel if ever he'd

heard it. Who needed to be challenged? He'd had more than enough challenges in his first marriage. Life was challenging enough as it was without getting involved with a woman who would drive you crazy.

He decided he'd had enough of the doc's checklist. She made finding the right person sound like a trip to the grocery store. Let's see, I want compatible. Check. Common interests. Check. Smart. Check, check. Hit the checkout stand, then take him home. Bah. Where did that leave any room for people to just plain fall in love?

He flipped back to the front page, where she'd inscribed, *Hold out for your prince.* What the hell was that supposed to mean? She should have written something like, *Glad to see you found your prince.*

He was everything Bambi wanted, or at least she acted like it. And she was everything he ever wanted. Well, almost. He had to admit, it would be nice if she didn't complain every time he wanted to see something on the History Channel. And they didn't always get in the most intellectually stimulating conversations. But she'd watch any action/adventure movie he wanted to see. She was good-looking, fun to be around, and easy to get along with. When it came right down to it, what more could a man want?

He left the book in his car when he got home. He was going to see Bambi on Wednesday. He'd give it to her then, as he was leaving. She could come out to the car and get it. That way she couldn't stumble on the List with him there, and decide to go through it together. He'd been with enough women to know that kind of activity always resulted in doing time discussing "our relationship," and there was no need to waste time talking about something that was just fine.

He got home to find a piece of lined school paper taped to his front door, with little boy printing on it.

Will you come to my gam on Sat? asked Robbie in his note. *Its at two. I sur hop you can be ther.*

Jeff smiled. "Sure kid, I'll come to your 'gam.'" And while he was at it, he could give the kid the autographed baseball he'd promised that day at the emergency room. Now that he and the doc were getting along better, she probably wouldn't mind. He supposed Bambi would be coming over, and she'd want to go. He just hoped she wouldn't bring up the subject of that book.

Suddenly, Jeff got the spooky premonition that he was carrying around a time bomb, and once he gave it to Bambi, it would go off.

He shook off the feeling. That was nuts. And that was the trouble with living right next door to someone who spent all her time poking around inside people's heads: it turned you into a navel gazer. Well, he had more important things to do in life than sit around contemplating his navel and rooting around in his id. Life was to be lived, not talked about.

And he'd have to remind Bambi of that when he gave her the doc's present.

Seven

WHEN THEY WERE FIRST DATING, BAMBI USED TO tune in to Jeff's show every night. She listened to it in her car on the way to the Sea Gals practices, while she was working out at the gym, or at home, struggling to memorize the names of the body's various muscles. The sound of that deep, friendly voice of his had been as soothing as a tape of waves on a beach, and knowing that KZOO's "Mr. *Jock Talk*" was her Jeff made her feel warm all over.

Of course, she still felt warm all over whenever she thought of Jeff, but she'd gotten past the need to listen to him talk for four hours straight about sports every night. Now, she just tuned into his show for the last fifteen or twenty minutes so she could make some nice comment when he asked her how she'd liked the program. That always seemed to satisfy him.

The sudden banging on her door announced Jeff's arrival, and she hurried to open it. He walked in bearing a takeout pizza and a fresh pineapple.

"I brought dinner," he said, giving her a kiss, then handing over the pineapple. "Something for each of us."

"Thanks," she said. "Are you actually going to eat some of this?"

"Maybe on my pizza. Or, if you chop some of it up, I'll put it over that ice cream I brought last week." He pretended to look at her suspiciously. "You didn't eat all my ice cream?"

Bambi shuddered. "That disgusting rocky road is right where you left it."

"Good," he said, following her into the living room. He plopped the pizza carton on the coffee table. "Because if you'd eaten it, I was going to have to spank you."

Bambi just shook her head at Jeff's goofy humor and headed into the kitchen to cut up the pineapple.

"So," he called, "did you catch the show?"

"Yeah," she replied. "You were great."

"What'd you think about that guy who thought we should have kept A-Rod? Who needs old Pay-Rod, anyway? Two hundred and fifty-two million for ten years. That's obscene. No ball club should be paying that kind of money and no player should be taking it when there are people starving in the world." He shook his head. "People seem to be losing track of the fact that baseball is not figure skating: it's a team sport."

That caller must have come on before she tuned in, but Bambi knew what to say when that happened. "You're absolutely right," she agreed.

"I tell you, you get all kinds," said Jeff, obviously satisfied with her answer. "Hey, looks like you rented us a movie."

"Yeah," called Bambi, and braced herself.

"A romantic comedy?" he asked, sounding pained.

Bambi stuck her head around the door frame. "Yes, a romantic comedy."

"Talk about spanking. What have I done to tick you off?"

"Nothing," said Bambi. "Now, come on. You know you like funny stuff." And there was funny stuff in this movie.

There were also some real three-hankie moments, but she wasn't going to tell him about those. If she did they'd never even get the video in the VCR.

Jeff's sigh could probably be heard over in the next apartment. He sank onto her sofa, flipped open the pizza box, and hauled out a huge, greasy-looking piece.

She didn't know a man who had worse eating habits than Jeff Hardin. At the rate he was going, he'd be dead by the time he was fifty. He *would* eat some of this pineapple, even if she had to force-feed him. She went back to work, spearing the bite-sized pieces with toothpicks and arranging them on a plate.

"So, is this one really funny?" he demanded as she joined him.

"It's supposed to be," said Bambi, handing over the remote control. "Anyway, last time we watched one of your favorites. It's my turn."

"Well, I don't want you not to get your turn," he said, waggling his eyebrows at her. "In fact"—he threw his half-consumed piece of pizza back in the box and moved closer—"maybe we should just forget the movie."

She had it for three days. She could watch it later.

But Jeff was a sport. They got back to the movie eventually, and he settled in to watch it, consuming his cold pizza, which he topped with some of the fresh pineapple. Bambi was pleased that he actually laughed at all the funny parts—she knew he'd like the movie if he just gave it a chance. Then they hit the first teary, emotional moment, and he went to the kitchen to hunt for ice cream. On the final, moving scene, where the dysfunctional family reconciled, Bambi held him down and insisted he watch.

The expression on his face made him look like a suffering actor in a pain reliever commercial.

"There," she said finally, taking the remote from him and stopping the video, "that wasn't so bad, was it?"

"No worse than going to the dentist," said Jeff. "What do you women see in these weepy movies?"

"They're good. They're all about . . . life," she finished lamely.

He gave a snort. "Life is tough enough without having to import misery."

Bambi knew Jeff's ex-wife was a bitch, but other than that he didn't seem to have it so bad. "Yeah, your life is sure tough," she said with uncharacteristic sarcasm.

He looked at her in surprise. "What's that supposed to mean?"

"I mean you seem to have it pretty good, so I don't understand what you've got against anything that has to do with being serious."

He shrugged. "I just don't see the need for it, at least not fake serious."

"Fake serious?"

"Yeah, fake serious. Death and sickness and taxes, now, there's real serious. But this kind of stuff," he said, waving a hand at the television set, "that's pretend, so why get worked up about it, or even watch it? If I'm going to pretend, I'd just as soon go along for the ride while some guy saves the world."

Bambi hated these conversations. She went into them knowing she had a valid point, but she could never quite produce the argument to prove it: the words that would make Jeff sit up and take notice always refused to come to her rescue.

"I guess," she said, giving up.

He checked his watch. "Well, babe, I should hit the road."

"You could stay here," she offered, even though she already knew what the answer would be.

"Nah. I've got all my stuff back at the house."

She sighed inwardly. It was as if she had used up her quota of his time and now he was anxious to get on to something else—probably one of those thick history books stacked by his bed.

"Oh, I almost forgot, I've got something for you. Be right back."

He jumped off the couch and dashed out the door, leaving Bambi to fantasize over what he might possibly have gotten her. Concert tickets? Who was coming to Seattle in the near future? Or maybe it was jewelry. Maybe even a ring. She smiled at the thought. It would be just like Jeff to start a proposal so casually. Her smile lost some of its shine. Yes, it would.

He was back in the door now, carrying a hardback book. *Not a history book, please.* Maybe it was something interesting, like a biography about a movie star.

"Here," he said, handing it over. "It's a gift from Kate, and it's autographed."

"Autographed! For me?"

"Yeah."

Bambi opened the book.

"I don't know why she didn't write something like 'glad you found your prince,' though," Jeff was saying.

"Oh, gosh, how nice! This looks great. Tell her I'll start reading it right away."

"Don't lose any beauty sleep over it," cautioned Jeff, grabbing what was left of his pizza. "I'd leave this for your breakfast, but I know that would be a waste."

He gave her a garlic-scented kiss, then disappeared into the night, tossing over his shoulder something about calling her.

She wasn't sure exactly what he'd said, because she had already opened the book to chapter 1, "Hello, Cinderella."

"WELL, JILL, IT COULD VERY WELL BE THAT YOUR strong punishment techniques are reinforcing the very habit you're trying to break. Ever find yourself telling a little white lie at work to keep the boss from coming down on you?"

"Well, yes," said Kate's caller reluctantly.

"Your daughter is doing the same thing. It sounds to me like she's fallen into the habit of lying out of self-protection. She lies to save her skin. Literally. Now, let's look at this incident you've just described. Do you think your child is going to be anxious to confess that she was playing in your makeup when she knows she's going to get a spanking?"

"Well, no, but I've got to do something."

"Yes, you do. But I suggest that you talk with her. Don't ask her again if she was in your makeup. You both know that she was. Instead of threats and punishment for what is simply a natural little girl curiosity, why don't you try using some positive reinforcement? Tell Cherry that if she doesn't play in your makeup this week, you will buy her something of her own. Get her some flavored lip gloss. You can go shopping for it together and let her pick out the flavor. Then next week, if she keeps the bargain, you can get her something else, like a little makeup bag of her own, or some nail polish. After three or four weeks, she should have enough of her own kid-version cosmetics to stay out of yours. And, the fun side benefit is that when you're doing your makeup, she can sit on your bathroom counter and do hers, too."

"That's a great idea, Doctor Kate. Thanks."

"You're welcome," said Kate. George had started the bumper music, so she closed the show with her usual, "We'll meet tomorrow for more life strategies. And remember, in real life we don't get to go back to start, so let's make the right moves along the way."

She sat back in her chair and let out a sigh. That last call had been the only easy one she'd taken since she went on the air. It had been a long day, filled with depressing problems: people in denial, people seething with anger, people trying to put their lives together in the wake of abuse, people who had made so few right moves along the way that their daily existence sounded like an emotional war zone.

And many of those problems could have been averted if the caller had just looked before leaping.

Pushing her fingers to her temples, she left the air studio and joined Wallis and George in the master control room.

"Boy, did you have some call-in misery today," said George. "I almost feel guilty for being normal."

"You are, indeed, a prince," said Kate. "Too bad we can't clone you."

Wallis was studying her. "Head hurting?"

"Just a little."

"You can't save them all, you know."

"I know, but I'll save as many as I can."

At that moment, Jeff Hardin popped in. "So, how's life in the nuthouse today?"

"If it isn't Ernie Empathetic," said Wallis in disgust.

"Hey, I'm as empathetic as the next guy."

"Which is why Kate has so many callers," Wallis retorted.

It was kind of her producer to go on the attack, and if she'd had any emotional energy left, Kate would have joined her.

Instead, she walked past Jeff, saying, "I need to catch a ferry. See you all tomorrow."

Jeff pulled his foot out of his mouth long enough to call after her, "Bambi loves your book."

It made Kate smile. "Then my life hasn't been in vain," she murmured.

IT IS ALSO HARD TO PULL TOGETHER WHEN YOU don't know what motivates each of you on the deepest level. A real prince not only wants to know your hopes and fears, but also trusts you enough to share his.

Bambi gnawed on her pencil. She wished she could mark "Yes" by this question about her prince sharing his real self with her. She loved Jeff, but was he her prince or just a frog with a glass slipper? And if she settled for him, was she not only cheating herself, but robbing some other woman of the man who would be perfect for her, like Doctor Kate suggested?

Bambi knew she couldn't expect perfection. Even Doctor Kate admitted that Superman didn't exist. Jeff was pretty close, but was he her Mr. Perfect?

He could be. Maybe they just needed to talk. She'd be at his place this weekend. It was as good a time as any.

K ATE RETURNED HOME FROM WORK FRIDAY TO learn that Amanda and Sommer had plans for Sommer to spend the night. Well, why not? Kate could return Sommer to her parents after Robbie's ball game the next day. Which, if this wonderful June drizzle continued, might just get rained out. She could always hope.

The bad weather didn't bother the girls at all. After consuming huge quantities of macaroni and cheese, they left Kate to her chicken salad and vanished into the den to check out the Seahawks Web site. Earlier in the week, Bambi had sent Amanda a poster with all thirty Sea Gals on it, plus a message that she could learn more about them by visiting the site.

After a few moments, Kate's curiosity got the better of her, and she went to peer over the girls' shoulders and see if the collective I.Q. made it as high as one hundred.

The girls had gotten to the group picture and were in the process of pointing arrows at each pretty face and clicking to bring up individual shots and bios.

"Isn't this cool, Mom?" gushed Amanda.

Kate checked out the picture of Athena and read her vital stats. Occupation: receptionist/cheer choreographer. College: Cornish College of the Arts. Cornish! The girl was no slouch. Kate read on. Dance background: eighteen years ballet, four years modern, four years jazz. Danced with the Joffrey Ballet for two years. Kate blinked. This was not what she thought of when she heard the words *Sea Gals*. Athena's favorite TV show was *Ally McBeal*, her most prized possession was her cat, and the place she was most interested in seeing was . . . Africa? The sound of crumbling stereotypes was deafening.

Kate lingered as the girls selected other pretty faces to learn their backgrounds. Occupations ran the gamut from public relations to hairdresser. Several of the women were in college, and all had many years of dance under their belts.

"Did you do Bambi yet?" asked Kate.

"Oh, yeah. We did her first," said Amanda.

"And what did you learn about her?"

"She's had eight years of ballet lessons," said Sommer, "and three of modern jazz. I'm going to ask my mom to let me take dancing lessons."

"Could I take dancing lessons?" asked Amanda.

"You're already taking piano lessons, and I have a hard time getting you to practice for those."

"I'd practice my piano if I could take ballet."

Amanda was definitely more musically than kinesthetically gifted, but Kate could see some advantages to playing "Let's Make a Deal."

"Well," she said, "we might be able to work out something. Why don't you show me you mean business by putting in your half hour a day on the piano this summer, and if you do, I'll spring for dance lessons."

Amanda jumped up and nearly hugged the breath out of Kate. "Thanks, Mom. You're great!"

She kissed the top of her daughter's head. "Just remember, you have to keep up your end of the bargain."

"Oh, I will," promised Amanda. She sat down again, saying to Sommer, "We could take lessons together."

"Yeah," said Sommer.

Kate left them to their dreams and went in search of her new paperback thriller. She could hear the rain hammering steadily on the roof now. Music to her ears.

She loved the sound of rain on the roof. It brought back memories of her childhood, when she would lie in her attic bedroom in their old house in Oregon and let the raindrops lullaby her to sleep.

Some things never changed. The gentle patter increased, and Kate didn't get more than five pages into her book before it convinced her to lay it on her chest and let her eyes fall shut.

She awakened some time around two to discover it was still raining.

Inside? No, she'd been dreaming.

A droplet splinked off her nose, making her blink. Kate sat up and caught another drop on top of her head. Sadly, she hadn't been dreaming. It was really coming down out there now. And in here, too.

"Don't do this to me," she growled, but the roof continued to leak, forcing her to shove her bed against the wall, then go to the kitchen to fetch some pots. On her way downstairs, she made a quick inspection of the other rooms and discovered she'd also be setting up a drip catcher in the bathroom, too.

"This is just too fun," she muttered, wiping a drop off her neck. "Thank you so much, Rob Stonewall for croaking your stupid self and leaving me alone to deal with this kind of thing." *Real rational, Kate.* So, who wanted to be rational at two A.M.!

By the time she got back to bed she was fully awake and the rain was no longer romantic or comforting. It was one more sniper in the army of circumstance taking potshots at her. First her car, then her house. What next? A fresh leak sprang over her bed's new location and caught her on the shoulder. Well, this, too, she could cope with. She shook her fist at the ceiling. "Go ahead. Make my day." As she marched to the kitchen for a fresh pot she had a fanciful image of Rob in heaven with a giant hose, playfully sprinkling her. Yeah, right. Saint Peter would never let him in: there were no sports in heaven.

• • •

THE STORM PLAYED ITSELF OUT SOMETIME IN THE wee hours of the morning, and blue sky and sun smiled on the day of Robbie's big game. Robbie was smiling, too, as he gathered up his gear.

Jeff had promised to be at this game, and Kate worried that Robbie would feel driven to perform well and impress him. And if he failed, it would be a sad day in Mudville. How she wanted this phase her son was going through to pass! Right now they were in a lose-lose situation. If Robbie did poorly he'd be unhappy, but if he had a good game, it would merely reinforce his fascination with the sport, and the nonsense would pick up again next spring. She remembered her words to a recent caller, a mother more worried about her popularity standing with her daughter than her parental responsibilities. *It's your job as a mother to do what is best for your child.* The nonsense didn't have to pick up again next spring. Other words to another caller popped up to taunt her. *Part of our responsibilities as parents is to find where our children excel and then allow them to do so.* Well, one hit did not qualify as excelling. If only Robbie didn't have a game today!

BAMBI ARRIVED AT JEFF'S HOUSE TEN MINUTES before they had to leave for Robbie's game, bringing along trouble in the form of a certain book.

"I missed a ferry," she explained. "But while I was waiting, I finished the book." She set it on the counter.

Jeff could almost hear the thing ticking. "Yeah?" he replied cautiously.

"Did you look at it at all?" she ventured.

"I scanned a few pages. Sounded like a lot of psychobabble to me," he added, hoping to disarm the bomb.

"Do you think we're right for each other?" she blurted.

Shit. He knew this would happen. He should have forgotten to give the thing to her.

"Of course we're right for each other," he assured her, pulling her to him. "We've got all kinds of stuff in common, just like the doc suggests. We have a great time together, and we get along well. Now, you can't say that about a lot of couples."

"Yes, but there are a lot of things we don't have in common, and we don't really share."

Share, share what? "Of course we do," argued Jeff.

"Not our deepest feelings."

Oh, that. "Come on, babe. Guys don't get into that stuff like you women."

"I feel like there's a lot about your life I don't know," said Bambi, looking up at him with worried blue eyes.

That did it. He was going to save mankind by blowing up his neighbor's computer. Hopefully, she hadn't copied whatever she was working on now onto a disk.

"Jeff," prompted Bambi.

"Look, we're happy. Why do you want to go and rock the boat?"

"Because I want to be sure that . . ."

He held up a hand. "Don't use the words *frog* or *prince*."

She frowned. "You're not taking this seriously. In fact, you don't take anything seriously."

"I do, too. In fact, I'm taking it real seriously that you want to let someone who doesn't really know either one of us have so much power over our lives."

"But I think she has a point."

"Yeah, she does: right on top of her head."

"See? There you go again, not being serious."

"I'm damn serious. And I'm ticked off. Come on, Bambi, do you really need a book and a checklist to tell if things are good between us?"

"Well." She stood there turning everything over in her mind.

Watching her, Jeff decided the revolution could take awhile.

"We don't have time for this right now. We've got to get

to the field for Rob's game. I promised the kid I'd go, and I don't want to be late."

"Okay," said Bambi, "but when we come back, we've got to talk."

"Oh, for crying out loud," grumbled Jeff. "Let's go."

WITH CONCERNED EYES KATE OBSERVED HER SON anxiously scanning the road to the field. The game had just begun and his team was up first. She knew he was praying that Jeff Hardin would arrive in time to see him get up to bat.

Kate asked herself how Jeff and company had managed to become so important so quickly to her children. Of course, the answer to that was easy: children needed heroes to look up to. And while parents were vital to a child's well-being, there was a special pedestal kids reserved for someone they could admire who hadn't been assigned by biology to love them. She supposed it was her own fault that Jeff and Bambi had been set on that pedestal. She hadn't exactly been busy presenting her offspring a lot of other people for the position. And with their friendly manner and interesting vocations, she could see how the couple would draw a child's admiration.

Her kids could pick worse idols, she supposed. This present fascination beat having Robbie following the exploits of some violent, oversexed basketball player, and Amanda wishing she could grow up to be an anorexic movie star with a troubled love life.

The first boy was up to bat now and the parents in the bleachers began to chatter.

"Come on, Dustin," called Janet. "Get us started."

Dustin got two strikes, and the crowd on the bleachers tensed. The third try, he hit a single, arriving safely on first base.

"Atta boy, Dusty," called his dad.

Three more boys got up to bat. One struck out, one got

a hit and made it to first, putting the first runner on second.
The third boy up to the plate also managed to advance
everyone a base. Now the bases were loaded and a new boy
stepped up to the plate while Robbie got ready on the side-
lines by taking some practice swings.

"Bases loaded," muttered Janet, and put a red fingernail
between her teeth.

Kate silently prayed that the kid would get a hit and
bring some of his teammates home. *Don't let Robbie have
to get up there and face being the third out with the bases
loaded.*

The boy struck out and Kate's breakfast omelet suddenly
sat heavily in her stomach.

The crunch of tires on gravel announced a new arrival
and she looked over her shoulder to see that Jeff had arrived. She shot her attention back to Robbie, who was just
stepping up to the plate, and knew by the tightly com-
pressed look that he, too, had seen Jeff. Great. More pressure.

The ball came and Robbie swung with all his might and
missed it by a mile.

Kate moaned and Janet patted her arm.

Jeff and Bambi were at the bleachers now. Bambi wore
white jeans shorts and a polo shirt. Her blonde hair was
caught up in a ponytail. Tanned legs distracting several of
the dads, she picked her way up to where Kate and Janet
sat, then settled in on the other side of Kate.

"I wasn't sure we were going to make it," she gushed.
"The ferry lines are huge." Before Kate even had time to be
polite, Bambi smiled across her at Janet and introduced herself, then turned back to Kate."Have we missed much?"

"No," said Kate. "It's the first inning."

"Oh, good. Jeff was crazy to get out the door. He was
afraid we'd miss seeing Robbie. Hit me a home run, Robbie!" she called.

Kate felt irrationally irritated. "You can do it, Robbie!"
she added.

Robbie probably didn't hear either of them. His concentration was all for the ball now. It sailed over the plate and he swung under it.

"Swing level," called Coach.

The one person her son probably wanted to hear something from stood by the fence, silent.

From the look on his face, Robbie could have been trying to decide which wires to cut on a bomb instead of trying to hit a baseball.

This was ridiculous, thought Kate. What were they doing here?

The third ball came and Robbie missed that one, too. His shoulders slumped and he dragged himself to the dugout for his mitt.

Oblivious to her son's pain, his teammates grumbled and headed for the outfield, and the opposing team rushed in like an attacking army.

"It's only the first inning," said Janet consolingly.

"He sure looks cute in his uniform," observed Bambi.

"It's the last time he'll wear it," vowed Kate.

She watched Jeff call to Robbie as he headed for the outfield. Robbie went reluctantly to the fence. They talked momentarily, and Kate wished she could hear what Jeff was saying to him.

Whatever it was, it worked magic. Robbie smiled up at him and Jeff tugged on the bill of his baseball cap, then her son rushed off to his position.

"I finished your book already," said Bambi.

Kate was having a hard enough time dealing with her baby's troubles. She wasn't in the mood to save the rest of the world today.

"Let's talk about it a little later, shall we?"

"Could we?"

Bambi sounded eager. Was there trouble in paradise?

"Yes," said Kate. "After the game."

Bambi nodded and shut up.

The innings marched on. Robbie let a fly ball bounce

from his mitt to the ground and got up to the plate two more times, where he hit two foul balls and one straight to the shortstop, who actually managed to stop it and get it to first base long before Robbie got there.

"Oh, that's too bad," said Bambi.

Kate gritted her teeth.

The final inning arrived, and with it Robbie's last chance to make his hero proud.

He shot a look toward Jeff, who called, "Watch it all the way to your bat."

Robbie nodded and set his jaw. Kate mirrored the action up in the bleachers.

The ball came and Robbie connected and sent it sailing into foul ball territory.

"Way to go," called Jeff.

The ball came again. Robbie swung the bat and it smacked the ball with a resounding crack, making it rocket out into the field.

Robbie stood for a second, following its progress in amazement. Every parent on the bleachers screamed, "Run!"

Robbie ran. First, second, third base.

Kate, Janet, and Bambi jumped up and down and hugged each other.

"He's wonderful," gushed Bambi. "Another Ken Griffey, Jr."

"You never know," said Janet, grinning at Kate.

The world will never know, thought Kate, determined not to lose her determination.

Jeff finally joined them, plopping down on the other side of Bambi.

"Hey, Doc."

"Thanks for coming," said Kate. "It means a lot to Robbie."

"I wouldn't have missed it for anything. You've got a great kid. I'm glad he could end the season on a positive note."

Janet's son was up to bat now and they concentrated on urging him to get a hit. He did, making second base and sending Robbie home, and, again, the parents went wild.

"Man, I love Little League," said Jeff as the crowd settled down to watch the next batter. "There's no game on the planet like baseball. It can be real good for a kid."

Kate couldn't resist countering, "And what about the child who doesn't do well?"

"He learns about the realities of life. Sometimes you win, sometimes you lose. He learns how to take the failures and go on to the next game. And if he isn't the best player on the team, he learns that teamwork can take him farther than he might be able to go on his own. Not bad lessons, I'd say. Would you?"

"No," agreed Kate. "But what about the other lessons?"

"Okay, I'll bite. What other lessons?"

"That you don't matter unless you can hit a home run."

"Oh, but you do matter. Not everybody can hit a home run. Some can catch, some are fast, some are good for morale. We're not all good at the same things. Isn't that how life works?"

"And what about the child who's not athletic?"

"He still learns about teamwork, and how to be a good sport. He takes those lessons with him through his life and maybe he hits a home run for his company."

"Maybe," countered Kate. "And maybe he just comes away thinking winning is everything."

"Learning how to win is part of life, just like learning how to lose," said Jeff.

Kate gave up the battle.

"I never win an argument with him either," said Bambi consolingly, which made Kate want to cut off her ponytail.

The game ended with Robbie's team winning by a narrow two points, and the kids came whooping off the field, ready for their celebration party at the Pizza Factory.

Janet reached across Kate and Bambi to shake hands with Jeff. "Hi, I'm Janet."

"Jeff Hardin," he said, pumping her hand.

"I know. My husband listens to you all the time. The team's going out for pizza. Would you like to join us? The kids would love it."

"Sure," said Jeff. "Why not?"

The Pizza Factory had been nearly empty until the team and their parents arrived. Now it fairly jumped with activity and racket. There had been a moment of reverence when Jeff presented Robbie with the promised autographed baseball, but that quickly ended. Now small bodies ricocheted back and forth between the arcades and the adults who held the key to happiness in their wallets. Shrieks and laughter and the whirl and ping of the fun machines punctuated adult conversation, and occasionally the pizza maker could be heard calling out an order number.

Jeff had made Robbie's day with a slap on the back and a simple, "Good job, man." Then he had achieved godhood with his autographed gift. That accomplished, he now rested at one end of the table, deep in conversation with Bill.

Bambi took advantage of the moment to corner Kate. "Could we talk for a minute?"

"Sure," said Kate. "How did you like the book?"

"I thought it was wonderful. But now I'm not sure if Jeff is my prince. It's not that I don't love him. I do. And we enjoy a lot of the same things, and he's easy to get along with, and sweet and kind."

"Sounds like he's pretty close to perfect," observed Kate. "So where's the problem?"

"I'm not sure we really communicate," confessed Bambi.

"A lot of women have that complaint," said Kate, "and, as I said in the book, you have to remember to differentiate between the way men and women communicate. He's never going to talk with you as if he were your best girlfriend."

Bambi nodded her head. "I know. And I don't expect

him to. It's just that, sometimes, it seems to me he's afraid to talk about his hopes and fears."

"That is certainly possible. Or maybe you haven't reached a point in your relationship where he feels secure enough to open up."

"We've been together for almost a year. You'd think by now that he'd feel comfortable." Bambi sighed and began to rearrange the remains of her salad with her fork.

Kate watched her and tried not to feel guilty about the two pieces of pizza now residing comfortably in her stomach. "Only you can answer the question of whether he's the right man for you or not," she said. "All I can tell you is that it's important to have the man you want to spend your life with open to revealing every side of himself. If he can't do that, you'll wind up living with someone very one-dimensional. And good luck having a full and lasting relationship with a poster."

Bambi nodded. "That's kind of what I thought you'd say."

"Take your time and don't rush into anything," continued Kate. "If there's one common mistake we women make, it's jumping into a relationship too quickly. We do more careful research on the cars we buy. Of course, the big difference between cars and men is the sexual attraction factor. But you can't get so caught up in the feeling you forget to be practical. You have to make sure a man's temperament and goals are a good match with yours. If they aren't, he's not your Mr. Right, no matter how nice he is."

Bambi bit her lip and nodded.

Kate patted her arm. "You'll sort it out."

"It's sure hard," said Bambi. "I mean, when you love someone."

Kate nodded. "They don't say 'love is blind' for nothing. Believe me, I know. I was blind once, myself."

And never again would she let hormones stuck in overdrive run her into a mismatched relationship. She'd learned her lesson the hard way. She wouldn't wish that kind of schooling on anyone.

$\mathcal{B}$AMBI WAS SILENT AS THEY DROVE BACK TO THE house, and it made Jeff about as comfortable as wearing jockey shorts that were a size too small. She'd been talking to the doc. Trouble lay ahead.

"So, did you have fun?" he asked.

Bambi was looking out the window. She turned and smiled at him. "I always have fun with you."

So far, so good. "That's good," he said, reaching across the seat to take her hand, "because I always have fun with you, too. I guess we're a pretty good match, huh?"

Half of Bambi's lower lip disappeared beneath her teeth. "What?"

"Do you think we are, really?"

"Of course," said Jeff. He could see that the rest of the day was not going to be pleasant, and he knew who to blame for that. He kept a firm hold on Bambi's hand.

"I mean, I know we have fun together, but sometimes I'm just not really sure how close we are," said Bambi.

"I was feeling pretty close last time we made love."

"Well, we are, but we aren't," she amended, freeing her hand. "Sometimes, Jeff, I think you're afraid to show me who you really are."

"You see who I really am! This is it. This is what you get."

She nodded slowly, and he realized that he had, some-how, said the wrong thing. "What, exactly, is it you're wanting me to show you, anyway?"

"Your emotions."

That ticked him off. "Oh, I get it," he said snidely. "If I'd just break down and have a good cry with you once in a while, then you'd be happy."

"I think you're afraid to break down and cry," said Bambi.

"I don't have anything to cry about."

"Even after almost a year there's so much I don't know about you. You don't share much from your past."

"That's because it's in the past."

"You don't share much at all. Everything's on the surface with us."

"Well, I guess I'm just not a deep enough thinker for you."

They had reached his driveway now, and he braked with a little more force than necessary, making his tires spit gravel.

"I didn't mean to insult you," said Bambi. "We both know I'm not as smart as you, so that's not what I meant."

He sighed and turned to look at her. "Well, you did insult me. I don't know what you want from me, kid. I am who I am, and it's all I know how to be."

"I know," she said slowly. "And who you are is wonderful, but I'm not sure if who you are is who is right for me." She stopped a moment, brows knitted, as if she'd gotten lost in her own sentence.

He understood perfectly. "It's that damned book, isn't it? I knew when Kate gave it to me that I shouldn't have passed it on to you. Everything was fine before you read it." Bambi sat silent for so long, he began to wonder if she'd heard him. "Well, wasn't it?"

She finally turned to look at him. "Actually, no, it wasn't. It wasn't like I wasn't enjoying being with you, and it's not like I don't love you. It's just that, well, I've been wondering lately, if we're a match. In fact, you remember the day you and Doctor Kate were playing in the water?"

"Hey, we were just goofing around," said Jeff quickly.

"I know. But there seemed to be something between you that you and I don't have."

"Oh, you are definitely imagining things," said Jeff. "Come on, let's go in the house and get comfortable. I'll prove to you you're wrong."

She shook her head. "I don't want just sex. That's body close. I want heart close."

"We have that," protested Jeff.

Bambi shook her head, making her blonde hair shimmer. "We don't. I hate to do this, but I know it's what's right for both of us."

Panic gripped Jeff, and he tried to stop her. "Don't say it."

She ignored his warning. "We're really not right for each other. I don't want to make a mistake and end up with a man who isn't right for me. And I don't want you saddled with a woman who's not right for you."

"But you are right for me," he insisted.

"I'm comfortable for you," she corrected.

"That's what I want, comfortable."

"I'm not an easy chair."

"Oh, for Pete's sake."

"We can still be friends."

Friends, the final insult.

"I don't want to be friends," protested Jeff. "I don't want some other guy to have you."

"Jeff, you're a wonderful man, but I'm afraid that, for me, well, you're a frog."

A frog! The words whipped up a hurricane inside Jeff's brain, blowing his thoughts every which way. Before it could settle, Bambi had gotten out of the car. He hopped out and got to hers just as she shut the door.

"Come on, babe, let's talk this over," he begged.

She started her engine. "We just did. I'll always love you, Jeff. I hope you find someone wonderful."

She put the car in gear and he jumped back before she could run over his toes.

Through a red haze of rage he watched her spin the car around and zip on up his driveway without so much as a backward glance. *Thank you, Doctor Kate.*

Eight

"I GOT A HIT YESTERDAY, GRANDPA," ANNOUNCED Robbie from the kitchen phone extension.

"That's my boy," said Kate's dad, his speaker phone making him sound like he'd placed the call to them from Atlantis.

"That's wonderful," added his wife, her voice sounding equally distorted.

"How far did you get?" boomed Frank Hewitt.

"Third base. Then James hit me home."

"Good job."

"And Jeff Hardin came to my game."

"Got your own fan club going already?" joked his grandfather.

"Jeff Hardin?" repeated Carol Hewitt.

"Catch any flies?" asked her husband, his attention still focused on baseball.

"I almost caught one," said Robbie. "And I stopped a grounder."

"Sounds like you had a good game," said his grandfa-ther. "When you and Amanda come down to visit us next month, you and I will have to go to the park and play some serious catch while the women go shopping, won't we?"

"Yeah," said Robbie. Then, to his mother, "When are we going to see Grandpa and Grandma?"

"You leave right after the Fourth of July."

"All right!"

Having said all he needed to say, Robbie hung up, then whooped his way out the door.

Kate leaned back in her chair in the living room and braced herself for the conversational whiplash about to come. She tried to prevent it by keeping them on the subject of the children. "Don't forget it's their first time traveling without me."

"We will be waiting at the gate," said her mother, then jerked them onto the subject Kate had hoped to avoid. "So, it sounds like things are going swimmingly with the attractive nuisance next door."

Kate could feel the little vibes of hope for a love connection creeping out of the phone receiver. She sent them back, saying, "Not that swimmingly, so don't be taking your mother-of-the-bride dress out of mothballs."

"Oh, I'd get a new one," said her mother.

"Now, Carol," scolded her husband, "don't go harassing your daughter about her love life."

"A very good suggestion," said Kate. "Anyway, my neighbor already has a woman in his life."

"I have to admit, I'm sorry to hear that. I was thinking perhaps Cupid might be gearing up to do you a good turn."

"Okay, enough hearts and flowers stuff," said her dad. "Tell me how your stock portfolio is doing."

"Oh, fine," lied Kate.

"Have you dumped that E-commerce stock yet?"

Kate wished she could say yes. "I'm going to hang on to it. I think it will turn around eventually."

"How about that other goofy venture that hit the toilet last week? I hope you unloaded it when I told you."

"Well. . ."

"Katie girl, I warned you about those dot-com stocks. Now, you can't be an expert in everything. You should listen to your old dad."

"I know," said Kate humbly.

"At this rate you're not going to be able to support me in my golden years."

"At this rate I'm not going to be able to support me in mine."

"So, how are you doing? Really?"

"I'm doing fine," said Kate.

"Are you sure?" asked her mother. "You don't sound all that fine."

"I am. I'm just tired. The roof has sprung a leak and my car has been giving me grief. It's just one thing after another."

"Let us know if you need help," said her dad.

How about finding me a tall, dark, and handsome brilliant man with a car that never breaks down and a cousin who's a roofer. "Don't worry," said Kate. "I'll be fine."

"I don't know how to break this to you, dear," said her mother, "but you never stop worrying about your children."

"We'll make an exception in your case and stop once you get your own TV show," added her dad. "How's that for a deal?"

"Sounds good to me. Love you."

"Love you more," he shot back.

They said their good-byes and Kate hung up, smiling. The irritations in her life hadn't disappeared—the biggest one still lived next door!—but she felt better. Everyone had to cut the umbilical cord, but an occasional patch into the parental unit to charge your batteries, well, that was okay.

Kate poured herself a lemonade, then settled on her porch to watch the sun diamonds dance their glittering ballet across the waters of Pleasant Cove. She took a deep breath of fresh air. Life was good. And she really did have a lot for which to be thankful. Robbie's baseball career had ended on a happy note, she had established diplomatic relations with her irritating neighbor, and her career was right on track, and it was a beautiful day. What more could she ask for?

She watched Robbie and Amanda racing back and forth across the lawn, playing some made-up game that involved a huge amount of screeching. More time with her children would be nice. But sole providers didn't have any choice but to provide. Anyway, she didn't have to work the long hours many women did, so she could be grateful for that.

Her mother's remark seeped into her consciousness, muddying her contentment just a little. She wasn't counting on any favors from Cupid. But it would be good for her children to have a father. As far as Kate was concerned, male and female was the best team for raising well-adjusted children. And having someone with whom to share her life—and bed—would be nice. In spite of all the people in her life, she sometimes felt very alone, like a child hovering at the edge of a playground watching the other children, or a ballerina trying to stay on her toes in a room full of waltzing couples. But, she told herself sternly, you play the hand fate deals you.

Still, if Cupid did want to do her a good turn, she wouldn't turn down an introduction to some perfect specimen of manhood. And, after the first one she married, he would definitely have to be perfect. Otherwise, the little guy with the arrows could go find some other sucker to use for target practice.

MONDAY MORNING BROUGHT MORE SUN, AND, after contacting the roofers, Kate went for a walk. It wasn't exactly the equivalent of hitting the gym, but it was a good beginning. Bambi was studying to be a personal trainer. Maybe next time she paid a visit to Jeff, Kate could

get Bambi to help her design a more effective exercise reg-
imen.

Kate was a quarter mile from home when Mr. *Jock Talk*
sailed past her in his Jeep. She waved at him, and he gave
her a polite salute in return. She remembered her conversation with Bambi on Saturday. Were things going badly
between the two lovers, and if so, was Jeff projecting the
cause of that trouble onto her?

She hoped not. Their truce had been so enjoyable, she
really didn't want to go to war again.

Well, she wouldn't. It took two to make a fight, and if
that was what Jeff was looking for, he'd find his real
enemy in his bathroom mirror.

Once at work, Kate's personal life was pushed aside as
she absorbed the problems and struggles of others. As always, the time evaporated, and before she knew it another
show was over.

"Good show today," said Wallis.

"Yeah," put in George. "I liked your advice to the caller
with the boyfriend who was bipolar."

"Speaking of bipolar," murmured Wallis, nodding in the
direction of the hallway, "it looks like our favorite jock
wannabe has experienced quite a mood swing since the
day he was in here playing frogman."

Kate watched Jeff striding down the hall, his usual
goofy grin replaced with a grimly set mouth.

"Oh, dear," she sighed.

"Maybe he should call you for advice," teased Wallis.

"I think, perhaps, he's already benefited from my advice," said Kate.

She headed down the hall toward the break room and
found Jeff there, pouring himself a cup of coffee.

"You look like you lost tickets to a Mariners game," she
observed.

He kept his back to her, concentrating on dumping
sugar into his cup. "I lost something, all right."

"Bambi?"

"That was positively psychic," he said snidely.

"I'm sorry."

Jeff turned to face her, his eyes hard and his lips curled in a sardonic twist. "Yeah, I'll bet you are."

"I am!" she protested. "I'm sorry you're hurt."

"I would think you'd be feeling pretty pleased with yourself. You just rescued another woman from some worthless man. How did we all manage before Doctor Kate and her how-to books came along?"

"Oh, come on now. You can't blame me for your breaking up with Bambi."

"*I* didn't break up with her. She broke up with me!" He pointed a finger at Kate. "You know, it's one thing to mess around in people's lives when they call and ask for it, but it's another to go poking your nose into somebody else's business."

"I didn't poke my nose into your business," retorted Kate, stung. "I gave your girlfriend a copy of my book as a gesture of kindness."

"Yeah, you're just full of kind gestures," growled Jeff, pushing past her.

She called after him. "If you were right for each other, she wouldn't have broken up with you."

He let her have the last word, stalking down the hall in silence. But he left part of his black cloud behind to hang over Kate. The cloud grew when, halfway to the ferry, her car engine gave a cough that threatened the onset of another automotive cold, and the black, dreary thing stayed with her for the commute and followed her home.

"What's wrong, Mom?" asked Amanda.

"I just had a long, rough day," said Kate. "Nothing a good night's sleep can't cure." As long as Jeff Hardin didn't sneak into her dreams and toss her around a baseball diamond.

This was ridiculous. She needed to put that incident at work out of her mind.

And she knew the best way to do that. "I think we

should see if Grace wants to come over and have dessert with us," she said, going to the phone. "What do you guys think?"

"Yes," chorused the kids.

Grace was over in five minutes, and Kate dished her up some raspberry sorbet.

"Fat free," she announced, handing her friend a bowl.

Grace eyed it. "One scoop?"

"Oh, sorry," said Kate, and added another.

"That's better," said Grace. "Just because you're miserable and dieting doesn't mean the rest of us have to keep you company. Right, kids?"

"Yeah," said Robbie, and drizzled more strawberry topping over his ice cream.

"Thanks," said Kate. "How about if you two take that temptation out onto the porch?"

The kids roared off, and Kate shoved the various cartons back in the freezer.

"Did you hear that Jeff and Bambi broke up?" she asked, keeping her voice casual.

"No! They seemed so perfect for each other. What happened?"

"Dr. Kate Stonewall, that's what happened."

"Oh, dear."

"Oh, dear is right. I gave Bambi a copy of my book. I guess they weren't as perfect a fit as they looked."

"And Jeff blames you?"

"It's easier than blaming himself."

"He'll get over it," said Grace, dipping her spoon into her sorbet.

"Yes, I suppose he will," agreed Kate with a sigh. "But meanwhile, guess who's been nominated as the villain in his life."

"Jeff's a smart man. It won't take him long to admit the truth."

Kate shrugged. "It would be nice if he would blame the real person responsible for his troubles. But then, how many of us find it comfortable to do that? Anyway, I'm really not sorry I gave the book to Bambi. There's truth in it."

"And sometimes the truth hurts," said Grace. "And people say a lot of stupid things when they're in pain, so try not to take whatever Jeff said to you today personally."

"How did you know he said something to me?"

Grace chuckled. "You may have the degree, but I've got the experience. Come on, now. Hike up your bra straps and get back in the fight. You've got a message to take to women, and you can't let one disgruntled man make you lose sight of your call."

Kate leaned across the kitchen table and patted her friend's arm. "What would I do without you?"

"I really don't know," said Grace.

THE REST OF THE WEEK WASN'T THE BEST ONE Kate had ever had. Her car coughed itself to death on Wednesday. No Jeff Hardin appeared to rescue her this time, and Kate had plenty of opportunity to reflect on the importance of extended warrantees while waiting for Andy to come tow her off the highway. What she tried hard not to think about was Jeff.

Even if he had driven by, she knew he wouldn't have stopped. This week she was the person he most loved to hate. He had been his usual sunny self with everyone at the station but her. With her he'd been polite and remote, just as she had once been with him. It hurt.

By Friday, she was ready for the weekend and some time away from the station. She fired up the loaner Andy had given her and took the kids to a movie.

Saturday morning, she made arrangements to go shopping with Janet so she wouldn't have to see the two-legged reason why she wanted to be away from the station.

They returned from the mall with packages galore, and Kate sent her offspring to their rooms to put away their new treasures. In her own room, she stood in front of her mirror and held up the pretty, lavender summer dress she'd bought one size too small. Beautiful motivation. She gave it a prominent spot in her closet, then proceeded to put away the less exciting cotton undies and the new bra she had purchased.

A Saturday symphony floated in through her half-open bedroom window: a bee looking for an entrance through her window screen, the hum of a distant lawn mower, the putt-putt of a boat coming into the cove. A metal screech added a sudden sharp note, and Kate looked out from her balcony to see that the usual view had been altered. Next to her dock sat a pile of lumber, and on the dock itself knelt a man, pulling up nails.

Until now, she'd forgotten Jeff's casual promise to fix her dock. Obviously, he hadn't. She hurried down to join him, stopping on the way for a glass of iced tea.

"Doing good to your enemy?" she asked.

He kept his attention on the nail he was pulling. "Something like that."

She shoved the glass under his nose, saying, "You don't have to do this, you know."

"Hey, one good turn deserves another."

"Okay, Saint Jeff, you've heaped enough burning coals on my head. You can go home now."

He took the glass and drained half of it, then squinted up at her. "I was kind of a shit this week, wasn't I?"

"Kind of."

"I'm sorry, Doc. I want you to know I've been doing some thinking."

"We're in trouble now," murmured Kate.

"And I had a lot of time to think last night, having no date and all," he added.

Kate said nothing. That remark was designed to make her feel guilty, something she had no intention of doing. She had no more cause to feel responsible for his breakup than she did for the problems of the people who called her during the week for advice.

"I hate to have to admit it," Jeff said, "but maybe you had a point. If everything was as great as I thought it was between Bambi and me, she wouldn't have split."

"She really does care for you, you know."

"Yeah, that's why I'm all by myself this weekend."

Kate sat down next to him. "You can care for someone but still not be suited for pulling in harness for a lifetime. Better to break up now than end up divorced."

"Been there, done that." He shook his head. "I don't know. Sometimes I wonder, are you women worth it?"

"I don't know. Sometimes I wonder the same thing about you men."

That lifted one corner of his mouth. "What? Doctor Kate isn't sure about something?"

"Doctor Kate isn't sure about a lot of things."

He grinned. "There is hope for the human race."

"Ha, ha." Kate motioned to the half-loose board. "I could hire someone to do this, you know. You really don't have to."

"I may as well since I have no life."

"I doubt that will last long," said Kate.

"Yeah, the women are lining up."

Kate shrugged. "Word hasn't gotten out yet. Would you like me to make an announcement on my program?"

"Everyone who listens to your program has problems," said Jeff. "No thanks. I'll find my own girl."

"I'm sure you will," said Kate. "What are you looking for in a woman?"

He shot up an eyebrow. "Want to apply for the position?"

Kate felt her cheeks warming and turned to study his house. "Maybe." Where had that come from? "Just kidding," she added hastily. "About applying myself, that is. But tell me what you're looking for. I might know someone."

"That you'd introduce to a sports nut? Come on, now. Be real."

"All right, then. Let's just say I'm curious. If you could log on to the Internet and special-order a woman, what would you order? "

"Hmmm, let's see." Jeff drained the rest of his iced tea, then turned his gaze toward the water. "Well, the first thing I'd ask for is someone who is stacked. She needs to be well built. And I don't want anyone who's smarter than me, and she should be a good cook." He stole a glance at her and caught her frowning.

His sly grin served to deepen her frown. "Very funny," she said. "We're not talking about the radio Jeff Hardin. Now, be serious, or I'll poke you with one of these rusty nails."

"Okay, seriously, I want someone I'm attracted to, but since I'm easily attracted, that leaves the field pretty wide open. And, contrary to what *some* people think," he said, giving Kate a friendly bump with his shoulder, "I do have other interests in life besides sports."

"So you say."

"It's true. I want a woman who's not only up for going water-skiing or to a ball game, but who'll watch the History Channel once in a while."

"Bambi liked the History Channel?"

"The closest I could get her was *Biography* on A&E," admitted Jeff. He scowled. "It doesn't seem right without her here."

Kate knew what he was talking about. Once you had a history with a person, that person's departure, whether for better or worse, left the landscape of your days looking empty.

"I remember walking through the house after my husband died," she said. "It seemed like it didn't fit me right anymore."

"Loved the guy a lot, huh?"

"The truth is, we'd been drifting apart for years. Still, I

missed him more than I could have imagined when he was gone. I felt abandoned."

Jeff shook his head. "That must have been awful."

"I survived. Just like you're doing."

"There's no comparison."

"Loss is hard, whatever form it takes," said Kate, not wanting to diminish his present experience. "But we all manage to go on. And speaking of going on, continue with your perfect woman checklist. What else do you want?"

"I'm a lover not a fighter, so I don't want someone who's always going to be picking a fight. I like women who are easy to get along with."

"And who have no opinion so you can always be right?"

"I didn't say that," protested Jeff.

"Not in those exact words. Could that be the reason you were perfectly happy with Bambi? She never made waves, never questioned you. You always got to be right. And could that also be a good part of why she left?"

"Because I was always right?"

"Because you were overpowering her."

"Me?" Jeff rapped on his chest. "Do I look like the kind of guy who goes around overpowering women?"

"Not deliberately," said Kate. "But you may have just been too strong a personality for Bambi. Ever hear the saying that if two people agree on everything, one of them is unnecessary?"

"Oh, brother," said Jeff in disgust.

"Well, it was a thought. I could be wrong." He opened his mouth and she put her hand over it. "Don't say it."

He chuckled and his warm breath against her fingers produced an unexpected flutter in her chest. She pulled her hand away. "So, go on. What else do you want in a woman?"

"That about covers it. She doesn't have to be perfect, just nice and fun-loving."

"You should have no trouble finding someone."

"I don't know," said Jeff. "It seems to me that these days most women have forgotten how to have fun. They're all busy working their butts off, and half of them have a grudge against the whole male race."

Kate eyed him. "I hope you weren't including me in that category."

His eyes widened, then his cheeks turned russet. "Well . . ."

"I try not to be a workaholic, and I really don't hate men," said Kate. "I'm just on a crusade to make sure women don't get involved with ones who aren't right for them. We've got a high enough divorce rate in this country as it is."

"It's not always the man who's the bad guy," said Jeff softly.

Kate remembered he had alluded to being divorced. "You're right there," she agreed.

"Well, I'd better get back to work," he said, blocking the path to his past.

"And I'd better go have some fun," said Kate. "Thanks again for doing this."

He already had the claw end of his hammer inserted under a nail head. "No problem."

She left him there, hunkered over his past like a troll guarding treasure.

BAMBI HAD MANAGED TO FILL UP HER SATURDAY with shopping, followed by a night out with her friends from the Sea Gals. But Sunday loomed ahead of her like a gaping pit. Saturday's nice weather had vanished, and looking outside her apartment window at the drizzling, gray skies didn't do anything to lighten the heavy mood that was settling over her. She called a couple of friends and only got their answering machines. What was Jeff doing today?

Hopefully, getting on with his life, just like she was. So, what was she going to do?

She was going to do the sort of thing she liked to do that she couldn't do with him, of course! She opened her Sunday paper to the movie listings. That new movie she'd been wanting to see was playing at three-fifteen. It wouldn't be much fun going to see it all by herself, but she had to start her new, Jeffless life somewhere.

With a package of red vines in hand, she walked into the theater at three o'clock and found it almost half full. Mostly women, of course. Bambi supposed a romantic comedy about love between an oncologist and his former breast cancer patient wasn't the kind of movie at which you'd expect to find a lot of guys.

The mostly female audience made the few men present stick out like dandelions on a lawn. One especially stood out. He was a broad-shouldered hulk almost overflowing his seat. Bambi was sure she knew that large frame, and she walked down another few steps for a closer look.

As people sometimes do, he seemed to feel her gaze on him and turned, giving her a full view of his face.

Sure enough, it was Don Bullman, Seahawks fullback. "Don?"

In repose, the Bull, as he was fondly referred to in sports circles, looked like he ate little children for breakfast. But when he smiled it changed his face completely, making him look like a big, friendly dog. Now he was grinning as if he'd just seen his long-lost mother.

"Bambi?"

It was all the invitation she needed to turn into his aisle and settle next to him. Sea Gals weren't allowed to date the players, but running into someone at the movies and sharing a seat next to him didn't count as dating. Anyway, the phenomenon of a man who came by himself to this kind of show was one that needed to be studied. And a girl certainly couldn't get in trouble for doing research. In fact, Bambi was sure Doctor Kate would approve.

"What are you doing here all by yourself?" she asked.

He shrugged. "It's raining out. It seemed like a good idea."

"You like this kind of movie?"

He looked embarrassed, and his chin jutted out defensively. "Yeah."

"That's amazing," breathed Bambi. "I've never met a man who liked chick flicks."

Don frowned. "I hate that expression. It's really sexist, you know. I mean, men can be sensitive."

Bambi smiled at him. "I think it's great that you're here."

"What are you doing here all by yourself?"

"I couldn't find anyone to come with."

"That's hard to believe. I thought you had a boyfriend."

"We broke up."

"Really?"

Don sounded so interested, she went on to tell him more.

"It doesn't sound like you guys were a match to me," he said at last.

"Yeah, I think I'd known that for a while. But he was so nice, I just kept thinking I could make it work."

"Well, that was nice of you," said Don. "But I think you were right to call it quits, not only for yourself, but for him, too. I mean, if you were wrong for each other, it means you were both right for someone else."

Bambi was impressed. "That sounds just like something Doctor Kate would say!"

Don looked embarrassed and quickly called her attention to the first coming attraction trailer.

It seemed every movie that attracted Bambi pulled an interested response from Don. "That looks good," he'd say, just as if he'd read her mind. It was amazing.

The movie began and they watched it in companionable silence, and when Bambi started crying, Don handed her a tissue.

After it ended, he said, "Man, that was good."

"Yes, it was," agreed Bambi. "Would you go out with a woman who had had cancer?"

"Yeah. Why not? I mean, there's no guarantee in life. You gotta grab happiness when you find it."

She nodded.

They stood there for a moment, neither one talking, then Don said, "I know you can't date the players, but since we've run into each other anyway, how about going someplace for a cup of coffee?"

It wouldn't be a date. Just a cup of coffee with someone she'd run into at the movie.

"I'd like that," said Bambi.

Two hours and three cups of coffee later, Don said, "You know, that new movie with Julia Roberts is still playing. I thought I might catch it Friday night. Have you seen it?"

"No," said Bambi.

"Well, I'm going to the seven-ten showing. Maybe I'll run into you."

Running into Don at a movie wouldn't be dating, and the thought of cuddling up next to him in a dark theater was too tempting to resist. "Maybe you will."

"And if I do, maybe you'll want to get something to drink afterward."

"Maybe," she agreed.

Nine

JEFF WOKE UP TO A SUNSHINE-DRENCHED MONDAY and decided since he had a couple of hours to kill before he had to get ready for work, he'd try to finish repairing Kate's dock. That was a fair trade: a new dock in exchange for a new outlook on love.

He'd had all of Sunday to go over their latest conversation and concluded that the doc had a point. Maybe he had overpowered Bambi. But if he had, it hadn't been intentional. And she'd gone along with it, so, they were both to blame. They'd become a habit. A fun habit, but there had definitely been something lacking.

Well, enough contemplating his navel. Time to go do the manly man thing.

He hauled his radio out with him, figuring he'd catch the last half of Harry Mann's morning show. Old Harry had that new finance guru scheduled for today, and Jeff was curious to hear what the guy had to say.

After the first ten minutes, Jeff could sum up the man's philosophy: the economy will be collapsing any moment, so get out of debt and save now, then pick up bargains at the end of the world.

Jeff shook his head. A guy had to live a little as he went along. What was the sense in waiting until you were old and gray to spend your money? Anyway, that kind of money-hoarding philosophy was bad for the economy. How could anybody stay in business if nobody bought? Well, he was going to do his part to stimulate the economy now. He grinned as he pictured himself in that tournament ski boat he was buying from Ski Masters, a sweet Toyota Epic with a Lexus twin dual overhead cam engine. Mr. Money probably wouldn't call such a purchase wise, but Jeff knew there were some things a man had to buy while he was still young enough to enjoy them. And that was what financing was for.

In between pounding and sawing, he listened to Harry's guest, grunting his agreement or disagreement with the expert's advice. Somewhere in between the sawing and pounding and grunting, Harry slipped off the air and Kate Stonewall came on.

Jeff was surprised to hear her voice at his elbow, as if she were standing over his shoulder, watching him work, teasing him with the nearness of her curves.

"Well, Clay, I understand how you feel, but it's not me you're going to have to convince that all these sporting events are important. It's the woman you're dating. Frankly, you'd never be able to convince me."

Jeff stopped his pounding. No male voice emerged via the airwaves to counter that Clay's woman should take a little time to find out what it was about those sports that interested her man. Kate had obviously cut the guy loose.

"To me sports are a waste of time," continued the good doctor. "But then, that's why I'm not dating someone who's into that sort of thing."

"That's why you're not dating anyone," corrected Jeff as he started packing up his tools.

"My prince," said Kate, "loves musicals and art galleries. But that's me. Who are you? Who you are will determine who your prince is. So, when you're looking for your other half, you've got to make sure the person you find is a match. Without common interests, you're going to have a hard time forming a glue strong enough to hold you together for the long haul. Don't think your kids will do it. They'll grow up and have lives of their own and then it will be just the two of you, staring across the kitchen table at each other, asking, 'Who are you?' "

Jeff scowled at the radio and demanded, "Well, what about learning something new? What about finding new interests in life and growing together? And what the heck is so bad about sports, anyway?"

Hmmm. Good question. Maybe it was one he needed to pose to his listeners.

JEFF STUCK HIS HEAD IN THE SOUND-STUDIO DOOR while the commercials before the last fifteen minutes of Kate's show were rolling. "Got your dock done."

"Oh, thanks," she said, and came over to him. She caught a tantalizing whiff of spicy aftershave, but she quickly advised herself not to comment on it. Instead, she said, "At this rate you're a shoe-in for the good neighbor award."

"That's me," said Jeff. "I caught part of your show while I was finishing up."

Kate was sure this was leading to something and braced herself. "Oh?"

"Yeah. Why don't you listen to mine on your way home. We're going to try and answer an important philosophical question."

"What's that, how many jocks it takes to screw in a lightbulb?"

"Something like that," he replied cryptically.

"Okay. I'll listen for ten minutes, which is probably longer than you listened to me."

"That's not true. I listened for fifteen." The look he

gave her told her she'd better extend him the same courtesy.

"I'll try to return the favor," she said.

I N HER LATEST LOANER CAR, KATE TURNED ON THE radio and Jeff's voice emerged from the speakers like a genie from a bottle. He had a great voice for radio, warm and friendly, and his presence seemed to fill the car. He'd gotten past his "Pop open a beer" greeting—thank God— and the first commercials, and was just launching into his opening remarks.

"I've got this cute friend," he was saying. "Let's call her Babe, Babe Ruth. She's my neighbor, in fact, and we have a good time talking together."

Cute. Good time. The words lifted Kate's mouth at the corners.

"Unless I mention sports," Jeff added. "Then it's all over. I mean, she hates sports as much as Doctor Kate. She can't see what us guys see in football, baseball, basketball, soccer, golf, handball, volleyball, you name it. I mean, this woman doesn't like anything that makes you sweat. Well, almost anything. There's one sport I haven't asked her about, but she's got kids, so I assume that one's okay."

That was supposed to be funny? That was what he wanted her to tune in to hear, him making fun of her? Kate frowned and reached to punch Jeff Hardin into silence.

"Now, don't touch that radio, Babe," cautioned Jeff, as if he'd seen her reach for the controls. "Because, like Bud, this one's for you. We're going to dedicate today's show to convincing you why sports are a necessary part of American life: what's good about 'em and why we need 'em. So, guys, and especially you women out there, I expect you to call in and give me some good arguments that will show Babe everyone who loves sports isn't a jerk or a doofus. Help me out here, people, because I'm not real good at coming up with stuff on my own."

Aw, shucks, folks. It's just li'l ol' dumb Jeff, askin' for help. Kate glared at the radio. That good-old-boy personality he adopted was incredibly phony and irritating.

But, contrary to what some people thought, she did have an open mind. She'd give him a chance to make his argument.

"Tim, you're on the air," said Jeff.

"Hi, Jeff," said his first caller. "Has your friend ever gone to a game of any kind?"

"Big league stuff? I don't know. Good question," said Jeff. "Hey, Babe, ever actually go to a game?"

"Of course, you nincompoop! I have a father. And an older brother, for crying out loud."

"Let's assume she has," said Jeff.

"Well, then," said Tim, "she's got to have seen how much people enjoy it. And sports are good for the economy."

"Oh, right," retorted Kate. "Let's talk about the cost to the taxpayers of all these stadiums we've built. I'm sure the people in eastern Washington would have a thing or two to say about how good they've been for the economy."

"That's a good point," said Jeff. "Having a professional sports team is good for a city."

"Especially its traffic," added Kate.

"And it keeps us in shape," Tim continued.

"True," said Jeff. "We don't work in the fields anymore. A guy has to do something to keep his weight down and his ticker healthy."

"And sitting on the couch drinking beer and watching the game will sure do that," said Kate, remembering Rob's marathon football weekends. "You are going to have to do better than this, Jeff Hardin."

Jeff pulled in another caller.

"It's important to learn good sportsmanship," said Jay.

"Yeah," drawled Jeff. "I agree with you, Jay. Thanks for calling."

Jay disappeared and Jeff continued, "Don't you wish

we could say we learn that good sportsmanship from the pros these days? I'm not sure we do. But on the local level, it's still alive and well. And here at KZOO, we're doing our part to help. Go to our Web site, KZOO.com, and click on *Jock Talk* and you'll see this year's winner of the Jeff Hardin Good Sport Award: Clint Curtis of Ballard High. Clint came up with something called the Sports Tutor program for kids. For all of you who haven't heard of it yet, it's Ballard High School athletes spending time giving one-on-one instruction to grade school and junior high kids, and they help 'em with everything from their free throws to their fielding skills. Way to go, Clint! Clint got twenty-five hundred dollars toward his tuition at the U of Dub next fall and season tickets to the Seahawks.

Kate had no idea Jeff had such an award. So, Mr. *Jock Talk* was a philanthropist. There was another word he probably couldn't spell, but he obviously knew the meaning of it. She remembered his degree. Okay, he probably could spell it.

"Sam, you're on the air," said Jeff.

"Hey, Jeff. Love your show," said Sam.

"Thanks, man. Hey, what do you want to tell my friend Babe about why she should appreciate sports?"

"Sports are good discipline," said Sam.

"Good point, Sam. People need challenges, and that's the beauty of sports: it's a man pushing himself to be all that he can be . . ."

"That's the army," said Kate in disgust.

". . . but still being big enough to offer his hand to the guy who beats him."

This was getting sickening. She'd listened long enough. Again, Kate reached for her radio.

"Hey, Janet. Thanks for calling in."

Janet? Kate pulled her hand away.

"What do you think about sports?" asked Jeff.

"I think playing sports teaches kids a lot about real life," said a familiar voice.

"Traitor," muttered Kate.

"I want my boys to try to do well at something. And I want them out getting exercise, not home, sitting in front of the TV. I also want them to learn that sometimes they'll win and sometimes they'll lose, but life will go on either way and they'll be loved no matter what."

"Good point," agreed Jeff. "What do you think so far, Babe?"

Kate rolled her eyes. "I think my fifteen minutes is almost up."

"I look at it this way," said Jeff. "Sports are the civilized version of war. You work out your aggressions, you try to beat the crap out of the other guy, but nobody gets killed. It works for me."

"Well, it doesn't for me," said Kate, switching stations. "Time's up."

THE KIDS WERE STILL IN BED, ENJOYING THE LATE June luxury of not having to get up for school. Kate sat on her porch swing, inhaling the aroma wafting from her tea mug and luxuriating in the view of morning on Pleasant Cove. Looking at her new dock, she resolved to invite Jeff over for dinner on Saturday and get that social obligation out of the way.

After she'd given him the promised reward for his manual labor, that would be the end of their socializing. She didn't need to be getting any chummier with Jeff Hardin, not with the effect he had on her every time he got close.

Of course, it was perfectly natural to find herself attracted to him. Biology was, once more, asserting itself, and Jeff was serving as a human barometer, indicating her body's rise in temperature. She was out of the deep freeze at last and ready to rejoin the human race.

But she wasn't going to be so naive as to rejoin and then fall for a completely inappropriate man. And the sooner she had Jeff out from under her feet, the easier it would be to find Mr. Right.

Of course, if she was going to meet anyone, she supposed she'd have to start redeveloping some of the interests she'd ignored the past few years.

Remembering those interests, she half chuckled. Single men would probably be few and far between at a women's fiction book club. She didn't think she'd find many interested in cake decorating, either. Well, maybe it was time she found some new interests: learned an instrument or took up folk dancing or photography.

"Hi."

She gave a start and looked up to see Jeff leaning on the porch railing, regarding her.

"You looked like you were making up your grocery list just now," he said.

"Something like that." Kate lifted her mug. "Cup of something?"

He shook his head sadly. "I never mastered the social art of coffee. To me, Starbucks will always mean football."

"That is a scary thought," said Kate. "But this is tea."

"Without ice? That's a woman's drink."

"I'm sure all the men of England would thank you for that remark," said Kate. She nodded in the direction of the dock. "It looks good."

Jeff grinned. "I'd say it definitely deserves a steak dinner."

"Steak, is it?"

"And baked spuds. You can skip the salad, unless you've got lots of bacon bits and dressing."

"Real men don't eat salad?" teased Kate.

"You got that right, little lady," he said in a John Wayne voice. "So, what did you think of the show last night?"

She should have known he'd bring that up. "I think you try too hard. You don't have to prove anything to me."

"Oh, yes I do. Convince the queen and the kingdom will follow."

"And what kingdom might that be?"

"Womankind," said Jeff, sprawling across her porch steps.

"You know I don't speak for all women," said Kate.

"You speak for enough of them. And to them. So, come on, what did you think?" he added, reaching out and giving her ankle a little squeeze.

The nervous flutter it produced deep inside her was just biology. Just damned, irritating biology.

"Don't do that," Kate commanded, pulling away her foot.

"What?"

"Don't touch me like that."

Jeff gave her a cocky look. "Does it make you nervous?"

"It's inappropriate. I'm not your girlfriend."

"Wanna be?"

"No." Her tone of voice sounded exceptionally snippy, even to her. She scowled at him. "You have got to be the most irritating man on the planet."

"Oh, I don't have to be," he said. "I just like to be. Come on, now. You're avoiding the issue."

"I think we should simply agree to disagree."

"In other words, nothing anyone said last night changed your mind."

Kate made a face. "Good for the economy? Oh, please. And I loved the remark about civilized war."

"I thought that was a great observation," said Jeff, looking hurt. "Sports really do teach a person a lot, not only about good sportsmanship, but self-discipline, and how to work together to reach a common goal."

"There are other ways a person can learn self-discipline," said Kate. "And working together to break other people's bones and trample them, all so you can have some little trophy, is not my definition of nobility. By the way, did you know that it takes three thousand cows to provide the footballs for an NFL season?"

"What? Where did you hear that?"

"On the radio."

Jeff let out a snort of disgust. "Not on my program."

"Wouldn't you say that's a lot of cows dying just so a bunch of grown men can scramble around in the mud and try to cripple each other?" continued Kate, determined to drive home her point.

Jeff missed it completely. "We don't call it scrambling: we call it scrimmaging."

"I call it stupid."

"Hey, I'm sure they don't skin those cows and leave their carcasses lying around to rot. They probably use 'em to make hamburgers. And speaking of killing cows, Miss Animal Rights, don't you ever take your kids to the Golden Arches? That's a lot of Bossies and Ferdinands dying so Robbie can get the latest movie tie-in McToy."

"What a preposterous comparison!" sputtered Kate.

"Why?"

"It's like comparing apples and oranges."

"They're both fruit. You didn't answer my question, you know. Is that the best you can do?"

"This early in the morning, yes."

Jeff shook his head. "Tsk, tsk, Doc. You know what I think?"

"I don't need to know what you think," retorted Kate, using her most condescending voice.

"Ever read *The Wizard of Oz*?"

"Of course," said Kate, "and last time I looked no one played any sport in that book."

"Nope. They just wore those shades around the Emerald City that turned everything green. Funny how you can look at something through colored glasses and not see it for what it really is."

"That was very deep," said Kate. "I suppose you think I'm wearing my own emerald glasses when it comes to sports."

"Well, I'm not sure I'd call them emerald," said Jeff.

"Brown maybe, or black. Do you think your own past experiences could have colored your thinking just a little? Is that possible, Doc?"

Kate cocked her head. "Are you trying to psychoanalyze me, Mr. Hardin?"

He shrugged. "Maybe. How'm I doing?"

She got up and walked past him, patting his shoulder as she went. "Don't give up your day job." She slipped back into the house, leaving Mr. *Jock Talk* with something to think about.

A moment later he knocked on the door.

She opened it and looked at him expectantly. "What do you want now?"

"I want to know when you're going to feed me. You know, so many cows, so little time."

She grimaced. "That was sick."

"Quit trying to change the subject. When's dinner?"

"Saturday," she said. A little quiver of excitement ran through her and she told herself not to be silly. It was just dinner.

Thursday morning she went on a cleaning binge. Spring cleaning a little late, that was all.

Friday she got her hair done. It was way past time for a cut and her ends were split.

Saturday she spent way more at the grocery store than she intended. But it wouldn't be right to make light of all Jeff's hard work on her behalf by presenting him an inferior meal.

Filet mignon, baked potatoes with sour cream, chives, and bacon bits, and a fruit salad loaded with whipped cream. And after dinner, she could administer CPR when his arteries clogged.

Amanda set the table, hauling out all Kate's best china and crystal, and Robbie hunted down his favorite video game for the after-dinner entertainment.

Jeff finally knocked on the door just when Kate was up to her wrists in biscuit dough.

"Somebody get the door for me," she called.

Both children ran to answer it. From the kitchen, Kate could hear them chattering at him.

"I got Ninja Warrior for after dinner," Robbie announced.

"Where's Bambi?" asked Amanda.

"We broke up," replied Jeff.

"So she's not going to come over and visit anymore?" asked Amanda, her voice heavy with disappointment.

"Oh, she might come over once in a while," said Jeff, sounding completely unconcerned with his Bambiless future. "But you won't see her every weekend."

"Hey, then you can marry our mom and we can all live together," piped Robbie.

"Robbie," scolded Amanda. "He has no tact," she explained.

Kate felt relieved she hadn't been in the room for that awkward moment. She washed the dough off her hands, shoved the biscuits in the oven, then went to greet their guest.

His eyes lit at the sight of her in her new black capri pants and red top. "You look slick."

Jeff was in his usual jeans, but he had substituted a white polo shirt for his usual T-shirt. His hair was slightly damp, as if he'd just showered, and she could smell his spicy aftershave. He smiled at Kate, displaying the secret weapon that would win him a new woman in no time— hopefully one better suited to him than Bambi had been.

"You don't look so bad yourself," said Kate.

His smile broadened. "We're a fine-looking pair." He held up two bottles of sparkling cider. "Hope you guys like this stuff."

"Oh, yeah," said Amanda. "We usually only have it at Christmas and Easter, though. Oh, and Mother's Day. We always buy it for Mom."

Kate took the cider. "Thanks. Although you didn't have to bring anything."

"I know. I just wanted to."

First her dock, now this. Okay, so maybe she had mis-judged Jeff Hardin. He actually was a very nice man. He'd make some lady wrestler a great husband.

At dinner he kept the conversation away from sports, talking instead with the kids about video games, movies, and the latest Harry Potter book.

"You read those?" asked Kate.

"I can read."

She felt her face flushing. "I mean, a lot of adults don't read them."

"I heard that a lot of adults do, and I wanted to see what all the noise was about. I think they're pretty clever. I do, by the way, read grown-up books, too."

"Don't tell me, let me guess: Tom Clancy."

"Sometimes. But I prefer nonfiction."

"Are you done yet, Jeff?" asked Robbie, who had been squirming in front of his empty dessert dish for the last five minutes.

"Yeah, I think I am," said Jeff.

"All right," whooped Robbie, hopping up from his seat.

"But before we start that game, let's real quick, haul these dishes out to the kitchen for your mom."

"Okay," said Robbie, cheerfully obliging and racing toward the kitchen, plates and silverware clattering. Amanda followed suit, picking up her plate and glass and moving almost as quickly.

"I want some of whatever it was that you slipped in their sparkling cider," said Kate.

"I'm a novelty. You've got the home court disadvantage."

"I thought that was home court advantage."

"Whoa, you know more about sports than you let on," teased Jeff, then disappeared into the kitchen. Kate could hear water running and the sound of china getting loaded into the dishwasher. Amazing.

The dishes taken care of, the kids towed Jeff to the TV and Kate followed behind.

She kicked off her shoes and claimed a corner of the couch, tucked her feet under her, and watched her children and their hero at play. Jeff kept up a steady patter all the way through the game, and he seemed to have an endless repertoire of silly noises and sound effects, all designed to make the kids laugh.

And the kids weren't the only ones having fun. Surprisingly, Jeff Hardin was very good company. He certainly wasn't her type, but until the right man came along, he made a nice family friend.

Wait a minute. They weren't going to make a habit of this sort of thing. This dinner was a neighborly thank-you, that was all. Jeff Hardin wasn't going to be spending his weekends parked in her living room acting like an over-grown child and playing video games. It was a one-time shot.

Watching her children sitting close to him like two needy foster kids, she remembered Robbie's earlier comment to Jeff. She would have to make sure her son understood that his mother wasn't in the market for a Jeff Hardin kind of daddy.

J EFF WAS WHISTLING WHEN HE WALKED THROUGH his back door. Visiting Kate's house had felt like Christmas at his brother's. Playing video games with Rob and Amanda while Kate sat on the couch and provided a back-drop of smart-ass cracks had been more fun than a double header, and had given Jeff a glimpse of what he could have had by now. Too bad he'd popped the right question to the wrong woman a lifetime ago. Would there be kids in his own house playing video games if he'd taken a little more care in choosing a wife? Maybe, and then again maybe only on weekends.

Love: it was all a crapshoot. Look at the doc. She hadn't

done any better than him. And for all her books and her talk of princes and how to choose the right guy, Jeff didn't see any applicants lining up at her door to become king of the castle.

There should be. She'd make a great better half for some guy . . . as long as the poor slob didn't mind being reminded on a regular basis that she was, indeed, the better half.

Maybe someday both he and the doc would find that perfect match. Meanwhile . . . Jeff wasn't sure where he was going with that one word, so he left it hanging at the back of his mind. He wandered over to the TV and realized he was humming "Help Me Make It through the Night." *Don't go there.*

He picked up the remote, turned on the tube, and started flipping through the channels. One station was playing *Leave It to Beaver.* For a moment he stood, watching Ward and June puttering around the house, Ward in his suit, June in her housedress. Ward and June, Jeff and Kate. He shook his head and turned off the TV. *Don't go there, either. Ward and June you guys ain't ever gonna be.* Funny, though. For just a moment back there in her living room, it had felt like they'd found the way to Ward and June's street. If they actually went out together where would they wind up?

"I THINK YOU SHOULD MARRY JEFF HARDIN," SAID Robbie.

"I think we'll just keep him as a neighbor instead," said Kate.

"Don't you like him?"

"Well, of course I like him," said Kate.

"You didn't at first," Amanda reminded her.

"So maybe you'll change your mind and want to marry him," suggested Robbie.

Kate knelt in front of her son. "I know you've missed having a daddy, sweetie, and I hope that sometime soon a man will come into our lives who'll be perfect for all of us."

"Jeff is perfect," insisted Robbie.

"Well, he might be perfect for you, but we need someone who is right for me, too. Because someday you and Amanda will move away and have lives of your own. But I'll be stuck here with that daddy long after you're gone."

"She has to be in love with him, Robbie," put in Amanda.

Robbie made a face. "Love. Yuck."

Kate rumpled her son's hair. "You say that now. In a few years you'll feel differently about love."

"I hate girls," said Robbie emphatically. "Except Amanda," he added, looking at his sister.

Amanda just rolled her eyes. "Can we watch a movie, Mom?"

"Sure."

Robbie abandoned the subject of marriage to Jeff to help Amanda paw through the wicker basket full of videos that Kate kept next to the TV, and she gave an inward sigh of relief. There, that had been easy. Now they all knew exactly where she stood.

Except, perhaps, Jeff, who seemed to think that one home-cooked meal had made him and her best buds.

"Lookin' good," he told her on Monday. "Have you lost weight?"

"Maybe a couple of pounds," said Kate.

"Don't lose too much. You look pretty good already."

"Thanks," said Kate, trying to sound appreciative but not encouraging. After all, she really didn't care one way or the other what Jeff thought about her weight.

On Wednesday, he joined her and Grace while they drank coffee on her front porch, and Thursday he appeared again almost as soon as Kate had settled herself on the porch swing. Had he been watching for her? She quickly slapped down the part of her that got excited at the thought.

"So, what are you guys doing for the Fourth?" he asked casually.

"We'll probably have a picnic with Grace," said Kate, hoping he would get the polite message that she was busy.

"Would your kids like to include riding in a ski boat as part of their picnic?"

"Who's got a ski boat?"

"Me. I just bought it. Grace is hot to take a ride. I figured Amanda might like to learn to water-ski. My dad will be coming over, and between the two of us, we should be able to get her up. Robbie, too, if he wants to give it a shot."

Great. That was all she needed, to have her children dragged through the water at high speed.

"They won't get hurt," he added, as if reading her mind. "In fact, I'm thinking we might even get you out there. What do you say?"

In a bathing suit? "Oh, I don't think . . ."

"You'll look fine in a suit," Jeff the Mind Reader assured her.

"Fine wasn't exactly the word that came to my mind," said Kate.

"Come on. You're a shrink. Aren't you supposed to know better than to let worrying about what people think of you stop you from having fun?"

"Who said being in such a totally out-of-control and potentially dangerous situation is fun?"

"I did. And when you master the skill, you're the one in control and it's a thrill. And you shouldn't knock it until you've tried it. You don't do that sort of thing, now, do you?" he taunted. "I mean you are open-minded about some things."

The big stinker! He was trying to intimidate her. "Is that a dare?" demanded Kate.

"No. It's an invitation. Are you going to accept?"

"I suppose," said Kate, sounding anything but grateful.

"Good. Hey, and if you're interested, there's the street dance on the third."

The street dance the night before the Fourth of July celebrations was a tradition. Island cops cordoned off downtown's main street to traffic, and families would throng it to buy food at the various booths, create street art with chalk provided by island merchants, and then dance to a local band. The kids loved it, and Kate always managed to find friends to visit with, although she sometimes felt like an outcast watching the couples dancing. It would be fun to go and have someone to dance with for a change. But would Jeff consider this some sort of date?

"We'd be going just as friends, right?"

"Of course," he assured her.

The lure of dancing was irresistible. "Well, then, why not?" She had finally completed the manuscript for her third book, and it was waiting in her car, ready to be mailed on the way to the station. She could afford to step off the work treadmill and have some fun.

"Great," said Jeff, and grinned. It was an infectious grin, which quickly spread to a corner of her heart that had been dark for many years. *Be careful, Kate. Remember your own advice and don't turn into one of your callers. This is nothing more than an evening out. Jeff Hardin is not your prince.*

She pointed a finger at him and reiterated, "Just friends."

He held up both hands. "What do I look like here, the Big Bad Wolf? Anyway, we'll have the kids with us. What do you think I'm going to pull in front of your kids, for crying out loud?"

"I'm just making sure you understand the boundaries," said Kate. *You and me both.*

"Come on, I've barely broken up with Bambi. Give me credit for some sense."

"Okay. I just want to make sure we don't end up with a problem."

"We won't," Jeff assured her. He smiled and gave her a wink. "See ya later."

Kate watched him stroll back to his own property. He was, indeed, an attractive nuisance.

JEFF POURED HIMSELF A BOWL OF CORN FLAKES AND pondered the neurotic mess that went by the name of Kate Stonewall. He couldn't remember when he'd seen a woman so afraid of getting involved with a man. And she had nothing to worry about with him, anyway. He was just looking for someone to hang out with until he found Ms. Right. And Kate, he was discovering, was fun to hang out with. So why shouldn't they do some things together? He enjoyed teasing her, and he could tell she liked the crazy discussions they had as much as he did. But that didn't mean he was after her.

Well, not exactly. He did have to admit that, crazy as it was, Kate kept drawing him to her. But that didn't mean anything, really. He was a man, for crying out loud, and men were attracted to women, even neurotic ones.

As for anything more than fun and some harmless flirting, well, Kate could put away her neuroses. He wasn't in the market for a sharp-tongued know-it-all.

With a great smile and nice kids. But still a know-it-all. And a good mom and a loyal friend. And, on very rare occasions, a woman capable of admitting she was wrong, which hinted at a more human Kate hiding behind that professional busybody mask. If he could pry away her stiff facade, would he find someone soft and sweet waiting to be loosened up?

He looked out the kitchen window and imagined his boat rocking on the waters of a moonlit Pleasant Cove as Kate settled a picnic basket in the stern. Then she joined him at the bow and he sped them out into the middle of Puget Sound and killed the engine. Kate cuddled up on his lap and wrapped an arm around his neck and smiled up at him with those big, brown eyes of hers. The strap of her bathing suit slipped off her shoulder.

"Oh, this thing is such a nuisance," she complained. "Maybe I should just take it off."

Jeff let out a low whistle. The Kate of his imagination looked pretty good. What did the real-life one look like?

No doubt about it. He was going to get that woman in a bathing suit.

K ATE'S CAR WAS HEALTHY ONCE MORE, BUT JEFF insisted they all take his Jeep to the street dance. "More fun," he said. "Right, guys?"

Amanda and Robbie were happy to agree with him.

Well, why not? thought Kate. Who wanted to go out in something so sedate as a car, when you could hit the party in a zippy red Jeep? They piled in and Jeff started the engine. The radio came on, filling the small space with rock and roll music. Jeff cranked it up.

"You don't know you're alive unless you feel the bass pumping in your chest," he informed Kate.

"And you don't know you're deaf when . . . ?" she retorted.

"What?"

She frowned at him in mock disgust, and he laughed and backed up the vehicle for the run up the driveway.

The Jeep leaped up the steep drive like a mountain goat, and they hit the road. The blasting radio and her singing kids drowned out the lecture from her common-sense self on what a bad idea this was to be going out with Jeff Hardin, even as friends. As they sped down the highway, the wind rushed into the vehicle, sending Kate's hair in every direction and magically whisking away any remaining whispers of Doctor Kate's common sense. Just as well. It was her night off. Even she deserved some time away from Doctor Kate.

Tonight she was not a voice on the radio or a lonely

widow. Tonight she was a woman ready to have a good time. The kids would gorge themselves on hamburgers and ice cream, and draw pictures on the street. And she would dance until she wore the soles right off her tennies.

She pulled the wild strands of hair away from her face and smiled at Jeff. "This is going to be fun."

"You've got that right. Tonight we are going to howl at the moon." To demonstrate, he threw back his head and let out a wolf call.

Robbie was quick to imitate, then Amanda joined in.

What the heck? Kate tilted back her head and let out a howl.

The street was well filled with people by the time they arrived. Dads strolled with toddlers perched on their shoulders, women stood in colorful clumps, visiting, grandparents watched small, fledgling artists create sidewalk masterpieces. People stood in line waiting for corn on the cob and hamburgers, and the smell of sautéed onions danced down the street as the band pumped out "Walk Like an Egyptian."

"There's Sommer," cried Amanda. "Can I go hang out with her, Mom?"

"Only if you promise to meet me at the bandstand at ten o'clock. Can you do that?"

"Yes!" squealed Amanda and darted off through the crowd.

"Ten o'clock," Kate called after her.

"I want an ice cream," said Robbie.

"That sounds like a good idea," agreed Jeff. "Life's uncertain: eat dessert first. Come on, guys."

At the ice cream booth, he ordered three ice cream bars.

"None for me," said Kate.

"Don't worry, I'll make sure you burn it off," Jeff assured her, and she gave in.

Well, why not? It was, after all, her night to howl.

Ice cream in hand, they moved closer down the street to where the teen swing-dance club was putting on an exhibition. Jeff hoisted Robbie onto his shoulder and positioned Kate in front of him where she could see.

She watched all that energy and enthusiasm hopping every which way with a jealous eye.

"Looks like fun, doesn't it?" said Jeff, reading her mind yet again. "Ever think of taking lessons?"

"Yes, but it would keep the only man in my life out past his bedtime."

"I'd take lessons with you," Jeff offered.

"They probably offer them on weeknights," said Kate quickly. Going to a street dance with her overly friendly neighbor was one thing, but they weren't going to be getting any more palsy-walsy.

"I'll bet there's somebody on this island who gives private lessons on Saturdays and Sundays," said Jeff.

Kate said nothing.

The exhibition ended to enthusiastic applause and the band started up.

"Come on," said Jeff, grabbing Kate's hand. He worked his way toward the curb in front of the bandstand, then swung Robbie down and placed him on it. "Okay, slugger. You sit here and finish your ice cream and I'm going to show you how a real man dances."

Before Kate knew it, her last bite of ice cream had been tossed into the garbage and Jeff had an arm around her and was twirling her with enough finesse to make Patrick Swayze jealous.

"It looks to me like you've already had private dancing lessons," she observed.

"I know a few steps," he said modestly.

"I never would have figured you for a dancer."

"Dancing is a great way to get your arms around a woman without getting your face slapped," said Jeff and spun her again.

She was breathless by the time the song ended, and happy to stagger back to her son and collapse next to him.

"Hey, they're doing the Hand Jive," said Jeff. "Know how to do that?" he asked Robbie.

Robbie shook his head.

"Come on over here, next to me. Come on, Kate. This is easy," he said, pulling her up from the curb.

He positioned them next to a line of people who were slapping their thighs and clapping their hands, and began the motions. "See, it's easy," he said to Robbie, demonstrating. "Just do the same thing over and over again."

Kate picked up the hand motions and fell into the rhythm of the song. It was simple and fun, and made her smile. It seemed everything tonight was making her do that. She felt so light she thought she might rise above the crowd at any moment, like a balloon in the Macy's Thanksgiving Parade. She had needed this more than she realized. It felt great. Life was great. She looked at Jeff, who was making his hand motions with exaggerated sweeps, and a laugh bubbled up out of her. He turned her way and smiled and she forgot what she was doing, and somehow, that, too, seemed worthy of a laugh. Everything was fun and wonderful, and she felt like a woman who had just been brought back from a near-death experience and taken to the Mardi Gras.

The band started a slow song, and Jeff steered Robbie back to the curb, then pulled Kate against him and began to sway them to the rhythm of the song.

He smiled down at her. "Having fun?"

"Absolutely. This was a great idea."

"I thought so," he agreed, and pulled her against him, starting a heat wave spreading through her body.

It's just a dance, she reminded herself. *And it's good to have this experience to remind yourself how easily a woman's hormones can betray her. You'll be able to better empathize with your callers.*

She was conscious of Jeff's leg between hers, and he was bending low enough to hum in her ear, his breath ca-

ressing her and sending shivers down her spine. *Research.*
Try to think of it as research.

Kate did a lot of research in the next two and a half
hours. She was glad when Amanda showed up at ten and
she had an excuse to end the evening. Any more dances
with Jeff Hardin and Kate was liable to develop amnesia
and forget why he was so absolutely wrong for her.

They drove home with the radio thumping a little less
loudly and the kids sitting subdued in the backseat. Kate
felt anything but subdued. Her heart rate was up and she
felt jumpy. Even her skin seemed to be twitching. She
hadn't experienced these extreme sensations since eighth
grade and her first necking experience with Roger Wilson.

They pulled into Jeff's driveway and he turned off the
engine.

"Thanks," she said to him. "It was fun."

"Yeah, thanks, Jeff," said Amanda.

"And thanks for the food," said Robbie.

They got out of the car and the kids headed off to the
house.

Kate started to follow.

Jeff caught her arm. "How about joining me on the dock
for a nightcap?"

"It's getting late," she said.

He raised an eyebrow. "Ten-thirty? Come on, Cinderella. The ball doesn't end until midnight. Remember?"

"All right. Just for a few minutes," said Kate, then
wished she hadn't.

Oh, what was she doing acting like a scared rabbit? She
could handle Jeff Hardin. Anyway, they were just going to
sit on the dock and visit for a few minutes. That was all.
He knew the boundaries.

She hurried the kids into bed, then, heart racing faster
than her feet, she rushed through the house and out the
door.

Jeff was already seated on her dock and he held up a
bottle to her. "Like wine coolers?"

She saw he'd brought out a couple bottles each. "Are you trying to get me drunk?"

"It would probably take more than a couple of wine coolers."

Actually, Kate didn't have much of a head for alcohol—she usually nursed a glass of white wine through a whole evening. She took the bottle, vowing to only take a couple of sips.

Jeff patted the wood next to him. "Have a seat and say hi to the man in the moon."

She settled herself next to him and he clinked his bottle against hers. "Here's to friendship."

"To friendship," she echoed and took a sip.

"I never thought when I first moved in that you'd turn out to be such a great neighbor," he said. "But you are. It's been fun."

"Some of the time," amended Kate, and downed more of her wine cooler.

"Most of the time," he said gallantly.

"Liar."

"I try. Well, then, here's to good relations between neighbors," he said, and they clinked bottles again and took another drink.

"You know, I used to be a pretty heavy drinker in my young and stupid days," said Jeff.

"A lot of people can say that."

He shrugged. "My mom died when I was in college. Parties and booze seemed like a good alternative to feeling sorry for myself."

"There's a difference between feeling sorry for yourself and grieving for the loss of someone you love," said Kate softly.

"Yeah, you're right. I didn't know that back then. Thought I was being a wuss." He took a swig from his bottle, then continued. "I met my first wife at a frat party. She was one wild woman."

Kate could well imagine. She'd never been a wild

woman, and somehow, tonight, that seemed like a loss. She took a deep drink from her bottle.

"I guess, being a shrink, you can figure out what happened," said Jeff.

"You sobered up, she didn't want to."

"Something like that. I guess it's made me a little cautious. Do you think that's why I picked Bambi, because deep down I knew I didn't want to marry her and so she'd be safe?"

"It's possible, certainly understandable. But I'm sure you know that in the long run that sort of reasoning's not very beneficial."

Jeff smiled and shook his head. "You talk like a dictionary. I don't think I've ever met anyone quite like you. In fact, you're a damned amazing woman, Kate Stonewall."

Somewhere in that speech, Jeff's voice had lost it's teasing note. He turned to look at her, and even before he set down his bottle, Kate knew he was going to kiss her.

Ten

THE EASY SMILE FELL FROM JEFF'S FACE, MAKING him look like a different man. Kate saw his gaze fasten on her lips, felt his breath warm them before they even touched. Then his mouth caught hers, bringing alive every cell in her body. Her eyes closed, pulling her into a dark theater of the senses. Jeff's musky scent swirled around her like incense, while under them, the dock rocked gently with the caress of lapping waves. He slipped an arm around her shoulder, drawing her to him, and she was so caught up with the sensations of his chest pressing against her that she was barely aware of the empty wine cooler bottle falling from her hand and hitting the dock with a clink. Somewhere in the distance someone started setting off fireworks.

Or was that something only she was hearing?

Their kiss deepened and she felt a clutch of anticipation deep in her gut. Jeff finally broke contact to move his lips to the base of her neck. His contact with that sensitive skin turned Kate into the human equivalent of a sparkler. Above them, fresh fireworks exploded against the night sky and fell in a shower of color.

Someone moaned. It was her. She drove her fingers through his hair and threw back her head. He took full advantage of the offer, tracing the line of her collarbone with his lips. He eased her down onto the dock, nestling her between his arms. For one magical, movie-like moment he studied her face, his own expression intense, searing. Breathing suddenly seemed so mundane she had to stop. The night hung in sudden silent anticipation. Slowly, Jeff moved his hand up Kate's midriff, setting off fresh sparks. He lowered his mouth to hers.

Then a new sound drifted into her consciousness: a small child's giggle. It immediately drenched the sparks, and Kate pulled away. Again the giggle floated out to them, and she turned to look at her house.

A curtain twitched at her window and she knew that Amanda and Robbie were not in their beds.

"Looks like we're busted," observed Jeff. He stood and offered a hand to Kate. "Why don't you come over to my place?"

She ignored the outstretched hand and scrambled up. "I need to get home."

"Come on, Kate, nothing's going to happen to the kids with us right next door."

"Nothings going to happen, period," Kate corrected him, and hurried up the dock.

He caught up with her in two long strides, turning her to look at him. "Kate."

She shook her head. "This was not a good idea. We're neighbors, that's all."

"Would it be so bad if we became more?"

She stared at him in disbelief. "Are you insane?"

"You tell me. You're the shrink."

"All right, I will," snapped Kate, turning her anger at herself on him full force. "For one thing, I'm not into sex without commitment. It's not healthy, especially when there are children involved."

"This wasn't anything I was planning on involving your kids in," protested Jeff.

"You know what I mean. My children don't need to be saddled with having to cope with my sexuality. And, furthermore, you and I have nothing in common."

"Oh, so you don't like to dance?"

"That's only one thing, Jeff."

"Did it ever occur to you that we may have more than one thing in common?"

"That would be an impossibility," declared Kate. "Let's not take this relationship down a road that would lead to problems, okay?"

He sighed. "Yeah, I guess you're right."

She couldn't resist saying, "Of course I'm right."

That erased the last of the frown from his face, replacing it with a reluctant smile. "Okay, Doc. You win."

"Shake on it?" She held out her hand.

"Why not?" He took the proffered hand and set off a fresh shower of sparks inside her.

She broke the contact, saying, "Thanks again for a nice time."

He nodded and said nothing, and she hurried her scorched body away to put out a fire of a different kind.

By the time she got into the house, both spies were in their beds feigning sleep. She let Robbie be, going after Amanda, who had probably been the instigator of the domestic espionage.

"I know you're awake, so you may as well sit up," she said, entering the room with arms crossed.

"What?" said Amanda, trying to sound sleepy.

Kate sat on the side of her daughter's bed. "Didn't I ever get around to telling you it's not nice to spy on people?"

"I don't remember," said Amanda.

"Well, it's not."

Amanda sat up in bed. "You like him, don't you?"

The words "Certainly not" sat poised to dive off the tip of Kate's tongue, but she called them back. That would be all she needed, to send her daughter mixed signals about sexual behavior.

"I do," said Kate. "But that kiss was a mistake."

"But if you like him," began Amanda.

"I like him as a neighbor and a friend," said Kate.

"And you think he's cute," added Amanda helpfully.

"And I think he's cute," admitted Kate. "But that was our first and last kiss."

"But Mom, he's really nice," insisted Amanda.

"He is, but that doesn't mean he's the right man for me."

"You may not meet any more men," said Amanda, her voice taking on urgency.

"I'm sure I'll eventually meet someone."

"Yeah, right," said Amanda, pulling out her preadolescent snot voice.

"Amanda," said Kate sternly.

"I'm sick of being the only girl in school who doesn't have a dad," cried Amanda. "Everyone but me goes to the father-daughter spring banquet. Even my friends whose parents are divorced have a dad they go see on weekends."

Her daughter's words splashed across Kate's heart like acid. She swallowed her tears. "Honey, I'm sorry. There's not much I can do about that."

"Yes, there is, but you just don't want to. You aren't even looking, and I think it's really selfish of you to not even give Jeff a chance." With that, Amanda threw herself onto her side, turning her back to her mother.

Kate touched Amanda's shoulder and the child jerked away.

Kate sighed wearily. "I'm sorry that life played you such a dirty trick. I really am. And I want to fix the problem and give you guys a dad. You know I think they're important. But I want the one I pick to last. I want us to be a family. And for that to work, it has to be somebody who will make a good husband."

Amanda was sobbing now. "You're never going to find anyone," she wailed. "I won't have anybody to walk me down the aisle when I get married."

"Hey, what about Grandpa?" said Kate softly.

Amanda sniffed, but said nothing.

"You know, most of us don't get to have everything perfect when we're growing up."

"You did," shot back Amanda.

"Yeah, I had it pretty good," said Kate. "But I had to put up with your Uncle Randy beating me up all the time. At least you get to be the older sibling."

"Yeah, but you won't let me beat up Robbie."

"Life is tough," agreed Kate. She leaned her chin on her daughter's shoulder. "I know it would be nice for you to have a dad, but at least we've got each other. And we're not doing so very bad, just the three of us. Are we?"

"No," said Amanda reluctantly.

"Then how about we concentrate on being thankful for what we've got?" suggested Kate.

"Yeah, I guess."

"You guess? That's all you can say, you guess?" demanded Kate, tickling her daughter.

Amanda's squeals brought Robbie running into the room. He jumped on the bed and draped himself over Kate's back, and before she knew it, both children were on top of her.

"Okay, I surrender," she cried. "Just name your terms."

"Ice cream," said Robbie.

What the heck? It was a holiday, after all.

An hour later, Kate finally made it to her own bedroom. For the first time since she'd moved in, it felt too big. She walked to the window that faced the cove and slipped aside the shade a crack. Looking out, she caught sight of a lone figure sitting on her dock, staring out at the water. For a moment she indulged her senses by letting them play with the memory of Jeff's hand caressing her, of his mouth on hers, of his sudden intense look of possession that had reached down and closed over the lonely corner of her heart. What would happen if she went back out there and slipped into the safe circle of his arms?

Her common sense rushed in and banged the door shut on that idea, forcing her to return to her right mind. She let the shade fall back into place and moved quickly away from the window, reminding herself that loneliness and wanting did not add up to love.

JEFF STARED AT THE MOON IN THE VAIN HOPE THAT the guy up there could explain to him why it was suddenly so important that Kate Stonewall want him. How had she gone so quickly from being his obnoxious neighbor to becoming his dream woman, anyway? Come to think of it, the transformation hadn't been quick. It had been happening ever since he and Kate started their verbal sparring matches at the station. Those had contained all the thrill of a Vegas boxing match, but without the black eye and split lip. Tonight Kate had morphed from a sparring partner to a sexy, laughing dancing partner who had made him hungry for more than a dance. And kissing her had been even better than dancing with her. Now he wanted her so badly he'd probably have to jump in the cove to cool off—an idea the good doctor would definitely applaud since she'd just told him to go soak his head.

The old noodle could use a soaking. It sure could use something, since it obviously wasn't working well these days. Jeff shook his head. This would get filed in his memory banks as the summer of stupidity. He'd blown it with a woman who had loved him just so he could chase after one who wanted nothing to do with him. Boy, he really did need a shrink. But if Kate was any example, all those mind benders were more screwed up than he was.

What was he saying? He wasn't screwed up. And there

was only one shrink he needed. He'd had his epiphany tonight, and he knew he and Kate were right for each other, knew it deep in his gut. She needed a guy like him who would bring out that great laugh of hers. She also needed a guy who would say "I do" and mean it, one who would hang in there for the long haul, love her and love her kids, too, as if they were his own. He was the man for the job. This was the woman he could commit to for the rest of his life: one who could always find something to say that would make him stop and think, who would give her all to those she cared about, the woman who could burn a hole in his heart when she smiled. With her sharp tongue and strong opinions, Kate sure wasn't his mirror image, but she was his other half. And he was hers.

So how did a man go about attaching his other half when she didn't want to attach? It was a frustrating problem for a guy who had never had trouble getting a woman. No, it was worse than frustrating; it was disheartening. Here he was, ready to hand over that most precious of all male possessions, his freedom, and the woman he wanted to give it to wasn't interested. Jeff tried to expel his disappointment with a sigh, but that didn't work, so he took another slug from his second bottle of wine cooler. That didn't help either. He poured the rest into the water.

What was Kate so afraid of, anyway? Dumb question. He knew the answer to that. She didn't want to repeat history. But Jeff wasn't the same guy her husband was.

He had to open her eyes, get her to see that. He knew she was attracted to him, that deep down under that rock-hard shell, hot lava bubbled. He'd felt the heat of it tonight. All he had to do was make Kate realize it was okay to listen to her heart and she'd blow like Mount Saint Helens. Jeff set his jaw in determination. He'd turn up the volume on her ticker so loud she couldn't help but hear it. He'd be Mr. Friendly, just like she wanted, and the more time they spent together, the quicker she'd realize, as he had, that they had something good going between them. But no more passes. Well, at least not for a while. If she wanted to skip chemistry to concentrate on psychology, he could do that. For the moment. Meanwhile, let the lava keep on heating.

L IVING IN THE SEATTLE AREA, YOU NEVER KNEW, even as far into summer as the Fourth of July, if it was going to rain on your parade or not. This year, the clouds had found some other locale to haunt, leaving both Seattle and the nearby island of Bainbridge to bask under azure skies decorated with delicate cloud streamers.

Standing on the balcony for a weather check, Kate could see it was going to be great weather for a parade.

She rousted the kids, then went downstairs to make pancakes.

She was stirring batter when the phone rang. "Hey, it's me, Mr. Platonic. I'm leaving to get my new boat. You haven't chickened out on going water-skiing, have you?"

The memory of their aborted makeout session on the dock sent heat rushing to the far corners of Kate's body. This was all her crazed hormones needed, another day of chumminess with Jeff Hardin.

"I think, under the circumstances, it would be best if we didn't—"

He cut her off. "Oh, come on. What did you think, that I was going to hold a grudge because you gave me a verbal slap last night? We're letting bygones be bygones, remember? Anyway, it's no fun to have a ski boat and nobody to take skiing."

"I'm sure you could find someone."

"I already did. You. Come on, Grace won't want to be the only woman at the party."

"Well, we're going to the parade this afternoon," said Kate. "You'll probably be all done by the time we get home," she added hopefully.

"Nope," said Jeff. "It'll take Dad and me till at least two

to get done fooling around with the boat. We can do some skiing when you get back, then fire up the barbecue and throw on the burgers."

It really wasn't a very good idea to be spending so much time with Jeff. It would only raise her children's hopes again. But they would love a chance to ride in a ski boat. Kate waffled, trying to decide what to do. Indecision was an unfamiliar experience, and she didn't find it pleasant.

"Come on, Kate," urged Jeff. "Get wild. Live a little."

This was the absolute last thing she was doing with Jeff Hardin. "Oh, all right," she said, sounding less than gracious. "We'll be there."

"Great. Come on over when you get back," said Jeff.

Amanda ambled into the kitchen just as Kate hung up the phone. "Where are we going?" she asked.

"Over to Jeff's later. He bought a ski boat and he's going to take us out in it."

"Water-skiing?" squeaked Amanda.

"Probably."

Amanda let out a shriek. "Oh, this is so awesome." She grabbed for the phone. "I've got to call Sommer."

Amanda was telling her friend the good news at a volume nearly as high as her velocity when Robbie bounced in, looking for breakfast.

"What are we doing?" he asked.

"We're going to the parade and then we're coming back and going out in Jeff's new ski boat," said Kate, trying to make herself heard above Amanda.

"Oh, boy!" exclaimed Robbie. "Is Jeff going to teach us how to ski?"

"He might."

"Yes, yes, yes," chanted Robbie, raising the noise level in the kitchen from loud to cacophonous.

Kate smiled and turned her attention to pouring pancakes. It would be a fun day for the kids. Actually, it would be a fun day for them all. Now that Jeff really understood the boundaries there was no reason she shouldn't enjoy herself. Not in a bathing suit, though. She hadn't gone swimming in two years, and she was sure she hadn't lost enough weight yet to fit into her suit. But maybe she'd try it on after breakfast just to see.

She found it buried under a stack of summer clothes she'd outgrown that she'd been meaning to take to the Goodwill. She picked up a pair of white denim shorts and held them against her. They looked like they might just fit.

She tossed aside her bathrobe and pulled them on. And got them zipped! They were a little snug, but she was in them, and that was what counted. She turned in the mirror to examine herself. Yes, her buns were definitely shrinking. And she hadn't been imagining it; she was getting a waist again. Her old jeans had been fitting more loosely, but she never dreamed she'd made this much progress. Another week or two and she might actually be able to face her bathroom scale.

Okay, now try on the bathing suit. She chewed her lip and regarded the pale blue, stretchy thing. Oh, Lord, it would cling to her tummy and make her look like she was four months pregnant. *Just try it on.*

She slipped off the shorts, discarded her night tee, and pulled up the suit. Breath held, she stepped back in front of the mirror.

Well, she was no Bambi, that was for certain, and she still had a pot. But her reflection wasn't terrifying; just mildly scary. She could wear a T-shirt over the suit when she rode in the boat. And if she got brave enough to get in the water, she'd keep the T-shirt on.

She grabbed the shorts, a pink, scooped neck, sleeveless knit top, and her bra and panties and headed for the shower. She may as well celebrate her weight loss and wear them to the parade.

"You have lost weight," observed Janet as they staked their claim on a piece of curb along Madison Avenue with the rest of the growing crowd.

"I haven't worn these shorts in two years," Kate confessed, handing Robbie a can of pop. "I feel like a new woman."

Janet took in Kate's fat ponytail, her hot pink visor, and the fish-shaped earrings dangling from her ears. "You look like a new woman. I've never seen you dressed quite so sporty."

"I had the wardrobe, just lost the figure."

"Well, you've certainly found it. You look great. It's a shame the only person who's going to see you looking like that today is Grace."

"Well, Grace and my neighbor," said Kate.

"Jeff Hardin? How does he come into the picture? I thought he had a girlfriend."

"They broke up."

"Oh," said Janet as if she now understood the outfit.

"It's not what you're thinking," said Kate. "This is just a block party."

"Oh? Who else will be there?"

"Well, no one that I know of."

"Small block," observed Janet.

"We're just friends."

"My, how things have changed," murmured Janet.

"Jeff's got a new boat and he wants to take the kids out in it. That's all."

"He seems like a nice guy," said Janet casually.

"He is," agreed Kate. "He'll make some jockette a wonderful husband."

"I hate to tell you this," said Janet, "but Mr. Perfect doesn't exist."

"No," agreed Kate. "But Mr. Right does, and I'm not settling for less than a man who is exactly right for me. I don't intend to find myself ten years down the road calling Doctor Laura under an assumed name."

"Well, you're the expert, so I guess you know what you're doing."

Janet's dubious tone of voice was hardly a vote of confidence. Well, thought Kate, a prophet is without honor in her own country. And it didn't matter what Janet thought. As long as Kate herself knew what she was doing; that was the important thing. She watched her children, sitting side by side, their legs stuck out in front of them, looking up the street for some sign that the parade was about to begin, and was glad she knew exactly what she was doing. She owed it to them as well as herself to hold out for the man who would be her perfect match.

JEFF EASED HIS NEW PRIDE AND JOY UP TO THE buoy, and his dad secured her. "Man, I can hardly wait to strap on the skis," said Jeff.

"She'll give you a good ride," said Sandy. "She handles great."

"So, I didn't make such a bad investment after all, huh?" teased Jeff.

"I didn't say that," said Sandy. "Talk to me in a couple years when you've discovered the second happiest day in a boat owner's life."

"Yeah, yeah," said Jeff. "I'm not selling this baby."

"That's what I said about the cabin cruiser."

"The cruiser may not have lasted, but you had that little speedboat for years," said Jeff. "I remember learning how to ski behind it."

Sandy shrugged. "That was when we had the place on Hood Canal. You couldn't have a summer shack and not have a boat."

"Yeah, I guess not," said Jeff. "Here, let's go ashore and get a beer," he added, steering them away from memory lane.

Talking about the good old days when Jeff's mom was alive wasn't a favorite pastime for either of them. Even after all these years, his dad could still tear up if they talked for very long.

They had popped a couple of cans of Bud and were

making a sizable dent in a bowl of chips when Grace arrived with a chocolate cake.

"Grace, love of my life," called Jeff, throwing his arms wide. "Marry me."

"You're too old," she retorted, handing over the cake.

"Darn," chimed in Sandy. "I guess that really lets me out."

Grace looked him up and down, and Jeff wondered if she saw the same thing he did: shaggy gray hair and matching chin stubble, and a body that had gotten downright scrawny in the last couple of years.

"I make exceptions," said Grace.

Sandy's lips split in a wide grin.

Jeff made the introductions, adding, "Grace is the best cook on Bainbridge Island."

"And you look like you could stand some of my cooking," said Grace.

"I can stand anybody's but my own," cracked Sandy.

And he'd had plenty of chances to sample other people's home cooking after Mom died. Before he decided to become the Solitary Man, Dad had taken up with two or three different women. But Mom was a tough act to follow and none of them had lasted. But then, none of them had been Grace.

She and the old man had already settled into a comfortable conversation about living in Seattle versus living on the island. Smiling, Jeff took the cake into the house and left them to it. Maybe, before the summer was over, both the Hardin men would get lucky.

IT SEEMED THEY'D BARELY GOTTEN IN THE DOOR BEfore the kids were scampering over to Jeff's with their bathing suits and towels. Their laughter drifted through the kitchen window to Kate as she pulled her potato salad out of the fridge. She had her bathing suit on under her oversized tee now, and so was ready to jump in the water to save her children should some freak accident occur. She'd be sure to instruct Jeff not to tow them very far; just enough to give them a little excitement and a new experience. That was all they needed.

As she left the house, she realized that her pulse was up and anticipation had quickened her pace. It would appear that the kids weren't the only ones looking forward to a little excitement.

She found everyone seated at Jeff's new redwood picnic table, which was strewn with bags of every imaginable kind of junk food. Jeff was entertaining his company by tossing black olives into the air and catching them in his mouth. Next to him sat a grizzled man who looked to be somewhere in his sixties. Jeff's father. The family resemblance was unmistakable, especially when the older man smiled.

Kate saw that now Robbie was attempting to imitate Jeff and a sudden vision of her son catching an olive in his throat made her voice sharp when she called his name.

The olive bounced onto the grass and Robbie turned to smile at her. "Hi, Mom."

By now Kate had reached the table. She set down her bowl, saying, "Robbie, don't do that. You could choke."

"But Jeff's doing it," protested Robbie.

"Hey, if your mom says no, then no it is," said Jeff quickly.

Kate felt as if everyone was staring curiously at her. "He could choke," she said defensively, and knew she sounded like a neurotic bitch. She didn't care.

"That potato salad looks wonderful," said the older man, diplomatically changing the subject.

Kate smiled politely. "Thank you."

Jeff made the introductions, then conversation died, smothered under the wet blanket Kate had brought to the party.

"Well," said Jeff, attempting to revive it, "what do you think of my mistress?"

Kate looked where he was pointing and saw a sleek, electric blue boat bobbing on the water. It looked fast and lethal.

"It's beautiful," she admitted. "How fast can it go?"

"Not fast enough to kill your kids," Jeff assured her.

"Can we take a ride in it now that Mom's here?" asked Robbie.

"We sure can," said Jeff. "And after that, how about some water-skiing?"

Both kids exploded in shouts and squeals.

"I guess that means yes," said Jeff. "Come on, Kate. I'll take you and the kids for a spin first, then we'll put Dad and Grace in the boat and we'll see about getting these guys up on skis."

"You do have life jackets for them, don't you?" Kate asked.

"Absolutely," said Jeff, directing her attention to the pile on the dock. "And one for you, too. You can even wear it when you're skiing."

"Oh, I think I'll just ride in the boat," said Kate quickly.

"I think you'll want to take a chance and try something new." Jeff eyed her chest and a wolfish grin spread across his face. "It looks like you've got your suit on under that T-shirt."

She felt a blush spreading its rosy fingers across her cheeks. "Yes. I thought I'd get in the water with the kids."

"You can if you want," he said. "I'm going to be in there with them, but you can stand by for moral support."

"That's very kind of you," said Kate sarcastically.

"I thought so."

Once in the boat, all bundled up in life jackets, Jeff headed them out of the cove. They skimmed along the water and watched houses and land slide by like so many attractions at a Disneyland ride. The sun touched Kate's shoulders with warmth and the wind spattered her face with spray. She looked back to where the kids perched and saw two faces awash in bliss.

She turned to Jeff. "Thanks for doing this."

"My pleasure."

And, from the expression on his face, she could tell it was. He looked like a man who had just closed a million dollar deal. She understood, because right now she felt the same way.

They rode for a good twenty minutes before returning, then Jeff and his father changed places, putting Sandy at the wheel of the boat. Grace took up the position at the stern with the understanding that she would report to Sandy immediately when a skier went down.

Robbie sat in the boat with them while Amanda, as oldest child, was given the privilege of going first. Although her expression betrayed a certain nervousness, she gamely clung to the ski rope, ski tips bobbing in front of her.

Kate stood beside her, shed of her shorts and shivering in her bathing suit and T-shirt.

Jeff crouched behind her, holding the back of the skis to keep them in place for her. "Just let the boat pull you out. Don't lean back."

Amanda nodded, and Jeff called to Grace, "Pick up some of that slack, Grace, and keep it tight. Once she's up you can start letting it out."

Grace pulled in the rope a bit, tightening it.

"Scared?" asked Jeff.

"Kinda," admitted Amanda.

Kate was sure he'd say something ridiculous, like "Don't be." Instead, he said, "It's always scary trying something new. I'm right behind you, though. And if you go down, Sandy'll stop the boat and we'll try again. Okay? Just remember, if you fall, let go of the rope."

Amanda nodded.

"Okay," hollered Jeff, and the boat moved forward.

Kate's heart lurched as Amanda rose from the water like a small Aphrodite. She went a few feet, leaned forward at an angle, then toppled, and Kate's stomach tumbled right along with her. Following Jeff's directions, Amanda let go of the tow rope, and it skipped off in the boat's wake without her, leaving Amanda bobbing in the water like a cork. Kate could hear Grace calling to Sandy. He immediately turned the boat and they got Amanda out of her skis and hauled her in, then returned her to Jeff.

"Not bad for your first attempt," he told her. "You almost made it. Want to try again?"

Amanda nodded, fierce determination on her face.

Sandy got the boat back into position while Jeff put the skis back on Amanda and got her set once more, saying, "Just relax and enjoy it."

She nodded, but her jaw remained clenched.

Jeff's voice was soothing. "You did really good not leaning back. Remember, you want to stand up, so don't lean forward too far. That's why you went over. You'll get it this time." To his dad, he called, "Start her out just a little slower, Dad."

Jeff handed over the tow rope and once again got behind Amanda, pulling out a litany of trite "You can do it" sports phrases.

The boat moved forward again, pulling Amanda out of the water. This time she got to a standing position, and they began to tow her out to the open sea.

"Look at that!" cried Jeff. "Up on her second try."

"How far are they going?" asked Kate nervously.

"Not that far," Jeff assured her. "Just enough to make her feel good about herself. Hey, don't worry," he added. "She's not going to drown wearing a life vest, and there are no sharks in Pleasant Cove."

He was right. She was being neurotic. Kate watched as the boat made a wide arc, pulling Amanda behind it. She made it almost all the way back before going down and Sandy quickly turned the boat and fished her out. Kate was relieved to see both legs working fine as they hauled her into it.

"Can I go now?" called Robbie eagerly once they were back.

"Sure," said Jeff. "Amanda, you can ride in the boat with Grace. Okay?"

Jeff repeated his instructions to Robbie, who was barely able to stay still waiting for takeoff. Then Jeff signaled his father to start, and Robbie popped out of the water and skidded off in the wake of the boat.

Jeff chuckled. "The kid's a natural. Does he get that from his mom?"

"I doubt it," said Kate.

She watched in amazement as her son followed the boat around the cove. They returned, and he let go of the rope and sank gracefully like a pro. By the time he was back with them, his mouth was set on high speed and he talked the entire time Jeff was removing his skis.

"Did you see me, Mom? I made it up. We went so fast! I've never gone that fast in my whole life. That was fun. Can I go again, Jeff?"

"You gotta wait your turn," said Jeff, who was now pulling a bigger set of skis from the shore end of the dock. Before Kate realized what was happening, he was back in the water and had an arm around her waist. "Your mom's gonna go now."

"What?" Kate sputtered. "No, I can't. You go. It's your boat."

"And you're my guest. Ladies first. Come on, Kate, you're not going to let your kids make you look like a wimp, are you?"

"I don't need my kids for that," Kate assured him, trying to pull away.

"Oh, no, you don't," he said, tipping her on her rump in the shallow water. "Let's see how these fit."

"You can do it, Mom," called Amanda from the boat.

Kate subsided and submitted to the fitting, realizing it would be silly to act cowardly in front of her children. But her insides were quaking. And the feel of Jeff's hand on her ankle was only heightening the shivers. She should have listened to her common sense and declined his invitation. What had she been thinking? Maybe the skis wouldn't fit.

But they did, and a few minutes later, she was crouched, shivering, in front of Jeff while he gave her the same pep talk he had administered to her kids.

"This is insane," she said between gritted teeth. "I am not a sports kind of person."

"You don't have to know baseball stats to water-ski," said Jeff firmly. "Take up the slack, Grace. Okay, Dad. Take her out slow."

The next thing Kate knew, her arms were being pulled with enough force to yank them out of their sockets and she was rising out of the water against her will. The boat pulled her mercilessly forward. She tried to balance and quickly found herself bent over, with the water looking ever closer to her face. She was vaguely aware of Jeff shouting, "Don't lean forward," before she pitched face first into the sound. He yelled something else now, but all she could hear was the frantic gurgling of water in her ears. It assaulted her face and went up her nose, trying to choke her. She twisted onto her side with angry waves beating at her. Still, she clung to the rope like a shipwreck survivor to a piece of flotsam. Then the force let up and her pace slowed, and next thing she knew, she was marooned in the water, waiting for rescue.

The electric blue monster pulled up next to her and a laughing Amanda called, "You're supposed to let go of the rope when you fall, Mom."

"Thanks."

"Do you want to try again?" asked Sandy. "We can do a deep-water start right here."

"No, I think I've had enough fun for one day," said Kate.

Sandy leaned overboard and helped her out of the unwieldy skis, then they hauled her in like an oversized fish.

"Why don't you want to try again?" asked Amanda.

"Because I'm not crazy."

"You almost had it," said Sandy encouragingly.

"Oh, I bet you say that to all the klutzes," retorted Kate.

They brought her back to Jeff, who insisted that she was indeed going to try again. "What kind of a pathetic mother would let herself get shown up by her own kids?" he teased.

"One who wants to live to raise them," said Kate, her teeth chattering.

"Come on, Kate. Don't give up."

"Oh, all right. One more time."

"Two," bargained Jeff.

She raised an eyebrow at him.

"Hey, you might make it up this time," he said, snaking an arm across her middle and sending shivers to places the water hadn't affected. "But just in case you don't, the third time will be the charm. Guarantee it."

The second time was different from the first. This time, determined not to get pulled over, Kate leaned back and experienced being dragged through the water on her back.

"This is the last time I'm doing this," she informed Jeff as he once more stood behind her.

"You're right, because this time you're going to get up. Screw up this time and I will call the *National Enquirer* and tell them you're neurotic."

"Oh, you would," snapped Kate.

"Just hold steady and let the boat do the work," said Jeff. "Take her up a little slower, Dad," he called.

The boat surged forward and this time Kate rose from the water to a standing position. And stayed. Now she was flying along the surface of the water like a gull. A feeling of power surged through her and she let out a whoop of triumph.

They got her halfway around the cove before she lost her balance and toppled. The water socked her hard and she came up coughing. She waited for rescue, keenly aware of aching arms and legs, and an incredible feeling of exhilaration. She had gotten up on water skis!

"So, was it good for you?" asked Jeff as he took off her skis.

She was already very conscious of his hand on her calf, and his remark conjured up images that activated her imagination.

"It was fun," she admitted. "Oh, stop looking so smug," she scolded. "Are you one of those people who gloats every time he's right?"

"I must be," he said. "Or maybe I was just smiling because I've found us another common interest. Who'd have thought a sports nut and brain would have anything in common, huh?"

"I am not going there with you," said Kate firmly.

He didn't say anything, but she noticed her words had done nothing to wipe the smug expression from his face.

Free of her skis, Kate wrapped herself up in a towel and watched from the shore as Jeff slalomed his way around the cove. "Show-off," she muttered.

Thinking of the way his shoulder muscles had rippled as he took off from the dock and the easy grace with which he crossed back and forth over the ski boat's wake, she concluded Jeff Hardin did have a few things worth showing off. But that didn't make him anyone she would be interested in spending the rest of her life with. She hoped he realized that.

SEATTLE'S WATERFRONT PARK WAS THE HUMAN equivalent of an anthill, its grass covered with blankets and the blankets covered with people, children, and picnic baskets. Darkness had fallen, lending even more anonymity to the couple on the red plaid stadium blanket.

She sat between his legs, with his arms draped around her as they watched the fireworks popping in the sky above them.

"It's so beautiful," breathed Bambi.

"It's like being in an open-air theater in space, right in

the middle of the Milky Way," agreed Don, and he planted a kiss on the top of Bambi's head.

They didn't say another word for the rest of the display, just oohed and aahed like the rest of the crowd. It was only when the last shower of sparks had fallen from the sky that Don said what they'd both known. "I'm in love with you, Bambi."

She nodded. "I feel the same way." And she knew what that meant: it was the beginning . . . and the end.

Eleven

"THAT NEIGHBOR OF YOURS IS A FINE WOMAN," said Sandy as the two men enjoyed a postpicnic snack of beer and chocolate cake.

"Yeah, but she's a nut."

"She seemed normal," said Sandy. "Has she got anyone special in her life?"

"Yeah," said Jeff slowly. "She just doesn't know it yet."

Sandy frowned. "Are we talking about the same neighbor?"

"Who are you talking about?"

"Grace, of course."

Jeff covered his embarrassment with a laugh. "No, she hasn't got anybody. I'm not sure she wants anybody, either."

"Well, we'll just have to see about that," said Sandy.

"So, you really liked her."

Sandy nodded. "She's good fun. And so is that boat of yours."

"Not such a bad buy after all, huh?" teased Jeff.

"Hey, it's the next fifteen years of your life, not mine. But you make the payments and I'll help you enjoy it."

"You've got a deal," said Jeff, and they both took a slug of beer.

"So," said Sandy, "the other neighbor, this Doctor Kate, she rings your bell?"

"Yeah," Jeff admitted. He shook his head. "I've got to be nuts to want that squirrelly shrink, especially when she doesn't want anything to do with me, but there it is."

"In a nutshell," cracked his dad.

Jeff acknowledged the pun with a grunt.

"For someone who doesn't want anything to do with you, she sure seems to like you."

"As long as I play the game by her rules and we stay friends."

"Friends," said Sandy in disgust.

"But she's falling for me," Jeff insisted. "She just doesn't want to admit it."

"I don't know, son. When a woman says she wants to be friends it usually means the game's over."

"This one's just heating up."

"I've got to admit, she seems to have a little more on the ball than Bambi, but, she doesn't strike me as easygoing. Not exactly your type of woman."

"She can be a firecracker," admitted Jeff.

"It's none of my business, son, but here's a friendly reminder: you can get burned by firecrackers."

Jeff thought of the fun they'd all had setting off the fireworks he'd gotten in nearby Suquamish. "Yeah, you can," he agreed, "but think how boring life would be without them."

"Well, then," said Sandy, raising his beer can, "here's to excitement for you and boredom for me."

"I'll drink to that," said Jeff.

• • •

KATE AND GRACE SAT IN GRACE'S KITCHEN, DRINK-ing tea. The great weather had decided to extend its visit beyond the Fourth of July, and the kitchen was awash in sunlight. A morning breeze made the curtains at the open window dance like gingham ghosts and brought in the smell of low tide to mingle with the aroma of freshly brewed vanilla tea.

"So, your kids have been gone for twenty-four hours," said Grace. "Are you going through withdrawal?"

"The house does seem empty without them," admitted Kate. "I feel like a World War III survivor, looking for an-other living human being. It could be a long three weeks."

"Your parents are probably thrilled to have them, though," said Grace.

"Oh, yeah. They'll have a great time. And with the new book coming out, I'm doing a couple of local book sign-ings on the next couple of Saturdays anyway, so it's just as well. But this is the last time I'm sending them off without me."

"This was the first time you've sent them off without you," pointed out Grace.

"That, too. Golly, I miss them."

"Go shopping," advised Grace. "That will help. Now that you're getting so skinny, you must need a new wardrobe."

"I could use a few things," said Kate. "Good idea."

"You certainly looked good on the Fourth," said Grace.

"I felt good," said Kate. "Another fifteen pounds and I'm going to really feel fabulous."

"Well, hurry up and lose it. I'm tired of not having any-one to bake for."

"Jeff still appreciates you," said Kate. "And, from the looks of it, you gained a new customer in his dad. Al-though it looked to me like your cooking wasn't the only thing Sandy Hardin is interested in," she added.

Grace's cheeks took on new color. "He's lonely."

Kate eyed Grace over her tea mug. "He's more than lonely. He's interested."

The color on Grace's face deepened. "That's ridiculous. Who's going to be interested in an overweight, middle-aged woman?"

"A nice, lonely widower, who has sense enough not to judge someone by her appearance."

Grace rolled her eyes. "Never mind me. Let's talk about you."

Now it was Kate's turn to blush. "Oh, let's not."

"You are attracted to Jeff, and you might as well come right out and admit it to Mother Grace."

"All right, I will. I am attracted to Jeff Hardin. But I'm not foolish enough to think that attraction is a firm foundation for a lasting relationship."

"Please," moaned Grace. "Don't play those psychobabble games with me. You like the guy."

"He is likable," admitted Kate. "But we're friends and neighbors. That's all. That's as far as the relationship is going to go. He's not the right man for me. We're too different."

"I think he'd be good for you," said Grace.

Kate shook her head. "A sports nut would be about as good for me as an arsenic milkshake. No, there's another Bambi out there somewhere for Jeff."

"I don't think he wants a Bambi," said Grace. "I think he wants someone he can argue with, someone who will challenge him.

"And I'm sure he'll find her." Kate checked her watch. "I've got to get going if I'm going to make my ferry."

"Very convenient," muttered Grace.

"THANKS, DOCTOR KATE," SAID STELLA, "I THOUGHT I did the right thing. I just wanted to be sure."

"You did the right thing. It's always the right thing to listen to your logical self. Stay on the line, Stella, and I'm going to have Wallis get your mailing address so we can send you one of my 'No Frogs' T-shirts. I love that shirt," Kate added. "For those of you who haven't seen it, it's got a little frog on the front dressed like a fairy-tale prince, and he has the circle with the red slash stamped over him. Very cute. I'll try to have enough on hand to give one away to the first twenty people who come to my book signing at the downtown Seattle Barnes and Noble this Saturday. Take a break from that yard work and come see me. I'll be there from one to three, signing copies of my new book, *How to Separate the Men from the Boys,* and I hope to see some of you there."

"The first twenty?" moaned Wallis in despair as they settled down to wait for the reporter who would be interviewing Kate regarding her upcoming book signings. "The promotion department tells me that the new order won't be in until next week. I'll be lucky if I can dredge up ten."

"I thought we had more of those left."

"Not at the rate you've been giving them away."

"Well, I think they're cute."

"So do your fans, who are going to be very aggravated if they show up and find out you mislead them about the number of available shirts."

"Okay, find out exactly how many I have and I'll make an on-air correction tomorrow. All right?"

"All right," said Wallis, mollified.

The reporter from the *Seattle Post-Intelligencer* arrived an hour later—the same one who had written the article about her syndication deal and referred to her as a shrink.

"Doctor Kate," said the man, extending his hand. "Good to see you again. You're hot copy these days."

"So it would seem," said Kate politely. "And just for the record, I'm also a psychologist, not a shrink. Shrink is what I claim has happened to my clothes every time I gain weight."

He laughed. "That's a good one. Can I quote you?"

"Sure." Kate motioned to the well-padded swivel chair

she reserved for visitors to her office, and took the seat opposite, in front of her computer. "Can we get you something to drink? Coffee? Soft drink?"

"No, thanks," said Clark Kent Jr. "I'm on a tight schedule."

"All right. Let's get started. Fire away."

"THAT WAS A GOOD INTERVIEW," SAID WALLIS later as they headed for Seattle's International District and their favorite Chinese restaurant. "We ought to get some good press out of it."

"Sometimes I wonder if there is such a thing as good press," mused Kate.

"Believe me, there is, and even though you didn't like being called a shrink, that last article was good. This one should be too. Our boy reporter thought you were funny."

"Great," said Kate. "That means he'll probably refer to me as a stand-up comic in this next article."

"Hey, whatever gets publicity," said Wallis. "Seafair has started, and you've got the Milk Carton Derby to compete with this Saturday."

Seafair was a city summer festival that had been going on since before Kate was born. It featured parades, a visit from the Blue Angels, who flew over the area any number of times and disrupted traffic, and culminated in hydroplane races on Lake Washington. The Milk Carton Derby, sponsored by the Navy, was part of Seafair. Scouts, teens, parents, and corporations flocked to Green Lake to see who could make the most elaborate seaworthy vessel out of milk cartons. It was harmless fun, but Kate couldn't imagine it offering her any serious competition.

"I'm not too worried," she said.

"They're giving away money and prizes over there," said Wallis.

"Yes, but they don't have 'No Frogs' T-shirts."

"There is that."

• • •

"I'M GLAD YOU WERE FREE," SAID KATE ONCE they'd settled at a linen-clad table and placed their orders. "The thought of going home to my empty house to eat leftovers was not a pleasant one."

"It's going to be a long three weeks for you, isn't it?"

Kate nodded. "But my parents had so many great things planned they wanted to do, it would have been totally selfish of me to cut the trip short."

"You could have taken some vacation time and gone with them," pointed out Wallis.

"No, this actually works out well. The kids don't feel deprived and grumpy that I have to cut their day in half working, and I don't have to feel guilty. Plus their grandparents get to hog them. And we still have August. It works out well for everyone."

"Just so you remember to adjust to the separation," said Wallis. "I'm not going out to dinner with you every night for the next three weeks." She gave Kate a mischievous grin. "Not that I'll have to. After that comment about having to say good-bye to your munchkins and be all alone, we'll probably get tons of calls from men offering to keep you from being lonely."

Kate made a face. "Yes, I can imagine the interesting characters who would call in."

"The way Hardin was eyeballing you this afternoon, I wouldn't be surprised if he's the first in line," said Wallis.

Kate shook a playful finger at her. "You're fishing."

"Damned right I am. You're tight as a childproof medicine bottle where he's concerned."

"There's nothing to tell. We have established friendly relations and we are now good neighbors. That's all."

"That's what you keep saying," scoffed Wallis. "And I'd almost believe you, except for one thing: I've seen the way you look at him lately."

"Oh, please," protested Kate.

"Don't worry. You do a good job of hiding it. The average person would never suspect. But this is your old pal Wallis you're talking to."

"Who needs her head examined. Now, drop the subject or I swear I'll eat your spring roll."

"All right," said Wallis, "but I think you need to get over these fear issues you have. You'd feel better if you got it off your chest and shared your true feelings toward a certain radio personality."

"That does it." Kate reached across the table and plucked Wallis's spring roll off her plate. "Don't say I didn't warn you."

Wallis scowled and signaled the waiter. "Another spring roll, please." She returned her attention to Kate, studying her until Kate began to feel an embarrassed warmth creeping up her cheeks.

"Hey, it was just a joke," said Kate. "I'll pay for the extra spring roll."

"You do know you're falling in love with him, don't you?"

"I am not falling in love with Jeff Hardin. He is completely inappropriate."

"You crack me up," said Wallis. "You and your reducing love to a formula.

"Not a formula," corrected Kate. "Common sense."

"One of these days you're going to find your common sense doesn't know as much as you think it does. Then you'll have to write a whole new book."

Kate rolled her eyes. "Maybe I should have gone home and eaten leftovers."

"Okay, okay," said Wallis. "I'll stop. You can poke into my love life."

"You broke up with Kirk. You don't have one."

Wallis gave her a cocky grin. "Maybe that's why it's so much more fun to talk about yours."

"If I had a love life, would I be here with you?"

"Actually, yes. It's one of the things I admire about you;

you would never stand up a girlfriend for a man. You might steal her spring roll, but I guess no one's perfect."

They moved on to new conversational territory, and finished their dinner discussing the local theater scene.

The waiter brought their fortune cookies and they broke into them.

"When opportunity knocks, you will answer," read Wallis.

"I hope that doesn't mean you're going to leave me to go produce Doctor Joy," said Kate.

"I like your giveaways better. What's your fortune say?"

Kate opened her slip of paper. "A new adventure awaits you," she read.

"Oooh, I wonder what that could mean," said Wallis.

"Don't go there," warned Kate, "or I'll take your doggie bag."

IT WAS A THURSDAY, WHICH MEANT TONIGHT WAS a Sea Gals practice. That would not be the best time for Bambi to do what she had to do. She put in a call to Shari Johnson, the dance troop's director, and asked to meet her at the Seahawks headquarters.

That had been a dumb idea, too, Bambi decided as she pulled up into the parking lot of the team's headquarters in Kirkland. She walked into the lobby, decorated in the blue and green Seahawks colors, and already felt homesick.

She was just about to ask if Shari had arrived, when Shari herself appeared.

The two women shared a brief hug, then Shari said, "I don't think anyone's using the press room. We can talk in there."

Bambi nodded and followed her across the lobby.

On Wednesdays, the two long tables in this room were filled with plates of food, and the blue chairs housed TV and newspaper people, all come to have lunch with the coach and get the latest breaking Seahawks news for the fans. Today, the room was empty and lackluster.

As Bambi took a seat opposite Shari at one of the tables, she thought about how much she'd miss this woman. Slim and tan, with blonde hair and perfect features, Shari had been a Sea Gal for years before she got promoted to choreographer. She was kind and fair, and all the girls loved her. Right now, she looked concerned.

"What's the matter, Bambi?"

"I have to quit," Bambi blurted.

"Quit?" Shari looked shocked. "We just had our retreat last month, just took the picture for this year's poster. What's happened?"

"Don Bullman."

Shari sat back in her seat and crossed her legs. "I see," she said slowly. "When did this happen?"

Bambi pressed her lips together, hoping for an eleventh hour ability to organize her thoughts so they would make perfect sense.

It never came, so she took a deep breath and jumped in. "I know we're not supposed to date the players," she said in a rush, "and I wasn't dating him, at least not at first. I just ran into him at a movie. And then I ran into him again, and . . ."

"Again," finished Shari. "And now you want to keep running into him for the rest of your life."

Bambi nodded. "I think I love him."

Shari sighed. "Well, you're right. If you want to date Don, you'll have to quit. It's policy and there's nothing I can do about it." She leaned forward and laid a hand on Bambi's arm. "Are you sure you want to do this?"

Bambi loved to dance. She loved being a Sea Gal, enjoyed the camaraderie with the girls and the attention of the fans. She enjoyed all the special appearances and the charitable work, too. But she could find other places to dance, and she could still have her career in fitness. And she could do charitable work no matter what her profession. What she couldn't do was find another man as right for her as Don.

She nodded. "Yes."

"All right," said Shari. "We'll miss you terribly."

"I know. I'll miss all of you, too," said Bambi.

"And if it doesn't work out with Don, you can always try out again."

Bambi remembered the way she had felt the night of the Fourth when Don kissed her. "I probably won't be back."

S ATURDAY MORNING KATE OPENED HER MORNING paper to find a very flattering picture of herself under the headline SEATTLE SHRINK KNOWS HOW TO SEPARATE THE MEN FROM THE BOYS.

So much for her words to the wise. But the title was cute. She took the paper and her morning coffee out onto the porch.

Dr. Kate Stonewall, who first made a splash with her book, The Frog with the Glass Slipper, *will be signing her latest offering,* How to Separate the Men from the Boys, *at several local bookstores this month, starting today at the downtown Seattle Barnes and Noble bookstore at one* P.M. *The good doctor, who dishes out advice to the lovelorn . . .*

Kate scowled. Advice to the lovelorn? She thought she had made it perfectly clear to that nincompoop reporter that she wasn't the Dear Abby of the airwaves. She dealt with serious family issues on her program.

. . . at Seattle's local talk radio station, KZOO. *Doctor Kate, a widow, promises romantic success to all women who follow their heads instead of their hearts into a relationship. This formula seems to have brought success to Stonewall, whose show has risen in popularity in the last year, and who recently signed a syndication deal with Premiere Radio Networks.*

"Formula!" Kate tossed aside the paper in disgust.

"Hey," called a familiar voice. "Is that any way to treat good publicity?"

Kate turned her scowl on Jeff as he plunked himself onto her steps. He was wearing a white undershirt that had been worn nearly to the point of transparency, and some ragged cutoffs. In spite of his scruffy dress, he looked freshly scrubbed and attractive. Unbidden, the memory of their kiss on the dock paid her a visit.

The unwanted company made her even more cranky. "That is not my idea of good publicity. Advice to the lovelorn? Formula?"

"The average person will read that and be impressed," said Jeff. "And the picture is great. You should get lots of people turning up at your book signing, thanks to that article."

"I suppose," said Kate. "It just irks me when I see what I do being trivialized."

"You know you help people. The people you help know it. That's what counts."

Kate gave him a reluctant smile. "I guess you're right."

His eyebrows shot up. "Really? I must go home and write that in my diary."

"Oh, stop."

He chuckled. "By the way, I won't be able to make it to your signing. I've already learned how to separate the men from the boys. Anyway, I have to be at the Milk Carton Derby."

"I'm crushed to hear that," said Kate.

"I knew you would be. Want to meet up for dinner later?"

He never gave up. "No."

He shrugged. "Your loss. I was gonna pay."

Kate just smiled and shook her head.

He stood up and stretched a kink out of his back, and Kate watched the movements of his shoulder muscles under his worn T-shirt and wondered idly how they would feel under her fingers. "Well, good luck."

"Thanks," said Kate.

She watched Jeff make his way back to his side of the property line and wondered if, pretty soon, there would be a path worn in the grass. Jeff Hardin was getting entirely too comfortable with just dropping in on her any old time. She was going to have to talk to him about that. They could just as easily be neighborly waving at each other from a distance. And with the way he was distracting her these days, distance was what she needed. Thank God he wouldn't be at the book signing.

K ATE DRESSED IN A WHITE LINEN SUIT AND CLIPPED up her hair. Looking in the mirror, she was pleased with what she saw. The suit, which she had found on a shopping spree at Nordstrom after work the day before, fit beautifully. And putting her hair up made her look very together and professional—just the look she wanted for her appearance. She transferred all her belongings to her new purse, grabbed the shopping bag of "No Frogs" T-shirts, then went to her car.

Was it her imagination, or was the thing running a little sluggishly? Hopefully, it was her imagination. Maybe she'd just trade Andy straight across for that Toyota he'd loaned her last time. Even though the Toyota was ten years older, she'd come out ahead on the deal. Her lemon was a money pit on wheels.

She forgot her car miseries when she arrived at the bookstore to find a good two dozen people already lined up in front of the table where she would be signing her books.

The stream of fans was steady, and at three o'clock, Kate was still signing. Finally, the line began to shorten, and the stream turned to a dribble. Which made it easy to notice the man in the slacks and polo shirt and sports jacket, who stepped up to the corner of the table and picked up a book.

He was tall and well built. His face was square chinned,

with perfect, even features, and dark hair just beginning to
be salted with gray. His skin was tanned, and fine lines
made tracks along the corners of deep blue eyes. She
guessed him to be somewhere in his early forties. He
glanced up and smiled at her, revealing perfect white teeth,
and she felt almost giddy.

She smiled back, and then returned her attention to the
fan standing in front of her. But not before checking the
new arrival's left-hand ring finger. No band of gold proclaimed him taken, and no band of white skin proclaimed
him a cheater. So far, so good.

He took his place in back of the woman now gushing at
Kate, and she found she could hardly concentrate on what
the woman was saying. She scribbled a quick hieroglyphic
inside the woman's book, handed it over, and smiled as the
stranger stepped up to the table. She hoped some of her lipstick was still on.

"Doctor Kate, it's a pleasure to meet you," said the man.

"Thank you," said Kate sweetly.

"I'm a fairly new Seattle resident, and I only recently
discovered your program."

"Oh? Where are you from?" she asked.

"Most recently? New York. My sister still lives there."
He handed over the book. "I think she could use this.
Would you mind autographing it for her?"

"Not at all," said Kate.

"Her name is Anne."

Kate scrawled out an inscription and handed over the
book. Their fingers brushed in the process and she felt an
electric charge shoot through her.

"You seem to have a good handle on human relations,"
said the man. "I like your logical approach to dating."

"So, you're a logical sort of man?" Kate hadn't meant
for her tone of voice to sound so flirty. Where had that
come from?

"I am now. I rushed into marriage fifteen years ago, and
it was the biggest mistake I ever made. I'm not in any

hurry now. I'll wait forever for Miss Right rather than make another mistake."

Kate nodded. "A good idea," she said approvingly. "So, how are you liking Seattle?"

"It's not as friendly a city as I'd heard," said her new friend.

"It certainly can't be as impersonal as New York," protested Kate. And someone so handsome surely had women falling all over themselves to make him feel at home.

"Oh, I'm sure I won't feel that way in another month or so. I'm probably just suffering from the new-city blues." He held out his hand. "My name's Grayson White, by the way."

Kate took it and, again, experienced that jolt. "It's nice to meet you."

Another fan came up and Grayson White stepped aside so she could talk to Kate. Kate was happy to see he didn't leave.

Once the fan had left, he motioned to the café section of the store. "I'd love to buy you a cup of coffee when you're done, if you've got the time."

"I think I can spare half an hour," said Kate. *Or the whole night, for that matter.* "Let me just sign this pile of books and I'll meet you."

He nodded and moved off, walking with an easy grace. Handsome, polite, intelligent, and, it appeared, single. Kate signed the books with record speed.

Ten minutes later, she sat opposite Grayson White, sharing life stories. She learned he was originally from L.A. and that he was a software/technology expert who worked as a business consultant. He had already purchased season tickets to the Seattle Repertory Theater and the 5th Avenue Theater, and was anxious to visit the Seattle Art Museum.

"No Seahawks tickets?" she teased.

He looked pained. "I'm not into Neanderthal sports."

"So, you're not a sports nut?"

"Let's just say I'm selective in my insanity. I do like tennis, and I manage to get in a game once a week. And, I have to confess, I've even gone to Wimbledon a couple of times."

Tennis. Wimbledon. The man was civilized.

Before she quite knew how it had happened they had exchanged business cards, and Kate found she had a date to meet him at the Seattle Art Museum after her second book signing on the following Saturday.

She drove onto the ferry, still wearing a triumphant smile. Everyone had laughed at her, encouraged her to settle for less, told her she would never find Mr. Right.

They had been partially correct. She hadn't found him. He had found her.

Twelve

"OKAY, YOU DON'T GET TO WEAR THAT SMUG look anymore unless you tell me what's behind it," said Wallis.

"After seeing almost sixty books walk out the door wearing my signature on Saturday, why shouldn't I look smug?" retorted Kate.

"I figured you'd move more than that, and so did you. Now, the real reason, please."

"I'm just in a good mood. I had fun and met some interesting people."

Wallis's eyes narrowed to an inquisitive squint. "Did one of them have a low voice and wear pants with a fly?"

"Well, I did happen to meet a man who's fairly new to the area."

"Ah-ha! I knew it. And?"

Kate assumed a casual attitude, picking up a pile of e-mail printouts and pretending to scan them. "And we're going to S.A.M. this Saturday after my morning book signing at the University Bookstore."

"KZOO's resident frog is going to be heartbroken. Give me the details," Wallis demanded.

Kate was happy to oblige. "And, amazingly enough, he's not a sports nut," she finished.

"He sounds like a perfect match," said Wallis.

"He looks promising," said Kate. "But promise is one thing, reality is another. I'm not holding my breath."

S HE MADE THE WORDS HER MANTRA ALL WEEK, but when she met Grayson White in front of the Seattle Art Museum's gigantic *Hammering Man,* she forgot them.

He took in her white linen pants and navy blazer and said, "You know, the picture in your book doesn't do you justice."

Kate detested flattery, which was manipulative. But judging from the appreciative look on Grayson's face, this was a sincere compliment, another thing altogether.

She would accept it as such. "Thanks."

"I'm glad you could join me," he said as they walked into the museum. "Did your book signing go well?"

Kate felt pleased by his interest. "Yes, it did. Thanks for asking."

"Fortunate for me that you had to come into the city," said Grayson.

"I'd have met you anyway," Kate assured him. "I enjoy visiting the museum."

He was quick to step in front of her to pay their admission. "I'm glad. Great art is good company, but I happen to be one of those people who enjoys it even more when I have a friend along to discuss it with."

"I'm not sure one cup of coffee qualifies me as a friend," said Kate.

"Perhaps not, but by the time we're done visiting the exhibits I hope we will be," said Grayson. "I read they've reinstalled the European galleries. Care to see Strozzi's *Hagar and the Angel*?"

"That sounds like a great place to start," said Kate.

They strolled through the European galleries, admiring the work of both Strozzi and Van Dyck as well as some lovely Renaissance bronzes and Italian terra-cottas.

By the time they had finished with the gallery where the Eastman Johnson paintings were displayed, Kate realized that Grayson was right. They were going to be good friends. Maybe more.

"Are you in a hurry to get home?" he asked as they left the museum.

"No. My children are visiting their grandparents in San Diego, so I'm footloose and fancy-free."

"Great. I found a café just a little north of Pioneer Square. We can grab something to eat and enjoy the sunshine. If you like, we can take my car, then I'll bring you back to get yours later."

It sounded like a good idea to Kate.

Grayson ushered her into a black BMW with luxurious leather seats. Unlike a certain car bound for the scrap heap, its engine purred.

"Music?" he asked.

"Sure," said Kate, and was surprised that he chose a soft rock station. "I figured you for a classical music kind of man."

"I'm a rock and roll guy. And I love to dance." He shot her a look and a smile. "Do you like to dance?"

"I do." The memory of herself gyrating with Jeff at the island street dance put a smile on her face. Actually, it was simply the memory of dancing that made her smile. Jeff had nothing to do with it.

"How would you feel about going dancing?" asked Grayson. "Or am I moving too fast?"

"I have another week and a half of freedom. I ought to take advantage of it," said Kate.

"I agree," said Grayson.

"And since this freedom is getting to me, I'd appreciate the distraction."

"Good kids, huh?"

"Oh, yes."

"So, tell me about them."

Showing an interest in her children: that scored Grayson White some more points. And Kate was happy to oblige.

"They sound wonderful," he said when she'd finished. "I always wanted children. Unfortunately, my wife decided she didn't. It was the main reason we split."

Kate sighed. "That's sad. Wasn't it something you discussed before you married?"

"Actually, it was. We decided to wait a couple of years before starting a family, though. And during those two years she got so attached to her great job and all the travel and perks that went with it that she decided she didn't want to risk losing it by taking time off to have a baby. She was sure that a child would change everything. I couldn't convince her she could do both."

"It's hard to do both," said Kate. "Maybe she realized that."

"It looks like you're managing."

"I am, but I'm a single parent. I have to."

"That has to be difficult," agreed Grayson. "The stress of paying bills, saving for your children's college education."

"Oh, I've got a good start on that," said Kate.

He nodded. "Smart woman. Have you got a good financial advisor?"

"Yes, me."

"You don't think being your own financial advisor is a lot like being your own lawyer?"

"I've done all right managing my own money so far," said Kate. Although she knew her dad might not agree. "Most of my investments have paid off well, and, in spite of my leaky house and a car that's trying to drain my savings, I'm doing okay."

"I hope you've invested in technology," said Grayson. "I've got stock in one company that's about to split."

"I have a couple of things. If my dad had his way I would be investing only in blue chip."

"He's a different generation," said Grayson. "These days it's important to diversify."

"So, do you have a financial advisor?"

He nodded. "You bet. But the professional who helps me the most is my sister. She's a stockbroker, and she's given me some very good tips in the past."

"Insider trading?"

"No, no. Nothing illegal," Grayson assured her. "But Anne has gotten me in on the ground floor of some great businesses."

"So, you have your sister to thank for this very nice car?" teased Kate.

"Partly," he agreed.

A man who wasn't too proud to give credit where credit was due. Chalk up another star for Grayson.

Dinner was long and leisurely, and after he returned Kate to pick up her car they stood talking in the parking lot for another half hour.

"I'd better let you go," he said at last.

She nodded, feeling reluctant to leave, and opened her car door.

His hand on her arm stopped her from getting in. "So, getting back to dancing. Will you go with me on Friday?"

"I'd love to."

"Good." He still had her arm and he moved her toward him. "Thanks for giving me so much of your time."

"Thanks for making it go so quickly," she said.

He leaned down and kissed her. It was a soft kiss, unthreatening and undemanding. He released her and rubbed her arm with his hand. "I don't normally move this fast, but it's a long time until Friday. Would it be pushing to suggest dinner on Wednesday?"

"Yes," said Kate.

He looked crestfallen, but immediately covered it up with a polite smile and nod.

He was about to say something, but Kate hurried to add, "But I don't mind pushing things a little since I'm free."

"Great," he said. "I'll call you." He made no effort to kiss her again. Instead, he let her get in her car, then politely shut the door for her. "Thanks again, Kate. I had a great time."

"Me, too," she said.

She managed to appear her normal efficient, in-control self until she got out of sight, but by the time she hit Coleman Dock she was singing with the radio at the top of her lungs.

She missed the seven–forty-five ferry by ten cars, but what did she care? She had plenty to think about while she waited.

JEFF'S PARTY WAS IN FULL SWING, HIS HOUSE ROCKing with his buddies and their girlfriends and their girlfriends' girlfriends. They had all spent the afternoon water-skiing, then fired up the barbecue and slapped on the steaks. They'd washed those steaks down with beer and wine coolers. And with each new raid on the ice chest the noise level escalated another notch.

Now Jeff stood talking to a cute little brunette in a bikini and sneaking surreptitious looks at Kate's house. It was nine o'clock and she wasn't home yet. And her appearance had been scheduled for eleven A.M. Even if she'd spent the day shopping she should have been home before this.

He took another slug of Bud and wondered if something had happened to her. Which was dumb, because what could have happened to her at a book signing for crying out loud?

Maybe some cuckoo had fallen out of the nest and come after her with a gun to make her pay for giving him bad advice. Maybe her car had broken down again. If her car crapped out on the island she called Andy. But who did she call in the city? Did she have Triple A?

"I loved watching you slalom," purred the brunette. "Will you teach me sometime?"

"Sure," said Jeff. From over her shoulder, he thought he caught a glimpse of Kate's car coming down her drive. He interrupted the brunette midsentence. "Excuse me. I've gotta . . . check something."

Jeff hurried away without waiting for an answer. He got to the back of his house in time to see Kate climbing out of her car.

"Hi," he called.

"Hi."

"Just getting back?" Duh. Of course she was. *Way to sound like a genius, Hardin.*

"Yes," said Kate. "It's been a long day."

And she hadn't spent it all signing books. "How'd your signing go?"

"Oh, fine," she replied airily, and headed toward her back door.

"Want to come over and tell me about it?"

"It looks like you're a little busy," she replied, nodding in the direction of his house. Someone had cranked up his CD player and the bass was now thumping like a gigantic heartbeat.

"Join the party. We've got plenty of food."

She shook her head. "No, thanks. I'm a little tired."

Who had she been with that had gotten her so tired? Jeff forced a smile. "Okay. Good night."

"Good night," she said. Now she was on her back porch.

"Kate," he called.

"Yes?" She sounded just a little like the old patience battery was wearing down.

"I'll make sure we turn the noise down by eleven."

"Thanks." Sweetness softened the sharp edge of her

voice, and he smiled. He wished he could have talked her into coming over. The kids were gone. She didn't need to turn into a hermit, not on a Saturday night.

He took another slug of beer and wandered back to his party, wondering again who Kate had been out with. Probably Wallis.

Not a guy. Couldn't be. Outside of her kids and him, Kate had no life. She couldn't have found somebody in just one day.

But what about last week? She could have met someone then.

Jeff's mind instantly rejected that suggestion. It absolutely couldn't be. What man in his right mind would want to buy one of her books?

He had to know for sure. He'd catch her the next day and give her a subtle third degree.

But he struck out the next day, too. By the time he got rid of the horde that had decided to spend the night, Kate was no longer home. Well, no matter. He had his spies. He'd find out if a man had surfaced in her life.

AFTER WORK MONDAY, KATE HEADED FOR NORDstrom to find a new outfit to complement her new life. She had just crossed the street when she heard someone calling her name. She turned and saw Bambi running up to her.

"Doctor Kate, how are you?" With her enthusiastic smile, Bambi could have just won the lottery.

"There's no need to ask how you are," said Kate. "You look great."

"I am," gushed Bambi. "And it's all because I read your book."

That was not surprising to hear. Kate tried to look modest.

"I've found my prince," Bambi announced.

"You're sure this one's a match?"

"Oh, I'm sure," said Bambi, nodding.

"So, where did you meet him?"

"Actually, I already knew him. It's Don Bullman."

Bambi dropped Prince Charming's name like it should be on the tongue of every woman in America, but it certainly wasn't ringing any bells with Kate. "Should I know who that is?"

"He's a fullback for the Seahawks."

Bambi had dumped Jeff, who had some brains, for a football-toting Neanderthal with none? Kate felt as if the wisdom in her book had been wasted, her pearls scattered before swine and trampled.

"He's the most sensitive man I've ever known," sighed Bambi, causing Kate to raise a questioning eyebrow. "No, really, he is. You know that movie about the doctor who falls in love with the woman who had chemo?"

"I've been meaning to see that. It sounds great.

"It is," said Bambi. "And that's where I met Don."

Kate blinked. "You met this man at that movie?"

Bambi nodded eagerly. "We wound up sitting together, and we went out for coffee afterward, and, well, we've been together ever since. He's just the most amazing guy. We talk about everything. It's so different than it was with Jeff."

Kate didn't think it was all that difficult to get Jeff to talk, but she kept the thought to herself.

A troubled expression now surfaced to cloud Bambi's earlier radiance. "Um, how is Jeff?"

"There's no need to feel guilty," said Kate. "He's fine."

The smile popped out again. "Oh, good. I don't want him to be miserable. He's probably figured out we weren't really right for each other by now." Suddenly shy, she added, "Actually, he and you seemed to hit it off real well."

Kate shook her head vehemently. "Oh, no. I'm not the right woman for Jeff."

"I don't know," said Bambi. "He's smart and so are you."

"That's a good combination for the gene pool," agreed Kate, "but we both know it takes a lot more than that for two people to be right for each other."

Bambi's nod seemed reluctant. "Well, yeah. And I guess you'd know. You're the expert. But there sure seemed to be something between you two that he and I just didn't have."

"Well, there wasn't," said Kate crisply.

Put in her place, Bambi nodded and looked embarrassed. "I guess I'd better be going."

"Me, too," said Kate. "And Bambi, I'm really happy for you."

"Thanks," said Bambi, still subdued, then hurried away.

Kate shook her head as she headed inside the department store to lay money at the feet of the fashion gods. She and Jeff Hardin a match. Oh, puh-leeze.

"GUESS WHO I SAW TODAY?" KATE SAID TO GRACE as they settled on her kid-stained couch to watch a video.

"Elvis?"

"Better. Bambi."

"Really? I always thought that girl was sweet. How's she doing?"

"Great. She says she's found her prince."

"She sure crashed the ball in a hurry."

Kate shrugged. "She claims he meets all the qualifications."

"Well, I've always heard you know when it's right."

"Maybe there's some truth in that," acknowledged Kate.

"Wait a minute. This isn't the Kate I know talking," said Grace. "What's making you sing a new tune?"

"I'm not singing a new tune," said Kate quickly. "I'm still all for being practical and following Santa's example: you make a list and you check it twice. But you could still have that feeling."

"You know this from practical experience?"

Kate tried to look mysterious. "Maybe."

"Okay, spill."

Kate spilled.

"My gosh, he sounds fabulous," said Grace when Kate had finally wound to a stop.

"He is," said Kate with a sigh. "He's like a dream come true. Of course, that doesn't mean I'm not going to take my time and make sure we're really a match. But, I've got to admit, it looks good."

Grace set aside her bowl of popcorn and leaned forward. "So, has he kissed you yet?"

Kate shut her eyes and relived Grayson's kiss. "Ummm."

"That good, huh? And he didn't turn into a frog."

"No warts, no ribbits."

"No kidding. I'm jealous."

Kate opened her eyes. "What, nothing going with Sandy yet?"

Grace's face turned pink. "He's coming over for lunch tomorrow."

"Well, well. It looks like we've all been ordering glass slippers," said Kate.

"Start the movie, already," ordered Grace.

"SHE'S MET SOMEONE?" JEFF SUDDENLY LOST HIS appetite. He pushed away his plate with his half-eaten roast beef sandwich.

"Hey, buck up," said his dad. "You haven't lost the war, just the first battle."

"I don't know," said Grace, pouring iced tea. "This Grayson White sounds pretty incredible."

"Maybe she wasn't the right one for you, anyway," said Sandy.

"She was. Hell, listen to me. I'm talking like I've already lost her."

"You never really had her," pointed out Sandy.

"Whose side are you on here?" demanded Jeff, his voice rising.

"Yours, of course," said his dad calmly. "And I want you to find a woman who appreciates you, like your mom did me. Find somebody sweet, like Bambi. Why do you want to go chasing a woman who doesn't want you?"

"She does want me," insisted Jeff.

Grace raised an eyebrow and Sandy outright guffawed.

"Well, she does. She just doesn't know it yet."

"I hope she finds out before it's too late," said Grace.

"Yeah. Me, too." Jeff checked his watch. "I'd better get going or I'll miss my ferry. Thanks for the lunch, Grace."

"Have a good one," said Sandy, and neither of them paid much attention as Jeff let himself out the kitchen door.

He left Grace and Sandy to enjoy each other and forget completely about his misery, and spent his ferry commute planning his strategy against his new enemy. This Grayson guy must have a gigantic amount of charm, for Kate to be so smitten. But he also had to have an Achilles' heel. Jeff just needed to find it. And meanwhile, he'd keep on being his usual nice self and do things to show Kate what a superior man he was. This Grayson White might have scored some points in the first quarter, but the game was still far from over.

K ATE WORKED FOR ANOTHER THREE HOURS AFTER her program Wednesday, then slipped into the ladies' room and changed into her new periwinkle blue dress with the scoop neck. She accessorized it with a gold chain and gold ball earrings and some strappy white sandals she'd found on sale at Bon Marche, a department store she loved nearly as much as Nordstrom.

Jeff was already on the air so she didn't have to worry about encountering him and having to endure his comments on her new dress or put up with a nosy interrogation over where she was going. Not that she'd been worried about encountering him, anyway. She would have simply thanked him for his compliment and told him her social life was none of his business.

The corner of her brain responsible for perverse behavior wondered what he'd say if he saw her this dolled up and suggested she wander back in the direction of the air studio just to see. Naturally, she ignored it. She didn't need Jeff Hardin to tell her she looked good. She knew she did.

The emotional lift she got at seeing her slowly slimming body in her hot, new dress was nothing compared to the rocket ride she took when she saw the light in Grayson's eyes as she entered the station lobby.

He quickly rose from his chair, looking freshly pressed and Cary Grantish in his gray suit, and came to meet her.

"How do you do it?" he asked.

"Do what?"

"Look better every time I see you."

"Oh, please."

"I mean it," said Grayson. "You look incredible."

She did look good, but with the pounds she still had to lose, incredible might be a slight exaggeration. Still, it would be rude to argue, so she thanked Grayson and let him escort her to his car.

He took her to Stuart Anderson's on the locks. A window seat, naturally. Vintage wine with dinner, of course.

"So, tell me. What led you to become a psychologist?" he asked over coffee and cheesecake. (She'd get back on the diet treadmill tomorrow.)

Kate shrugged. "I thought it would help me to make sense of my own life and the mistakes I'd made."

"You seem too together to make mistakes," observed Grayson.

"I wasn't when I got married."

Kate blinked. Where had that come from? The wine bottle, obviously. She certainly hadn't intended to make such a personal confession, at least not on their second date.

"It's easy to be fooled when you're young," said Grayson. "But you're older now, wiser."

"Yes, I am. I won't rush into anything."

He nodded. "I understand. You have to be careful, not only for your own sake, but for your children's as well."

Grayson White was no fool. "Exactly," said Kate, pleased that he understood.

"I feel the same way," he said. "I don't want to make my life or anyone else's miserable. I want something lasting, and I'm willing to wait until I find the perfect woman."

Here, indeed, was a sensible man. Kate could hardly believe her good luck in finding him.

"What is your perfect woman?" she asked.

He didn't hurry to answer. He remained thoughtful a moment, then took a sip of coffee. Kate ruthlessly curbed her impatience as she waited.

At last he said, "For me, the perfect woman would be, well, obviously, someone who enjoys the same activities I do. But she has to be more than that. I want someone who's intelligent and willing to think for herself, and who's brave enough to tell me when I'm wrong. I want someone who will believe me when I say I'm sorry, and someone who will let me spoil her with presents and not worry that I've spent too much. I've got the money and I like to spend it on people I care about."

"I can't believe you've had trouble finding that woman," scoffed Kate.

"You can't? And you call yourself an expert on the human mind? I've been looking, Kate, believe me. Until now, I'd just about given up hope that such a woman exists."

Kate set down her coffee cup and smiled at him. "I know the feeling."

"Now it's your turn," said Grayson. "Tell me about your Mr. Perfect."

"Well, like your perfect woman, he needs to be someone who enjoys what I enjoy. And I don't want a sports nut. I hate baseball and basketball and football."

"And tennis?"

Kate smiled. "I can put up with that, as long as it's not an addiction."

"So, you wouldn't be averse to going to Wimbledon?"

"Not if I was rewarded with a play in London."

Grayson chuckled. "Okay, what else?"

"I want someone who's smart and kind, someone who's not threatened by my success. And you don't know how hard that is to find."

"I think I do. Most men are threatened by other people's success, no matter what their sex."

"How about you, Grayson? Do I threaten you?"

He reached across the table and took her hand, sending a shock wave clear down to her toes. "What do you think?"

She thought she was falling in love, that was what she thought.

Grayson parked his car and rode the ferry with her. They let all the other foot passengers disembark first, giving them an excuse to linger in a dark corner of the passenger deck. At last Grayson gave Kate a good-bye kiss that made her want to stay on and ride back to Seattle with him.

"Thanks for a great evening," he murmured.

"My pleasure," said Kate.

Pleasure was probably an understatement. Thrill came closer. She was humming like a power line as she made her way to the ferry parking lot. This was, without a doubt, the most right man she had ever met in her entire life. At last, here it was, her grand finale, her reward for her disappointing life with Rob, for the loneliness and struggle she'd endured as a widow.

It's early, she warned herself. *You don't know him well enough to be sure.*

True enough. She'd go slowly. There was no hurry.

Three days until Friday. How would she ever be able to wait?

Thirteen

"SO, WHEN I REFUSED TO PAY HER CHARGE CARD bill, she got mad, told me I was a selfish jerk, and left," said Fred.

Poor man. Kate sighed inwardly. "How soon into the relationship were you sexual, Fred?"

"Well, um, fairly soon."

"And how soon is that?" persisted Kate.

"The third date," confessed Fred, sounding sheepish.

"You didn't waste any time, did you?"

Fred gave an embarrassed half-laugh. "No, I guess we didn't."

"Well, Fred, I don't think she's coming back. And, let me tell you, that's not a bad thing. You established a gold digger–sugar daddy relationship right from the start with all the presents you bought her, and that was how she wanted to continue. When you tried to equalize the relationship, she split. If I were you, I'd change the locks and try again."

"Yeah," said Fred reluctantly. "I thought that was what you'd say."

"You thought right," said Kate. "And you sound like a nice guy. Go find someone who will appreciate you for who you are, not what she can get out of you."

"Okay, Doctor Kate."

"And, Fred."

"Yes?"

"I know you're biologically programmed to get out there and make as many little Freds as you can, but how about going a little slower next time?"

"Yeah, you've got a point there," agreed Fred.

"Keep it zipped. You promise?"

"I promise."

Kate said good-bye to Fred and climbed up on her soapbox. "People, I know biology is a strong force, but let's go easy when looking for that Ms. or Mr. Right. It's easy to mistake physical attraction for intimacy, but they're not the same. And you don't want to make sexual intimacy the first level you hit of a relationship. Make sure you're compatible on a social and intellectual level first. Then make sure your values line up. If you interact well, share common interests and values, chances are things will line up just fine in the bedroom. Get the order reversed, and eventually, even the bedroom won't work for you."

Kate took the next call, which was almost as bad as the last. "Let me get this straight," she said after her caller had shared her sad story. "Half your wedding guests left the reception to go watch a sporting event on the TV in the hotel lobby, and you're wondering whether you were wrong to have been upset? My God, Linda. I wasn't even there and I'm upset for you!"

"It *was* a championship game," said Linda, trying to be generous.

Kate sighed. "I understand you're trying to be tolerant, and we both know that sports take precedence over every other human activity these days. But that kind of behavior is just plain rude. Were these people friends? I mean, you didn't just pull them in off the street, did you?"

"They were friends," said Linda, sounding ashamed over her poor taste in people.

"Well, you have my blessing to keep right on referring to those particular friends in the past tense and start looking for some new ones who are a little less selfish and a little better mannered."

"Thanks, Doctor Kate," said her caller, sounding relieved.

Kate looked to the op board and saw Jeff had arrived on the scene and was yucking it up with George.

If that wasn't typical of Jeff Hardin! He probably thought poor Linda's problem was hilarious. She could easily imagine the Frog Prince being one of the first guests to sneak away from a reception to rivet himself in front of a TV and watch grown men playing some infantile game.

She reined her thoughts back to the task at hand and took one last call. She finished with the caller and George managed to tear himself away from encouraging Jeff in his mockery long enough to start the bumper music.

"It looks like that's it for today, everyone," she said, keeping her voice pleasant in spite of the anger sizzling in her blood, "but we'll meet tomorrow for more life strategies. Until then, remember, we don't get to go back to start, so let's make the right moves along the way."

"Good show," Jeff said to her when she came out.

"I assume you heard that second-to-last call," she said stiffly.

"I did," he replied, donning a scandalized expression. "And I was shocked."

"Sneaking away from a wedding reception to watch a game is, of course, nothing you would ever do."

"You've got that right. They don't serve food in hotel lobbies."

George guffawed and Kate headed for the door, murmuring, "I wonder how many of those wedding guests were *Jock Talk* listeners."

"Probably not even one. My listeners have better man-

ners than that. And they don't have problems," he added,
making George chortle.

Kate did not dignify his remark with an answer. She just
waved good-bye to Frog Man and kept on walking. She
would never again drink wine coolers in Jeff Hardin's
presence, because sober she would never be so stupid as to
kiss the idiotic, irritating man.

J EFF SCOWLED AT KATE'S DISAPPEARING BACKSIDE.
"What put her in such a bad mood, anyway?"

"Do you need three guesses?" replied Wallis.

"What did I do this time?"

"You'll have to ask her," said Wallis.

"I think I will," said Jeff, irritated.

The next morning he paid Doctor Pill a visit. She was
out watering her roses, dressed in a T-shirt and some
shorts.

He couldn't help smiling as he noted that her choice in
tops was running to a more form-fitting style now that
she'd lost some weight. And she'd painted her toenails
pink. She had cute feet, an intriguing contrast to his size
eleven and a half clodhoppers.

She was humming to herself and didn't hear him approach. He ducked behind her and tapped her on the shoulder. "Hi."

Startled, Kate dropped her hose and it began to writhe,
squirting water at both of them.

Jeff pounced on the plastic water snake and handed it
over to a disgusted-looking Kate, saying, "Sorry. I didn't
mean to startle you."

"I'm sure you figured the eyes in the back of my head
would see you coming."

That snotty tone of voice she liked to use didn't even irritate him anymore. It was just her way of keeping a level
playing field.

"I hear all you mothers have them," he replied.

She sighed deeply. "Did you want something?"

Now, how to find out what last night's skirmish was about without escalating the conversation into a war. Jeff rubbed the back of his neck, looking for just the right words.

"Did you want to tell me about it before I have to leave for the station?" prompted Kate.

"Funny you should mention the station. That's what I came to talk to you about. Was it just my imagination, or were you ticked at me when you came out of the air studio yesterday?"

Now it was Kate's turn to be silent. She stood for a long moment, watching the hose rain on her roses. She was probably gathering up the big artillery for the upcoming verbal battle.

"Go ahead, let me have it," he said. "I know you will anyway."

"Since you asked, yes, I was mad."

"Why?"

Her eyebrows shot up. "I had a caller who had been very hurt by other people's behavior, someone who had a genuine concern, and you were out there laughing about it with George, and you have to ask me why I was mad?"

"Laughing about? Whoa. Let's back this pony up. I wasn't laughing with George about that. I was just trying out a joke on him that I was going to use on my show. Geez, Kate. Didn't they teach you in shrink school not to jump to conclusions about people?"

Her mouth dropped as if she couldn't quite believe she'd been wrong. "I guess I was absent that day. Gosh, I'm sorry."

"Well, you should be," said Jeff, full of righteous indignation. "I wish you'd spend as much time getting to know me as you do pigeonholing me."

She hung her head and pushed at a pebble with a pink-toed foot. "You're right," she said humbly. Then she looked up into his face with a sweet expression that made him want to grab her and kiss her. "I'm so embarrassed. And I'm sorry. Please forgive me."

"I just want you to give me the benefit of the doubt once in a while," said Jeff. "Do you think you can do that?"

She nodded. "I can try."

"Good, then prove it and go out with me."

She looked wary. "I don't think that's a good idea."

Jeff held up his hands. "No passes, I promise."

She started to shake her head.

"Don't you think after being so snotty to me that you at least owe me a date?"

"No. I owed you an apology, which I gave you."

"Sometimes an apology's not enough."

"Are you trying to manipulate me?" she challenged.

Jeff stood his ground. "Nope. Just trying to get you to lose your prejudice."

"I am *not* prejudiced."

"Okay, scarred for life. Just say yes, Kate."

"Oh, all right," she said grudgingly. "But I'm not going to any sporting event with you. That would be like getting the death penalty for shoplifting."

"I think I can manage to think of something you'll like," said Jeff. "How about tomorrow?"

"Tomorrow night?" She looked like a pirate who had just been ordered to share his plunder.

What, Jeff wondered, did she have going on Saturday night? "Actually, what I have in mind we can do during the day," he said.

"Okay, but not too early. I have plans for tonight and I want to be able to sleep in."

"Eleven then, and don't eat breakfast."

"All right."

Jeff said good-bye and returned to his side of the property line feeling like he had accomplished something.

Until he remembered her comment about having plans for the evening and her reluctance to commit her Saturday night. The specter of the other man rose in front of him: a stud in a three-piece suit with an Eastern Seaboard accent and money sprouting out of his pockets like weeds, who would lure her to his house full of expensive art and seduce her with vintage champagne.

Well, if this guy was better for her, then Jeff wouldn't stand in his way. He was a believer in the motto "May the best man win," and Kate deserved to be happy. But until he knew that his rival really was the best man for Kate, Jeff was staying in the game.

KATE BROUGHT HER DANCING CLOTHES TO WORK with her: a silk floral print dress with spaghetti straps, and white flats. She clipped up her hair to show off the pearl earrings her parents had given her for Christmas, and regarded herself in the restroom mirror. The lines of the dress were slimming, which was a good thing considering she'd had a couple of diet relapses. She'd probably have looked better if she'd worn heels. But her feet would have protested after half an hour, and anyway, it would be just her luck to turn an ankle dancing in them. She gave her makeup one final inspection and decided she looked pretty darned good. Hopefully, Grayson would think so, too.

He did. "That is quite a dress," he said as he escorted her out of the lobby. "In fact, you look even better than you did on Wednesday. How did you manage that?"

"Optical illusion," said Kate.

"I thought we'd try out one of those clubs in Pioneer Square," he said. "But first what do you say to dinner at one of the restaurants near my condo on the waterfront. If you want to, you can leave your car there and we'll taxi to Ivar's or that place on Pier Seventy."

The condos that stretched along the downtown Seattle waterfront were fairly new and extravagantly expensive; further proof that Grayson White had done very well in the world of business.

"That sounds like a good idea," she said, and wondered

if he would invite her to come see his place after they were done dancing.

The view from their window seat was as delicious as the restaurant's salmon, but it was Grayson's company that made the evening special.

Halfway through dinner their conversation turned to her program. He had caught part of the show when he was working at home on Thursday, and had been disgusted with the story of the guests who had abandoned the wedding reception in favor of a sports event on TV.

"That's pretty low," he said. "I think your advice to that caller was spot on. And I enjoyed your conversation with, oh, who was the sugar daddy? Fred."

"Oh, yes," said Kate. "Poor Fred."

"I think it was good for your listeners to hear that men can get used, too."

It was all Kate could do not to be tacky and ask him point-blank if he had been used. Handsome and rich as he was, he had to have any number of women chasing him.

"It pays to be cautious," he continued.

"Are you a cautious man?" asked Kate.

"I am now. I want someone who has the same value system I do."

His comment pleased Kate. And as they talked, she couldn't help but be impressed by how many things they agreed on. Like her, he felt that people should be more careful when choosing a mate.

"I learned the hard way that attraction isn't enough when you're choosing a life's companion."

Kate knew he was remembering his first wife, the woman who hadn't wanted to have a family with him.

"Are you thinking about what happened with your wife?" she asked gently.

He smiled at her and gave a little shrug. "Not anymore. Of course, she put me through hell, but things have a way of working out. Here I am, having dinner with a lovely, intelligent woman, so I can't complain."

Grayson's desire to make the best of whatever life handed him showed a good, positive attitude. She liked that.

Kate soon found she also liked how he held her when they danced. Close, but not the *Dirty Dancing* style preferred by a certain uncouth radio personality.

He smiled down at her. "Having fun?"

She nodded.

"Me, too," he said, and kissed her temple, making her stomach do a flip-flop.

There wasn't any kind of dancing Grayson couldn't handle. He did it all, from disco to salsa. Even the freestyle, shake your bon-bons kind of dancing that made so many men look like idiots was no problem for Grayson. When they weren't dancing, they were snuggled together at a table, flirting and laughing, him running his fingers along her forearm and driving her crazy.

A little after one, he suggested they go to his place for a nightcap.

She checked her watch and calculated the time. The last ferry to Bainbridge left at two-ten, and if she missed that she'd be stranded in Seattle. Maybe Wallis would take her in. If Wallis could hear her knocking past the earplugs and the white noise she kept going at night. On second thought, she'd make sure she caught the two-ten.

"I think I've got time for a quick cup of coffee," she said.

At his condo, Grayson took her sweater, then let her explore. It was spacious and airy with its cream-colored walls and wide-open floor plan. The floors were hardwood, covered with antique Persian rugs, and the modern oil painting hanging over his beige leather couch looked very expensive. Kate eyed his glass-top coffee table with envy. She would love to park something like that in her living room, but it would never survive life with Robbie.

An old Queen Anne desk sat in one corner, and on it a silver-framed picture of an attractive, dark-haired woman.

Kate went over to look at it. "She's very pretty. Who is she?"

"My sister, Anne. She's promised to come out and visit before the end of the year. I think you'll like her," he added as he headed for the kitchen.

Kate waited until he was done grinding coffee beans, then asked, "What's she like?"

"Smart, confident. A little opinionated, sometimes. She's also fun-loving, and one of the most generous people I know."

A man with family loyalties, that was good. "She sounds wonderful," said Kate. She wandered to the window and stared out at the water. "Your view is incredible."

"It is," he agreed. "And it will do until I can find a house I really like."

Houses. Kate suddenly realized she had neglected considering what the permanent addition of a man in her life would do to her living situation. That had been stupid, especially since Amanda and Robbie would be profoundly affected if said man didn't want to live on the island.

If that turned out to be the case there would be no man, then. She wasn't going to uproot her kids.

"What kind of house do you want?" she asked.

"Waterfront of some sort, but not in the city. And although the East Side would be convenient, it doesn't appeal to me. I've been considering either Bainbridge or Vashon Island. Does the commute bother you?"

Bainbridge? Excitement rose in Kate's chest. "No," she said. "I like it. I use the ferry ride to read, and it gives me downtime before I get home."

He crossed the room to join her. "How would you feel about me invading your island someday?"

Kate caught a sudden vision of Grayson seated on her deck, drinking his morning coffee.

"I wouldn't mind, and I think you'd like it."

"I think I'd like being near you," he murmured, and tilted her chin for a kiss.

A moment later, she was standing on tiptoe, pressed against him, her arms around his neck, her lips magnetized to his. The kiss went on until she thought she would melt. He pulled away long enough to whisper, "You are exquisite," then claimed her lips again. Her calves hurt, and the muscles in her neck protested the extra burden she was putting on them, but she refused to break the kiss, letting Grayson's hands slip down her back to wedge her even more snugly against him.

The antique grandfather clock she'd seen in the hallway chimed the half hour and she knew she had to go. Reluctantly, she pulled away. "I guess I'll have to take a rain check on that coffee."

"I know," he said regretfully. "The ferry. I'll walk you to your car."

At the car he gave her another kiss for the road, then murmured, "Can I take advantage of your temporary carefree status and get you to go out with me tomorrow night?"

"Yes," she said, glad she'd kept the evening free.

"Great. Why don't I come your way? In fact, maybe we could get together in the afternoon and look at houses."

Kate remembered her date with Jeff and could have kicked herself for letting him manipulate her into spending the day with him. "I'm afraid I've got plans during the day," she said. "But how about dinner? Come over on the six-fifteen as a foot passenger and I'll pick you up and take you to Ruby's Restaurant."

"Sounds great," he said.

She started the car, then gave him one final wave as she pulled away.

He waved back and remained watching until she was a good two blocks down the nearly deserted street, probably making sure she was safely on her way. His chivalry pleased her.

She wished their time together hadn't flown so quickly, wished she hadn't had to leave his place so soon.

She supposed it was just as well. Neither she nor Grayson wanted to rush into anything. But the more time she was spending with him, the harder she was finding it not to.

Tomorrow she'd bring him back to her place and they'd take up where they left off. The thought made her smile greedily.

Until she remembered who lived next door. It would be just like Jeff to decide to drop in and make a nuisance of himself. Hopefully, there would be a game on by the time she and Grayson returned from dinner, and Mr. Jock Itch would be tucked away in his house, glued to the set and guzzling beer.

GRAYSON HAD JUST WALKED BACK INTO THE CONDO when the phone rang.

"Well, I'm surprised you're home," said a throaty female voice.

Anne. "Just," said Grayson, "and I'm glad you didn't call any sooner. You would have ruined a very romantic moment."

"Oh? So, how's it going?"

"Great. By the way, I got you a present."

"Jewelry, I hope," said Anne.

"No. Doctor Kate's latest book. Now you can learn how to separate the men from the boys."

"Darling, you know I learned how to do that years ago."

"Consider it homework," said Grayson. "It's even autographed by Doctor Kate herself."

"My, my. How do you rate? I suppose it says something like 'To Grayson, a man among boys.'"

"No. It's signed to you, of course," said Grayson.

"That was very thoughtful of you. So, tell me more. Does the good doctor meet your qualifications?"

"She's perfect."

"But not as perfect as me, I'm sure," said Anne lightly.

"You're too modest," said Grayson.

His sarcasm didn't phase her. "False modesty is disgusting."

"Why aren't you in bed asleep, anyway?" asked Grayson.

"Just a touch of insomnia. I must have been worried about you, all alone in a new city."

Grayson chuckled. "Aren't you sweet?"

"You know I'm not. And now I'm going to bed before you start telling me the sordid details of your evening."

"An excellent idea," approved Grayson.

"So, keep me posted?"

"Of course. And don't call me. I'll call you."

"Yes, sir. And send me my book."

"It's in the mail."

"Yeah, right. Don't forget to call me."

"I won't," promised Grayson, and hung up. He poured himself a glass of Scotch and went to the window to admire his view. Seattle was a beautiful city. He should have come here years ago.

JEFF COLLECTED KATE PROMPTLY AT ELEVEN AND whisked her to the Blackbird Bakery for coffee and scones.

After they had settled in at a wooden booth, he casually said, "So, you got in late last night. That must have been some date."

"Actually, it was," said Kate, glad the subject had come up. If Jeff had any silly ideas left about the two of them getting together this knowledge would certainly drive them from his head. "I was out with a very charming man."

"So where'd you meet this guy?"

"He showed up at my first book signing."

Jeff looked incredulous. "He wanted to know how to

separate the men from the boys? Are you sure you want to get involved with a guy like that?"

"He got the book for his sister."

"I suppose he's a real prince among frogs," said Jeff, and stuffed a gigantic chunk of scone in his mouth.

"Cute. He certainly has better table manners than some people," observed Kate.

Jeff managed a muffled "Ha."

"And yes, he is a pretty amazing man."

"So tell me what's so wonderful about Mr. Amazo."

"His name is Grayson White."

"What kind of a name is that?" sneered Jeff.

"A very distinguished one, just like the man."

"Okay, he's distinguished. Well, that's a must. What's he do for a living, anyway? Wait a minute, with a name like that, he probably doesn't even work. I know," said Jeff, snapping his fingers. "He's a lawyer."

"You are a bit of a reverse snob, aren't you?" said Kate in disgust. "And no, he's not a lawyer. He's some sort of computer expert and he works as a consultant."

"And I suppose he's scored a hundred percent on the Doctor Kate perfect man test."

Kate broke off a dainty bite of scone. "As a matter of fact, he has. He enjoys the same activities I do."

"No sports?"

"Just a little tennis."

"And, of course, he agrees with everything you say."

"We see eye to eye on a lot of things."

"Well, I'll bet he can't dance," said Jeff, sounding like a man who was very sure of himself.

"There isn't a dance he can't do."

Jeff frowned. "This guy sounds too good to be true."

"Oh, please," said Kate in disgust.

"Look, Kate. The man has to have some faults."

"If he does, I haven't found them."

"In case nobody told you, Jesus Christ already came. This guy ain't him."

"I'm sure as we go along I'll discover he has some flaws," said Kate stiffly, scooting out of the booth.

Jeff followed her. "Yeah, I can tell you're looking real hard. You'd better be careful, Kate. You don't want to go skipping down the primrose path and end up falling on your face into the thorns."

She scowled at him over her shoulder as she marched for the door. "Don't worry about me. I'm a grown woman and I know exactly what I'm doing and where I'm going."

And to prove it, she collided with a woman balancing a two-year-old, a muffin, and a glass of orange juice.

The juice sloshed onto Kate and made it's cold, sticky way down her chest, staining her white top.

In the midst of their mutual apologies she could hear Jeff behind her, saying, "Yep, she knows where she's going all right."

"I guess we'd better take you home to change," he said once they were out on the sidewalk.

"I think we'd better take me home, period. This is not working."

"Oh, no," said Jeff. "You don't get off that easy. A promise is a promise."

"I didn't promise to spend the day listening to you insult my taste in men."

"I'll be good," he assured her.

And he was. He took a freshly clad Kate to the Bloedel Reserve, a favorite spot for island nature lovers. They spent the next two hours strolling the paths that led through the formerly private estate and admiring the scenery, which morphed from bird marsh to English landscape, complete with reflection pool, to moss garden, and then to Japanese garden. The sun was shining, the birds were singing. This did not strike Kate as a natural habitat for Jeff Hardin.

"I never would have figured you for a man who'd like

to do this sort of thing," she said as they made their way
back to where his Jeep was parked.

"I like to do all kinds of things," he said. "I'll bet you'd
be surprised to know that I've even been to the Rep once
or twice in my life."

"The Seattle Repertory? Who made you go?"

"Probably my date," said Jeff, and opened the Jeep
door for her.

"I won't deny I enjoy how I make my living," he said
once he was behind the wheel. "But sports aren't all there
is to me any more than examining people's psyches is all
there is to you."

"You're sure working hard to prove that," observed
Kate.

"And I think you know why," he said softly.

The look on his face produced that annoying, purely
physical reaction in Kate. Fortunately, she knew the difference between physical attraction and love, so was able
to ignore it. The person who seemed to need the education
was Jeff.

"You're wasting your time," she said. "There's nothing
between us."

"It didn't feel like nothing when I kissed you on the
dock."

"Funny, I could have sworn you kissed me on the lips."

Jeff Hardin, the king of the ill-timed jest, glowered at
her. "I'm being serious here."

"No, you're being stubborn and stupid. I spent our entire breakfast together telling you there is another man in
my life and you're acting like your hearing aid was un-
plugged the whole time."

He took a deep breath. "Okay, maybe I'm just being
jealous and immature. Of course, if this guy is as great as
you say, then I'm happy for you. You've had some rough
sledding, and you deserve a break."

So, backed against a wall Jeff Hardin could be mature.
She smiled at him and said, "Thank you."

"You're welcome," he said, and started the engine. "And I suppose you have a date with him tonight."

"I do."

"Then I guess I'd better get you home so you can put swamp mud on your face and do your nails."

"I'm fresh out of swamp mud, but I do need to get home and change."

"Into something more comfortable, I suppose."

Kate refused to rise to the bait.

J EFF MANAGED TO KEEP UP THE SMALL TALK ALL the way home, but by the time he left Kate he was drained. He'd thought he was miserable when Bambi dumped him, but that had been Little League stuff compared to what he was feeling now. Kate Stonewall was, without a doubt, the most exceptional woman he knew, and it tore at his gut to think of some other man getting her. But he had to admit, the guy sounded like just her type.

So for her sake he'd be a good sport and quit chasing her and let her enjoy her romance in peace. Hell, he'd even dance at her wedding. If Grayson the Perfect would share the dance floor.

Jeff scowled. Chivalry sucked.

B Y THE TIME KATE HAD TIDIED THE HOUSE, TAKEN a bath, and done her nails, it was time to pick up Grayson. She'd heard Jeff's lawn mower buzzing earlier and assumed he was still home, which was, thank heaven, where he'd stay now that they finally understood each other. She and Grayson could enjoy their evening together and she wouldn't have to worry about Jeff popping over just when he was least wanted.

He had covered his disappointment well, but she knew he had been hurt by the news of Grayson and the finality of her rejection. Still, she couldn't help that. If ever there were two people not destined to be together, she and Jeff were they. In spite of the fact that he kept trying to show her things they had in common, the truth was that they were two very different people who inhabited different worlds, and even an unforgettable kiss under a sky filled with fireworks couldn't connect them. She knew what she wanted, and Jeff Hardin wasn't it.

That's what I want, she told herself, watching Grayson jog toward her car. Today he was wearing khaki slacks and a summer-weight black ribbed top, with a black windbreaker hooked over a finger and slung over his back. He looked like a male fashion model coming down a runway. Phony?

Oh, thank you, Jeff Hardin, for planting that ugly little seed in my mind!

Well, she could hardly blame him. Insecurity motivated people to say all sorts of ridiculous things.

Grayson opened the door and slipped into the passenger seat.

"Hi, there," she said. "Long time, no see."

"Too long, in fact," he said. "Thanks for picking me up."

"My pleasure," said Kate. She watched as he tossed the small gold box he'd been carrying in his other hand onto the back seat. "And what might that be?"

"I thought I heard you say once on your program that you liked dark chocolate."

"Like is a bit of an understatement. Thanks."

"Don't thank me yet. This gift comes with a string: you have to share. I happen to like dark chocolate, too."

"It'll be hard, but I'll try," said Kate. "Our reservation isn't until seven-thirty. So you want to drive around and see a little of the island?"

"Great idea," he said. "Let's see what some of those water views look like."

She showed him Eagle Harbor, Point White, and, lastly, Pleasant Beach.

"I'm almost hooked," he said. "But first I have to see if the restaurants are civilized."

"They are," Kate assured him. "And this is one of my favorites," she added as she parked in front of Ruby's.

Grayson pointed to the quaint Lynwood Theater next door. "That looks like a slice of Americana."

"It's been around since the nineteen thirties, and the lobby has that feel. But the seats don't: they've replaced the old wooden ones."

"Let's take in a movie after dinner," he suggested.

"Fine. Just remember, tonight I'm paying for everything."

"I guess I can live with that," said Grayson, and held open the restaurant door for her.

Ruby's was small and cozy, with European cuisine and fine wine.

"Very good," said Grayson, setting down his wineglass. "And you say the other restaurants on the island are this good?"

"Absolutely."

"I think I'll have to come back again and try another."

Kate smiled at him. "I think so, too."

They left the restaurant and strolled arm and arm to the theater. Grayson beat Kate to the ticket booth and paid their admission, so she sprang for the popcorn. They settled into their seats in the dark and he put an arm around her and pulled her against him. Gentleman that he was, he let her consume most of the popcorn.

The ending credits were just rolling when he kissed her, then whispered, "Now let's go see how your view compares to mine."

Good idea.

He entered her living room with its kid-worn furniture and slightly stained Berber carpet and smiled as if he were entering a designer home.

"It's great," he said.

"Compared to your place?" teased Kate.

"As a matter of fact, yes. Your house looks lived in. I'll bet you pop popcorn and watch movies in here with your kids."

"I do."

"I can almost smell it," he said.

She laughed. "No, that's me." She held her hand to his face and he caught it and kissed her fingertips, supercharging her nerve endings.

He led her to the French doors in the dining room and looked out at Pleasant Cove. "I could live with a view like this."

She opened the door and they stepped out onto the porch. The smell of saltwater greeted them.

"Let's go down to the dock," he said.

The image of Jeff spying on her from his living room window flashed through Kate's mind.

Let him spy. This was her property, and if she wanted to go stand on her dock with a handsome man she could. Anyway, a visual aid would serve to reinforce their earlier conversation.

She and Grayson walked hand in hand down the lawn and out onto the dock. Kate could hear the water lapping below them. "It feels like we're on a movie set," said Grayson, "too beautiful to be true. Is this really happening? Are you real?"

"I am," said Kate.

He drew her to him. "Prove it."

His lips on hers set off the fireworks just as effectively as Jeff's had, but there was one big difference: Grayson was the right man. Kate arched her back and slipped her arms up and around Grayson's neck with a moan. The entire moment was perfection.

As the perfect moment continued, that same tightness she had felt the night before returned to Kate's neck. And as their kiss became increasingly more intimate, the tightness changed to an ache that began to creep up the back of her head.

She stepped out of Grayson's embrace and rubbed her neck in an effort to cure it.

"What is it?" he asked, concerned.

She shook her head. "Sorry. The angle is a little uncomfortable."

"Of course. What was I thinking? Here, let's go back inside."

As they walked back up the lawn, Kate expected the ache would disappear, but oddly, once started, it didn't.

Even after she and Grayson were settled on her couch with cups of coffee and the dark chocolate he had brought her, it still nagged her.

"Your head still hurts?" he asked.

"Stupid," said Kate. "I never get headaches."

He reached over and began to gently massage the back of her neck. "Does that help?"

Kate felt herself going limp and the pain receding. "Oh, definitely."

After five minutes she was completely relaxed. She leaned back against the couch and smiled up at him. "I feel much better."

"Good," he murmured.

Kissing from this position was definitely more comfortable, thought Kate, as Grayson slid her down among the sofa pillows. And he was the most delicious kisser.

So what was with this headache returning! She'd just ignore it.

And she tried, but soon, the pain had grown too big to ignore. She broke the kiss.

"What is it, Kate?" he asked, looking at her in concern.

"I'm afraid the headache's back," she confessed. "I'd better take an aspirin."

"And I'd better head home and let you get some rest."

"There's no need for you to leave so early," said Kate, determined not to ruin the evening.

Grayson ran a finger along his chin. "None other than the fact that you look dead on your feet. We'll have other nights together."

She sighed. He did have a point, and her head was aching fit to split.

"Would you like me to call a taxi?" he offered.

Kate was impressed with his thoughtfulness. "No. I'll just take that aspirin and be right with you."

JEFF HADN'T MEANT TO SPY. HE'D JUST HAPPENED to be in the kitchen cutting himself a slice of ham for a sandwich and looked out the window to see Kate and Mr. Perfect out on her dock going at it. He sawed at the ham with a new vehemence and reminded himself that he wanted Kate to be happy.

And since he wanted himself to be happy, too, he determined to throw the ham on some bread and retreat to his movie without another glance out the window.

But watching Kate lean into this guy like she was kissing Superman had a sick, hypnotic effect on Jeff, keeping his feet rooted to the kitchen floor. He noted the guy's great build and the fact that he seemed to know what he was doing, and felt a very unsportsmanlike urge to go push the creep in the cove.

Then, to Jeff's surprise, Kate pulled away, rubbing her neck and shaking her head. Crick in the neck? Maybe the guy didn't know what he was doing.

But they went back in the house and Jeff spent the next half hour imagining what was going on in there on Kate's couch. Or worse yet, her bed.

He was grinding his teeth on his sandwich when he heard her car start. He raced for his back door, stubbed his toe on a chair and hopped the rest of the way. He poked his head out just in time to see her heading up her driveway with her guest riding shotgun in the passenger seat.

Fifteen minutes later, she was home again. She must have taken White to the ferry. But why so soon?

Jeff remembered her actions on the dock and a grin crept onto his face. *Not tonight, dear. I've got a headache.* Maybe Mr. Perfect wasn't so perfect after all.

Fourteen

GRAYSON CALLED ON SUNDAY, JUST TO SEE HOW Kate was feeling. They talked for two hours. Monday they went to dinner, Tuesday Grayson took her to the Arboretum, laid out a blanket, and plied Kate with purple grapes, wine, and Brie and crackers. The wine gave her a headache, though, which ended their evening together just when things on the blanket were getting interesting.

"I'm afraid I don't have much of a head for alcohol," she confessed, "even the expensive kind."

He reached across the car seat and took her hand. "Next time I'll bring sparkling cider."

Kate sighed. "It's probably just as well to call it an early night. Tomorrow will be a long day."

"That's right. Your kids come home. You've probably missed them something fierce."

Kate smiled at him. "Not as fiercely as I'd anticipated, thanks to a certain dark-haired man."

He looked away from traffic long enough to shoot her a dazzling grin, and squeezed her hand. "That's a high compliment. Thank you."

"Think nothing of it," said Kate lightly.

"Not a chance."

She raised his hand to her lips and kissed it. How wonderful it felt to be in love again, and with the right man this time.

K ATE WATCHED HER SMILING CHILDREN AND THEIR flight-attendant escort emerge from the jetway and felt her heart catch. They appeared to have survived their first trip without her. Amanda even looked older from the responsibility of having to watch over her brother while in the friendly skies. They were both growing so fast. Too fast.

They spotted Kate and broke into a run. The minute they reached her, Robbie's mouth took over where his feet had left off. He was so full of his adventures he could barely stand still for a kiss, and Kate had her hands full trying to listen to him, show her identification to the attendant, and give Amanda a proper hug.

"Grandpa got me a new baseball glove, and he took us to see the Padres."

Thank you, Dad.

"And we went to the zoo. We went once in the day and once in the night to nighttime zoo and they had magicians and everything."

"And Grandma took us to the mall," put in Amanda.

"Where you got a ton of cool new clothes for school," guessed Kate. "So, you had fun?"

"Yeah," said Robbie.

"But we missed you," added Amanda.

"Good, because I missed you guys, too. Come on, let's go get your suitcases."

The kids kept up a steady chatter all the way home from the airport, filling Kate in on their every adventure. All in all, it had been a great trip. She just wished her dad hadn't encouraged Robbie's baseball mania. Well, he was home now, and signed up for drama classes in August. Come fall she'd enroll him in the island kids' choir. He'd find other interests.

Once they had dumped their dirty clothes in the laundry room both children came to the kitchen for the root beer floats Kate had promised. They were just scooping the ice cream into glasses when the phone rang.

"I'll get it," said Amanda, snatching the receiver before it could ring a second time. Her eagerness changed to politeness and she said, "Just a minute, please." She held out the receiver to Kate. "It's for you."

Feeling all the eagerness her daughter had just displayed, Kate took it and said hello.

"Hi," said Grayson. "I see you made it back with the kids."

"All safe and sound," said Kate.

"Then I won't talk long."

"It's okay," said Kate. "Robbie, pour that root beer slowly or it's going to overflow the glass."

"Celebrating?"

"Yes, as a matter of fact, we are."

"Good. I just called to see how the headache was. It sounds like you're feeling fine."

"I am," said Kate.

"Good. Say, do you think the kids would let you out one night this next weekend? I'd love to see you, and I think the Torchlight Parade is this Saturday night."

She wanted to see him, too, and the parade sounded like fun. "I think we can arrange something. How about if I call you in a couple of days?"

"Sure," said Grayson. "I'll go ahead and see if I can get grandstand seats."

"That sounds wonderful," said Kate.

"Thanks again for last night."

"I enjoyed it."

"Enjoyed what?" asked Amanda after Kate had hung up.

"I went out last night," said Kate.

Amanda's eyes widened. "With that man on the phone?"

"Yes, as a matter of fact."

"What's he like?" asked Amanda.

"Is he going to be our new dad?" added Robbie, looking anxious.

"He's very nice, and I don't know."

"Is he as nice as Jeff?" asked Robbie.

"Yes."

"Does he play baseball?"

"No, but he plays tennis."

"Tennis, yuck," muttered Robbie. "I hope he doesn't become our new dad."

Kate rumpled his hair. "Don't worry, slugger. That decision is still a long way down the road and I'm not going to import a new dad nobody likes. Okay?"

Robbie nodded. "Okay."

"Now, guys, no eating those on the couch. Take them outside or eat them at the table." The kids wandered out the kitchen door, spooning froth-covered ice cream into their mouths as they went.

Kate took a spoonful of ice cream to keep her taste buds from whining, then poured herself a glass of root beer and followed them out, making herself at home on the porch swing.

Jeff was on vacation. He had friends over, and they were barbecuing and water skiing. The activity drew the kids to Kate's dock to watch. They plunked themselves down, feet dangling, and Kate knew they would spend the next hour watching *Jock Talk* meets *Beach Blanket Bingo*.

Would they be as fascinated with Grayson as they were with Jeff? She wasn't sure. Grayson, after all, wasn't an oversized kid. He apparently liked children. But she couldn't imagine such a suave man playing video games.

Kate reminded herself that to be good with children an adult didn't have to behave like one. Her kids didn't need more friends. They needed someone they could respect, someone who would guide them and have their best interests at heart. That was the role of a parent, and Grayson looked like he could handle it.

If things continued to work well between them she would introduce him to the kids and see if they got along. She wasn't expecting miracles: the kids didn't have to slavishly adore him, and he didn't need to prove his desire to be friends by donning a clown suit. Anyway, one clown in the neighborhood was enough.

"Hi!" Kate turned to see Grace coming her way, glass of lemonade in hand.

"Hi. Have a seat."

Grace collapsed onto a patio chair. "I see the kids didn't pick up any rare disease or die in a plane crash."

"They did fine, and next time I talk to my dad I'm sure he'll point that out."

"So what are your plans for tonight?"

"We're going to McDonald's and then a movie. Then tomorrow it's back to the salt mines for me and back to tormenting you for them."

"I'm ready to be tormented. I've missed them. In fact, I've missed them so much I'll even take them for you one night this weekend if you want."

"Now, how did you know I was going to ask?"

"Feminine intuition. Things are still going well with Grayson, I take it."

"Better than well. He's wonderful."

Grace nodded in the direction of the dock. "And how will he compare to their hero?"

"I guess that remains to be seen. I think they'll like him. And they'll have to trust me to know who's the best man for all of us."

"Well, with Jeff next door, it looks like they'll get the best of both worlds: Grayson when they want *Family Matters* and Jeff when they want *Wide World of Sports.*"

Kate smiled at her. "Something like that. Thanks for not campaigning for Jeff."

"My philosophy is that once you board the *Love Boat* it's every woman for herself."

"And how are things going in your corner of the deck?" asked Kate.

"We're not just playing shuffleboard." Grace's smile was infectious.

"Well, here's to a bon voyage for both of us," said Kate, and they clinked glasses.

KATE AND GRAYSON SAT CUDDLED IN THE VIP grandstand and watched a lighted float glide by. "Oh, that's lovely," she said.

"To me, it's missing something."

"Oh? What?"

"You should be up there with King Neptune."

"I think the king likes his water nymphs a little slimmer," said Kate.

"Well, then, he's been underwater too long," said Grayson firmly. "You look fine the way you are."

"I will look more fine another thirteen pounds lighter," said Kate. "Oh, look!" she pointed to the Chinese Drill Team in their colorful costumes.

She felt Grayson's gaze on her and turned to see him smiling indulgently at her. "What?"

"You look like a little girl at the circus," he said. "It's so charming."

"I feel like a little girl at the circus. This is magical. Thank you for bringing me."

"Thank you for coming. I take back what I said when we first met about Seattle not being a friendly city."

"Whatever I can do for public relations," said Kate.

"Really? How about coming to my place after the parade?"

Kate's conscience piped up to remind her she had been

gone since five, and to stay out 'til all hours would qualify as taking advantage of Grace. "I'd better not. Give me a rain check?"

"Of course," he said. "I hear it rains a lot here."

"Don't worry," said Kate. "It does."

IT WAS MONDAY MORNING, AND JEFF WAS DOING some touch-ups on his porch trim when Robbie came skipping up the steps.

"I got a new mitt," he announced, holding it up for Jeff to see.

Jeff let out a whistle. "Pretty cool. Who got you that?" Not Kate, he'd be willing to bet.

"My grandpa. Amanda and me went to see my grandma and grandpa in San Diego."

"I think I remember hearing something about that," said Jeff.

"We went to see the Padres play."

Jeff dipped his paintbrush into the paint can and carefully scraped off the excess. "So, are you gonna play for the Padres when you grow up?"

"I want to play for the Mariners," said Robbie. "My grandpa played catch with me when we were there. I'm getting pretty good. I wanted to go to baseball camp, but Mom says I can't."

Jeff had seen Kate's car disappearing for visits to the garage, and the major roof overhaul going on next door was probably costing her a bundle. He knew her book was doing well and she'd signed that syndication contract, but maybe all those unexpected expenses had given her a temporary cash flow problem. A small thought crawled into his mind.

"Did you know I sponsor the baseball camp that's starting next week?" The *Jock Talk* Baseball Blast was something Jeff had put together with the island park department. He had players from the University of Washington running

the drills, and some Mariner celebrity appearances scheduled. He also offered scholarships, and last he'd heard
there were two left.

"That's the one James is going to." The expression on
the kid's face reminded Jeff of a basset hound watching a
German shepherd eat a bone.

After he'd finished painting, Jeff sent the kid on his way
and went inside to make a phone call. "Hey, Jean, are those
two scholarships for my baseball camp still up for grabs?"

"Just one," replied his park department buddy.

"One will do," said Jeff. "I want it to go to Robbie
Stonewall."

"Doctor Kate's son? Oh, I love her!"

Me, too. "Sign the kid up. I'll make sure the rest of the
paperwork gets filled out."

The thought that this was not going to endear him to
Kate haunted Jeff, but he reminded himself that it would
only initially make her mad. She'd be glad he'd done her
this favor once she saw her son having such a great time.
He still remembered how pleased she'd been when Rob
got that hit at his last game. Kate could say what she liked
about sports, but the bottom line was that she wanted her
son to be happy.

Kate didn't seem to be interested in the bottom line
when he told her the good news Friday morning. In fact,
judging from the look on her face, the only thing she was
interested in was clubbing him on the head with a baseball
bat.

She smiled tightly while Robbie ricocheted all over the
kitchen. "I'm going to have to leave for the station in a
minute," she said to her son. "Why don't you take the last
of your toast and go on over to Grace's, okay?"

He bounced out, shrieking all the way, and Kate turned
on Jeff. "I can't believe you'd have the gall to do something like this without asking me. You've put me in a position where I have to act like a villain in my child's eyes."

"Hey, I'm sorry. I wanted it to be a surprise. I should

have asked you first. But, honestly, would you have said yes?"

"No! What on earth made you think you had the right to decide what's good for my child?"

"The thought that maybe, with all the car and roof repair expenses, you didn't have the cash on you right now to send him."

Kate still looked mad, but she looked like she was trying to be fair, also. "You could have asked. My finances are just fine. In fact, you should have known that I didn't want to send him because I don't want him to play."

"I'm sorry, Kate. I really am. But can't you just let the kid do this? He wanted to really bad."

"Oh, he didn't even know about it," snapped Kate.

"Yes, he did. He told me all about it earlier in the week."

He saw hurt that her child had kept his dream from her flash across Kate's face, but she quickly shoved her angry mask back in place. "Well, he should have told me." She grabbed a sponge and began attacking her countertop.

"Why do you think he didn't?"

Her scrubbing slowed and she leaned on the counter and sighed. "I hate sports. I hate baseball."

"I know," said Jeff gently. "But your son doesn't."

He saw a hand reach up to brush at her cheek and longed to go stand behind her and hug her. He settled for laying a comforting hand on her shoulder. "It's got to be hard letting him grow up. And away."

She was looking out her kitchen window now. "My mom wanted me to be a lawyer."

"You'd have made a good one. My dad wanted me to play pro ball."

She turned to face him, forcing him to drop his hand. "If I let Robbie go to this camp it's going to be under one condition."

"Oh?"

"That you never again, for any reason, interfere in my life."

As if he would. Jeff nodded. "Deal."

She held out her hand. "Shake on it."

He took her hand and forced himself not to pull her into his arms. "Deal."

"I THINK YOU DID THE RIGHT THING," SAID GRAYSON, when Kate told him over dinner about the mess with Jeff.

"I hope so," said Kate. "Funny how easy it is to run other people's lives, but with my own . . ." She didn't bother to finish the sentence.

He set down his coffee cup. "When you look at all the trouble kids get into these days, sports seems like a pretty safe addiction. And, anyway, he's only how old?"

"Seven, but he'll be eight in November."

"And one year closer to hearing about drugs from some thug hanging around the edge of the school ground. If he's going to love baseball, he's going to love baseball. And all the drama lessons and choirs in the world won't change that."

"You're right, of course. Maybe you should take over my show."

Grayson smiled and picked up his coffee cup. "No, thanks. Anyway, you're doing fine. You know, Kate, it's not easy raising kids alone, having to be both mom and dad. I think you're handling it amazingly well."

"Thanks," she murmured. "I have to admit, it is good to get a male viewpoint."

"And this neighbor of yours, is he someone who would like to give you help with your kids on a permanent basis?"

"If you're asking if you've got competition, you don't."

Grayson looked relieved. "I must admit, I'm glad to hear that."

"The only part Jeff Hardin plays in my life is to irritate

me," said Kate, and she could feel herself getting angry all over again.

Grayson reached across the table and patted her hand. "He's not here now, Kate. Let it go."

Of course, she was acting ridiculous. "You're right," she said.

"How about a walk on the waterfront?" he suggested.

"Perfect," said Kate.

And it was. Strolling hand in hand with Grayson among the tourists, she could forget she was a woman with children and responsibilities. It was so incredibly freeing. And so romantic, especially when Grayson suggested they take a ride in one of the many horse-drawn carriages parked along the curb.

She barely had time to agree before he was fishing a wad of bills from his wallet and handing them up to the driver. "You know, this is something I've always wanted to do, but have never taken time for," he said. "I can't think of a better person to do it with."

They settled in to the back of the carriage with Grayson's arm around Kate, and the driver set the animal clopping forward.

"I feel like the luckiest man in the world right now," he said.

Kate smiled at him. "What a coincidence, because I feel like the luckiest woman."

"I hope our luck holds out. Forever," he said, and kissed her.

They had just finished their carriage ride and were about to go to his place for coffee when his cell phone rang. "White here. Yeah, Harry. What is it?"

Uh-oh, thought Kate. Evening over.

"Can't it wait? No, sure. I understand. I'll be there in an hour." Grayson disconnected and looked apologetically at Kate. "I'm sorry."

"Don't be," she said. "That's what happens when you're a mover and a shaker."

He shrugged. "I developed the software. When there's a problem . . ."

Developed software? No wonder Grayson was so rich. "Does this sort of thing happen to you often?"

"Often enough. After tonight I'm wondering why I'm still working."

"We all have to do that."

He laughed. "Not all of us. I could easily live off the royalties and my investments. I like working, though. It gives me a feeling of purpose. I just wish I wasn't needed tonight."

"We'll have other nights together," said Kate.

"I'm holding you to that promise," he said. "Come on, I'll walk with you to the ferry dock."

"YOU LOOK LIKE A WOMAN IN LOVE," SAID GRACE when Kate walked in the door.

"I am," said Kate.

"So when do I get to meet Mr. Perfect? Or more to the point, when do the kids meet him?"

"Soon. I want to be doubly sure, find out a little more about him first."

"How much *do* you know about him, by the way?"

"You mean his personal life? Only that he doesn't need to work and he has a sister who's a stockbroker who gives him hot market tips."

"Well, then, hurry up and introduce me to this man," said Grace. "On second thought, skip the middle man and introduce me to his sister."

"OKAY," SAID JANET. "I'LL THROW ROBBIE IN THE backseat with James and haul him home from base-ball camp, but it's going to cost you."

"It's already costing me plenty just letting him go," grumbled Kate.

"Yeah, what's with that?" demanded Janet. "How did you suddenly get to be Jeff Hardin's pet charity?"

"Just unlucky, I guess."

"Is there something going on between you two?" asked Janet suspiciously.

"Good God, no! And the only reason Robbie is going to this is because he wanted it so badly and I didn't have the heart to say no, especially since he could be finding worse things to get hooked on," she added, and realized she was quoting Grayson.

"Well, you're right about that," said Janet. "And he'll have the time of his life. If you want I can have him come over and play with James afterward."

Kate thanked her and hung up. Janet was right, of course, and so was Jeff. Robbie would have the time of his life, and he'd probably improve his skills. Or he wouldn't improve and he'd decide to give it up. Now, there was a comforting thought.

AFTER DAY ONE, HER SON SHOWED NO SIGNS OF giving up on baseball. "We had batting practice today and I hit a triple. My coach said I'm awesome."

Well, good self-image was important. "That's great," said Kate.

"Johnny Inch sprained his ankle," he added as an afterthought. "It got all big like a balloon, and the coach got this bag of little white beans and punched it and then it turned green and got really cold and they put it on Johnny's ankle. He was crying and everything."

Wonderful.

"A kid could sprain his ankle playing in his own backyard," said Jeff when the subject of Robbie's camp adventures came up at the station.

"Yeah," agreed George.

"Yes," said Kate. "A backyard is a dangerous place. It's a good thing my son is safe at baseball camp."

• • •

"NOW, BE CAREFUL," SAID KATE ON THURSDAY AS she handed Robbie his sack lunch. "We don't want you on the casualty list." It was the same parting statement she'd given him all week—a talisman to ward off evil baseball spirits. So far it had worked. All they had to get through was today and tomorrow.

"Okay," he piped, then exploded out the car door and ran off to join the swarm of boys already tearing around the ball field.

It was good to see him having fun. But, Kate reminded herself, he would have fun learning how to act, too. At this age, children enjoyed all kinds of activities. It was adults who channeled them into these competitive sports and drove them. Maybe she'd spend a few minutes on her program today talking about that.

She was just organizing the e-mail messages she wanted to read on the show when Grayson called. "Do we still have a date tonight?"

"Absolutely. Both my little dears are going to be spending the night with friends."

"So," said Grayson, "no curfew for you."

"It doesn't look that way."

"Good. I've found a great little restaurant on the East Side I think you'll like. We can catch a movie after if you want."

"That sounds great," said Kate.

"Now, I guess I'd better get back to work and let you get on the air."

They said their good-byes and Kate hung up to find Wallis giving her a very knowing look.

"I can see the title for the book now," said Wallis. "*How to Fall in Love,* by Doctor Kate. Subtitle: *See? I am Human.*"

"Everyone knows that," said Kate.

"I don't know," Wallis drawled. "I think some of our listeners don't think you take the ferry home. They figure you just walk right over the tops of the waves."

"There have been times after seeing Grayson when I felt like I could fly home," admitted Kate.

"Well, I hope it works out," said Wallis. "You deserve a chance to be happy."

"Thanks."

"And next time you're out with Prince Charming ask him if he has a clone."

"I'll try to remember."

It was two-thirty, with only half an hour of the program left when the call came in.

"We're going to a commercial break," Wallis said into Kate's earphones. "Your neighbor's holding on line three."

A boulder settled in the pit of Kate's stomach. "We've got to take a break," she told her listeners, trying to sound calm. "Hang on for more life strategies."

She picked up the phone and punched the blinking line.

"Kate," said Janet. "I'm sorry to bother you at work, but I'm here at the baseball camp. Grace wasn't home and I was next on your emergency phone number list, so they called me."

"What's happened?"

"Well, now, it's not as awful as it's going to sound," began Janet.

"Tell me what's happened," cried Kate.

"Robbie got hit on the head with a baseball."

Fifteen

K ATE FELT SICK.

"He's not unconscious," said Janet quickly. "Although he was stunned for a couple of minutes. I have that permission note you wrote for me to take him to the doctor and we're headed for the Winslow Clinic."

"Okay. I'm on my way. If I leave right now I think I can make the three o'clock ferry."

"I'll call you on your cell when we get to the clinic."

Kate hung up and rushed out of the air studio.

"What's happened?" asked Wallis.

"Robbie got hit on the head with a baseball. They're taking him to the clinic. I've got to go."

"Okay. We can handle things," said Wallis. "George, play the plug for Kate's book. Then we'll air the public service announcements."

Kate snatched her purse and raced out of the station. She fumbled her keys into the ignition, started her car, and attempted to roar out of the parking lot. The inspiration for the lemon law did not respond like a finely tuned machine: she hit the street and set off at the pace of a dying snail.

"What is wrong with you, you piece of crap!" Kate growled.

More to the point, what was wrong with her? How could she have allowed herself to be persuaded against her better judgment to allow Robbie to attend that stupid baseball camp? Anger surged through her and she slammed down the gas pedal and did a poor imitation of zipping into another lane of traffic, receiving an angry blast from the car behind her.

She screeched up to the Coleman Dock ticket booth, handed over a ticket, and careened onto the dock just in time to see the three o'clock boat easing out of the slip. The whistle blew, mocking her.

She swore and pounded the steering wheel, then burst into tears. Her son was wounded and she was stuck on this stupid ferry dock until three-fifty. She assaulted the steering wheel one more time, then fell back against the seat, and worked on resigning herself to her fate.

She was waiting on the dock, drumming on her abused steering wheel, when her cell phone rang.

"Okay," said Janet, "he's almost good as new. Grace is home now and we're taking him there and putting an ice pack on his head. You're to keep him quiet tonight and wake him up every hour. And a liquid diet for the next twenty-four hours."

"Thanks, Janet," said Kate. "I'm stuck here waiting for the three-fifty. Tell Grace I'll get there as soon as I can. And make sure she keeps his head elevated."

"We will. And don't worry, everything's fine."

Just peachy. "I'm sorry I turned your day upside down."

"Hey, what are friends for?"

Once on the ferry Kate called Grace and repeated everything she'd told Janet. Grace sounded calm and in control. Okay. Everything was all right. This sort of thing happened when you had kids. It was just one of life's curve balls.

Kate scowled. Surely she could find something other

than trite sports metaphors to comfort herself. She went up on the passenger deck, bought a cup of coffee, and spent the rest of the ferry commute trying to control her antsiness by reminding herself that Robbie was fine and there was nothing she could do for him that hadn't already been done.

Except be there. She was his mother. It should have been her taking him to the doctor.

And he shouldn't have even had to go to the doctor! *Thank you, Jeff Hardin.*

The ferry finally docked and Kate tried to speed home to her wounded son, making dire threats to her unresponsive car all the way.

She finally rushed into Grace's family room to find Robbie on the couch, wearing an ice pack chapeau. He sat propped up with pillows, drinking ginger ale and watching a video.

He saw her and smiled. "Hi, Mom."

She wanted to cry again. Instead, she put on a smile and knelt beside him.

"So, what happened to you?"

"I got hit with a baseball. It really hurt. I even saw stars," he added in an awed voice.

"How did you get hit?"

"I was in the outfield and we were working on catching fly balls."

"And you didn't see the ball coming."

Robbie looked chagrined. "There was a bee, and I was swinging my mitt at it and it wouldn't go away. It almost stung me."

"So while you were trying to hit the bee the baseball hit you."

"My head hurts," Robbie confessed.

"I can imagine," said Kate, and gave him a hug.

"But it will be fine by tomorrow," he added.

She knew where they were going with that conversation. "No baseball camp tomorrow," she said firmly.

He looked like she'd threatened to cut off his toes. "I have to go," he said, his voice rising. "We're going to get our T-shirts tomorrow."

"I'll make sure you get a T-shirt," Kate promised.

"I want to go." Now the tears were coming. He was going to become distraught and make his head hurt even worse.

"It will be okay," she said, hugging him.

"But I want to go," he wailed.

"I know," she said. "But I think your head wants a day off. In fact, I think it's kind of mad right now about getting hit."

"It hurts," he sobbed.

"I know, sweetie."

Kate continued to hold him until he settled down. "Now," she said softly, "do you want to finish watching your video before we go home?"

He nodded. "Can I still spend the night with James?"

"We need to keep an eye on you tonight to make sure your head doesn't hurt worse. How about if we have James over tomorrow instead?"

Robbie didn't look completely thrilled with her proposition, but he nodded.

"Now, the doctor wants you to just drink liquids tonight so you don't get your tummy upset. How about if I go to the store and get some more ginger ale while you're watching the movie?"

"And Gatorade?" asked Robbie hopefully.

"Okay," said Kate.

"Can you keep him while I make a quick run to the store?" she asked Grace.

"Sure. Too bad you had to cancel your dinner plans."

Dinner with Grayson. Kate moaned and rubbed her head. "I completely forgot. He's probably at KZOO by now, wondering where I am."

"You're welcome to use my phone," said Grace.

"I'll just call him on my cell," said Kate. "Be back in a little bit."

Seated in her mobile phone booth, she dialed Grayson's cell phone.

"White here."

"Stonewall here."

"Stonewall where? I'm at the station but you're not."

"I know. I'm back on the island. I'm afraid I'm going to have to take a rain check on dinner. Robbie got hit on the head with a baseball at camp."

"Your people were just telling me. I'm sorry. Is he okay?"

"It looks like it. But I'll be spending my night waking us both up every hour."

"Poor Kate," said Grayson.

"Stupid Kate. I should never have allowed Jeff to talk me into sending Robbie to that camp. It serves me right. I knew better."

"Kate, you couldn't know this would happen."

"On a subconscious level, I did. I think sometimes we're better off listening to our instincts than our voice of reason. Instincts can't get persuaded into stupid behavior."

"I'm not sure I'd go so far as to label letting your boy go to baseball camp as stupid behavior," said Grayson gently, "and I don't think you should blame yourself for this. It was an accident."

"Yes, but one that didn't need to happen." Her own head was hurting now. "I'm sorry I turned your evening upside down."

"Don't worry about it. Actually, I've been having a good time hanging out here. I've been getting to know your producer."

"Oh, great," joked Kate, "competition."

"Not possible. You're peerless. So, what do you think, should we try for tomorrow night?"

Kate remembered her promise to have James over. "I'm afraid tomorrow night's taken."

"Okay, how about Saturday?"

"If I can get someone to stay with the kids that would be great."

"Let me know, then," said Grayson, "and if you want someone to talk to while you're doing your bedside vigil tonight, I'm here."

Kate was touched by his thoughtfulness. "Thanks, that's sweet of you."

"Not sweet," corrected Grayson. "Selfish."

They said good-bye and she started the lemon and headed for the store.

While waiting in the checkout line, she made arrangements to pay a visit to Andy the following morning and swap cars again. "I want this thing fixed this time," she said.

"If it turns out to be the heads, you'd be better off driving it into the sound," said Andy.

"That's not what I wanted to hear," said Kate.

"I know. I just thought I should warn you."

Kate put away her cell phone with a sigh. Life should not be this complicated. But it was when you were alone. Maybe she would call Grayson later.

EVERY TIME THE NEWS CAME ON JEFF DEBATED whether or not to use the break and call Kate and see how Robbie was doing. And every time he chickened out. He was sure the kid was okay. Kids were tough, after all. But he could imagine what kind of mood the doc was in, and just who she was blaming now for her latest misery. She was right, he shouldn't have interfered.

But he'd just wanted to do something nice for the kid, for crying out loud. Sometimes it didn't pay to be nice, and this was looking like one of those times. The odds had been stacked against him before this. Now they'd grown from a stack to a skyscraper.

The news ended and he donned his radio personality again. "Well, guys, we're back talking about the M's beating the odds. Can they do it?" *Never mind the Mariners. Can I?*

K ATE DIDN'T EXACTLY BEAM AT JEFF AT THE STATION the next day.

"Hey, I'm sorry about Robbie," he said.

"Fortunately, there wasn't any lasting damage," said Kate stiffly.

"So you're still pretty ticked at me?" guessed Jeff.

"I'm still pretty ticked. Period," said Kate. "I'm mad at myself for allowing him to go, and mad at you for starting the whole mess."

"So you're equally mad at both of us?"

"Something like that."

"Does that mean when you get around to forgiving yourself you'll forgive me?"

"Something like that."

"And how long do you think that will be?"

"About a decade."

Jeff nodded. "Ten years, that's not so bad. I could have gotten life."

"Don't you have any siblings with kids you can ruin?" demanded Kate irritably.

"None close by."

"Maybe they'd like their uncle Jeff to move closer."

"Come on, Kate. It's not that bad. Anyway, you can't put your kid in a bubble."

"And how many kids did you say you have?"

"Hey, I had brothers, I was a boy."

"A boy what?"

"A boy wonder."

"Well, Wonder Boy, maybe you should do my show since you're so good at figuring out what's wrong with other people's lives."

"I know what's wrong with yours," snapped Jeff. "Your kid needs a man in his life."

"Well you're not the man he needs," snarled Kate. "I meant what I said. Stay out of my business."

Jeff watched her march down the hall, kicking himself harder mentally with every step away from him she took. *Strike three, Hardin. You're out.*

"WELL," SAID ANDY WHEN KATE SHOWED UP AT HIS garage on Saturday, "it's like I thought. You've got burned valves. And I removed the heads and found you've got cylinder problems, too."

"But it can be fixed, right?" asked Kate.

"You don't want to pay what it's gonna cost."

"But this car is not that old," Kate protested.

"I know, but it's had it."

Kate groaned. She hated all things mechanical, and just the thought of having to go car shopping was enough to raise her stress level.

"I tell you what I'll do," said Andy. "I'll take it off your hands."

"I can hardly wait to hear the generous offer you're going to make me," said Kate.

"The best offer you'll get, believe me."

"Okay, just take it. Fix it up and sell it to somebody in South America so I never have to see it again."

"My friend Buzz has a Toyota dealership in Puyallup. I'll call him and see what he's got," Andy offered. "You can't go wrong with a Toyota."

"Okay. You can see what he's got, and if the price is right and I don't find anything better in Poulsbo, I may pay him a visit," said Kate. "I don't want something brand-new that's going to depreciate the second I drive it off the lot. Last year's model will do just fine, and I'll take every warranty he can give me."

"Okay," said Andy.

"And tell him it has to be a pretty color," she added. After all, aesthetics were important.

• • •

KATE COLLAPSED ONTO THE SEAT OF GRAYSON'S car. "You are an oasis in the desert."

"Things are that bad?"

"Let's just say the last couple of days haven't been the most carefree ones of my life," said Kate. "My son is doing well now, but my car has an incurable disease and I have to get a new one."

"It didn't look that old."

"It's not," said Kate. "It just hates me."

"So, what's wrong?"

"It needs new heads." She sighed. "I hate having to deal with this sort of thing."

"I know a little about cars," said Grayson. "If you need help picking out a replacement, I'll be happy to help. You want to make sure you get a car that's sound, with the best possible financing."

"I have no intention of making payments on something that's only going to depreciate," said Kate. "I'll pay cash."

"If you can do it, that's great," said Grayson. He was silent a moment, then said, "I know it's not my business to be giving you financial advice."

"But?"

"Well, if I were you, I wouldn't draw my last penny out of the bank just to avoid car payments. That money could be better spent earning interest in a good mutual fund. I'm sure you know that when the market is good you can earn from fifteen to twenty percent. Compare that to your interest rates on a car loan, which will run anywhere from eight and a half to nine and a half percent if you finance through your bank or credit union. Myself, I like to keep a good chunk of change available for investment opportunities."

"A very good idea," said Kate. "But you probably have an edge on me there. I suspect you have more play money than I do."

"How do you think I got that play money?" said Grayson.

"Well, you've also got a sister who's a stockbroker. I don't have one of those."

"I'll share."

Kate smiled at him. "Looks like I've got friends in high places after all."

"Something like that," he said. "Anyway, I understand you have to spend your money as you see fit, but I care about you, and I want to help you if I can."

I care about you. The words nestled against Kate's heart and warmed her. "Thanks for caring. And thanks for listening. It seems like I've been dumping on you a lot this last week. It's just so hard to have to always be putting out fires."

"Maybe in the future you won't have to do it alone," said Grayson, and reached for her hand.

His fingers closed around it, lending strength.

"Maybe," murmured Kate.

He took her to his condo, and they ate crab salad and croissants on the balcony, enjoying the sun and the view. He put on Vivaldi to underscore the sounds of the city that drifted up to them.

"I could stay here forever," said Kate, watching the waterfront trolley go by.

"I wish you would," said Grayson. He stood and held out a hand. "Join me on the couch?"

Kate was happy to join him, but her worries wouldn't let her relax in his arms.

"You're so tense," he said, rubbing her neck.

"I'm afraid you've caught me at a tense time of life," said Kate.

"Is that all it is?" he asked. "I'm not pressuring you to be intimate, Kate, believe me. But I do sense that every time we start to get close you pull away. If it's because you're worried my only interest in you is sexual, you're wrong."

"I don't think that," said Kate quickly.

"Good. Then relax. I agree with your ideas on how to build a good relationship, and I'm not going to push you to a level of intimacy you're not ready for. You're in charge of the time line. You set it and I'll follow it."

Chalk up another point for Grayson White, who was not only romantic but who also understood the necessary steps for building a solid relationship.

"And I hope that time line is going to include me getting to know your children," he added.

"That's probably a good next step," agreed Kate. "If you still feel that way at the end of the month, I'd like them to meet you."

"If they're anything like their mother, I'm going to love them," Grayson predicted and pulled her into his arms.

ON SUNDAY GRACE DROVE KATE AND THE KIDS ON a tour of Kitsap County's car lots, ending with Andy's friend clear down in Puyallup, where she became the proud owner of a pale green—Crystal Ice was the official color name—Toyota Camry with air-conditioning. She decided not to pay cash, opting instead to pay the car off in five years. She wasn't sure her father would approve, but, she decided as she drove her new baby off the lot, he didn't have to know. Grayson was right, of course. Her money could be better spent in investments. And if, when the day came and she met his sister, that sister just happened to have a hot stock tip, she would want to have a nice chunk of change handy to invest. She wondered if Anne was planning on coming to Seattle for a visit any time soon. If she was anything like Grayson, Kate knew they would become good friends. She tooled down the highway in her new car, while Amanda twiddled with the radio, making it blast all manner of noise into the car. It didn't matter what the radio was playing; in her head Kate heard only love songs.

• • •

"SOMMER'S MOM SAID THAT IF IT'S ALL RIGHT SHE can spend the night," said Amanda. "So can she?"

Kate threw the last armload of clothes in the washer. "Sweetie, I've got a date, remember?"

"You've always got a date," said Amanda in tone of voice that didn't exactly project happiness for her mother's good fortune.

"Once a week does not count as always."

"Can't you just stay home this Friday?" pleaded Amanda.

"This from the girl who wanted a father like all her other friends?"

"We haven't even met him yet."

"Well, you will."

"When?"

"How about next week?"

"Okay," said Amanda. "And will you stay home tonight?"

"No. I'm meeting Grayson after work and we're going to an early dinner and then a play. But I will stay home tomorrow night and Sommer can spend the night then and go to Grace's garden party on Sunday. How's that?"

"All right," said Amanda sulkily, and dragged herself off to call her friend.

"And thank you, Mom, for working things out so my friend could come over," muttered Kate, digging the last of the laundry soap out of the box.

"I THINK IT'S TIME YOU AND MY CHILDREN MET," SHE said to Grayson after they had ordered.

"That's fine with me," he said.

"Next week?"

"I'm free on Saturday."

"Would you like to come over for dinner, then?"

"I have a better idea," he said. "How about if I spring for dinner?"

"You've been buying enough of the dinners lately," said Kate.

"I don't mind, believe me. Anyway, I was thinking of some place like McDonald's, which won't break the bank. Then we can go to the Seattle Center afterward and hit the rides."

"Which will break the bank."

"Don't worry," said Grayson. "I'm still solvent."

"Well, all right. I still wish you'd let me cook."

"Next time," he promised.

Kate didn't argue with him any more. She suspected he wanted to make a good impression on the kids. And what he had planned couldn't fail to do the trick.

What had she done to deserve finding such an incredible man? Maybe it wasn't her. Maybe it had been Rob, up there in the great beyond, putting in a good word for her. *If it was, you're off the hook for dying on me.*

GRACE'S PARTY WAS IN FULL SWING WHEN JEFF AND his dad arrived, bearing bags of potato chips and several containers of dip.

Jeff was wearing cutoff jeans and a loose-fitting, ragged T-shirt with the sleeves cut out that proclaimed him a 1998 park department volleyball champion. It should have said something like Best Biceps, Kate decided, watching him. Not that she was interested in getting her hands on those biceps. It was just a casual observation.

"We haven't missed the yodeling contest, have we?" he asked Amanda, who had raced Robbie to get to him and won.

She giggled.

Funny, thought Kate, how quickly one man's presence could turn a simple gathering into a party. She had to admit, Jeff had a gift for making life fun.

"You think I'm kidding?" Jeff said to Amanda. "Didn't

Grace tell you? Grace," he called, "didn't you tell Amanda about the yodeling contest?"

"It completely slipped my mind," said Grace, relieving Sandy of his chips.

"You can yodel, can't you?" Jeff asked Amanda.

"I don't think so," she said, looking at him like he was crazy.

"Well, that's too bad, because the prize is Mariners baseball caps." He reached around to his back pockets and pulled out two caps, and both kids began to squeal and jump for them. "Nope. You gotta yodel first."

"I don't know how to yodel," said Robbie.

Jeff demonstrated with a pathetic sound that would make a Swiss man gag. Robbie did a fair imitation and was rewarded with a cap. Amanda followed suit and was equally rewarded.

"What about me?" asked Sommer, who had arrived late on the scene.

"Let's hear you," said Jeff.

Sommer, too, let loose, and Jeff said, "You know, that was so good, you are going to get the grand prize." He reached into his back pocket and pulled out his wallet. Out came two tickets. Kate noted that his dad's eyes grew wide, and she suspected that this particular prize was an ad lib.

"Here you go," said Jeff. "Two tickets to next week's Mariners game. You can take your dad."

"Oh, man," whined Robbie as Sommer skipped off, clutching her treasure.

"My feelings exactly," said Sandy, scowling at his son. "You didn't have any more hats back at the house?"

Jeff shook his head. "Sorry, Dad. It was the only thing I could think of. I'll make it up to you."

His father clapped him on the back. "It's okay, son. I think I'll go see if I can butter up the kid into taking me instead of her old man."

"That was nice of you," said Kate, after Sandy had wandered off.

"That's me. Mr. Nice Guy," said Jeff, and plunked down at the picnic table. Grace had covered it with a bright yellow tablecloth and used a Mason jar filled with daisies for a centerpiece. He took one out and began pulling off its petals. "So how's Mr. Perfect these days? Found any faults yet?"

"Sorry. None."

Jeff gave a grunt and tossed a petal onto the ground. "So, the guy's a hunk and the best lover since Don Juan DeMarco."

"He's very romantic. And he also wants more out of our relationship than an express lane to my bed."

"So he's still in the slow lane, is he?"

Jeff's snide tone of voice was beyond irritating. "This will come as a surprise to you, but some men want more than sex from a woman."

"I wanted more than sex from you!"

Kate's face flamed, and Jeff looked guiltily over his shoulder, then lowered his voice and repeated himself.

"Yes," said Kate. "You wanted more. You wanted to tell me how to raise my children."

"Oh, and of course Grayson the Perfect doesn't butt in."

"No, he doesn't."

"And he never disagrees with you. What a guy. Is he real or is he Memorex?"

"Just what is that supposed to mean?"

"Kate, he's a fake."

Jeff's words stunned Kate, leaving her speechless. She saw he was looking almost as stunned as she, but that didn't make her feel any more charitable toward him. In fact, if she didn't walk away from him this very moment, she would probably club him over the head with the Mason jar. She stood up.

"That's a ridiculous accusation to make. You are out of control. You need help."

"Kate, you're the one who needs help. You've built such a thick suit of shining armor around this guy that you can't see who he really is. It's not like you to be so impractical. You're not thinking."

"Oh, I'm thinking, and you don't want to know what." She walked away, saying over her shoulder, "I need to help Grace bring out the food."

"Kate, wait," he called.

She picked up her pace, refusing to let his conciliatory tone distract her from her mission: to see if Grace had anything messy and disgusting in the kitchen that she could dump over Jeff's head.

JEFF RAN HIS HANDS OVER HIS FACE. HE'D DONE IT again. Opened his mouth and stuck his foot right on in.

Even though he'd been a clod, he knew there was some truth in what he said. Something was off with this Grayson character. Nobody was that perfect.

The thought irritated his mind until he couldn't stand it anymore. This was one itch he had to scratch right now. He slipped back over to his place, dug out his phone directory, and made a call.

A recorded voice picked up on the other end. "You've reached the Nase Detective Agency. We can nose out what you need to know. Leave your name and number and Gary Nase will call you back."

"Gar, it's Jeff. I need a favor, man. Call me."

Jeff hung up, feeling better. Until he remembered his promise to Kate not to interfere in her life anymore.

But what the hell? She already hated his guts. What did he have to lose? Compared to what she stood to lose if his hunch was right, nothing.

Sixteen

"I DON'T KNOW, GAR," JEFF SAID TO HIS OLD HIGH school buddy. "There's just something about this guy that doesn't ring true. From what I hear, he's got it all: looks, money, charm. He likes all the same things Kate does, enjoys the same kind of food, even thinks the same way she does about everything. It's all too perfect, too pat. He's like a chameleon who's parked on top of all Kate's fantasies until he fits right in."

"Hmmm," said Gary Nase thoughtfully. "The guy could be running some kind of sweetheart scam. Has Kate got a lot of money?"

"She's got to have a chunk of change squirreled away somewhere," said Jeff. "She had a book on the best-seller list, and she just signed a big syndication deal."

"Oh, yeah. I think I saw something about that in the paper. That's the kind of stuff the really good con artists look for. She's high profile and single. The guy wouldn't have had a hard time finding her. He could be a roper, setting her up for a sting further down the road."

"How much further down?"

"Well, he won't wait forever," said Gary. "It's hard to imagine one of these guys wanting to try and outthink a shrink, though. But then, a lot of them have pretty big egos. It would be a challenge."

Jeff looked out his kitchen window and watched Kate kneeling in front of her porch, weeding her flower beds. Hard to believe any man would be low enough to take advantage of a widow. Hard to believe that particular widow could get taken in. He'd never even met Grayson White. So what made him think he knew what was going on in the guy's head? Was he just making White a bad guy because he wanted him to be? Maybe, but he had to be sure.

"Do some snooping on old Grayson and let me know what you come up with," he said.

"You are paying me for this, aren't you, Hardin?" asked Gary suspiciously.

"Hey, do you want good seats for the Seahawks this fall or not?"

"Okay, okay. But if this turns out to be a lot of work I don't want to miss a single home game."

KATE HUNG UP THE PHONE. "WELL, GUYS, HOW would you like to go to the Fun Forest this Saturday?"

Ear-piercing screeches and much jumping around answered her question in the affirmative.

"Can Sommer come?" asked Amanda.

"Not this time. We already have a friend coming, someone I've been wanting you to meet."

"Grayson White?" guessed Amanda.

"Is he going to buy us cotton candy?" asked Robbie.

"I'm sure he will. He's very generous."

Amanda sat a moment, staring at her corn flakes. "Do you think he'll like us?"

Even though her daughter talked about wanting a father, meeting a potential one had to be scary. Kate swooped down on her and gave her a hug. "Of course he will. What's not to like?"

Amanda shrugged.

"Just be yourself. And remember, he's probably just as nervous about you not liking him."

"Is he going to be our new dad?" asked Robbie. "Will he take us to see the Mariners?"

"I don't know," said Kate. "He's going to be my friend for a long time before we think about adding him to the family. So for now, let's just see if we have fun on Saturday. Okay?"

Robbie nodded. "Okay. I hope we get cotton candy," he said to his sister.

GRAYSON PICKED THEM UP IN HIS BMW AND DROVE them to the McDonald's across from the Seattle Center. After saying hello to Kate, he wisely concentrated on the kids. He scored instant points with Amanda by asking her what radio station she'd like to listen to, then went on to win Robbie by asking him how he had liked his baseball camp. Then, before Amanda could totally switch off, he brought her back into the conversation, complimenting her on her lime green fingernails. After loading the kids up with hamburgers and french fries, he insisted they have sundaes for dessert.

"You, too, Kate," he said. "No diets today. We're just going to have fun."

It had been so long since her tongue had tasted hot fudge. Grayson didn't have to work very hard to persuade her.

The Seattle Center stood at the heart of the city, offering twenty acres of landscaped areas, plazas, and performing arts halls. It was home to all the major performing arts organizations in Seattle, but most important to the kids, it housed the Fun Forest, which offered a plethora of rides and carnival booths. Robbie could hardly contain himself as they made their way to the Center from the parking garage across the street.

Grayson ponied up for ride tickets, then bought the kids cotton candy, fulfilling Robbie's every dream. And he wasn't above going on the rides, either, which was fine with Kate, who preferred to watch. Actually, she didn't even like to do that. It did bad things to her stomach watching her children sailing through the air in flimsy little metal buckets.

Finally they came to the Orbiter, the modern-day version of the Octopus, which had swirled Kate so jarringly when she was young and foolish enough to give fate the raspberry.

"Come on, Kate," urged Grayson. "Go on this one with me."

"Yeah, Mom," said Amanda. "It's really cool."

The last carny ride Kate had taken had been in junior high school. She had hurled her popcorn and hot dog on her best friend, who shortly thereafter resigned the position. Getting locked into a bucket of steel and allowing herself to be dipped and spun like a sock in a dryer held little appeal for Kate.

"I think I'll just watch."

"Oh, Mom, don't be such a chicken," said Amanda in disgust.

"Just call me Cluckie."

"Come on, Mom," put in Robbie, taking her hand and pulling her toward the gate.

"Oh, I don't know," said Kate, wondering how Grayson would feel about wearing her lunch.

Grayson came alongside her and slipped an arm around her waist. "How about it? Just one ride."

"Those things really do give me the heebie jeebies. I just don't like feeling out of control."

"Most of life is. Let's see how it feels to face it together."

When he put it that way. "All right," said Kate, "but

you're not going to make a habit out of asking me to do this sort of thing, are you?"

He squeezed her. "No, love. I promise."

The kids scrambled into one bucket of the ride and Grayson and Kate climbed in the one behind them.

Kate felt a nervous ripple in her stomach. "I haven't done this in years."

"You know, before today, I hadn't either. I've got to confess, it's kind of freeing."

"I just hope it doesn't free up the hamburger I ate."

Grayson put an arm around her. "These slacks will wash."

The metal creature started slowly, but it didn't take long for it to pick up speed. Soon it was a fierce alien, moving at warp speed, throwing Kate against Grayson. She hung on to the metal bar in front of her with all her might and screamed. The world became such a blur she could have been traveling through a black hole or in a time machine.

She felt Grayson's arm tighten around her shoulder and closed her eyes and turned and wrapped an arm around him, pressing her face against his chest.

"I've got you," he told her.

And as they spun and dipped crazily around, she felt Grayson's firm chest under her cheek, felt his arm around her like a band of iron, and realized how exciting it felt to spin out of control pressed against him.

The ride slowed to a stop and she looked up to find him smiling down at her. "We survived," he whispered.

"Yes, we did," agreed Kate. She smiled up at him and he kissed her.

LATER THAT NIGHT AS SHE WAS TUCKING IN Amanda she asked casually, "So, how did you like my friend Grayson?"

"He's awesome."

"Then you think this is someone you could stand to spend more time with?"

"Oh, yeah."

R OBBIE, IT TURNED OUT, LIKED GRAYSON WELL enough to talk about him to Jeff.

"I hear you guys had a good time at the Center," said Jeff as he and Kate passed in the hall at KZOO.

"We did, thank you," said Kate politely.

"Robbie seems taken with him."

"Both the kids are," said Kate. And repressed the impulse to add, *So there.*

Jeff nodded. "Well, good. I'm glad it's working out."

"It is," said Kate.

Here was the perfect opportunity for Jeff to confess that he had acted like a complete toad at Grace's party, and to admit that he had been wrong in defaming Grayson. But, of course, he didn't. Instead, he just nodded and continued on toward the air studio.

What could you expect from a male air personality but ego and pride, anyway?

I 'VE MET HER KIDS," GRAYSON SAID TO ANNE.

"So, things are getting serious?"

"Yes, they are, and I think it's time Kate met my sister."

"And I am dying to meet the famous Doctor Kate. This should be fun."

"Did you finish the book?"

"Yes. It was the best bedtime story I've read since *Cinderella.* I will, of course gush over it."

"That's my girl," said Grayson. "Plan to come after Labor Day. We'll show you the sights."

"There's only one sight I'm interested in seeing," said Anne.

"I know, I know," said Grayson, and hung up.

• • •

"YOU'LL NEVER GUESS WHAT YOUR FATHER GAVE ME for my birthday," said Kate's mom.

"Airplane tickets to Seattle."

"You guessed."

"Who do you think suggested the idea to him?"

"Aren't you a clever girl!"

"Oh, we both know who the clever one was," said Kate. "All those broad hints about how nice it would be to just get on a plane and come for a quick visit. Very subtle, Mom."

"But effective."

"So, you're flying out right after Labor Day?"

"If that's convenient. We'll get in on Tuesday night."

"Absolutely. I'm planning on you staying here all week. You can finally meet Grayson."

"Yes, I must admit that's another reason I've been dying to get up there. He sounds wonderful."

"He is. I think you'll like him."

"I just hope he and your father will hit it off. If he doesn't like sports, what on earth will they find to talk about?"

"Business, of course, and Grayson can tell Dad all about his travels. And we'll take you out to dinner at San Carlos to celebrate your birthday."

"Be sure to include the children."

"Of course. I'll invite Grace, too, and we'll make it a party. How does that sound?"

"Memorable," said her mom.

Kate had barely hung up the phone when Grayson called. "You'll never guess who's coming to town," he said.

"Santa Claus?"

"My sister."

"Oh, wonderful! I finally get to meet part of your family. When's she coming?"

"Week after next," said Grayson.

"Oh. That's the week after Labor Day."

"Is there a problem, darling?"

"No, it's just that my parents are coming up that same week for my mother's birthday, and I'm wondering how either of us will get to know the other's family well."

Grayson was silent a moment. "I tell you what. I'll see if Anne can juggle her schedule and come out this next week instead."

"I don't want to turn her vacation upside down," said Kate.

"Let me at least ask. I really want you two to have a chance to get to know each other."

"Well, it would be good if we could stagger things just a little," said Kate. "I want to be able to spend time with your sister, and that would be hard the way things stand now. But if we have some overlap, it would be fine. In fact, it would be really fun if she could stay in town long enough to join us at one of our local restaurants for my mother's birthday party."

"That sounds good. Let me talk to Anne and I'll get back to you."

Kate hung up, feeling as excited as if she were making plans for her senior prom night. This was going to be quite an event.

Grayson called her back an hour later. "Okay, tell me how you think this will work. Anne is going to come out the week before Labor Day and stay through the following weekend."

"I hope she didn't rearrange her trip just for me," said Kate.

"No, she did it for me. She knows how badly I want you two to have a chance to really get to know each other."

"Well, I can hardly wait to meet her," said Kate.

"Good. Are you up for dinner at the Space Needle? I know Anne will insist on going there."

"I haven't been to the Space Needle in years."

"Who goes to their own city's tourist spots unless they have out-of-town company? How about Friday night? I can pick up Anne at the airport, get her settled in my spare bedroom, then we'll come collect you. We can have dinner then take in some of that Bumbershoot art festival."

"Great," said Kate. "Then you guys can come over and spend the day on Saturday."

"She'll love it," said Grayson.

"I HAVE TO SPEND ALL SATURDAY WITH HER BRATS?" demanded Anne.

"Anne."

The tone of his voice brought out a surly "All right. I can stand anything for one day."

"That's right. Be your sweetest self. Bring some cookies for the boy . . ."

"I thought zoos don't let you feed the animals."

Grayson ignored the crack. ". . . And give the girl a compliment. She'll be your friend for life."

"Just what I always wanted, a ten-year-old friend."

"You're not going to get bitchy on me?" chided Grayson.

"Don't worry," she said, sounding resigned. "I'll be a good girl at the party."

"Good. See you soon."

JEFF SCRATCHED AT THE LABEL ON HIS BOTTLE OF beer. "You haven't found anything yet?"

Gary poured the last of his into his glass and signaled the waitress for another. "You know, I do have paying customers."

"I'll pay you, already. Just get to work on this. Grace tells me he's about to bring his sister out for a visit. At the rate you're moving, Kate's going to be married to this goon before you do anything."

"He's probably a bigamist. She could get it annulled," said Gary.

"I'm trying to prevent her from getting her heart broken here," said Jeff between clenched teeth.

"She's already in love with the guy, isn't she? So it's a given that's going to happen."

"Well, I don't want her to get taken and make it even worse."

"Okay, okay. I'll get working on it," promised Gary. "Now, relax. Have another beer. The Nose is on the job."

"Sleeping on the job," grumbled Jeff. Maybe he needed to do a little investigating himself.

"SO, WHAT ARE YOU GOING TO DO TO CELEBRATE Labor Day this weekend?" asked Wallis.

"Grayson's sister is coming to town. We're taking her to the Space Needle Friday night, then she's coming over for the day Saturday. I imagine we'll do something Sunday or Monday, too."

"Well, this is getting serious," said Wallis.

"It's moving that direction."

"So, have you slept with him yet?"

"Aren't you getting a little personal here?"

"As your producer it's my duty to make sure you're practicing what you preach and not jumping into bed with this man too soon."

"I'm sure it's in your contract."

"It is. So, have you?"

"No."

"Do you want to?"

"I'd have to be dead not to."

"You're right there. That man is, without a doubt, the finest specimen of manhood I've ever seen."

"Yes, he is," said Kate dreamily.

"Well, if I were you, I wouldn't be able to keep my hands off him."

"Yes, I know. And to cure those nympho tendencies, I

prescribe three chapters of *The Frog with the Glass Slipper* before bedtime."

"Only if there doesn't happen to be anyone in my bed," said Wallis.

There was no opportunity for Kate to set her straight. It was time to go on the air.

WHEN KATE CAME TO COLLECT THE KIDS FROM Grace she learned that Amanda had been invited to go sailing with Sommer's family for the weekend, and Robbie and James were in the process of wrangling a two-day adventure at James's house that involved a pup tent in the backyard.

"Looks like that leaves you free," said Grace. "I wonder how you'll fill the time."

"Pining for my children, of course."

"In between activities with Grayson and his sister."

"Yes, dinner at the Space Needle Friday night will be a hardship without my offspring along. And maybe it's just as well if they're not on hand when Grayson brings his sister over on Saturday. I do want to make a good first impression."

"Oh, she's probably just like him and loves kids," said Grace.

"Yeah, I'm sure you're right."

"Well, I wish I was going to be on hand to spy on your little threesome, but I'm going camping with Jeff and Sandy."

"You little devil."

Grace nodded and gave a self-satisfied smile. "We're going east of the mountains where the sun actually shines, taking Sandy's trailer, a tent, and three mopeds."

"Who's the tent for?"

"The men. I get the trailer all to myself. Isn't that chivalrous?"

"I'll bet chivalry has nothing to do with it," scoffed

Kate. "They just want to be able to belch and pass gas without having to excuse themselves."

"Probably," agreed Grace. "But this will give me the chance to give the ultimate test to Sandy."

"Oh, no, not that."

Grace nodded. "If he cheats at cards, he's history."

"Very sensible," approved Kate.

"No frogs for me."

"It looks like we're both going to come away from the ball with a prince," said Kate.

"I've got my fingers crossed for you," said Grace.

JEFF SAT AT THE TABLE IN THE SEAHAWKS PRESS room, ignoring both his teriyaki chicken and the coach's remarks. Instead, he sat mulling over his unsuccessful stint as a private investigator. It would have helped if he'd been able to get into Grayson's condo. Gary hadn't been even remotely interested in breaking and entering for a good cause, and so far Jeff had been unable to discover anything damning by camping in his car and surveying the condo through his binoculars. He'd thought he was pretty hot stuff when he'd been able to figure out which one was Grayson's, but that had been short-lived. So far he'd watched the place three nights in a row, and all he'd gotten for his trouble was a crick in the neck and a good scare the night that cop car had cruised by. From what Jeff could tell, White was the most boring man on the planet. All he did was watch the tube, talk on the phone, and drink. Last night had looked promising when White emerged onto his balcony, drink in hand, all dressed up to go somewhere. Jeff had tried to tail him, but lost White when he'd sailed through a very orange traffic light on First Avenue. Jeff had caught sight of the patrol car half a block down and killed the urge to follow. By the time he got back in hot pursuit, there was no one to pursue. Then, to cap the evening, he'd missed his boat.

"Hey, Hardin, what's with you," asked Pete Muldrew from KWOW. "Did somebody cut out your tongue or are you still pouting 'cause Bullman got your woman?"

Jeff pulled himself out of his reverie. "What? What woman?"

"I didn't know you had more than one."

"Who are you talking about, Muldrew?"

"Bambi, of course."

"Bambi and Bullman?" How long had that been going on?

Muldrew just shook his head.

The meeting broke up and it was time for the media to hit the locker room and the field and interview players. Jeff tracked down Bullman just as he was heading onto the field for practice.

"So, Don, how's it going?"

Bullman looked at him warily. "Fine."

"I thought you might like to talk about some of the plays you made this summer. On my girl."

"Hey, she wasn't your girl by the time I met her. You guys had broken up."

"Well, you didn't waste any time moving in on her, did you?" said Jeff, stepping up to the tower of muscles in the football jersey.

"She's happy with me, Hardin. And I'm happy with her."

"Yeah, well, I was happy with her, too."

"You weren't right for her. She told me. You guys weren't a match. You were a frog. I'm her prince." Don's chin rose as if daring Jeff to make fun of what he had just said.

Jeff half scowled. "Yeah, the world is full of princes these days. I seem to be the last frog left."

"Hey, man, I'm sorry," said Don.

Jeff realized he'd been acting like a jerk. His heart wasn't breaking over Bambi's defection: the only thing hurting here was his pride. A certain freckle-faced doctor was the one who had his heart on the rack. He shrugged. "She's happy. That's the main thing. And she's got a good guy."

"Thanks, man." Don clapped him on the arm, nearly knocking him off balance, then loped off to practice his American gladiator skills.

Jeff leaned up against the wall of the building and thought again of Kate. It was looking more and more like he was going to lose again. And there was more at stake this time around than pride. He thought of Grayson White and his perfect condo, his perfect clothes, his perfect looks. He suddenly realized his upper lip had lifted and he was baring his teeth like an angry dog. Jealousy alone wasn't going to do him any good. He had to find a way to rip off his rival's mask. Heck with the mask, he'd rather rip off the guy's face. Of course, that would win Kate's enduring love.

Jeff headed for his Jeep, grinding his teeth as he went. Kermit had it right. It wasn't that easy being green.

Seventeen

THE MEN HAD FINISHED PITCHING THEIR TENT NEXT to the camper, which was now snugly parked among the other hundreds of R.V.'s squeezed into a campground full to overflowing with people getting away from it all. The smell of dripping meat grease sizzling on barbecue coals filled the air, and a variety of radio stations played with varying levels of volume, depending on the age of the campers.

The picnic table at the Hardin site was now loaded with bowls of tossed and potato salad, a basket of sourdough rolls, and a platter piled high with cold ham. Off to one side sat a pie.

"What kind of pie is that?" asked Jeff, breaking off a piece of crust.

"Blackberry."

"Okay, Dad, let's eat!" called Jeff and plunked himself down at the table.

"You might want to wait until I get the cutlery out."

"I don't think so," said Jeff. "Just slide that pie in front of me and I'll put my face right in it."

Grace went back into the camper for plates and plastic utensils, and Sandy joined his son, saying, "Boy, does this look good."

Grace returned and dealt out paper plates, then sat down next to Sandy. "Yes, Kate can keep her Space Needle dinners. Me, I'll take simple fare and comfortable clothes every time."

"Hear, hear," said Sandy.

"Space Needle?" Jeff turned to Grace, who suddenly looked like she'd just betrayed a state secret. "I suppose she's there with Mr. Perfect." He knew he shouldn't have agreed to come along on this trip. He should be back home with his trusty binoculars. And watching Grayson paw Kate? On second thought, maybe it was a good thing he was here.

"I'm sorry," said Grace. "I've got a big mouth."

"Who goes to the Space Needle besides tourists?" muttered Jeff. He knew he sounded like a surly fifteen-year-old, but he couldn't help it.

"Well, they're taking a tourist. Grayson's sister is in town."

"His sister, huh?" Jeff speared a piece of ham and shook it onto his plate. "Does she live around here?"

"No," said Grace. "She lives in New York. She's just come out for a visit."

"Isn't it a little early for him to be introducing her to his family?"

"I don't know," said Grace. "She introduced him to the kids."

Jeff shook his head. "It seems to me that the good doctor isn't exactly practicing what she preaches."

"And what's that?" asked Grace.

"Well, doesn't it seem like she's moving this relationship along at a pretty fast pace?"

"It's not like she's getting engaged," countered Grace. "She's simply spending time with Grayson and his sister."

She laid a hand on Jeff's arm. "I'm sorry I opened my big mouth. I hadn't meant to even mention it."

Jeff shrugged. "It's okay. I'm not going to go drown myself in the river or anything. And if Kate's happy, then I'm happy for her." He just wished he'd known about her plans for the weekend. He'd have stuck around home and kept an eye on her.

K ATE TOLD HERSELF IT WAS SILLY TO FEEL NERVOUS. If Grayson's sister was anything like him, they were bound to get along great. The fact that she was nervous spoke volumes, however, and she reminded herself that she shouldn't be placing too much significance on this meeting. It was early days yet. It would be another six months before she could be sure that this relationship was going to go somewhere. In spite of her logical self-talk, her emotions took charge of the situation, keeping her insides jumpy and making it hard for her to sit still.

The boat docked and she followed the herd of people off it and found Grayson waiting in the terminal for her with a slim, beautifully dressed woman at his side. Kate recognized the pretty face and dark hair from the picture in Grayson's condo. She commanded herself not to sweat and moved toward them.

The woman saw her approaching and touched her brother's arm. Grayson turned his head and his face lit up at the sight of Kate. His sister, too, was smiling now as Kate approached.

"Hello, darling," said Grayson, and gave Kate a quick kiss and a warm look. "I'd like you to meet my sister, Anne."

"I feel like I know you already," said Anne, reaching out to shake hands. "Grayson can't stop talking about you."

"And can you see why?" he asked.

Kate felt embarrassed. Compared to Anne, with her

slim waist and stylish clothes, she felt like plain potatoes. "Let's not put your poor sister in a position where she has to lie," she said quickly.

"Don't be silly," said Grayson, giving her a hug. "I thought we'd just take taxis tonight," he said. "After hearing what a crowd shows up for Bumbershoot, I figured it would be easiest."

"Good idea," said Kate.

"I loved your book," Anne said to Kate as they crossed the street to where several taxis stood waiting. "In fact, I loved it so much I went right out and bought your first one. She shook her head. "It seems I've kissed a lot of frogs in my time."

"Haven't we all?" agreed Kate.

They climbed into the taxi and Anne settled back and looked out the window. "This is a lovely city."

"This is your first time here?" asked Kate politely.

Anne nodded. "I've been to the west coast, seen L.A. and San Francisco. I did like San Francisco, but I must say, their Fisherman's Wharf can't hold a candle to what you have here."

"I agree," said Kate.

They continued to chat about different cities each had been in until the taxi let them off. The Center was thronged with people, all come to celebrate Bumbershoot, what *Rolling Stone* magazine termed the mother of all arts festivals.

"My God, what a mob!" exclaimed Anne. "I feel right at home."

"I understand we'll be exposed to everything from dance to drama," said Grayson.

"And music," added Kate. "You name it, it's all here this weekend, everything from classical to Cajun."

Anne turned to Grayson. "This was worth changing my plans for. And, of course, I wouldn't have wanted to miss a chance to spend time with Kate," she added, smiling at Kate.

They stepped into the Space Needle's elevator and rode up to the Sky City restaurant at the top. There, too, they found a crowd.

"It looks like we'll have a wait," said Kate as Grayson made his way to the reservations desk.

"That won't bother me," said Anne. "I'm on vacation. My clock has stopped."

"Grayson tells me you're a stockbroker."

Anne nodded.

"That sounds like a pretty interesting way to earn a living," said Kate.

"Bear market or bull, I love it," said Anne. "There's nothing quite so exciting as watching new companies that I've recommended to my clients grow. I love making 'em rich. And my brother, too," she added as Grayson rejoined them.

"Bragging?" he teased.

"Just a little," said Anne.

"So what growing company are you excited about these days?" asked Kate.

"I have one I've invested in that really has me excited. In fact, Grayson, it's the one I was telling you about: TechEase." Anne turned back to Kate and explained, "This company has created a new user interface even better than Windows. Remember how many millionaires Microsoft created? I'm predicting that investors in this company will be the next wave of technology millionaires."

Millionaires? Kate had an instant vision of yawning lazily as she wrote the checks to her children's Ivy League colleges while stretched out on a deck chair in the stern of her yacht. "Really?" she said. "What are the stocks going for?"

"Right now? Two dollars a share. I bought two hundred and fifty thousand shares before I left. Within two months I'm predicting it will be going for thirty."

Kate thought of that nest egg she was sitting on and imagined it doubling in size with one smart investment.

"Now, don't be trying to suck Kate into your schemes," cautioned Grayson.

"But what if I want to get sucked in?" protested Kate. "Anyway, how two-faced can you get? One minute you're counseling me not to pay cash for my car so I have plenty of liquid funds ready for that great investment opportunity, and the next, when opportunity's knocking on the door, you're hoping I won't answer."

"There are all kinds of investment opportunities," argued Grayson. "New technology can be a gamble."

"This from the man who once said I should have stock in technology?"

Grayson shrugged. "I'd hate to see you lose a bundle. That's all."

"And when have you ever lost on one of my tips?" demanded his sister.

"Very hypocritical," observed Kate.

Grayson looked sheepish. "Well, I can afford to gamble a little."

"So can I," said Kate.

"I know we all hear a lot about people making a killing in the market," he said gently, "but what we don't always hear about is the man who loses his shirt. It can happen in a blink. So far Anne has been lucky."

Anne's pleasant expression hardened. "I am not lucky. I have good instincts and I know what I'm doing. And if you don't think I do, then maybe I don't have to share any more stock tips with you."

"Not share? What would Mom say?" teased Grayson, and she stuck out her tongue at him.

The tense moment passed, and Kate changed the subject. But long after they were seated and Grayson and Anne were deep into childhood reminiscences Kate was still thinking about that new company.

After a leisurely dinner, they left the restaurant to become part of the crowd of celebrants enjoying Bumbershoot. Kate watched the interplay between Grayson and his sister as they went from stage to stage, taking in the different acts, and was impressed by their closeness. A man who was good to the women in his family would be good to a wife.

At twelve, they decided to call it a night. Grayson found them a taxi and they returned Kate to the ferry dock.

"I think this is where I go take an avid interest in the display case," said Anne. "I'll be looking forward to seeing your house tomorrow and meeting your children."

"Well, no children," said Kate. "As it turned out, they both got a better offer."

"Oh, that's too bad," said Anne. "Well, I'm sure I'll get a chance to meet them before I have to go back." She smiled and strolled away, leaving Grayson and Kate to enjoy a kiss and a hug.

"So, how do you like my sister?" he asked.

"She's great."

"I thought you two would hit it off. Can we bring anything tomorrow?"

Kate shook her head. "Just your bathing suits."

"See you around noon, then," he said.

People were starting to board the boat, so he gave her arm a squeeze and she reluctantly left him. She gave one last look over her shoulder as she joined the line of late night passengers and saw him standing where she had left him with Anne back at his side. They both waved goodbye and she waved in return and headed for the walkway.

She had a lot to think about on the ride home, how things were progressing with Grayson, how very much she liked his sister . . . and TechEase.

GRAYSON AND ANNE ARRIVED FOR LUNCH WITH Anne bearing a bottle of white wine.

Kate was touched. "It will go perfectly with the crab salad we're having."

"Oh, good," said Anne. "Wine can be the most perfect gift, but it can also be the most awful failure."

"I don't have much of a head for alcohol," Kate admitted, "but I do like to nurse a glass of white wine occasionally."

"I'd better confess right up front, I'm a lush," said Anne. "So you nurse and I'll guzzle."

"You're supposed to be making an impression," scolded Grayson.

"She is," Kate assured him. "I like honesty."

After lunch Kate took them to the Bloedel Reserve, and Anne exclaimed over everything. "Why do I bother to go to Provence in the summer when I could just come here?"

Provence in the summer? Kate thought again about TechEase and vowed to find out more about it. Of course, she didn't want Anne to think she was only interested in her for the money she could make. But, Anne had opened the door the night before, and when an opportune moment came, Kate saw no harm in reintroducing the subject into conversation.

She had her chance after they returned to the house to go for a swim. Grayson was still doing a marathon crawl, but the women had packed it in and were lolling on the dock. Kate hadn't felt too bad looking at herself in her blue tankini in Bon Marche's dressing room, but comparing herself now to Anne, who was looking svelte in a black number with a plunging neckline, she felt like the Pillsbury doughboy's sister.

"I swear I've gained five pounds since I came out here," complained Anne, slathering sunblock on a perfect, thin thigh.

Kate found it hard to sympathize. Anyway, she didn't want to talk about weight issues, she wanted to talk about money.

"You know, I've been thinking about that new company you mentioned."

"TechEase?"

"Do you really think it's a good deal?"

"I wouldn't have bought two hundred and fifty thousand shares if I didn't," said Anne.

"Your brother doesn't appear to be quite so impressed."

"Oh, don't mind him. I know for a fact he's planning on buying a hundred thousand shares. He's just concerned that if you were to invest and didn't double your money or, worse yet, if you lost money, you'd blame him."

"That's ridiculous. Why would I?"

Anne grinned. "That's what I asked him last night. Anyway, if you want to know more about it, check the OTC Bulletin Board. If it sounds good we can talk again."

Grayson returned from his swim and joined them on the dock. He had the most beautiful body Kate had ever seen: well muscled and tanned, with a fascinating smattering of black hair on his chest.

"I hope Anne wasn't telling you all my childhood secrets," he said to Kate.

"No, we were talking about investment opportunities."

Grayson rolled his eyes. "Don't tell me she's still trying to part you from your hard-earned money."

"If I part from it, it will be because I decided to," said Kate firmly. "I've been managing my money quite well for some time now."

"If you think you should invest in this company Anne's so wild about, who am I to stop you?"

"Especially since you're going to invest," pointed out Kate.

"Well, yes, I am," he admitted. "But I can afford to lose money."

"I told you before, so can I," said Kate.

"But neither one of you is going to, so that's a moot point," said Anne. "What about having lunch with me one day next week and we'll talk a little more. I'll even leak all those childhood secrets of Grayson's. Oh, that's right, you're on the air, aren't you?"

"I'm afraid so," said Kate.

"Well, then, let's grab an iced coffee after you get off."

"That sounds great," said Kate.

"How about Tuesday?" suggested Anne.

"I'm meeting my parents at the airport at five. Filling in the wait after work will be great."

"Good," said Anne. "We can talk about Grayson to our hearts' content without worrying about him showing up to eavesdrop," she added, bumping him with her shoulder.

THE OTC.BB WASN'T THE NASDAQ, BUT KATE FIGured since it was administered by the National Association of Stock Dealers it was just as good a source of information. She got the kids off for their first day of school Tuesday morning, then logged on to her computer, brought up the bulletin board, and did a search for TechEase. Sure enough, there it was in all its glory. The stock had been moving, and now it was selling for not two, but three dollars a share.

A knock at her kitchen door told her that Grace was up and ready to share her camping adventures. Cup of tea in hand, Kate went to let her in.

"So, how is life over there in cowboy land?" she asked.

"Warm and sunny," said Grace.

Kate poured a mug of tea for her friend and handed it over.

"Funny coincidence, it was warm and sunny here, too. Come on back in my office. I was just on the computer checking a hot stock tip."

"Oh, that's right. Grayson's sister is in town. So, did you two hit it off?"

"Yes, we did."

Kate sat back down in front of the computer. "Look at this," she said, pointing to the screen. "This stock is now selling for three dollars a share. Last week it was two. Anne is predicting that within two months it will be up to thirty."

"What kind of company is it?" asked Grace.

"It's a software company, and Anne thinks it's going to make millionaires out of everyone who invests. Well, providing you invest the right amount of money."

"At the right time," added Grace.

"It looks to me like the right time is now."

"So, this sister of Grayson's . . ."

"Is the one partly responsible for the fact that he could quit working tomorrow if he wanted," said Kate.

"Hmmm," said Grace thoughtfully. "Maybe I'd better ask my broker about this."

"I'm considering buying some," said Kate. "I think I'll watch it today and see how it does."

K ATE LOGGED ON TO THE OTC.BB AGAIN AFTER she got to work and saw that more TechEase stock had moved. "Oh, my."

"Oh, my, what?" asked Wallis. "What's this?"

"A hot new company that Grayson's sister the stock expert told me about. She thinks this is going to be up to thirty dollars a share in two months."

Wallis looked again at the current stock price. "That's a nice profit."

"I'd say so," said Kate. "Got some money you can invest?"

Wallis sat for a moment, chewing her lip. "About ten thousand."

"Grayson's sister seems to think TechEase stockholders will become the equivalent of Microsoft millionaires," said Kate thoughtfully. "What would you do if you became a millionaire?"

"Quit this job," said Wallis. "Not that I don't love producing you, of course."

"Of course," said Kate. "Quit and do what?"

Wallis's face took on a dreamy expression. "Buy into a

radio station. I always wanted a station of my very own. What would you do with a million dollars?"

"Who's getting a million dollars?" asked George, walking in on them.

"We are if we invest in this company," said Wallis. "Got some spare change in your piggy bank, George?"

K ATE FOUND IT DIFFICULT TO CONCENTRATE ON her callers' problems. Her mind kept visiting a pleasant future where she flew the Concorde to France, cruised in the Greek Islands, and visited the pyramids in Egypt. She also had her own personal trainer—Bambi—and her own chef, who knew one hundred and one recipes for non-fattening chocolate desserts.

"I think I'm going to invest in TechEase," she told Anne as they sat at a café table in the Westlake Mall that afternoon and drank iced coffees.

"Funny you should mention that," said Anne. "I've been thinking about what Grayson would do to me if you invested your hard-earned money and didn't make a profit."

"Absolutely nothing," said Kate. "I think I made it plain to him that I'm fully capable of making my own financial decisions."

"Not that that's going to happen anyway, mind you," added Anne. "I've checked this out pretty carefully, and have advised my clients to buy now."

"That's good enough for me," said Kate.

"Well, it still might not be good enough for Grayson. I know you're a big girl, and so am I, but I'm still the man's sister, and we're close. So, I think I've come up with a way to do better for you and keep Grayson happy, too. Like I said when we first met, I've got good instincts, and lately my instincts have been telling me that we're going to end up being sisters."

Kate felt her cheeks warming.

Anne hurried on before she could speak. "Having read your books, I know it's too soon for either of you to be talking about anything seriously, but, frankly, when there's money to be made on the stock market, you can't take the same length of time you do to develop a relationship. If you wait, you lose. So, here's my proposition. I bought my stock at a dollar a share. How about if I sell you fifty thousand shares for what I paid?"

Kate looked at Anne in shock. "Anne, I can't let you do that."

"Sure, you can," said Anne. "I do this kind of favor for Grayson all the time."

"Yes, but we're not related."

"Yet," added Anne with a grin. "Don't worry, Kate. It won't break me. But if it will make you feel better, when the stock hits thirty dollars a share you can pay me the two-dollar difference between what I paid and what it's going for now. Okay?"

"That's a deal," said Kate.

"Meanwhile, if you've got friends who want to make a killing, I'd get them in on this."

"Actually, I've already told a couple," admitted Kate.

"Good. There's enough for everyone."

"I think you and Grayson are coming to my mother's birthday party on Sunday night," said Kate. "How would it be if I gave you a check then?"

"Fine," said Anne.

"*Y*OU LOOK WONDERFUL," SAID CAROL HEWITT after she and Kate had hugged. "Being in love agrees with you."

Kate laughed. "It's either love or the killing I'm going to make on the stock market."

"Oh, what's this?" asked her dad.

"I'll tell you on the way to the baggage claim," said Kate, and proceeded to fill them in as they all made their way down the concourse. "And Grayson's sister is selling me fifty thousand of her shares for the same price she paid: a dollar a share," said Kate as they stood scanning the luggage riding the carousel.

"My goodness!" exclaimed her mother. "Things must really be getting serious between you and Grayson."

"I don't know," said her father. He leaned over and hauled off a huge black suitcase marked with a pink ribbon, then set it down with a grunt. "I'm always a little leery of these technology companies."

"Which is why the young people are making all the money these days," said his wife. "Come on, Frank, you have to change with the times or you get left behind."

"And just what are you saying?" demanded Frank Hewitt.

"That we should think about investing in this company while the stock is affordable," said his wife.

"We can check the OTC.BB tomorrow and see if it's moved," said Kate.

"A good idea," agreed her mother. "Now, tell us all about Grayson."

Kate obliged and that kept them talking clear from baggage claim all the way into Seattle and onto the ferry.

"Well, we're glad you've found someone you think you can be happy with," said Kate's father.

"It's looking more and more that way," admitted Kate.

"And I guess he's more your type than the guy who does the sports show," he added.

"Sorry, Dad."

"Don't be sorry, kidlet. It's your life. We just want you to be happy."

"I am," Kate assured him.

"THIS STOCK SOUNDS LIKE SOMETHING I OUGHT to invest in," said Sandy after Grace had told him about TechEase over hamburgers.

"I think you should," said Grace. "It's already doubled."

"I've got a few thousand tucked away for a rainy day."

"Well, it's raining," said Grace. "Get your umbrella and call my broker."

THE NEXT MORNING SANDY CALLED JEFF. "HI THERE, son, are you awake?"

Jeff looked at his clock. It was only eight-thirty. "I am now," he groaned.

"Good, because I've got a hot stock tip for you."

"Since when are you a stock expert?"

"Since I talked to Grace last night."

"I didn't know Grace was an expert."

"She got the tip from Kate, who got it from her boyfriend's sister the stockbroker."

Jeff was fully awake now, and the hairs at the back of his neck were standing at attention. "Have you put money in this, Dad?"

"Yep," said Sandy. "I took that four thousand I've had sitting in savings and put it to good use."

Jeff felt sick. "And how about Grace, how much has she put in?"

"I think about seven thousand," said Sandy.

"Dad, you get your money back right now and tell Grace to do the same."

"What? What are you talking about?

"It's a scam."

"That's the dumbest thing I ever heard," said Sandy in disgust. "You think Grace's stockbroker is going to be in on a scam?"

Jeff's racing blood pressure settled. "You got it through her stockbroker?"

"Yes, it's perfectly legit."

Okay, maybe he'd jumped to conclusions.

"And the information is right up there on that stock bulletin board on the Internet."

"I'll check it out," said Jeff.

"Well, you should," said Sandy, his voice stiff with insult. "I only paid three dollars a share, and the stock is supposed to be up to thirty dollars a share in two months. I'd say that's a pretty good return on my investment. Wouldn't you?"

"Yeah," said Jeff.

He got out of bed and went to the desk where his powerbook was sitting and booted up. He hit the over-the-counter bulletin board and found TechEase listed there. It should have made him feel relieved. It didn't. Everything looked right, so why was his gut telling him something was wrong?

"Because you're a jealous idiot," he muttered. *And in a few months you'll be the only man at KZOO who isn't a TechEase millionaire.*

"YEAH, I DON'T KNOW, EITHER, HARRY," FRANK Hewitt said to his stockbroker. "I tell you what, buy me five hundred shares and let's watch this carefully."

"You're such a big spender," teased Kate as her father hung up the phone.

"I believe in being cautious. So does my stockbroker."

"That's not how you get rich," said Kate.

Frank pointed his coffee mug at her and countered, "That's not how you get poor, either."

"Oh, enough, you two," said Carol. "Let's talk about something more pleasant, like what we're going to do tonight when Kate gets home."

"How does dinner at Bill and Janet's sound?" suggested Kate. "Bill's planning on barbecuing salmon, and he and Dad can talk sports to their hearts' content."

"That sounds like a good idea," said Frank.

"And I'm sure Grace will want to visit with you this afternoon," said Kate.

"Well, while the women visit I think I'll tackle that leaky faucet in your bathroom," said Frank.

WHILE FRANK POUNDED AND SWORE AT THE plumbing in Kate's bathroom, Grace and Carol sat on her porch swing, drinking lemonade and discussing Kate's radio program and the kids.

"Tell me, what's Grayson White like?" asked Carol.

"I haven't met him yet," said Grace, "but according to your daughter he is the most perfect man who ever drew breath."

"They all do look that way when you're in love, don't they?" said Carol.

"This one does sound like something, I've got to admit," said Grace. "And probably a better match for Kate than Jeff, but I've got to admit I was partial to him."

"The neighbor?"

Grace nodded. "He's quite a guy."

"He seems to have made an impression on the kids," said Carol. "Robbie, especially, dropped his name a lot."

"He is a doll," said Grace, "but he and Kate had a few misunderstandings, and it started the whole relationship off on the wrong foot."

"Well, Kate knows human nature, and she certainly knows what she wants. I'm sure we'll like Grayson when we meet him."

"We'd just better be sure to have our sunglasses handy," said Grace. "All that dazzling brilliance may be hard on the eyes."

THAT NIGHT WHILE THE KIDS WHOOPED AROUND the backyard and the adults sat at the patio table, Kate shared her stock tip with Janet and Bill. "I'm giving

Grayson's sister a check Saturday night for fifty thousand shares," she concluded.

"Hmmm," said Bill thoughtfully. "Maybe we should see if we can scrounge up some money. What do you think, babe?"

"I think I want to be a millionaire," said Janet. "I suppose this means I'll have to learn to like champagne."

"Probably," said her husband. "But you could make the sacrifice, right?"

"Anything for family," she said. "Tell Grayson's sister we'll name our next child after her. Oh, that's right, I had my tubes tied. Tell her we'll name our next dog after her."

"She'll be touched," said Kate.

"So, HAVE YOU BOUGHT SOME OF THAT HOT STOCK yet?" asked Luke, Jeff's producer.

"Oh, not you, too," moaned Jeff.

"Hey, George told me it's going to be up to thirty bucks a share in a month. Why not?"

A month? When he'd talked to his dad it had been two months. This just got better-sounding with each new buyer. He didn't care. He still didn't like it.

"Because . . ." Jeff stopped. What could he say? Because Grayson White's sister suggested it and I hate Grayson White? Who did he think he was punishing by not buying into this company, anyway? Certainly not White. "I don't know," he finished weakly. "It just sounds fishy to me."

"Fishy? How? My stockbroker bought it for me, and he's an on-the-level guy."

Jeff scratched his nose. "I don't know. Something's wrong here, I just feel it."

Luke looked at him like he was nuts.

Maybe he was, he thought later as he sat in his car, watching White's condo. If Kate knew what he was doing she'd tell him he was sick and obsessed. Well, okay, so he was sick and obsessed, just like that poor fool in *Of Human Bondage*. So maybe someday, somebody would write a book about him and it would become a classic. Meanwhile, he was going to follow this obsession and see where it led.

Eighteen

JEFF'S OBSESSION LED HIM NOWHERE. HE FELL ASLEEP listening on his car radio to a talk show that specialized in weirdness and dreamed he got kidnapped by aliens. His bug-faced kidnappers were cutting into his big toe to plant a tracking device when he awoke with a start. Rubbing his foot, he checked his dashboard clock and saw it was almost two.

Great. If he stomped the gas he'd just make the last ferry. He looked up at White's condo. Naturally, it was dark. White had probably come in after Jeff dozed off and had, himself, been sawing logs for a couple of hours. Only idiots and insomniacs were awake at this hour during the week. Idiot Hardin swore and headed for the ferry. He thought of Snoopy from *Peanuts* shaking his paw and growling, "I'll get you, Red Baron." What he was doing made about as much sense as Snoopy's threats. Snoopy was a dog. What was his excuse?

• • •

HE WAS STILL STEWING OVER HIS STUPIDITY when Grace arrived on his doorstep with a plate of cinnamon rolls. "I haven't seen you in a while," she chided.

"I've been keeping out of sight so I won't rain on anyone's parade," he said, stepping aside to let her in.

"Probably a good idea, although I suspect Kate's dad has been hoping to meet you."

"And I know Kate's been hoping for a chance to introduce me."

Grace didn't say anything to that. Instead, she said, "Your father tells me you don't have much faith in Kate's hot stock tip. Why?"

He shook his head. "No good reason. I just don't trust White."

"Could you be a little biased?"

"I could be a lot biased, but I still don't trust him, and I wish everyone would quit throwing money at him and his sister."

"It's too good a deal to pass up," said Grace.

Jeff plucked a cinnamon roll off the plate and tore into it. "Yeah, I guess. How much has Kate paid in?"

"Nothing yet, but her mom told me yesterday that Anne is selling Kate some of her stock at a dollar a share. She's going to give Anne a check for fifty thousand dollars when we go out to dinner for Carol's birthday Sunday night."

Jeff sucked in his breath and choked on the roll. After much coughing and back-slapping he managed to croak, "Fifty thousand. What the hell is she thinking of?"

"Doubling her money, I guess. I wish I had fifty thousand and a generous friend."

"Yeah, well, this woman sounds a little too generous to me," muttered Jeff.

"For a future sister-in-law?"

Jeff set what was left of the cinnamon roll back onto the plate with the others. Suddenly he'd lost his appetite.

• • •

BY FRIDAY IT LOOKED LIKE EVERY FRIEND AND relative Kate had was buying into TechEase. This had to be on the level, thought Jeff. What would it be doing on the OTC.BB if it wasn't? Still, he couldn't get his earlier conversation with Gary Nase out of his mind. What if this was some sort of sweetheart scam?

He called Gary. "Gar, can you run a stock scam and have it show up on the over-the-counter bulletin board?"

"Sure," said Gary. "The OTC.BB has a much lower reporting requirement than NASDAQ, so it's easier to slip stuff in."

"I think Kate's about to get swindled. What have you found on Grayson White?"

"Not much yet," said Gary. "Tell me why you think that."

Jeff related what he'd been hearing about Kate's activities and mentioned the other people who had invested so far in TechEase.

"It's possible," said Gary. "And with that many people chasing them with their checkbooks, these guys could easily walk away with a hundred thousand dollars. And that's just Kate and her circle of friends. Chances are, White could be working the same con on at least one other woman in the area, so he could easily double or triple that number. Not bad pay for a couple months of sweet talking."

Jeff swore. "You've got to pull out all the stops, Gar. We've got to get this guy and fast. Kate's handing over a check to his sister day after tomorrow for fifty thou."

"Sister," scoffed Gary. "You can bet this woman ain't his sister."

"Well, find me the proof and get your butt over to the island first thing tomorrow," said Jeff. "I'm not going to see Kate get taken."

Saturday morning Gary was still assuring Jeff that the Nose was on the case, and Jeff was feeling so nervous he felt ready to burst out of his skin. They only had one day left. What if Gary didn't get all his evidence gathered in time? Kate would hand over her check and the Bunko Kids would disappear into the night.

He had to warn Kate. Without evidence, she'd never believe him, but he might at least be able to convince her to be cautious and wait another day or two to turn over her money. It would buy Gar some time to finish up his research, and keep Kate safe another couple of days.

And as much as she respected Jeff, she'd listen to anything he had to say. He sank onto his couch and dropped his head into his hands. He couldn't do this. It was hopeless.

Laughter from next door crept in through his open window and he thought of all the people who would suffer if White and his accomplice succeeded. Kate would be ticked at him for butting in. Better ticked than broke and humiliated. He had to make her understand, explain to her how these guys worked, get her to step back and look at this situation as Doctor Kate, specialist in human behavior, instead of Kate Stonewall, infatuated woman.

Okay, here's what you do, Hardin. You just wander over and say a neighborly hello, then you ask to talk to Kate for a minute. You present your case logically, detail by detail. And hope she doesn't kick you in the shins.

It would look better if he came bearing gifts, something for her folks, maybe? What did he have sitting around the house that he could take?

He suddenly remembered the two tickets to Monday's Mariners game presently residing in his wallet. Those tickets were promised to Gar, but, hey, Gar would understand. This was for a good cause. Jeff pulled them out, then headed next door.

Kate's expression looked less than welcoming as he approached her porch, where everyone was gathered. His guts turned to jelly, but he forced himself to keep walking.

Robbie called his name and both the kids hopped off the porch and ran to greet him, each one grabbing an arm and towing him to the other adults.

"Nice day," he said once they reached the steps.

"It was," said Kate. "Mom, Dad, this is my neighbor, Jeff Hardin. These are my parents, Carol and Frank Hewitt."

Jeff saw that Frank was smiling, obviously neutral, and Carol was looking at him like he was on sale for fifty percent off. The parents weren't as prejudiced as their daughter. That was a good sign. Kate didn't offer him either a drink or a seat. That was not a good sign.

He cleared his throat. "I just came by with something I thought your dad might appreciate." Jeff held up the tickets. "I've got a couple of tickets to the Mariners game on Monday, and I thought if you were still going to be in town you might like to go."

"Oh boy!" cried Robbie. "Can you and me go, Grandpa?"

"We don't have plans for that night, do we, Katie?" asked Frank.

"No," said Kate, clearly untouched by Jeff's generosity.

"Then, we'll accept," said Frank, and Jeff handed over the tickets.

"Would you like some iced tea?" offered Carol Hewitt, taking up her daughter's hostess slack.

"Actually, I was hoping I could talk to Kate for a minute," said Jeff, and his heart began to thud violently. "It's, um, business."

"Come on into my office," said Kate, then led the way through the kitchen door and back through the house into what looked like a spare bedroom fitted out with a desk and computer and a bookcase full of psychology books.

Jeff noticed the diplomas and awards decorating the room, and his hands started to sweat. Kate was no dim bulb who didn't know what she was doing. She was an intelligent woman who understood the human mind. And now he was about to try and convince her that the man she loved was a fake and the stock she was about to buy was phony, and the only proof he had was his own gut feeling.

"What did you need to talk to me about?"

His T-shirt was strangling him. He craned his neck. "Well."

"Oh, come on, Jeff. My parents are here. I don't have time to watch you go through your thinking ritual. What are you here for?"

He gnawed the inside of his lip, trying to find a delicate way to put it.

She turned and headed for the door. "Call me when you remember."

"Wait." He reached out and grabbed her arm.

She stopped and looked at him, eyebrows raised. "Wait," he repeated.

"Wait for?"

"Another day or two before you hand over the money for that stock."

"What?"

"You're getting this from Grayson's sister, right?"

"Yes," she said slowly. "Who told you?"

"Never mind that. Just promise me you'll wait another day."

"You are making no sense."

"Kate, I think you're being taken."

She removed his hand. "I don't know what you're talking about, but—"

Jeff didn't let her finish. "I think Grayson White is running some kind of con on you."

Her eyes flew open wide at that. She looked like the human equivalent of a deer caught in the headlights of an oncoming car. But only for a second, then she morphed into a Rottweiler. "How dare you!"

"I know it sounds crazy," said Jeff quickly.

"It sounds worse than that. Have you got proof of this, a police photo, some sort of rap sheet?"

"Well, no. Not yet."

"Not yet? What is that supposed to mean?"

"Well, I have this friend who's a private detective."

"You set a private detective on Grayson?"

"Not exactly."

Kate pulled open her office door so hard Jeff thought she was going to take it right off the hinges. "Scram."

"Kate, just let me explain."

"Get out of my house. Don't ever even think of crossing so much as a toe over my property line again. If you do, I'll get a restraining order."

"Oh, God, Kate. I'm not trying to make you mad."

"You don't even have to try! Get out."

"Kate, you've got to listen."

"If you don't get out right now, I will call the police."

Jeff admitted defeat and got out and she slammed the door after him. He sighed. *You handled that well, Hardin.*

KATE PACED THE ROOM, TRYING TO IMAGINE THE best way to murder Jeff Hardin. Tie him up and tow him to sea behind his ski boat, then feed him to sharks? Much too sporting. Make him eat quiche and listen to old Tiny Tim records? Not nearly cruel enough. Her pacing picked up speed. Of course, his behavior was nothing more than immature acting-out, spawned by jealousy.

But look what he was doing to her: he was turning her into an out-of-control, ranting idiot. "I hate you!" she cried, and stamped her foot.

She heard a tap at the door, followed by her mother's voice. "Kate, are you all right?"

Kate pulled herself together. "I'm fine," she called. "I'll be out in a minute. As soon as I'm sane again," she added under her breath.

"All right," said her mother, sounding far from reassured.

Kate fell onto the nearest chair and took several deep breaths. Okay, that was better. Now, she was going to go back out onto the porch and enjoy her family. Tomorrow she would go out with Grayson and his sister and all those who were close to her and celebrate her mother's birthday. And it would be a wonderful, memorable occasion because by then she would have wiped Jeff Hardin's childish accusations from her mind completely. Con artists, indeed! How silly and sick, and . . . typically Jeff Hardin!

I T WAS LATE SUNDAY AFTERNOON WHEN GARY called Jeff. "Hey, man. I think I've got your boy. And if he turns out to be who I think he is you've caught yourself a big one."

So he was right. *Great, just great.*

Gary talked on, dutifully sharing the mountain of dirt he'd dug up on Grayson, or whatever his real name was. It was more than Jeff wanted to know, certainly more than he wanted to tell Kate.

"Okay. I get the picture," he said. "Now get over here and help me explain all this to Kate before it's too late."

G RAYSON AND ANNE WERE ALREADY IN THE TINY lobby of San Carlos restaurant when Kate and her family arrived. As always, the place was hopping with bustling food servers and people waiting for a table and a chance to try the restaurant's award-winning Southwestern cuisine. People sat under umbrellas outside, enjoying margaritas and fish tacos or the restaurant's award winning white bean chili. The laughter drifting in to the waiting patrons promised good times. So did the smiles her family and friends exchanged as Kate made the introductions.

Lee, the owner, came out of the kitchen to greet his guests, then they followed the hostess down the stairs and into what must have originally been the living room in this converted old house.

They seated themselves around the table, with Grayson and Frank on each end, Grayson having Kate and her mom on either side of him. Anne, who was looking glamorous in a plain, black knit dress with half-carat diamonds glittering in her ears, sat next to Frank. On one ear she also wore an expensive gold hoop, and Kate knew after they got home Amanda, who now sat between her and Kate, would be asking for another hole in one of her lobes. On the other side of the table, Robbie got settled between Grace and Carol, and Kate noticed he was already fidgeting in his seat, waiting for the restaurant's popular freshly made chips to arrive so he'd have something to play with.

"Mrs. Hewitt, I can see where your daughter gets her good looks," said Grayson as soon as they were all settled.

Carol blushed and waved away his compliment, and he easily steered them into conversation about her life in San Diego.

Kate let her gaze stray to where her father and Anne sat, and from the snatches of their conversation, she could tell they were already in conversation about the stock market. Although Anne was too deep into her favorite subject to notice Amanda, the girl was nonetheless hanging on Anne's every word as if Anne were discussing the latest article in *Disney* magazine. Grace was listening to Anne just as avidly.

Kate smiled. Everyone had hit it off beautifully. This was the perfect dinner party. And after dinner, they'd all go back to the house for cake and ice cream, and the kids would read the poems they wrote in honor of their grandmother's birthday.

Grayson caught her eye and smiled, concluding his conversation with Carol by saying, "Well, I'm glad your daughter wound up in Seattle. If she hadn't I might never have met her."

He took Kate's hand and gave it a squeeze, and she smiled at him. How perfect life was when you just held out for your prince! This had all been worth waiting for.

The busboy arrived and poured water, and the waiter took their drink orders. Everyone ordered margaritas and piña coladas, and Kate ordered virgin piña coladas for the kids.

"Be careful and don't spill," she cautioned Robbie when his arrived.

He nodded and grabbed it with both hands.

Anne broke off talking with Kate's father and directed her attention to Amanda. "Amanda, how old are you?"

Her tone of voice seemed a little condescending to Kate, but she supposed, being a single career girl with no nephews or nieces, Anne didn't have much experience with children.

Amanda didn't seem to notice it. "Almost eleven," she said.

"Have you got a boyfriend?" teased Anne.

"No," giggled Amanda.

"Got somebody you like?"

"Maybe," said Amanda mysteriously.

This was news to Kate, and she stared in surprise.

"Is he cute?"

Amanda nodded.

"And does he like you?"

Amanda simply shrugged, then asked, "Have you got a boyfriend?"

"I'm still looking," said Anne. "Do you know anyone cool I should try for?"

"Jeff Hardin," put in Robbie, and some of the adults chuckled. Kate frowned and took a slug of her drink.

"And who is Jeff Hardin?" asked Anne.

"My competition," said Grayson.

Kate gave a snort of disgust. "Hardly."

"He's Kate's neighbor," explained Grace. "He does a sports talk show at her station."

Anne wrinkled her nose. "I'm afraid I'm not much of a sports nut."

"You and my daughter both," said Frank.

Conversation eddied into several directions after that, and Kate found herself visiting with Anne.

"I never thought I'd hear myself say this, but I'm going to hate to go back to New York," said Anne with a sigh.

"The pace here is so much more relaxed than on the east coast. I feel like a whole different person out here."

"It is nice," agreed Kate.

"But I do like what I do, and I love being at the center of things."

"Speaking of which," said Kate, grabbing her purse. She pulled her check made out to Anne from her wallet and handed it over.

"I'll make sure this gets taken care of first thing tomorrow," promised Anne.

"Thanks again for doing this. I still think it's awfully generous."

"I believe in sharing the wealth, especially with future relatives," said Anne. "There's enough of this pie for everyone."

"Are we having pie?" asked Robbie, making Kate smile fondly. Anne changed the subject.

JEFF SNATCHED UP THE PHONE RECEIVER AND snapped, "Hello."

"It's me," said Gary.

"Where the hell are you? You were supposed to be here an hour ago."

"I missed the boat."

"Well, that's just great. They're all at the restaurant, and for all I know Kate's already handed over the check."

"Are they coming back to the house afterward?"

"I don't know," said Jeff, kicking himself for not thinking to check out that possibility.

"Well, the boat's just loading, and it's only a thirty-five–minute crossing."

"They could be gone in thirty-five minutes. They've already been there for almost an hour." Jeff came to a sudden decision. "Don't come to my place. Go straight to San Carlos. I'll try to hold them there." He gave Gary directions, then hung up and pawed through the clutter on his desk for something he could use to hold off the bad guys until the good guys arrived, with the hard evidence.

THEY WERE NEARLY DONE, AND IN ANOTHER minute the waiters would come out to sing "Happy Birthday" to Carol. "Don't anyone order dessert," said Kate. "We've got cake and ice cream back at the house."

"That sounds good to me," said Grayson. He looked at his sister. "What do you think, Anne?"

Studying her new friend's face, Kate suddenly knew why Anne hadn't been contributing too much to the dinner conversation the last twenty minutes. Her eyebrows were drawn together and her mouth looked pinched. She was obviously not feeling well.

Anne managed a weak smile, but shook her head. "I hate to miss out on cake, but I think I'm getting a migraine."

"Oh, I get them sometimes," said Carol. "They're no fun. The only thing that helps me is to take those magic pills my doctor prescribed and lie down in a darkened room."

"I think that's where I'm headed," said Anne. "I'm sorry, Grayson, but you'd better get me home right away."

"Of course," he said, and started to rise.

At that moment Robbie's face lit up and he called, "Hi, Jeff."

Kate's blood pressure shot up and she turned in her seat to see Jeff Hardin approaching their table, a manila folder tucked under one arm and his mouth set in a grim line.

He strode to Grayson's side and pushed on his shoulder, lowering him back to his seat. "Where are you going? The party's just starting, and you don't want to leave yet, Mr. White. Or should I say Andrew Long? Or is it really Oliver Macaphrey?"

"What are you doing?" demanded Kate, jumping up.

Grayson looked up at him coldly. "Who are you?"

"This is my obnoxious neighbor, Jeff Hardin," said Kate. "Who I told to leave me alone," she added through clenched teeth.

"More to the point," said Jeff, ignoring her, "who are you? Really?" He held up the folder like a lawyer presenting evidence.

"This folder says you're a grifter, a con man. You've worked every major city from L.A. to New York, and you take women for large amounts of money."

"You're insane," said Grayson coldly.

"At least I'm not a celebrity like you. I haven't made it onto *America's Most Wanted.*"

Kate looked at the folder. This was impossible. It simply couldn't be. "Grayson?"

"Oh, for heaven's sake, Kate," said Grayson in disgust. "You don't believe this preposterous fabrication, do you?"

"I suppose you read about Kate's syndication deal in the paper and thought she'd be an easy mark," said Jeff. "A lonely widow with a bestseller, a syndication deal, and money in the bank."

"I don't have to sit here and take this," said Grayson, rising again.

"Oh, yes, you do," said Jeff, shoving him back so hard his chair nearly tipped.

"You little creep," snarled Grayson, jumping back up. "I'll sue you for everything you've got."

"From jail?" taunted Jeff.

"That's enough," cried Kate, taking Jeff by the arm and turning him to face her. "If you have so much proof that Grayson is a criminal why aren't the police here with you?"

"They will be," said Jeff. "Any minute."

"Well, you'll have to excuse me, but I have no intention of staying here to be insulted. I'll call you tomorrow, Kate." Grayson straightened his jacket. "And I suggest you consider carefully before you start throwing around wild accusations, Mr. Hardin. I have a very good lawyer."

He started to walk past Jeff, saying, "Come on, Anne. Let's get you home."

"Oh, no, you don't," said Jeff, grabbing his arm.

"Why don't we just see what's in that folder," suggested Frank, coming around the table.

Grayson attempted to shrug off Jeff's hand and push past him, but Jeff held on. "Take your hand off me," said Grayson in a low voice.

"In your dreams."

Their waiter had rounded up a few other servers and now they were approaching, bearing a small bowl of ice cream with a candle in it and singing "Happy Birthday."

Grayson shoved Jeff, and Jeff shoved back.

"Happy birthday to you?" sang the waiters dubiously as the shoving match became more violent.

"Let's just stay calm," said Frank, his voice rising.

The men locked together like two warring bucks fighting over a doe and began to career around the floor. They barreled past Kate and into the impromptu chorale, causing them to warble "Whoaaa," and dive for cover. All conversation in the restaurant had now changed to horrified gasps and screams as the two men ricocheted from table to table. From the far end of the room Kate heard Lee hollering, "Call the cops."

The men spun like a gigantic top, finally landing backward on a table, which promptly tipped and spattered refried beans and guacamole in all directions. The two middle-aged women sitting at it jumped up. One screeched and another one grabbed a glass of water from a nearby table and threw it on them, shouting, "Stop this right now!"

Frank rushed into the fray and attempted to separate the combatants, and they got tossed against more tables, sending rice and enchiladas flying.

"Food fight!" cried Robbie in glee and grabbed the remains of his refried beans and hurled them at Anne.

They hit her squarely on the backside, earning him an endearing epithet, "Little Shit."

Rubbing at the stain with a napkin, she headed for the bathroom.

"Stop that woman!" yelled Jeff right before Grayson punched him in the jaw and sent him sprawling onto a horrified woman's lap.

Kate was unable to stop anyone. She found all she could do was stand rooted while Grayson and Jeff tore up the restaurant and Anne went to repair the damage done by her son. Surely this was a bad dream, or a Groucho Marx movie. Any minute Harpo would come skipping in, honking his horn. She watched in growing horror as Grace went to take Anne's arm, saying, "I think we'd better wait for the police."

Anne jerked away, snarling, "Don't touch me, you bitch."

"Don't you yell at her," cried Amanda, and grabbed the back of the departing Anne's dress, making it rip.

Kate closed her eyes. This was not happening. Think of a field, a field of wildflowers.

The commotion grew and she opened her eyes to see that nearly every able-bodied man in the restaurant had now joined the fray. The Groucho Marx food fight had deteriorated into a barroom brawl.

Four of Bainbridge Island's finest made their entrance, and the sight of them ended the brawl, but not the heated accusations, which were flying faster than the food had been earlier.

"Officer, this man assaulted me," said Grayson. "I want him arrested."

"Actually," put in Frank, "I think it was you who threw the first punch."

"That's how it was," agreed Grace, who was holding onto a glowering Anne by the scraps of her dress.

As the waiters started to set tables upright and scrape food off the floor, the officers separated people and began to take statements. They were most interested in what Jeff and Grayson had to say.

"Officer, this man is a con artist," said Jeff. "He and his phony sister are running some sort of stock swindle, and she has my friend's check for fifty thousand dollars in her purse."

"I'm a stockbroker on the New York exchange," said Anne between gritted teeth, "and I'm going to sue your ass off, little man."

The officer was writing in his tablet. "That's a big accusation to make, sir."

"Well, it's true," said Jeff, "and I can prove it."

"Show them your folder," suggested Frank.

"Um," said Jeff.

Frank scooped the folder from where it had fallen, brushed the rice off it, and shoved the papers back in.

"My friend the detective should be here any minute," said Jeff. "His information is more up-to-date."

"Let's look at this," said the cop. He took the file and opened it, then looked at the top paper. He frowned. "This is notes about some golf player."

Nineteen

Kate glared at Jeff. "That's your big proof that Grayson is a con artist? You started a fight in a restaurant over that?"

The cop's eyes narrowed. "This is going to be a pretty costly joke."

"It's not a joke," said Jeff. "I was just trying to stall that creep until the private detective got here with the real proof."

As if on cue, a short, stocky man with a military-style haircut hurried into the room bearing a manila folder similar to Jeff's.

"Well, it's about time you got here," said Jeff.

The man walked up to the officer standing with Jeff and Kate. "My name's Gary Nase. I'm a private investigator, and I've got some information here about Grayson White that you're going to want to see."

The officer opened the folder, and, after a cursory glance, decided that he did, indeed, want to see it, along with Grayson's fingerprints. Since Grayson had assaulted Jeff, Grayson had already won a free trip to the police station. Sister Anne, the policeman decided, was eligible, too.

The nice officer promised to contact Kate later that evening, and prepared to escort Grayson and Anne on their all-expense-paid tour of the station.

Grayson looked at Kate sadly. "Kate."

"Grayson. Or should I call you Andrew, or Oliver? Or would you prefer Tom or Dick or Harry?"

"Let's go," said the cop.

"Kate, don't believe it," he called as the officer led him away. "This was all a mistake."

"It certainly was," said Kate and turned her back to him.

Gary looked around him. "This place is a mess."

"Better this place than Kate's life," retorted Jeff. "Remind me never to hire you again."

"Hey, I got the info," retorted Gary. He held out a hand to Kate. "Hi, I'm Jeff's friend Gary. You must be Kate."

"I'm afraid I must," said Kate, taking his hand.

"I've heard a lot about you," said Gary.

"I can imagine," she said dully. "So it's true?"

Gary looked extremely uncomfortable. "I'm afraid it is. But you shouldn't feel bad. This guy's good, a real master. He's taken almost fifty women just in the last year."

Kate nodded. Her head was aching and she felt sick to her stomach. And she wanted to slap Jeff Hardin's face. But the knowledge that she was projecting her anger at Grayson onto him stopped her. In actuality, she should be pinning a medal on Jeff. *The Lone Ranger saves the day.* Unreasonably, she just wished he'd get on his horse and hi-ho away. On second thought, she'd do the hi-hoing.

"Thanks for rescuing me," she said to him. She knew she should say more, tried, but the lump in her throat was impossible to talk over. She just shook her head and clamped her lips together.

"I'm sorry, Kate," he said. "I really am."

She nodded

"Let's get out of here," said her father. "Come on, kids."

"But why is Grayson going away with the police?" asked Robbie, and Kate burst into tears.

J EFF SAT IN THE PRESS BOX, WATCHING THE MARINERS game with absolutely no interest. He was supposed to be taking notes for tomorrow's show, but somehow, after everything that had happened in the last twenty-four hours, what was going on down there on the field didn't seem important. Maybe Kate was right about sports.

Maybe she was right about a lot of things, like them not being a match. The thought made him almost sick. If they weren't a match, how could he be so crazy about her? How come his most important goal in life had become to protect her from heartache? And how come it was killing him knowing she was hurting?

He thought of finding her dad during the seventh inning stretch and asking how she was doing, but decided against it. After the ruckus he'd created yesterday it would probably be a good idea to keep his distance from the whole family. He could still see poor Lee's face as he looked at his restaurant, newly redecorated in south-of-the-border brawl. And the image of Kate crying would forever be embedded in his brain, like a tumor. Jeff wasn't sure how else he could have handled things, though. And he'd only done what he did to help Kate. But he'd humiliated her. And, even worse, he'd taken a sledgehammer to her dreams. Love should operate like a ball game: if you scored, you scored, and nobody cared how. Sadly, it didn't work that way with women. He'd saved Kate's bank account, but fumbled her self-esteem in the process. Just one more proof in her eyes that he was a frog.

Damn it all! He'd meant to come to her rescue like a modern-day Prince Charming, riding in on his white horse and snatching her from the clutches of the bad guy. It shouldn't have turned out that, in the process of trying to scoop her into the saddle, he'd managed to drop her in the mud. *Way to go, Hardin.*

Well, he'd recover. He was tough.

But what about Kate? How much battering could a woman take before she just gave up and forfeited the game? He wished there was something he could do to help her. Sadly, he'd already done enough to help.

K ATE HADN'T GONE IN TO WORK. SHE'D FELT TOO drained from the torture of her weekend. After they returned home, Carol had given a subdued Robbie and Amanda cake and ice cream while Kate had another chat with two policemen and endured the humiliation of listing all the people she had roped into this con. Then she had called everyone and given them the bad news. Today, she knew they had all been busy talking to their stockbrokers and giving statements to the police. Some favor she'd done for her friends.

No one seemed to hold their misfortune against her. Instead, they had all been sympathetic and ready to storm the police station and lynch Grayson. After hearing what the ruckus in his restaurant was about, Lee had refused to take any money for damages from Kate. Wallis had insisted she take a couple of days off and regroup. A couple of days? How about the rest of the year? Or, better yet, the rest of her life.

I T WAS TUESDAY. THE KIDS WERE IN SCHOOL, AND her parents had decided to give her some solitude and had taken the ferry into Seattle for the day, leaving Kate to enjoy the quiet and baste herself in guilt. She put on her tankini and went to sunbathe on her dock. Bad idea, she decided as she laid out her towel. It brought back vivid memories of Anne spreading sunblock on herself while she covered Kate in B.S.

Kate stretched out on her stomach and looked out at the water where Jeff's boat bobbed at its anchor in the cove. She still owed him a king-sized apology, and the thought of paying it made her sick. Not that she didn't want to apologize. She did. She just didn't want her face rubbed in her foolishness, didn't want to be reminded of the grief she'd caused her friends. She looked over the edge of the dock and into the water. That was what a stupid woman looked like.

The sound of approaching footsteps invaded the silence of the moment and shot a feeling of dread though Kate. She looked up to see Jeff approaching.

"Be careful," he said. "You know what happened to Narcissus."

She pulled away from the unpleasant view and sat up. "Narcissus was beautiful."

He walked onto the dock, making it shake under his feet, then plopped down next to her. "Yeah, and you're a real ugly customer. Nice bathing suit, by the way. You look like you're wearing some kid's underwear."

She ignored the remark and got down to business. "I owe you an apology."

"You already apologized at the restaurant, so let's not go there. Did you get your check back?"

"The police are keeping it as evidence." Kate's sigh was shaky and her voice cracked when she said, "I should have known."

There. She'd said it. Now he could puff out his chest and crow.

Instead, he sat silent. Finally she ventured a look at him to see if he was still breathing. He was, and contemplating the water.

At last he turned to face her. "I've been thinking about that myself, and I don't think you were as taken in as you say."

"Yes, that's why I rushed to give that monster fifty thousand dollars."

"Well, I didn't say you knew up here," said Jeff, tapping her head. "I think you knew down here, in your gut." He touched her midriff and the contact sent out an unnervingly pleasant ripple. "I saw you and Grayson on the dock the night you brought him over here."

"You were spying on us?"

"No, I was making a sandwich." He looked at her. "Okay, I was spying."

"And what did you see?"

"A love scene that would never make it in Hollywood. Why did you stop kissing him?"

"My neck hurt."

"And so you went in the house and . . . ?"

Kate felt her cheeks warming. "Never mind."

"He didn't stay long," said Jeff.

"I got a headache."

"Did that ever happen before when you kissed him?"

"Well, maybe once or twice," said Kate, "but that's not surprising, considering the stress I was under. The car was acting up, Robbie had gotten hurt."

"Mm-hmm," said Jeff. "How do you know those headaches weren't more than stress? How do you know it wasn't your instinct for survival trying to warn you? Consciously you thought this guy was great, but on a subconscious level, you knew different."

Jeff's words sounded like something she might have said to one of her listeners. When had he gotten so smart and she so dumb?

"Maybe you're right," she said.

"Definitely I'm right. And if you knew, deep down, then you weren't as dumb as you thought. You just got a little sidetracked by that book of yours."

"As in pride goeth before a fall? Are you saying there's nothing valuable in my book?" Now she was sounding emotional and defensive. She could feel tears of self-pity gathering. Embarrassed, she blinked and looked away.

"No, I'm not saying that exactly."

Kate sniffed. "Then what are you saying?"

"That I think you had a theory on how human relations were supposed to work, and you got in trouble when your pride insisted you stick with it, even when, on some deeper level, you knew it wasn't working."

"Not very bright of me," said Kate bitterly.

"But human." Jeff put an arm around her shoulder and hugged her, and she suddenly felt just a smidgen better. He hooked a finger under her chin and turned her face to look at him. His smile was undeservedly tender and pulled up a fresh tide of tears. "Hey," he chided softly, "remember, none of us is perfect. Not even me."

That drew a smile from her, as she knew he'd intended it to.

He gave her another squeeze, saying, "Lighten up on yourself a little, kid. We all screw up, say and do dumb things, spend days, sometimes years wishing we hadn't. But sooner or later we start again. Right now you're still down, and I'd say that's normal. But I'm betting that pretty soon you'll get up, dust yourself off, and get back in the game. And maybe you'll put this in a book somewhere down the road, and other women will read it and not get taken in by slick operators like White. I mean, that's what it's all about, right? Letting each other learn from our mistakes so we can all live a better life."

Seeing the sincerity and kindness in Jeff's face was like really seeing him for the first time. Maybe she was.

"Thanks," she said. "That was profound. Would you like to do my show for me?"

He grinned and shook his head. "I hate wearing panty hose."

He released his hold on her and she was surprised to find how oddly bereft the loss of physical contact with him made her feel. "I'd better get going," he said, hoisting himself to his feet. "Don't drown yourself while I'm at work. And if you get lonely, feel free to listen to my show."

"If I do that I'm sure to drown myself," she retorted.

He grinned. "I can see you're feeling better already."

BETTER MAYBE, BUT NOT GOOD. "I'M JUST SO DIS-gusted with myself," she said to her mom as they sat at her kitchen table drinking tea later that afternoon. "It all seems so obvious now. Like Grayson's advising me not to pay cash for a car. Of course, he wouldn't want me to use up any of the money he planned to steal from me. And then there was his so-called sister generously selling me some of her stock for the rock-bottom price she paid. For stock in a company that didn't exist."

"But she did tell you that you could pay her back," said Carol. "That made it perfectly believable."

"Even that was done so casually. What kind of businessperson doesn't get a written agreement on a deal like that?"

"Someone who thinks you're going to be family," said her mother. "Things were already looking serious between you and Grayson. She thought—"

"She didn't think anything," burst in Kate. "She was a con artist, and his girlfriend, to boot. Good God. Why on earth didn't I see any of this when it was so obvious? What kind of a psychologist am I, anyway?"

"A human one," said her mother. "You're not God, Kate. How could you know?"

"I should have," Kate insisted. "Oh, and don't forget the cute little headache act Anne performed at the restaurant. No need to come over for cake and ice cream when they already had what they'd come for: my money. They probably planned to go home, pack up, and get out of Dodge that same night." She gave a snort of disgust. "And that slick condo. I bet he rented it from someone, furniture and all. Even the so-called business call he took when we were together one night—it was good old Anne, calling him at a prearranged time."

"The man was very smooth."

Kate shook her head. "Too smooth, now that I look back on it. You know, Jeff suspected there was something wrong with him almost from the first. He tried to warn me, but I thought he was talking out of jealousy." She gave a bitter laugh. "Grayson White, the perfect man: my prince. Boy, can I pick 'em."

"There is no such thing as a perfect man," said her mother. "But if you can find one who's honest and kind you'll be close enough."

So much for those books on frogs and princes and how to pick gems. Her mother had summed it up in one sentence. But surely some of what Kate had preached was right on. Wasn't it? And if it wasn't, maybe she needed to find a new line of work.

"Sweetheart, this isn't the end of the world," said her mother. "Your money is safe, and it's looking like your friends are going to get theirs back, too, eventually."

Kate nodded. "I know. It's more than that. I'm just wondering if I can keep doing what I do and feel good about it." She shook her head. "All that training, and for what? What do I know about anything? I should have seen through this guy. Instead I only saw what I wanted to see."

"Listen to what you just said. Isn't that something valuable and important to pass on to your listeners?" suggested her mother.

"Maybe it is," said Kate.

"You're hearing the best of Doctor Kate this week," said Kate, "because I'm away from the station, working on a very important show for Monday. You won't want to miss it, so plan on joining me then and tell all your friends that we'll be meeting for one of the most important life strategy sessions we'll ever do."

"That's a take," said George.

"And quite a tease," said Wallis.

"It's going to be quite a show," said Kate. "Now, I'm going to get out of here before I run into Jeff and get the third degree over how my psyche is doing."

"So now he's Doctor Jeff?" joked Wallis.

"He should be. He helped me get my head on straight," said Kate, then left Wallis with her mouth hanging open.

• • •

JEFF HAD HEARD THE RADIO TEASE, AND WONDERED what Kate was up to. He cornered her at her flower bed on Friday, and tried to pry the secret out of her. "You're not quitting, are you?"

"This show is top secret," said Kate. "No one knows what it's about but my producer."

"Can she be bribed?"

"Not even with a ton of chocolate."

"Kate, just don't do anything rash. Okay?"

The concern in his voice warmed her clear through to her heart. Then made her feel guilty. Unkind as she'd been to Jeff, she didn't deserve this level of concern. She set down her trowel and looked up at him. "You're a very nice man. You know that?"

"Of course I do. I tell myself that every morning when I'm shaving."

"Positive self-talk, that's a good thing."

"Yeah, well, make sure you use some of it on yourself," advised Jeff.

"I will, don't worry. And just make sure you're listening on Monday."

AT ELEVEN A.M. JEFF AND GRACE SAT ON HIS COUCH and listened to the bumper music fade as Kate's voice came over the radio.

"Well, hello, everyone. And welcome to all our new listeners across the country. For those of you who haven't met me yet, I'm Dr. Kate Stonewall, and I'm here to help you plan your strategies for a successful life. As all my regular listeners know, we normally devote our time together to sharing e-mail, and I try to help you with problems in all those relationships that are so important by answering your questions. Today is going to be a little different, because today we're going to talk about my problems."

"What?" cried Jeff. "Has she flipped?"

"This summer I was conned."

"She's ruined," moaned Jeff. "She'd have been better off quitting."

"I don't think so," said Grace. "Just listen."

"I was taken in by a very smooth operator who tried to involve me in a stock swindle. And from what I hear, a couple of you who may even be listening at this moment were taken in as well. 'So,' you may be asking yourself, 'how did a smart woman like Doctor Kate get taken in?' Good question. Like everyone else, I want to be loved. So, the man who conned me made sure he fit my description of a perfect man. I've made no secret on my show of the fact that I'm not much of a sports fan. So, naturally, neither was he. He had also learned through listening to my show that I enjoy theater. So, naturally, so did he. He was a chameleon, able to easily blend into my picture of the perfect man. After a certain amount of time, he had gained my confidence, and that was the first step in the con. Later, when I met his so-called sister who just happened to be a stockbroker, she did her part by playing on my greed—something a good con artist can find in all of us if they know how to dig for it."

Jeff knew what it was costing Kate to share this, and while he felt for her, he couldn't help admiring her guts. He also couldn't help wondering if she'd have a job by the end of the day.

"If I was the only fool in the pool I might not be sharing this with you all today," continued Kate, "but the truth is, people are conned every day, and we all need to know how this works. So, I've got a special guest in the studio with me. Private investigator Gary Nase from the Nase Detective Agency is here to explain to us how some of these cons work."

"Oh, boy. Leave it to Gar to turn this into free advertising," muttered Jeff, and Grace shushed him.

"Gary, let's start by talking about 'sweetheart cons.'"

Gary cleared his throat into the microphone, making Jeff wince, then said, "Well, they can vary. The one pulled on you was pretty sophisticated: a kind of combination stock swindle and sweetheart con. Sometimes the scammer—"

"That's the crook," interjected Kate.

"Yeah. Sometimes the scammer is just scamming for sex, sometimes for money, and the pigeon—"

"The victim," inserted Kate.

"The victim might be met by chance or stalked. You were probably stalked, Kate. But no matter how they find you, these guys all fit a certain profile. They're antisocial. For them, there is no such thing as doing the wrong thing. They're charming, attractive people, and they're excellent improvisational actors. As for victims, they fit a profile, too. They can often be professional businesspeople who later think they ought to know better."

"Ouch," said Kate.

"Or they can be single parents, struggling to make ends meet. But every one of them is vulnerable to attention and wants to believe in love."

"Or the perfect man," added Kate.

Her tone of voice didn't even hint at the misery she still had to be feeling. Jeff hurt for her.

"What are some signs that you're about to be taken by a con man?" asked Kate. "What questions should you ask yourself?"

"Well, the first thing you have to ask is, Does this really make sense? For example, a woman showing interest in a man old enough to be her grandfather. Do young women normally go after guys living on Social Security? Your next tip-off comes when money gets introduced into the relationship. For example, I had one client whose boyfriend had a problem with the ATM eating his card on their first date and she ended up paying for the meal. That should have been a clue. She didn't pick up on the fact that he was using her until he'd gotten a lot of money out of her."

On they talked, mentioning any number and combination of rip-offs, and every time Kate referred to herself Jeff winced. At last he left for work, leaving Grace to keep listening on his radio while he tuned in in his car.

By the time the ferry had docked Kate and Gar had gotten down to the specifics of Grayson and Anne's scam.

"They set up a 'shell' corporation, a company with no assets or business, but it's quoted and appears to be real stock. They move it around to look like there's action on it when in reality it's just the con artist, buying from himself. The only real money in the game is yours."

"But how can they do that?" asked Kate. "Doesn't the Securities and Exchange Commission catch this?"

"The Internet has complicated things, and although both the NASDAQ and the OTC.BB—"

"Over-the-counter bulletin board," explained Kate.

"Yeah. Although both of them are administered by the National Association of Stock Dealers, the BB has a lower reporting requirement. Stuff gets by."

Kate's sigh spoke volumes. "Let's take some calls. We have Tracy waiting. Tracy, you're on the air."

Jeff drove to the station, feeling sick as he listened to the stories of the callers who had been snookered by fast-talking swindlers. As far as he was concerned, the death sentence was too kind a punishment for the Grayson Whites of the world.

Once at the station, he continued to listen to Kate as he got ready for his own show, and by the end of it, he was seated with Wallis and George, watching Kate and Gar.

"Thanks for sharing your story, Stef," said Kate at last. "I know it was hard, but by being so brave you've probably helped another woman with a similar problem. I'm afraid that's all the calls we have time for today." She smiled at Gar and said, "Thanks for being with us today, Gary. I think we've all learned a lot. I certainly hope we've learned to be careful. It's a big, bad world out there, so remember, if that certain someone seems just too good to be true, it's probably because he is. Look out for frogs wearing masks.

"And now, before we close, I have someone else I need

to thank. Jeff Hardin, if you're listening . . ." At that moment, she turned her head and saw Jeff. A crimson tide flowed up her neck and covered her cheeks, but she held his gaze. "I want to thank you for staying my friend, even when I was a complete nincompoop. Thank you for putting up with my anger, my insults, and my general stupidity. People, we all need friends, and if you have ones who are brave enough to hold your face up to your mistakes, then get down on your knees and thank God. That's it for today. We'll meet tomorrow for more life strategies."

George pushed up the bumper music, and in the air studio Kate and Gary stood and shook hands.

They entered the control room and Gary saluted his friend, saying, "How do you like that? I'm a radio personality."

"You did great, man," said Jeff, clapping him on the back. "At this rate, you might just get your own show."

Gar's eyes lit up. "Say, Wallis," he said, taking Wallis aside.

Jeff smiled down at Kate. "You are one gutsy woman."

"And you are one smart man."

"I never thought I'd live to hear you say that," joked Jeff.

"Well, you had me fooled for a while there," said Kate.

"And you had me worried. I thought you were going to quit."

"No, I decided I should learn from my mistakes and share what I learned. A very smart man gave me that advice."

"Not all that smart," said Jeff. "Just a guy who cares." The impulse to reach out and touch her cheek was too strong to resist. Probably not a good idea, though, because the contact with soft skin just made him hungry for more.

She blushed and smiled, and looked like she was going to say something, but his producer appeared on the scene, breaking the spell.

He congratulated Kate on a great show, then turned to Jeff. "You're on in two minutes," he told Jeff, and handed him a paper with game scores on it.

Jeff sighed inwardly. "Guess I'd better go hit the salt mines."

Kate nodded. "Thanks for listening."

The phone rang. Wallis answered it then turned to Kate. "It's for you. The *Times*."

Jeff turned and entered the air studio, wishing for the first time in his life that he didn't have to go to work.

KATE SPENT THE NEXT HOUR DOING PHONE INTER-views while Wallis fielded calls. The show had obviously been a hit. It was at least some consolation for wounded pride and a crippled heart, thought Kate.

AFTER HER SHOW, KATE'S PARENTS INFORMED HER she was going to survive, and made plans to return home. She tried to talk them into extending their visit, but they left at the end of the week, reminding her before their plane took off that they would all have Thanksgiving to look forward to.

Left alone in her castle once more, Kate swept away the remains of her broken dreams and got back into the rhythm of her single-parent life. Between her job and the kids, she had plenty to keep herself busy. Robbie was now in the island kids' choir and acting as though he were serving time. Amanda was happily taking dance lessons one night a week and appeared to have resigned herself to having no father. This, Kate decided after a few weeks, could have something to do with the fact that Jeff was getting into a habit of inviting himself over on Saturday nights to play games or watch videos. Amanda seemed to think he made a good surrogate, always making sure she got included in the wrestling matches he and Robbie enjoyed.

As September marched into October, Kate realized she liked having Jeff around as much as the kids did. Other than his sports obsession, he was actually quite normal, and she was finally forced to conclude that her original intense dislike of him must have risen not so much from righteous indignation as from a subconscious feeling of insecurity and jealousy. Of course, that didn't mean he was any more right for her than Grayson.

But what about the fact that she was wearing perfume for the first time in years on those Saturday nights? That behavior could be easily enough attributed to simple female pride. Other behavior wasn't as easily explained away: like the fact that she often found herself wishing Jeff would leave the damned beanbag chair he camped in with the kids when they watched a movie to join her on the sofa and tuck her under his arm. And the way she was eyeing the play of the muscles in his back lately when he sat playing video games with Robbie could only be described as greedy. It looked like Amanda wasn't the only one developing a crush on their neighbor.

Well, it was natural, Kate reasoned. Even though he had been only an illusion, Grayson White had given her a glimpse of what she could have with the right man. She had gotten near enough to love to feel the warmth, and now that the door to that happy ending she'd envisioned was shut, she was filled with longing. It was only loneliness that had her eyeing Jeff's body with such hunger. Only restless longing that kept her playing with the memory of a July-hot kiss indulged in under the influence of wine coolers. It would be foolish to build the longing into something more. Jeff made a wonderful friend, but she wasn't about to confuse loneliness with love. He was not her prince.

"I JUST DON'T GET WHY YOU THINK THAT," SAID Grace as the two women did their morning walk around the cove.

"Because we don't have—"

"Don't say 'common interests,'" Grace cut her off. "You've found things in common. If you don't have anything in common what's he doing over at your house on Saturday nights?"

"Just hanging out. The kids like him."

"And so do you. You enjoy being with him, and you know it."

"I'm perfectly willing to admit that," said Kate. "We've been having a good time together."

Grace gave a snort. "Have you turned into the queen of understatement! You've been acting like a sixteen-year-old with her first boyfriend lately."

"Okay, I admit I've been enjoying myself. It's nice to have a man around," said Kate in her own defense.

"Yes, it is, and this one wants to stay around. So what's the problem?"

"We're just too different," insisted Kate.

"Yeah, you're a woman and he's a man. Most people manage to overcome that. Come on, Kate. How about forgetting your perfect man shopping list and just checking in with your emotions. You can't build a relationship on a checklist. I think you proved that with Grayson."

Kate cringed. "Please. Don't remind me."

"You need reminding. I'm beginning to think you need glasses, too, since you can't seem to see what's right in front of your nose."

Maybe Grace was right. Maybe Kate did need her vision checked.

"You also need another way to test a potential love of your life than what you used on Grayson."

Another way?

JEFF SAT SLOUCHED ON HIS COUCH, DOWNING CHIPS and salsa and watching the Denver Broncos play the San Francisco Forty-Niners. It looked like he was forever doomed to mere friendship with the girl next door, but at least he still had football. And this was some game. The score was twenty-eight to twenty-three in favor of the

Broncos, but the Forty-niners were working their way to a touchdown. And Jeff had bet Gar twenty bucks that they'd beat the Broncs this year.

The players came out of their huddle and faced each other for battle. "It's first down on the Broncos' forty-yard line," said the announcer. "On the snap, it's a pitch to the tail and a sweep around the left end. He's knocked out of bounds on the twenty-five-yard line, which brings up another first and ten."

"You can do it, guys," cheered Jeff.

The doorbell rang. Of all the times for company, he thought. Even Grace with a pie wouldn't be particularly welcome at this crucial point in the game.

"Come in. It's open," he yelled, keeping his gaze riveted on the screen.

"Oh, you're busy. I can come back."

Jeff recognized the voice, the tentative tone was new. He jerked his head around to see Kate hovering uncertainly in the doorway.

"No, come on in. The game's almost over." He moved his snack to the coffee table and patted the cushion next to him.

She sat down and looked at the TV. "Big game, huh?"

"Yeah, it's a good one," said Jeff. "But I'm sure you didn't come over to watch the game. What's up?"

"Oh, nothing. I just stopped by to say hi." She turned her gaze to the TV. "So this is what civilized war looks like."

Jeff remembered he'd made that comment about sports once. He was surprised Kate did.

"Believe it or not, a lot of strategy goes into this game. That's why I like it." But, of course, Kate hadn't come to talk football strategy. He shot her a sideways glance. "Okay, now, why are you really here?"

She looked like a swimmer getting ready to plunge into icy water. "I've been doing a lot of thinking lately . . . about what you said to me on my dock."

Jeff did a quick trip through time and tried to remember everything he'd said to her on her dock.

"I think maybe you were right."

The players were coming out of their huddle now. Jeff pulled his gaze from the TV. "I was right? That makes twice in one year. Tell me again what I was right about."

"My subconscious. I think maybe I have been ignoring my instincts far too long."

Jeff nodded. "Mm-hmm." He wasn't sure he was up for a shrink session with a shrink. What was she getting at? On the TV, the two teams were lining up on the twenty-five-yard line.

"I think I've gotten a little confused in my definition of perfect," Kate continued. "And I think while I was chasing an illusion of perfect, the real thing was right under my nose."

Him? Did she mean him? Impossible.

"So I've come to ask a favor. I want you to kiss me."

Jeff stared at her. "Am I hallucinating here, or did you just say you want me to kiss you?"

She nodded. "Please."

Did it get any better than this? He grinned. "Well, if you insist."

Kate snuggled next to him and he put an arm around her and captured her lips with his. Full-contact sport had never felt so good. She didn't seem in a hurry to end the kiss, so he kept at it.

When she did pull away, she still had her eyes closed. She smiled, then sighed.

In the background, Jeff could hear the announcer calling the play, but he didn't bother to turn his head. Watching the dreamy expression on Kate's face was infinitely more fascinating.

"No headache," she reported. "Not even a hint of one. But just to make sure, would you kiss me again?"

Jeff pulled Kate to him and happily complied. She let out a tiny moan and slid a leg against his.

"Um, Kate," he said against her mouth. "What are you doing here?"

She nibbled on his cheek. "Listening to my instincts. You don't mind, do you?"

"No, no. I'm all in favor of good listening skills."

Now she had her fingers in his hair and was sampling his ear, and her breath was hot. So was he. She slid onto his lap and he wondered when he'd wake up. Well, he might as well enjoy the dream while it lasted. He slid his hand down her back and indulged in another long, teasing kiss.

"On the snap, the quarterback rolls to his right, spots his split end all alone in the end zone," said the announcer, his voice taking on energy.

"I made a mistake," said Kate.

"I hope you're not talking about now."

"I was an idiot and I misjudged you. I'm sorry for all those times I treated you like a frog when you're really a prince."

That was good. But it wasn't enough. "Whose prince?"

The smile Kate flashed him promised steamy, rock 'n roll nights and days filled with the laughter of kids. "Mine," she murmured.

The announcer's voice throbbed with excitement. "And he throws a perfect strike. That's it, folks. Touchdown!"

Jeff grabbed the remote from the cushion on the other side of him, aimed it at the TV, and fired. "Who cares?" Then, feeling like king of the world, he kissed her again.

ᗪear ᖇeader,

I hope you enjoyed reading about the adventures of Dr. Kate as much as I enjoyed writing them. She may not know everything there is to know about the stock market (who does!), but she knows just enough about love to be dangerous. And her bestseller, *The Frog with the Glass Slipper*, is affecting women all over the country. You can meet two such women in my next book, *Lookin' for Love*, the story of Angel West and Trish Lyles, a couple of Nashville rising stars who are determined to quit messing up their love lives and start following the good doctor's practical advice on how to pick a prince. With sexy men like Jake Wilder on the scene, that is going to prove hard to do. Keep an eye on my website (sheilasplace.com) for a sneak preview of a tale of crooked cops, bumbling crooks, and true love.

Sheila (but not Dr. Kate) can also be reached at:

SHEILA RABE
P.O. BOX 4573
ROLLING BAY, WA 98061-0573

Praise for the novels of Sheila Rabe

Be My Valentine

July 6/15

"Tongue-in-cheek romance that lightens your spirit and brings a smile to your lips. Great fun!" —*Rendezvous*

"Don't miss this delightful look at modern love, filled with humor and heart."

—Susan Wiggs, bestselling author of *The Mistress*

All I Want for Christmas

"A delicious array of . . . characters keep this story hopping. Want to be uplifted and get in the holiday spirit? Grab a copy of this story and enjoy.'" —*Rendezvous*
"

"All the warmth and cheer of Christmas . . . A must-read for the holidays." —Jill Barnett, bestselling author

"Laughter and tears await you . . . pour a cup of hot chocolate and prepare to enjoy the magic of Christmas."

—*Old Book Barn Gazette*

"A Christmas romance reminiscent of . . . classic holiday films." —*The Romance Reader*

"All you'll want for Christmas is Sheila Rabe's thoroughly delightful story. Cuddle up by the fire . . . and get ready to be immersed in the joy of the season."

—Debbie Macomber, *New York Times* bestselling author

"This light, lively, family-filled romance takes an appealing premise, provides a cast of likable characters, laces it with humor, and overlays it with . . . seasonal sparkle."

—*Library Journal*

Titles by Sheila Rabe

ALL I WANT FOR CHRISTMAS
BE MY VALENTINE
A PRINCE OF A GUY